Contents

Acknowledgements

OUR HORSES IN EGYPT

Rosalind Belben

CHIVERS

British Library Cataloguing in Publication Data available

This Large Print edition published by BBC Audiobooks Ltd, Bath, 2009.
Published by arrangement with The Random House Group Ltd.

U.K. Hardcover ISBN 978 1 408 43242 6
U.K. Softcover   ISBN 978 1 408 4 3243 3

Printed and bound in Great Britain by
CPI Antony Rowe, Chippenham and Eastbourne

Acknowledgements

Two dear people, Penelope Hoare and Anthony Sheil, have presided with grace and patience over the writing of *Our Horses in Egypt*. I am very grateful to them for their tireless help.

I have benefited from works by the Marquess of Anglesey, Lieut.-Colonel the Hon. R.M.P. Preston, General Sir George de S. Barrow, Field-Marshal Viscount Wavell and Lady Butler, in particular; from the memoirs of Australian and New Zealander mounted infantrymen and British yeomen; from official histories, including that of the Veterinary Service; from the essential War Office publications of the time, *Cavalry Training* and *Animal Management*, and from a range of books and other documents. I have no cause to be excused howlers.

Without Wendy Dobell's generosity, and without the singular, unforgettable personality of a bay mare ... wherever she is now ... it is improbable that this book would have come into being.

Dorothy Brooke wrote so eloquently about the

horses (*For Love of Horses, Diaries of Mrs Geoffrey Brooke*, edited by Glenda Spooner) that it has been hard to quote more than a few lines without rendering the rest pallid.

R.B.

I PROVISIONS

Not only Army horses, but those given up to their country by countless hundreds of patriotic people—favourite hunters, cherished friends of many families, born and bred in English fields—were at the close of the war sold to bondage in a foreign land. Fourteen long years of toil in the hands of strangers—in scorching sun, in sand, in a land where water is scarce, where flies are a torment, and where, owing to the poverty of their owners, the work has been far beyond their wasted strength! Many hundreds still survive, pleading for release—old, utterly weary, so deserving of a kindly redemption. 'Home' now can only be represented by a peaceful death, but what a release that is, what further suffering it saves!

Mrs Geoffrey Brooke, *Morning Post*, 8th September 1932

Some of the British residents in Egypt were strongly averse to Army horses being sold to Egyptians, basing their objections on grounds of cruelty and imperfect supervision by the civil authorities. Letters appeared in the local and home press in support of this view, and political pressure was brought to bear on the War Office, with the result that all sales were prohibited until the termination of the war, when many horses were sold by the thousand throughout the whole country.

... Under proper supervision, Egyptians can take as good care of English horses as anyone else.

A HISTORY OF THE GREAT WAR BASED ON OFFICIAL DOCUMENTS: VETERINARY SERVICES, edited by Major-General Sir L.J. Blenkinsop and Lieutenant-Colonel J.W. Ramsey

1 A bolt

Smiling sweetly, Griselda Romney's mother, Mrs Lupus, climbed into the back of the motor.

Mrs Lupus said to her chauffeur, Maurice, 'Shake the children off at five miles an hour.' As they dropped from the running board, plop, plop, she watched. She gave a benign wave. Mrs Lupus reported to her elder daughter, Ida, at Quarr, that Griselda had gone mad and was proposing to take Nanny to Egypt.

'Egypt?' said Ida. 'What for?'

'Ida,' said Mrs Lupus, 'I quite thought you'd condemn it!'

'Why Egypt?' Ida was hesitant. 'Can there be "a man"?'

'I haven't heard so. Unless one credits Captain *Palsy* with more than meets the eye.' Mrs Lupus pronounced the name 'Palsy' with hauteur; pityingly. 'Griselda imagines herself able to cope with lessons, and she swears *ad infinitum* that Amabel must have Nanny. She says Amabel could read and write at the age of four.'

'What child cannot?'

'Oh, well, the slow ones ... And tell the time, and can tie shoelaces. Amabel will soon lace a boot.'

5

'Why then must Amabel go to Egypt?'

'Griselda . . .' a high snort '. . . cannot expect to return in any hurry. '*Imperative* to take Amabel and Nanny'!'

'Why go at all? There is unrest in Egypt, Ma. You don't read your newspaper?'

'She is going . . .' in a bursting tone '. . . to trace her horses.'

A grin escaped Ida. 'She has no money.'

'You'll be staggered,' Mrs Lupus said. 'Staggered!'

Ida stared.

'Reversionary interest!'

'May she do that?'

'It does seem so.'

The portion of capital secured in the Trust would have gone, on the death of Arthur's mother, Irene Romney, to Arthur and the Grazebrook cousins, had they lived. Arthur and Alan had been killed. Arthur's widow Griselda, a future beneficiary (whenever Irene Romney chose to die), had been, evidently, able to get her hands on some money.

Reversionary interest didn't work to the advantage of any beneficiary that wasn't desperate.

'Rash,' said Mrs Lupus. 'And, I omitted to relate, they have started to read *Masterman Ready*.'

'For the voyage?'

'She means the child is forward. It was, I recollect, a *solid* book.' A reflective silence. 'In

6

which a ship is wrecked. Well, whom do we know out there . . . ?'

Ida drove herself over to Bark Hart.

To Ida, Griselda said, 'I have to keep Nanny. She's bored at Bark Hart. Unless I act, I shall find myself without anybody. Nanny will adore the sea.'

'One sails to Egypt so as to entertain one's children's nurse?'

'There will be other nurses, other children. Going out to India, I dare say.'

'Ayahs.'

'Not all.'

'And Egypt? How suitable is Egypt for a small child?'

'If Amabel isn't "too old for India", she can't be too young for Egypt.'

'Oh,' said Ida. 'What does Nanny say?'

'She doesn't want us to go. She has never travelled, or lived overseas.'

'Nanny won't care for the food, or the heat, or the flies, or the . . .'

'Don't forget, I took that beastly one to Malta.'

'Malta was awash with Navy families.'

'Cairo will be awash with Army families.'

'Are you positive?'

'I can't consider Nanny's nerves. It will do her good to get over them.'

'Why does she like you so much!'

'She likes Amabel.'

'This is very vague.'

7

'I have reason,' said her sister, 'to suppose Conker ... dear Conker ... was killed in the Charge at Agagiya. I've seen Nick Flower! He was spiffing!'

'Nick Flower ... oh, yes,' said Ida, ruminatively.

'Philomena was alive at the end of the War. He says she would have gone to Remounts in Cairo. Philomena is in need of *rescue*.'

'Isn't that fanciful?'

'I ought to make the effort. If you, Ida, had gone all through the War, almost certainly been wounded, only to discover an ungrateful and parsimonious War Office had sold you off in Cairo, would you not prefer me to look for you, and bring you home?'

'Um ... sentiment?'

'Responsibility,' said Griselda. 'We can't exercise it for every animal on earth. I don't say that. Do you? For our own, we can!'

'Why must Nanny and Amabel exercise theirs for a horse on which neither has laid eyes?'

'Amabel is conscious that the English hunters were plucked from green fields and warm, airy stables.'

'Is she?'

'Philomena doesn't understand Arabic.'

Ida laughed.

'She will have picked it up,' she said.

'Or Greek.'

'The estate can't, you know,' said Ida,

'underwrite you. If in difficulty you won't be able to count on support.'

'I had grasped that,' said Griselda, with dignity.

Ida's head waggled; as if to say, goose chase.

As it happened, Ida did consider it had been ghastly. She simply didn't believe such matters behoved one to dash off.

Scandalous, yes. Dash off, no.

'Well, we'll have Georgie in the holidays.'

'Darling Georgie!'

2   Mrs Romney's horses

Every day, Nanny had tea with Mrs Romney. They sat in the garden in summer and by the open fire in the hall in winter. Nanny never sat down in the drawing-room. They were much of an age.

Mrs Arthur Romney had been gay, and would be again. She wasn't unfeeling. The blows dealt her hadn't made her oblivious. The War had made many oblivious. Nanny had lost all six of her brothers.

Railings were things for which not even a child could have felt very much. 'When the railings went,' Mrs Romney said, 'we smiled.'

'Did you, madam?'

'The more iron we were good for, the prouder we were.'

The railings had not been the first to go.
Upon sailing in the spring of 1914 for Malta,
Mrs Romney had sent her hunters to her
mother-in-law; to Mrs Romney, senior, at
Toller Bottom. 'They would have enjoyed their
summer rest, and been brought into condition
as per usual. Instead, the War started. Their
groom rushed off . . .'

'Oh my!'

'Our horses had to serve the country. One or
two dismal people had their favourites shot.
Thoroughly low of them. Nobody we knew.
Contemptible to pass a good horse off as a
crib-biter, or order a groom to create, with
chisel and rasp, fake incrimination in the stall!'

'I'd say!'

'Children's faces, I gather, Nanny, were
pale.'

'Wrong to have encouraged them to stand
around in the stable-yard at all?'

'Oh, I concur! D'you see, our sensible
hunters were ideal, and what the cavalry
wanted.'

It was one of those topics.

Nanny had heard Mrs Romney's sister, Miss
Lupus (Aunt Ida, to the children), pleading
with Mrs Romney.

'Oh, Griselda, how could it have been better,
had you sent them to me! How could I have
hidden them! Scarcely rational to suppose they
would have fared otherwise than they did . . .
parked on Arthur's mother.'

'*Entrusted* to H.H.G. !'

Miss Lupus was a lady who liked to see things as they were. Miss Lupus, thought Nanny, was so brave, hiding a broken heart, so diminished.

H.H.G. stood for 'Her Human Ghastliness'. A fine way for Mrs Romney to speak. Mrs Romney's cheek had turned hot and she'd wrung her hands. 'I must have been mad!'

Mrs Romney never forgot her horses. Nanny twitched her lips kindly at the mention.

Before the War's end, Mrs Romney had shingled her hair, and said suddenly, 'D'you know, Nanny, I find myself hard up.'

'Do you, madam?'

'I shall surrender the lease. I mean to buy a house. It may not be what you are used to. Will you consent to managing without a nursery maid?'

A house in the country.

'There won't be any pavements. I do very much want you to stay with us. I paint it in poor colours now, so you can't be disillusioned. I don't expect there will be other nurses. Or dancing lessons. Or parks. Please, Nanny! The Commander would have wished you to have remained with us.'

Mrs Romney had charm.

Mrs Romney had bought a place in a hamlet that boasted no other gentry. The lanes had been muddy and splattered with cow dung. They still were. The fire in the hall had

11

smoked and the chimney at times spouted flames. It still did. The upper floor was limited, the downstairs primitive.

Nanny had gritted her teeth.

Mrs Romney, senior, was 'critical'. About Bark Hart, Mrs Romney, senior, had been *very* critical. Nanny and her own Mrs Romney took umbrage with a grandmother that picked rusty nails from the lawn. In dealings with Her Human Ghastliness they were united.

Whenever Nanny evinced grief at the conditions at this Bark Hart, her Mrs Romney reminded Nanny of 'the disastrous nurses'. The first had gone with them to Malta before Georgie could speak, and trussed him in sticking-plaster, ripped off before breakfast, to correct unfathomable defects; and had tied his legs together at night. The second had forced purgatives down his throat until he'd had no inside that wasn't inflamed. Neither the least loving.

Both had smacked.

Horrors with nurses were commonplace. A Georgie well able to string words together had merely smiled; smiled his anguished, maddening smile.

Old Mr Romney had expired bankrupt. The Commander had given his life. So had his cousin Mr Alan. Bereft, Nanny's Mrs Romney had considered Amabel to be a stiff little girl. These facts had helped Nanny to make sacrifices in the matter of that to which she was

12

used.

Mrs Romney, so gay and companionable, now *chose* to maroon herself in Up-Nyland, at Bark Hart, without servants. Without anybody, thought poor Nanny, to make us comfortable.

Mrs Romney tried to compose meals. These meals made their way, in Mrs Romney's own hands, up to the nursery. Mrs R. got down on her hands and knees and scrubbed the floor. Her behind in the air, and a kneeler to save her stockings.

3 Bark Hart

Georgie was always smiling; that was what he was, a pale and smiling boy. Georgie had nice manners.

Georgie was Mrs Romney's favourite.

It had been Nanny who had realized he needed spectacles.

'How can he shoot! With short sight!' said Mrs Romney.

'Oh, Griselda! *Really!* Why shouldn't he be useful with a gun?' said Miss Lupus. 'Why couldn't you have established yourselves closer!' Miss Lupus often said. Quarr and Bark Hart were at opposite ends of the county. Bark Hart was closer to Grannie Romney's place. One of those puzzles.

'He must take after H.H.G.'

The more 'Muzz' doted on Georgie, the more scope for chagrin, thought Nanny.

An 'animal' on loan had been sent over by his Aunt Ida.

This Giggle's paces were sedate. Only eleven hands! And aged about *thirty*. No fun.

'Darling,' had said Mrs Romney to Georgie, 'I *appeal* to you! Be patient! Grown-ups ride ponies such as Giggle on the Moor ... ! Urgent that Amabel should learn.'

Nanny had started a rearguard action to stop Amabel from running wild. Pretty frocks cascaded from the sewing-machine, in delicate materials.

Mrs Romney had no horse; and foresaw a future without her own stable. On the bicycle, Mrs Romney hurtled when she could hurtle; for the fun of it. Otherwise, the bicycle served her for taking Amabel out on the leading-rein.

Georgie's 'dear Muzz', as she trudged up the stairs with a tray of food for the nursery, would give him a grin. Nanny could imagine that the smell-less smell of washing-up soda and the squeezed soap in its wire cradle would seep into Georgie's dreams, mixed with Mrs Romney's scent, the bloom of her face powder and the kid of gloves; for Georgie helped in kitchen and scullery.

Mrs Romney's dreaming was peculiar. Once she'd heard a horse's cough.

Mrs Romney gutted and skinned and plucked: she'd never learnt to boil an egg.

14

Since Nanny's fancy was for a white egg, Mrs Romney had acquired point-of-lay Leghorns, teaching herself to scramble and poach as well.

Cotter scribbled '*Soak night*' and '*Slow oven*' on the parcel; but no village butcher could remember that brains with their skin on might not appeal to the nursery. And the job Mrs Romney had to induce junket to set!

'I see that I shall have to stand over you, madam,' would pronounce a mournful Nanny. 'Blood heat is not very warm at all. It's not even tepid. You test it with your finger.'

And, '*This* milk is hotter than you, madam!'

4   Master Bun

Amabel sailed along in the bicycle's wicker seat behind Nanny with glee. A solar topee, which belonged in the dressing-up and fell on the child's nose, had been pronounced 'ever so much lead in my saddle-cloth'. Nanny knew how to reason with Amabel.

Amabel's friend 'Peter' cantered 'his blue roan mare' beside them, often on the other side of a hedge. The hedges were old, dense, or double. The banks had ditches. Amabel was perpetually craning. Amabel kept causing the bicycle to lurch.

Why had there been the *haste* to have the Commander's ancient dog, Master Bun, put down? Nanny had kept mum on the matter. Others spoke out.

The sister, Miss Lupus, had been impatient. 'I expect he *was* in a bad way . . . yes, I dare say! I can lay hands on people, you know I can. Why not the vet? Hasn't Pritchard been demobbed? Ours is back! Or an Army somebody!'

'In the old days, we managed.'

'These fellows you found . . .'

'They said they knew what they were about.'

'You're so gullible.'

'I shan't be again. I had chloroform myself when Georgie was born.'

'It didn't put you down.'

'How could it, a whiff or two! I was glad of it.'

'Poor Bunny.'

'Oh, oh, don't!'

Two men had claimed, turning up at the back door, to put a dog to sleep peacefully.

'I did have the forethought to send Nanny out on the bicycle with Amabel to the weir.' Nanny herself didn't go much on the weir, a nasty, dangerous spot.

'Magnificent!' Miss Lupus had seemed troubled. 'Arthur was attached to him.'

'I was attached to him too. You have no notion. And it upset the other dogs.'

Bunny had voiced his anguish. The old boy hadn't been ready to part with life. In a voice thickened by the water on his heart; with dull, hopeless, already pain-filled eyes; his curly tail limp.

'I was so *sorry*. I should have stayed with him, they carted him off to the barn and his howling started. He howled and howled. It was hellish.'

'As a child you had more sense. How could you be that idiotic!'

Mrs Romney had 'felt' it.

'The animal was suffering, madam,' Nanny had said, after Miss Lupus's departure, 'and you did what you thought right. His lungs were clogged up, and he couldn't stand on his legs, he was embarrassed because he couldn't be clean. There is a limit. He was eighteen, didn't you tell me, and didn't you tell me that was a good age . . . even for a mongrel?'

Adding, 'Although he was a nice old gentleman.'

'The trouble is, I so bungled it. My husband would have been miserable. I stupidly liked the sound of chloroform. For a dog to be seized by two strange men, carried into a barn, a *wood*shed, and forced to breathe from a wad, and not to go to sleep at all but to resist . . . It isn't that we're the least sentimental. My sister was right. One has an obligation to stay, and comfort a faithful dog, a *very* trusting dog. It was frightful of me.'

'The first and last time.'

'I'm not myself, Nanny.'

'Better not to dwell on mishaps. You didn't mean to fail, if fail you say you did.'

'I don't believe that *intention* is the whole picture.'

5 Captain Palsy

Children, instead of being repelled by the sight, since the War, of wounded heroes (absent arms, legs, noses and minds), generally had to be told not to goggle.

Palsy took it in good part.

He was well aware that Nanny had christened him 'Mummie's beau'.

'Dear Jack, don't go getting soppy over me,' Griselda had said, in headlong fashion.

'I imagine that you, Griselda, lying in bed at night and in view of the housework tired ...' (in her rather lonely bed) '... must have been wondering why on earth you, who crave fun, and company, ever moved to a quiet spot.'

'I wonder, more, you know, whether Philomena, who had no friends among the horses, was tolerated or could have been lonely. Whether she won any hearts, don't y'see?'

'Good Lord! You are a funny old lady.'

Arthur had been killed in 1918, on St George's Day; and not until the spring of 1919 had Griselda begun to notice the scolding of a wren in the garden. 'My dear Griselda, you will feel truly yourself once you've had *a morning with hounds,'* Palsy had said in 1920, in September.

In other words, mounted by him.

'Well, it would be a chance for Georgie to come out on Giggle.'

Palsy had risen genially to the latter proposition, anticipating the start of the term.

They'd met at Shap Spinney, with the purpose of dispersing the young foxes. Done nothing there. A dog-fox was seen away from the withies close to the Kennels at Nyland. The rising sun, breeze stiff, air cool. The music, breaking on Griselda's ears (surely) like *balm*.

Palsy's gelding, that gelding, with the Army's broad-arrow brand on his quarter, had been rather over ... trembly ... at the knees. She'd said frankly that she wouldn't, once, have had her saddle put on such a crock let alone gone out with hounds but that someone so *delighted* to be out (*delighted* to be loaned an animal *at all*) couldn't spare a lot of compunction ... Or, not just after the War. That was what she'd said herself!

When Jack Palsy opened his mouth, his arms shot about like trombones. His horses were inured to it. If his feet were on the ground, he stamped one or other of them to amplify his speech, though involuntarily. His chin stuck itself forward and shrunk forthwith into his neck. The neck was more corkscrew than join for the skull. His articulation of words was

19

explosive.

Gassed. He'd been lucky.

When Griselda had chosen to remember her own horses, to Palsy that had meant 'Conker', the bay.

'How sagely . . .' (she'd say) '. . . he carried me for three seasons before the War. I've pictured him, brave and bold, in a cavalry regiment, his life one of trumpet-calls and parades and thrill! If disagreeable in other aspects.'

Palsy reflected. Her voice still throbbed in his ears now . . . 'Conker must have done his officer proud!'

The other, the mare, hadn't been with Griselda for many months. A brown (her light colour had suggested common breeding), with a mealy muzzle. Philomena had been . . . indeed, would have remained . . . 'hoity-toity'. 'Oh, look here,' she'd say, 'am I not boring on!'

True, there had been the converse about 'holes'.

'. . . Conker's foot had never gone in. In the split second that Conker sensed that his foot had touched sheer air, he'd altered his stride.'

'So! An animal, this gelding of yours, didn't drop a foot in a hole! Good Lord!'

'Had *you* put your foot to a hole, *you* wouldn't have been able to pull it out. At least, I shouldn't imagine you would.'

'That's why I ride a horse,' he'd said, indulgently.

Then, when she'd asked her sister, Ida had looked at her with pity: 'If you hadn't been so slap-dash, so dashing, so keen to ride, rather than ride *horses*, you ... Why wait until you're grown up to discover the nature of what carries you?' Ida Lupus was a consummate horsewoman. Miss Lupus's petrifying eye could bring Palsy's cheeks up pink.

'I grew up in the shade of a consummate horsewoman,' Griselda would say.

He'd mounted her all season; and got no farther with her.

'Why,' she'd said to him (even back in 1920), 'haven't I bothered to find out about my horses?'

Palsy invariably gagged.

'Why!' she'd cried.

'Um!'

'I must try ...'

'Must you? Better not.'

'Why!'

'Make you unhappy.'

'I'm not easily overcome.'

'Um.'

6 The true confiders

'People are so uncommunicative, darling.' Georgie was the treasury of all Muzz's secrets.

'The troops in France suffered the sight of

horses left to die of their wounds. Horses that screamed with horribly fractured legs in the mud, or sat half buried, sinking through the crust; or, lying out, raised their heads, with bellies torn by shrapnel, with flesh turned to a mush by high explosive. Troops that bore the agonies of their fellows stoically were sore at the plight of horses and the mules. But you couldn't leave the ranks to put an animal out of its misery: your officer, who carried a revolver, stopped when he could.'

Muzz and Georgie were thrown together at Bark Hart.

Muzz *adored* Georgie and Georgie adored Muzz.

'Our horses were sold throughout the latter years of the War to be turned into bully at the *abattoirs hippophagiques* of France. With this on our consciences, we supplied the *abattoirs hippophagiques* with humane-killers. Grey transport horses at the front were painted with Cundy's Fluid and, when Cundy's Fluid was exhausted, with coffee. Appalling logic, darling, darkening the greys didn't protect them. Men in the trenches must have longed for coffee to *swallow*. These days nobody appears to answer letters.' Muzz had no telephone at Bark Hart. 'And Remount officers have chips.'

Georgie had said, 'I see.'

He did not. But he worshipped.

Grannie Romney had happened to visit them

22

at Bark Hart, to find Nanny and the children alone.

'London!'

Grannie Romney at Toller Bottom was eight miles from Bark Hart.

The true confider had seen little harm in boasting that Muzz was lunching with a chum 'at the War Office'. Grannie Romney's blue eyes had popped.

It was Georgie who had first heard of Paleface.

Out hunting, Georgie attracted approving looks. Georgie never complained about Giggle, whom he'd outgrown. He presented a cheerful face, hid his mortification: Giggle was a frightfully game pony.

One of the Egmont boys had spoken of a whip's horse with their neighbouring pack (the Maurward). Paleface (and you could imagine the great white blaze) had gone all through the War, in Palestine.

The story of Paleface perpetually revived Muzz.

Paleface had vanished at the behest of the Purchasing Committee, vanished with his man that rode him. Paleface had sailed off with the Dorset Yeomanry to Egypt, been wounded at Gaza, seen action throughout ... Paleface, purchased back from the Army, hadn't been obliged to rely on the War Office ... Paleface had found himself embarked from Tripoli in the grander company of two ex-chargers. To hunt again.

Still the penny hadn't dropped.

Muzz had never dreamt that her horses might have gone to Egypt. She'd pictured them in Flanders. Aunt *Ida* had known more than she'd divulged. This was because Muzz hadn't asked her.

'I could have nudged her in the right direction,' had said Grannie, splodgy with rouge, and her veins.

Muzz hadn't *wanted* to be nudged by Grannie.

7   Mustering, 1914

Sir Greville Selwood, acquiring one hundred and three Riding horses for the Dorset Yeomanry in Stag Westover and district, was to get forty-eight of them by 4 p.m. of the 1st Day to temporary HQ at Milborne Castle.

Mr Henstridge, the Purchasing Officer around Lackham and a member, likewise, of the Lord Lieutenant's Committee, had orders to send, by 6 p.m. of the 2nd Day, to the Old Artillery Barracks in Fawernbridge, eighty-seven Riding horses, three Pack, three Draught and a two-wheeled cart.

And so on.

Sir Greville Selwood passed Toller Bottom by.

Irene Romney's pastures and echoing stable-yard offered a permanent retirement to two aged ex-chargers, deposited there by her nephew, Captain Grazebrook; to her son Arthur's pensioner, the grey Romulus; and ease to the roan pony that went in the trap.

Griselda's groom, Dare, hadn't got his two up until late in July; and they were, even now, turned out in the over-lush paddocks at night, and doing but gentle road work.

There'd been no need to bring the horses into condition for the cub-hunting.

As for Dare ... Dare told Albie that Mrs Arthur was, on account of the outbreak, a-hastening back.

Dare himself was obliged (and were keen) to bugger off, and did so by the evening of that first day, to his yeomanry regiment in the next county. With a fond pat to each. Philomena was sleepy. She'd made the most of the summer grazing: she'd put on a belly.

The weather was warm.

Remounts had advertised *their* Purchasing Post in the *Chronicle*. It was for 7th August, at the Egmonts' place, Rivers House, three miles from Toller—Ida Lupus's, at Quarr Grange, was another, and Cuckenbry another.

Old Mrs Romney, pink about the gills, her mind on Arthur, on Alan Grazebrook too, her mind full, to capacity, of the imminent Threat, roused herself to do her duty and send Griselda's bay gelding and brown mare to

25

Rivers House.

Lazily, Conker and Philomena jogged over with Albie.

The yard was crammed with horseflesh. Folk's decent hunters, carriage horses, Mr Egmont's hunt horses, halfway horses off of the farms and the like. Albie got busy in swapping greetings with his acquaintanceship.

There was a flush in the air.

The Remounts officer was knowledgeable, pleasant; clean of tooth. Philomena pulled her lip away. She put her ears back. 'Thik yere d'belong to Mrs Arthur Romney. They baint the mistress's own,' stated Albie.

'Were they in your care at the time of the census?'

Albie was seventy, bow-legged; and John Chiswell's only hand. Dare, what was on for young Mrs Arthur, had fetched them up previous at Toller Bottom in April.

Philomena fidgeted.

The old lady had said to Albie, 'The country has a call upon our horses, and . . . and I *know* Mrs Arthur would be proud. Mrs Arthur would be *the first*. It's simply that Mrs Arthur can't give the say-so, and we can't reach her . . . since she is at sea. Will you say that? Will you remember? Have you *got* that, Albie?'

So Albie maintained stoutly, 'We'm not to let they go! They baint the missus's. Sir.'

The Purchasing Officer was seeking honest temperament, action that was true, well-formed feet; and a roomy middle piece.

He'd tried three himself.

'Her neck isn't set on well,' he remarked of Philomena.

'Grand charger,' said Albie, 'but she baint avaylible. Sir.'

The Purchasing Officer stood back. 'The gelding is a good 'un.'

The Army was paying sixty pounds for a charger, forty for a troop-horse.

Old Mrs Romney's glossy Daimler (what Albie didn't hold with) had already gone from the coach-house.

Remounts could take no more than fifty per cent of a stable.

Albie returned with the two animals and bad news: being missed in the census never made no difference.

'Requisitionin', Mrs Romney mum, be requisitionin',' said Albie. 'Thas what 'tis!'

'How remiss of me, Albie, I ought to have written a note for you to have shown the officer.'

In the early sunshine, a sergeant marched a mounted detail of the Field Remount Section in at the gates. They led in with them the organ-maker's cherished grey, Dalliance. The column swelled on out of the old lady's carriage-drive.

In cavalry 'halters', bridoons in their mouths, one out of every three stood with the rein passed through the back-strap of the halter of a companion. One of the fellows managed the reins of two on his near side and of another on the off.

The Field Section had kit strapped to hunting saddles! The beginning of the War was seeing shortages.

Old Mrs Romney hadn't risen up out of her bed. Anyways, Albie reckoned, 'twould a-bin the brandy until cockcrow . . .

Conker turned his head and gazed thoughtfully. With a scraping of gravel, they was off.

Folk had lined the street from the butcher's to the Chapel. A cheer was raised. The village's salute to the horses. Philomena stepped out. It was such a palpable occasion. The jackdaws laughed and flapped and hopped around the church tower.

This was August 9th.

It was boiling and the flies would be bad.

A sombre, abstracted mood was abroad; mixed with this queer elation.

In the brambles were tethered goats. Twice they met a driven pig and Dalliance widened her nostrils. Acres of corn had been cut. Not a breath of wind. The day held itself, shimmered.

Peacocks had alighted on the buddleia. A labourer waved his apron. A cow-dog darted up and was sent packing with tail between his legs. Bees hummed.

Conker was a gent. If asked to catch a loose

horse in the hunting-field and canter him back to a fallen rider, he made no fuss. He got on terms with the Field Section animal; and with the firm hand, the khaki breeches, khaki puttees and the toe of a boot.

Conker ignored Philomena.

Conker's was a grass cough. His head went down and he barked. Then the gruff voice would observe, 'Hold up, old fellow!' and, 'I d'trust that baint infictious!'

Philomena put her ears back and tried to kick away a horsefly from her belly.

She was puzzled.

The route was meandering. The halts were frequent. The men dismounted, slackened girths and brewed up. Sometimes, and on every hill, they marched at the horses' heads. And Philomena rested a foot in various stable-yards until the column formed again.

Early in the afternoon, they went into a sweet-tasting stream. A grey heron, arrested, with glazed expression, flapped into the air.

The Field Section horses were unsaddled. They could have a shake. Under the *numnah* their coats were dark with sweat.

The hedges of hawthorn, blackthorn, hazel, holly, elm, sweet briar and field maple were draped in bryony and hops. A tiny boy, perched on a five-bar outside Bew Hinton, saluted. Dalliance and Philomena hungered for shade.

The sun sank lower in the sky. The worst

29

flies went. The oil of citronella, Albie's last thought to their welfare, glistened still on poll and dock. The scenery of the Vale was replaced by woodland. The land rose and fell.

In the evening, on the road beyond Almsbury, a black cob picked up a stone.

Tired, they plodded on. Out of the village of Milton Ducis. On to the edge of the railway-line. On for a quarter of a mile in the dusk. Philomena's head came up. They could scent horses. They could hear horses. There was a casual order.

Philomena felt a tug.

Conker followed the khaki, willy-nilly. Three together, they were led to a trough. The water tasted spoilt.

Those that didn't drink at once or drink their fill were disturbed by the company.

With their halters exchanged for stable headcollars, tied by a knot that Conker, at least, knew how to undo, to a fixed rail between piles, and by both hind fetlocks to a peg, they found themselves in horse-lines. The shackle was a leather thong around the pastern. The rope ran free on the peg in a V.

Philomena was affronted. Never in her life held like that by the heel, she accepted the fact meekly; as though her foot had been caught in a fence.

If they felt some bewilderment, in company there was reassurance. The stars sailed in a clear sky. Their quarters were into the lightest

30

of breezes. Well after dark, nosebags arrived. In hers, Philomena found crushed oats, bran and chaff.

Nosebags were succeeded by pokes of hay. Philomena made haste to clean hers up.

Conker, calm as ever, sneezed.

At dawn, water was offered in a bucket. The horses were given a strapping. Then another feed. This was not home. At home, water had followed feed.

8 Unravelling it

Griselda said to Captain Palsy 'And *now*, only *now*, so smug and ingenuous, H.H.G. remarks, "In his letters, Alan mentioned your Philomena, you know. And Conker." Oh, give me *patience*!'

'Don't take to the old crow, do you!'

'Does anybody?'

'Heaps, Griselda, heaps.'

'Oh. Did you ever run into Alan? He was my husband's cousin.'

'Not often.'

'And, I said, "You *kept* it from me . . . ?" Alan corresponded with my mother-in-law; through his having been, in boyhood, parked on her at Toller.'

Palsy was devoted to Griselda.

'Don't let me bore you, Jack. H.H.G. said, "I

did consider telling you." And I said, "That wasn't kind." Mild, for me!' Griselda sighed. 'Alan must have assumed that she would have passed on what he'd written to her about my horses, don't you agree, Jack? So she said, "Well, somehow I did not!" I said, "May I hear now?" When she'd had "time to sort them into what was for general consumption"! I said to her, I murmured, positively murmured, "Were you not attached, ever, to horses?" My mother-in-law shook out a fold of her skirt . . . sheer affectation . . . and said, "Arthur and Alan gave their lives for their country." How dared she!

'I said, "Alan and Arthur aren't alive, *are not living*." She said, waspish as ever, "I don't suppose for a minute that Conker and Philomena are either. If you can speak of *horses* in the same breath! You must be *unnatural*."'

Palsy cleared his throat. Uneasy.

Working herself up, he thought.

'I said, "What about my dear Conker? Were they together?" She said, "You *harp on and on*. Conker was an *ugly* brute. And that *haughty* mare of yours." She said . . . can you believe what she said, Jack? . . . she said, "Philomena threw her head up whenever you tried to stroke her nose." I feel dreadful, you know I left them with her, in her care, when I should have sent them to my sister Ida. Arthur expected it.

'She said, "It doesn't cease to surprise me how thoroughly *stupid* horses are. It must be plain to them that persons who approach to pat them and to stroke their noses are benign, that no ill will come of it, and yet they throw up their heads, over and over again. *So* dense!" I goggled at her . . .'

Palsy noticed that Griselda was scrutinizing his face, to determine whether or not he'd got the point. Into the corners of Griselda's eyes a quizzical smile had crept.

He tried to look obtuse.

'One didn't, at Quarr devote much *thought* to the Yeomanry. We weren't those brave spirits that assembled in *drill-halls*, and tore off to Weymouth Downs each summer to sleep in tents, gallop about and . . .'

'There you go again!'

'Although they were people one knew. So many familiar names. *So* many! Until Gallipoli, it hadn't registered with me.'

'Hm!' he said.

The notion that Conker and Philomena could have gone to Egypt hadn't entered her head. Not only had she first got wind from her H.G. mother-in-law but she'd had to grovel.

Paleface had been brought back to England by an Egmont, an Egmont from Rivers House in Nyland. Having gallantly restored Paleface to Lord Maurward's, Bobs Egmont had toppled his motor into the millrace, and drowned.

'So he was of no use.'

To Palsy, Griselda explained how she herself had *implored* her mother-in-law. 'Would you *reveal* to me what Alan wrote to you?'

Alan had been posted to Palestine from the 8th Hussars in France.

'She said, "Oh, censorship caused letters to be so dull." I said, "I'd be awfully glad to hear, though, what he did vouchsafe on the subject."'

Griselda's wasted months!

'I might have been of use to you! *Real* use!' pleaded Palsy. 'Introduced you to the old Colonel, Stocks-Moyle. He knows everything there is to know! The county is full of chaps that served with the Dorset Yeomanry in Egypt and Palestine.'

'Occupied me for almost a year.'

'I've had no idea,' Palsy said, with utter helplessness, caught by one of his paroxysms.

At last, Irene Romney had produced the few morsels in Alan's letters. *Flower says Conker was killed in the Charge at Agagiya. For certain.* In Alan's pencil. *Philomena is flourishing.* The Jordan Valley. *Would you tell Griselda!*

Then, from Baalbek, *Philomena is flourishing, and here with me in Syria. I'll contrive to get Philomena cast, she can travel with my grey. Do tell Griselda!*

'Darling Alan!'

Griselda had travelled to Fawernbridge, not thirty miles from Up-Nyland, by train, via Quarr and Aunt Ida, to interrogate Captain

Flower, a man with whom, for her entire life, she'd had slight acquaintance. Shared her flask in a hailstorm up to their hocks in mud near Eastover Wood. Danced with.

'Oh Jack, I can't be said to have *lived* in the county since I was a child. I married. What is familiar to Ida has been a closed book.'

Palsy had to nod gloomily.

All a bit thick, thought Palsy.

Nick Flower had known Philomena so well. Nick Flower, whose face had been worn by Egyptian dust and Palestinian sun, had smiled at the memory. 'I've dug out a photograph,' he'd said. There, in a tiny, cracking print, had been a gaunt horse, unsaddled, in a headcollar. In pencil on the reverse side: *'Turnham with Philomena.'*

'Turnham?' said Jack Palsy, dully.

Griselda shrugged.

Nick Flower *believed* Philomena to have gone in 1919 among the sound and fit ('well, fairly') to the Remount Depôt in Cairo.

It was enough.

'Darling Georgie understands.'

9 Unsatisfactory daughter-in-law

'I *am* improvident, I am *aware*, it's what you all say!' a belligerent Griselda said. 'I've managed!'

'So peculiar,' said Mrs Romney, senior.

'I do think of Georgie, I do!'

Irene Romney assumed her 'glum' look, the prerogative of her generation. A face of despair.

'I don't see,' Griselda remarked, 'that I've had so much help from people that I need to justify myself.'

Irene Romney sighed.

'Won't you miss the hunting?'

'Nothing to hunt.'

'There is that agreeable friend of yours, Captain Palsy.' Griselda liked men.

'Captain Palsy is quite five years younger than I.'

'Won't he continue to mount you? And you can go over to your sister. How glad you must be to have the train.'

'There will be another season,' said Griselda, 'and, after that, another. Besides, Giggle is trotting lame. The shoulder. A pity, for the child's sake. Amabel, I mean. Georgie may go to Ida for the holidays. He'll leap at it. Or at night he could be at my mother's.'

It was a thrust.

'Master George may find a welcome with me.'

'Yes, how kind,' said Griselda.

'He might prefer my house.'

'He might. I'll ask him.'

Irene Romney drank. She made no secret of it. Irene Romney never saw her own back door: she candidly believed there was a pile there and that every so often the odd-man loaded the bottles into a wheelbarrow and buried them in the spinney.

'Well, consider it.'

'I'll consult Nanny.'

The conversation negotiated a turn.

'There are the dogs! I suppose you'll land your sister with them.'

'I shall miss the dogs. That,' said Griselda, 'is true. Dogs do have to be left behind. Married to Arthur, I had to learn that.'

'Nobody coerced you into following him.'

'It was better I did. He was inclined to forget us.'

'What nonsense!'

'Chaps,' said Griselda, 'become absorbed. The ship can be wife and children. When he remembered us, he was an excellent husband and a most endearing father.'

'A waspish remark!'

'Not at all. And to think I might have let Amabel have her own dog!'

'Reversionary interest, Griselda, is *wicked*! It's a very last resort! For an emergency! Why didn't you consult a *man*?'

'I ought to have gone last year.'

Mrs Romney drew a breath that was discourteous.

'The people were helpful.'

'They *would* be!'

'To whom else was I to have applied? What

is lucky,' said Griselda, 'in respect of Arthur's being killed, is that as a naval wife I am familiar with money, and investments, and paying the bills. It is a shock to many women.'

'That Arthur was killed was *lucky*?'

'I've arranged to have a fraction of what I shall get under the terms of the Trust *in the end*.'

'You say some dreadful things!'

'I am practical.'

'So practical you are ready to go off to Egypt, with no heed to cost, or climate, or children.'

'Great heed!'

With a daughter-in-law such as Griselda, one had the sort of relationship one had, thought Irene Romney, with a cardboard Easter egg once the contents had been eaten or had disappeared.

'Your four hundred pounds for Bark Hart . . . *that* outlay . . . was a necessity!'

'Mm,' said Griselda.

'A stupid whim is not in the same league.'

Griselda waved a hand in agreement.

'Let me have a chat with Nanny,' said Irene Romney.

'Please don't! Nanny is my affair.'

10   Remounts

The first nights, at Milton Ducis, were without shelter. That was agreeable. The first day was without shelter. That was disagreeable. The horses twitched without cease. The Army took none with short docks: oddly, not all were long-tailed.

They were used to stalls. But there wasn't a partition. Each was allowed three foot.

Seasoned hunters, when picketed, were expected to give no trouble. Yet a few *were* alarmed. The noises unsettled them. When the lines were shifted, a night was suffered within thirty yards of canvas. The canvas creaked.

There was the day when a dark brown gelding scratched his ear with a hind foot and got that foot over his head rope. On another, a bay mare, with a dish face and nervous ears, went down and panicked, injuring herself and a neighbour.

Within the experience of many had been 'sales'. This was an interminable day at the sales.

Water was not at hand. They went away to be watered. Two horses to one man.

The ground was already sour.

There was a dearth of hay-nets. The rations tossed and blew.

Standing for hours on end did no animal any

good. Sometimes Philomena was loose in the *chukker*. The horses milled until urged to head all in one direction. It was tricky: a stampede could have ended in catastrophe. Remounts juggled the need for increased fitness and exercise with the routine of the Depôt; which was to sort the good from the poor.

The horses were *losing* condition.

There were in the region of fifteen hundred at Milton Ducis; and, in men, two squadrons.

In a test for the carrying of glanders, Philomena had drops in the eye. Had she displayed pus and inflammation within twelve hours she would have been destroyed.

A full veterinary inspection followed.

She was trotted up. She was felt over; and was sounded for wind (the Purchasing Officer had put his ear to her chest). Her teeth told her age and she was measured at the wither. Each foreleg was lifted, fingers went under the toe and the leg was pulled forward from the shoulder. Putting a foot on the blacksmith's knee, yet higher. She stamped each hoof down again.

Intimate note was made of conformation, colour, markings and blemishes; down to the last white hair.

Conker was 'gelding, 10 yrs, 15.3 hh., bright bay, irregular star, broad race'. The markings of his legs boiled down to 'off hind leg, near fore fetlock partly'. That meant he had a white stocking on the off hind and pretty much of a

40

sock on the near fore.

His name had been recorded.

Others were viewed with severity. Cow hocks, straight shoulders, razor-backs, curby hocks, stag knees, gummy legs, sickle hocks, cat-hams ... Such faults tended to call into question the Purchaser's judgement.

The pale colour of two of Conker's hoofs was frowned upon. Dark hoofs were reckoned the harder. High frogs were favoured. The flat-soled, with large, fleshy frog, merited a sigh. Conker's sat well in the sole.

Of Philomena, the A.V.C. captain said, 'A free mover ... excellent feet. Deep through the heart, ribs well-sprung. Ill-set neck. Pokes her nose.' At least she wasn't ewe-necked or cock-throttled. 'Whole-coloured light brown, mealy muzzle, tan to darkening points.'

Her legs weren't mealy.

Philomena was spared a twitch when approached by a fellow with a funny-smelling piece of metal ... as black-hot as a shoe ... on the end of a pole-handle. She had a man at her head, and rails on her off side. She instinctively bunched up.

Philomena didn't even kick out when a stinging pain seared her behind the stifle, on the thigh: she grunted. But she lowered her head in shock.

She was Army property and bore the broad-arrow brand that marked even a box of ammunition or a crate of hoof-picks. She went

41

stiffly on her near hind for four days.

The cavalry of the line, contrary to popular opinion, was not perfectly keen to be drafted people's quality and part-bred hunters. The heavies desired bone. They wanted Irish horses. Lancer and hussar regiments prized endurance above bone. Quality thoroughbreds were appreciated by infantry officers. The R.E. required the stolid and solid.

Despite the rush to achieve full mobilization, regiments would disparage horses: the latter found themselves returned to depôt so that more could be drawn.

To bring regiments up to war establishment, Remounts sought to supply anything decent that stood for preference 15.1 hh. to 15.2 hh. and no higher than 16 hands; and was, in age, of six to ten years. No greys, unless to fill a special order: in practice, multitudes of greys were to go to France.

To the territorial batteries of R.H.A. went Cleveland Bays; to the field artillery the more raw-boned draught-horses and all heavy horses. To every regiment, sundry animals for their transports. Many an odd 'un, down on the forehand, or herring-gutted, flat-sided or tied at the knee, would end as a pack animal, harnessed to a water cart, or to an ambulance; or hustled off among the tolerable to the Army Service Corps.

Yeomen, smelling, as it were, of the hunting-field, appreciated the sorts with which they had supplied themselves in peacetime, and which they had brought with them, obliged to sell them *pro tem* to the Army. In hastening to bring themselves up to strength in horseflesh *and* recruits, they didn't cavil at greys.

It was an unspoken desire that the local yeomanry should get a useful bunch.

Conker, Philomena and Dalliance ... 'the three friends', said the A.V.C. captain, but Conker wasn't so fond of Philomena ... were clipped (their summer bloom), their manes were freshly hogged. They were re-shod regardless. They were issued with one spare front shoe and one spare hind. Also the regulation Universal Pattern saddle, *numnah*, surcingle; breast plate, halter, bit and bridoon.

Being entrained was no surprise to a hunter that went to distant meets—accustomed to a ramp that allowed a horse to be led from the platform into a roofed carriage with coconut-matted sides, and inner partitions, mangers and hay-nets. Three to each box; facing forwards.

This train was open. Nine in together. A cram of heads, each hitched short to a bar, to face the platform.

A sensible one would be led in first.

Though subdued, the horses, once in, squealed, and humped, and pinched their nostrils. A black was heaved by linked arms. Rather forthright encouragement was employed. There was, nevertheless, great

43

effort to 'act quiet'.

A callow gelding insisted on leaping the ramp.

Quite ten mares were in season.

It was a thirsty sort of summer's day.

There was a great deal of hanging about, and shunting; although theirs—'the three friends' —was to be the shortest journey.

Yet it was a stiff Philomena that came onto an unfamiliar platform. Frantic whinnying; and she, who thrilled to sudden excitement, called back. The nervy sweat sang in Philomena's nostrils.

Her ears flickered.

This was a quiet countryside. A smell of heath floated over the water meadows. Their shoes hammered on the metal and sparks flew off the flints. Sixteen horses, of which three were but halter-broken. The metal gave out directly. After the bridge, a slight incline. She heard the muffled crump-crump of shod feet on the white, summer dust.

They scented the air, tossed their noses. Philomena was getting into one of her fevers of impatience.

There was a cough; and a sneeze from Conker. It cleared his windpipe.

'That there d'sound healthier like,' said the friendly voice of their march across the county; rather as though it shouldn't be talking. Conker carried his pal in the saddle. No Field Section horses with them. Conker had been chosen: he always would be chosen.

Yellow gravel, lain by road-menders, swelled in the ruts. The chalk ridge behind the river valley reappeared to their near side; and down from it blew a salt tang.

The lane curled and the green fields shrank; retreated.

The horses were the sole objects that moved in a wide and lonely place. They hadn't gone two miles.

There was a buzz of insects.

A hutment, bell-tents and picket lines sheltered in the wide, shallow bottom of a leeward, sandy slope that rose gently to east and north. The horses of the column, with their keen eyes, were set alight by a weird vision. Out of the haze there cantered, in a wavering, confused fashion across bruised gorse and bracken, a loose, bay horse, with a straw dummy on his back; pursued by four mounted figures, whooping, with pointed swords.

The voice spoke to Conker. ' 'Tis goodbye to 'ee, fellow . . . no service overseas for you divils, and . . . and . . . *good hunting!*'

11 Amabel

Amabel had the sea in her blood. Friends of her father had told her so. They also said how

like her father she was. Amabel hot and
bothered reminded them of him; of his rages.
Rages so spectacularly funny. She was quick,
and bright. It didn't matter what she did, in
floods or over-excited ... they said she was
going to inherit his temperament; the gloom,
the elation.

'Dreadful for you, Amabel, to be so like
him!' was what they said, roaring. It was a
compliment. Nanny thought they'd made her
cocky, and that cocky little girls didn't go down
well.

Amabel slept with her father's sword above
her bed. Looking at medals made Amabel cry.
Muzz couldn't, herself, remember having cried
as a child. Muzz pinned the dress-set into the
smocking of Amabel's frock.

'Darling, for you and Nanny, Egypt will be
an *adventure*.'

And for Georgie?

'Georgie may choose. Quarr with Aunt Ida.
Or Toller Bottom ... but I don't believe I
could have a moment's peace ... with H.H.G.'

Amabel was gratified.

Nanny was aghast.

To Mrs Romney's own mother, Nanny said,
'I've been put in a quandary, Mrs Lupus, I'm
sure you feel for me ... I consented to come
with Mrs Romney to Bark Hart, where the
household arrangements were *not* to my liking,
and if you could suggest to Mrs Romney that it
is beneath her to get down on the floor,

46

besides doing irreparable harm to her hands ... It never entered my head that we should be setting foot on board a ship. And where our support is I have yet to discover ... I'm too old to be stranded ...'

'Nanny, you're hardly *old*! And why should you be stranded?'

'... and I expect to be met with typhoid, and infantile paralysis, and ringworm, malaria. I never have had a dispute with Mrs Romney over my handling of the child, it seems the outside of enough to take Amabel to Egypt, or trust her welfare to a foreign doctor ...'

'Nanny, the Army is in Egypt.'

'Army doctors!' scoffed Nanny. 'I've heard we have Colonials there. I can't have Amabel under a dago.'

'The Australians will have gone home by now. And the Indian Army regiments. Let's be optimistic and trust that Amabel isn't ill at all. Cairo is civilized.'

Mrs Romney said to her mother, 'Oh, Nanny is suspicious of medical men.'

To Mrs Romney, senior, the Toller Bottom grannie, Nanny said, in her nursery voice, 'Oh goodness me no! There isn't the remotest need for anxiety. Mrs Romney has it down to the last detail. We are in for a very nice trip. Back in no time! The child is cock-a-hoop. Of course, it will be new to me but I wouldn't be parted from Mrs Romney for the world. Oh no, Mrs Romney, *we* have no qualms.'

The Commander's mother smiled incredulously.

'You may confide in me, Nanny . . .'

Nanny closed her lips.

'Mrs Romney and I,' Nanny said, 'we *ask* Amabel whether we may peep at her pictures.'

There was a gasp.

'How absurd you all are!'

Nanny was of the opinion that absurdity was the spice of a happy childhood. If Amabel wanted to be rolled up in the nursery carpet Nanny wasn't the one to fuss over dirt in Amabel's pretty hair. The mat was shaken out of the window by Mrs W. daily. If Amabel wished to be carried down the stairs and around the garden, rolled up in clean, stringy blue mat, Nanny summoned the man, Baiter.

Nanny encouraged Amabel to garden.

If Nanny desired Amabel, at bedtime, to lie down and go to sleep, Amabel did so. When Amabel woke up crying, Nanny came running. Nanny wasn't fond of the bats. Amabel was. Well, so long as they didn't drop fleas. Nanny had no fault to find with furniture piled to make a carriage, or with the chairs harnessed to it, or with the reins and a whip brought in from the dirty outside. Nanny was sound out-of-doors. She blew eggs, and was that special thing, 'observant'. Pottering along the hedgerows and watching birds, butterflies, dragonflies and beetles was far more a delight to her than a duty.

Amabel *never* minded that Georgie was Muzz's favourite child.

Then Captain Palsy ('Take care of Mrs Romney, and bring her safely home!') went and daunted Nanny.

12 Eldon Heath

Conker's career as a trooper ended when Captain Neville's groom descended on the horse-lines and led him away to a different life.

Conker went; looking about himself with interest.

The inspection by several pairs of knowledgeable eyes, and a further test for glanders, since three remounts had been destroyed as carriers and the Regiment had undergone a period of quarantine ... the inspection by these knowledgeable eyes culminated in the sizzling by the shoeing smith of the letters DY into the wall of Philomena's off hoof, below the crown; and, to match that on the near, 541. She was issued to 'A' Squadron. As they grew out, these brands would be renewed. The unsettling air of the Depôt had been exchanged for the better.

'Off-saddles' meant that Private Mudge, with his shy smile, rubbed and knuckled her back; restoring circulation to numbed muscles. He'd lead her to loose sand and dribble water onto her loins. It gave her an irresistible urge to roll.

She was lucky in Mudge. He had all the knack.

Philomena could queen it over grey Dalliance, on her off side, and a meek, bay mare. The troop-horses were picketed not in breast-lines but tied by the head to a peg, and then with a single heel rope. The shackle was above the fetlock joint, and stiffer. Where its padded edge fell on the joint there was irritation. Horses could gall themselves.

The troublesome had their head ropes shortened; and, with ears laid back, they sulked. Not every officer noticed. Not every man was as good as Mudge.

Whereas the slugs had to be ridden strongly, what was difficult (to one with a long, free stride) was learning to walk at four miles an hour, to trot at eight; and at no more than four or eight. Measuring sticks marked the quarter-miles. Horses liked moving in a body. Philomena's belly and lack of condition helped her.

The instructor blew a short blast on a whistle to draw attention to commands. He was like a person who bellowed at a deaf dog. Commands were accompanied by signals. He'd waggle his hand; hold it up flat; or pump a fist up and down at his breeches.

Work was simple.

Inspections and assembly caused those of the experienced men on the Heath to shiver with shame. Through a halcyon recollection of what should have been rather than an appreciation of what had been. In a time of peace, the Regiment's muster had been two hundred and eighty-two.

What galled the officers was the shortage of mobilization equipment.

All ammunition had gone to the Front.

The yeomen did *try* to train like regulars. Their Adjutant had served in a *pukka* cavalry regiment. There was no lack of zeal. But, during 'Stables', saddles weren't cocked on the ground: they were strewn all anyhow, amid a shocking confetti.

The War cut training short.

Mudge was a freckly fellow; sweet of breath. In weight, he was nine stone ten; below average. With Philomena Mudge was well pleased.

When they were inspected in full marching order, she accepted with equanimity the copious quantity of items attached to the saddle and to Private Mudge himself.

Yeomen could be duffers at packing the Universal Pattern saddle. The very buckles undid themselves. Picketing gear, blanket, great-coat, ground-sheet, water canteen, two nosebags . . . all plumped off like pheasants; and, seeing this, the horses would flick their ears. Or slouch hats blew off. These the men *fell out* to retrieve. Frightful.

Philomena was unused to carrying a deal of

weight. And still without a bandolier slung around her neck. The introduction was necessarily gradual.

Early of a morning, they ambled ('marched in column of half-sections') along the narrow lanes. A halt was ordered after a mile or two: she could stale and her girths be tightened. In *every* hour there was a ten-minute halt and 'Off saddles'. Mudge would remove the bit and bridoon to let her graze. If hot, she might roll. The men had their brew. In the ten minutes before that halt Private Mudge would march on foot. Philomena learnt to adapt her ideas.

She was asked to show her paces, and do half passes, in the makeshift *manège*.

Far from being unnerved by the noises of a camp, Philomena felt reassured. She began to understand the orderly trumpeter. The lovely, four descending notes of 'Feed' were soon engraved in her heart. 'Reveille' was heard with a satisfaction that said 'Stables' had soon to follow.

They were watered on the way back from exercise; and, since they were in camp, they would be taken upstream right into the river, three further times in the day.

Then there was a strapping, for an hour, more thorough than the earlier brief brushing down.

And then ... then the four tilting notes ... four falling and *poop poop-poop poop-poop-pet-teee*, a high one! And so on, in that vein.

Much pawing and whickering!

Mudge was meticulous. He would turn the finished nosebag inside out and air it in the sun. Without breast-lines, a hay-net made fast at each end to lie like a lozenge wasn't possible. Any wind, and Mudge weighed down her poke.

They were kept off the new hay.

Private Mudge had sympathetic hands, rare in a man of his education. He was amused by Philomena's oddities.

There were fellows that bumped in the *manège* with their stirrups crossed (off-side *over* the near-side) in front of the pommel, or practised 'pursuit' in which one man had to touch another while the other tried to elude him, or 'wrestling' at which one had to grasp the other around the waist and the other to parry . . . *Not he!* Mudge had assembled a day per month in a drill-hall; gone every summer to Camp.

The remounts had an introduction to knee-haltering; and to hobbles. Not to nose-to-tail linking—that was put off.

Picket-lines had their orientation shifted with the weather.

Bewilderingly, horse-clothing was issued to 'A' Squadron; fitted, rolled and withdrawn by the S.Q.M.S. to Stores.

At noon, they heard the four blissful notes again.

Mudge had foot drill; and, named as a flank

53

guide, mounted drill on foot; skill-at-arms, or sabre thrusts; a deal of toiling and polishing; refreshers in rudimentary map-reading and sketch-drawing; use of a compass; perceiving cover; eschewing public troughs; thinking *of* and *for* the horse at all times; never striking the horse. Never.

Initiative and dash.

In the cool, there was more exercise, in the *manège* or over the Heath; the 'Watering Order', 'Stables' ... and last rations were issued.

If Mudge's hands seemed full, the *heads* of the recruits were by 'Guard Mounting' a-whirl; and the fellows (able with horseflesh though they might be) would reel into their tents and stick their toes at the pole; or propped their eyes open, on duty.

Genuine troop drill, mounted, was as yet a dream.

Nature at Eldon Heath offered aids to cavalry training. As well as the *manège* and the larger riding-school with *cavalletti* poles and jumps, there were slopes to slide; and a level expanse upon which an entire regiment could mass, manoeuvre, form line and charge.

'Horrible sights' were supposed to feature for troop-horses and chargers alike. Fallen stock had been hailed in the shape of a Red Devon carcass at the edge of Farmer Tilcot's six-acre.

Internal gases were heaving inside the cow.

There wasn't *so* much stink for the wind to carry off. A horse's sense of smell was keener. There might have been a snort or two.

In the freshening air, however, a daft spark had laid gun-cotton in the carcass.

This explosion startled a black gelding: he cannoned into Private Payne's leg and shattered the knee in it. Morsels of ruby cow-flesh had flown onto the two chestnuts. A bay was dripping blood.

Mudge held Philomena together.

The clump of gorse bushes was making 'haw-haw' noises. Philomena broke out a sweat on her shoulder.

'Idiots!'

That was one day. The next was funnier.

Dalliance was a novice ride. Perfect for a recruit that in peace would have been confined to drill on foot and to the riding-school until he could go bareback, with his arms crossed, over all its jumps.

Private Gould, aged sixteen years, had fibbed in the juvenile aspect. A physical specimen, having bronze hair and a broad chest, he could write his name on the ceiling with half a hundredweight suspended from his little finger.

Dalliance was to the rear of Philomena.

Gould's attributes didn't help him to notice that his Dalliance had started to tremble. There was no carcass; just a patch of rank, squashed grass. Dalliance had turned to jelly.

Gould was blithe: the lad hadn't witnessed the explosion. Her ears flickered, were laid back; and her eyes rolled, flashing the whites.

In a frantic plunge, Dalliance was gone.

Gould was dragged for a distance. When his boot fell from the iron he was unconscious. Dalliance bolted on, stoking panic.

With a huge jerk and snort she pulled herself up when she stepped on a rein.

Her foot released the rein and, with a louder, longer snort, she set off again, tail a-cock. Her saddle had slipped. The fright increased; but she circled, to head back towards the lines.

At a dry ditch in a bottom she executed a wild leap, and tipped over, hitting her neck a crack on timber shoring. Here she lay winded.

She struggled to her feet.

They were riding to cut her off; Mudge and Ashmore, with Corporal Worth . . . Whinnying like a filly, Dalliance careered on, towards the interested horses of 'A' Troop.

Philomena, with her long stride, outstripped the others.

At that juncture, the grey collapsed in a tangle; thrashing. Mudge jumped off and sat on Dalliance's head.

Philomena, well-mannered hunter that she aspired to be, whose turn of foot had been noted by Lieutenant Flower, for he eyed her in a considering sort of way, stood impassively over her own reins.

13   The younger Pardoner

Since this Mrs Romney didn't appear to be at all high in the instep yet was a 'real' lady, neighbours had done their mostest to make Bark Hart more conformable. If their lady had but consulted a soul over the two travelling fellows with their chloroform, she'd a-bin set aright.

A matter of pride 'twere that children, *boys* what wore coarse cloth next to the skin, could wander in and out of Bark Hart, and be treated to bread and jam, even bread and cold bacon, or dripping.

Nanny's starched uniform did strike a clang in the heart of village queerness. Nanny's grey cloak, white pinafore and blue-grey uniform drew mirth *and* respect. Nanny herself had a modest face, and zigzagged cowpats with the air of a camel.

In memory, a fair dozen from Up-Nyland had gone off into service.

Nanny had turned out, *not* in her uniform, for a village social down at Riversmeet, and won folk over.

Francis Pardoner reckoned Mrs Romney had a pleasant way. Francis dawdled the hours in staring at passers-by. Mrs Romney, on spotting him in his chair beneath the eaves, would have a cheery word.

Frank had lined, fresh cheeks and a thin body and above the knees his legs ceased to be. One had been amputated shorter than the other. He had 'new', and they pained him. With born delight, Francis Pardoner had watched little Miss Amabel on her pony. Miss Amabel rode astride; and sat a treat. He'd missed the sight no end. With Giggle unsound and that.

Mrs Romney had jumped down from her bicycle, once, to ask Father how rosehips made into a syrup. Four or five time, she'd wanted 'Mr Pardoner' to wring a neck. Polite, like.

The fifth hen's neck and Mrs Romney said, 'I don't even know where it was that you were wounded, Francis. The Western Front?'

'Palestine, Mrs Romney, m'm,' blurted Francis, straight out. 'Up from Gaza, like, to Beersheba, and into they Judaean hills.'

And his regiment? The Queen's Own Dorset Yeomanry. Francis Pardoner had joined up in May 1915, when the Third Line had been raised for to supply the first with reinforcements. He'd had fortune. The poor fellows of t'other sister unit, the 2/1st Dorsets, was to have their horses took away in 1916 and be stuck on bicycles. Think of doing cavalry drill on bicycles! There having been no drill book else. And very sick, by all account; officers and other ranks both. Francis had gorn in a draft, out to the Regiment in Egypt . . . winter of 1916.

Mrs Romney said, merry, hoicking Miss Amabel off of the basket-seat, 'Oh, Francis, good heavens! Would you be astonished if I were to tell you that my two hunters went to the Dorset Yeomanry from Milton Ducis? So Captain Flower has informed me. One of them, a brown mare, with a mealy muzzle, a great character, was *with you in Palestine*!'

Francis Pardoner was well acquainted with Mr Flower. Francis fancied he'd known each and every darn charger and troop-horse. To one on 'em, he'd owed the shatter of his second leg.

Frank could discover in himself no recollection, special, of a brown mare. 'Nor of any Filly Mina neither.'

'Captain Flower has a snap of her!' the lady said gaily. And, 'When you were in the Jordan Valley, Major Grazebrook was Second-in-Command ... you remember *him*! Major Grazebrook was my husband's cousin. Won't you,' the lady begged Frank Pardoner, 'tell me all about your War?'

II SAILING

In a remote oasis in Upper Egypt an Arab chieftain said this to me: 'Your people treat the dog as your friend, and the horse as your slave. With us Arabs it is the other way. Ours is the better plan . . .

'Every man should have one horse that he cares for beyond anything else. If he makes friends with a dog the horse will know, and he may lose the friendship of the horse.'

LORD MOTTISTONE (General Jack Seely), *My Horse Warrior*

I recollect the time when the Yeomanry did a small amount of drill and duty every year, learning certain manoeuvres and performing them as well as we could. But in those days we certainly, from the colonel downwards, were not fit to take our places alongside regular soldiers in the field, as the Yeomanry have so fully become. But we did our best.

VISCOUNT PORTMAN, *speaking 8th May 1918 upon the occasion of the presentation by the subscribers and the unveiling of Lady Butler's painting, 'The Charge of the Dorset Yeomanry at Agagia, Egypt', to the County Council.*

14 Preliminaries

Mrs Romney made the convoluted journey by bicycle and train to take Georgie out. Without that, Mrs Romney couldn't have borne it. They had luncheon together, and tea; and she tipped Georgie riches. Nanny found it a wrench, the abandonment of Georgie.

Nanny felt for small boys.

They would join at Plymouth, rather than toil to Gravesend; to render it easier for Nanny. It had put Mrs Romney in a slight fuss. Mrs Romney had no desire to sit 'at the Surgeon's table'. Mrs Romney had moved heaven and high water to obtain a passage for them: many ships were still in government service.

'Won't they know you're coming?' asked Nanny.

The trunks set off for Plymouth.

Dog baskets, bowls, leads, Mrs Romney, Amabel and Nanny were fetched by Miss Lupus. Nanny had looked forward to this. The Grange was less of a bind than Bark Hart in October. The dogs were to be parked.

In the Swift, Mrs Romney said, 'Ida, if you could bend your thoughts, dearest ... Bandages, lint, cotton wool, mackintosh, all our ointments, liniment, thermometer, sulphate of zinc, paraffin oil, grease,

63

Stockholm Tar, boots, louse powder, tweezers, scissors, black drinks, paring knife, rasp, blisters, arsenic tonic, enema kit, poultice bags, iodine, carbonate of ammonia, turpentine, Epsom salts . . . um, lime water . . . knife. What have I forgotten?'

Being practical was their creed.

'A finger-stall,' said Nanny.

Miss Lupus said, 'For a horse?'

Since Peter could canter through the fields and jump the yellowing hedgerows and clatter over or under the bridges, Amabel was silent. Only a dog managed to dribble and, in defiance of the open window, be sick.

Amabel was in awe of her Aunt Ida. Praise from that quarter was treasured. The dread lay in having to shake hands with the ancient with which the Grange was furnished, and 'shout'.

With her feet on the ground, Amabel disappeared to the stables. Peter's blue roan mare had to be found an empty loose-box; and Peter shown where to fill the hay-net and where to put up the feed. This would mystify and entertain. The stables reckoned Miss Amabel a duck.

Nanny kept away from all stables.

The comments of the Quarr staff, skeletal though this staff was, reached right to Nanny's nerves. Nanny had supported the notion of Egypt so far. She now wished she'd never said she'd go. Had she not, she and Amabel would have been parked. Nanny had never thought she'd envy a dog.

Instead of racketing after Madam, they might have enjoyed a pleasant visit to a very nice part of the world.

The grandmother at Quarr, over the park wall, was as straight as Grannie Romney was treacherous. The Commander had been a dear man. His mama was *rum*. By all accounts the Commander had been fond of H.H.G. Nanny had never known the cousin, Mr Alan, but he had too. So the woman must have had some good in her.

That her own Mrs Romney had nourished a tender feeling for Mr Alan, Nanny was *well* aware. The memory of Mr Alan was still wreathed ... indeed, Mrs Romney so rarely spoke of him and, when his name cropped up, displayed languor; *highly* conspicuous!

And a smile had come to Nanny's kind lips.

'I couldn't say it in front of Nanny,' Griselda was saying. 'D'you know, *Palsy* wanted to escort me!' They went into hoots. 'It isn't as though we'll be away for long.'

'Are you counting on things?'

'On my usual luck!'

Ida looked grave and said, 'You *are* dotty.'

'You're echoing Palsy. And it did annoy me, extremely much.'

'Do you even *like* him?'

'I can't bear it,' said Griselda, 'when one is diverted from a course of action, which, had one only taken it, would have diverted another

65

event from occurring.'

'What are you talking about?'

'Conker,' said Griselda, 'and Philomena. Leaving them at Toller Bottom.'

'Oh, Grizel!' said Ida.

Having 'lost' Georgie to Quarr, H.H.G. had been tricky over Plymouth. H.H.G. had been tiresomely determined to wave from the dock. Griselda had imagined the sheer frightfulness of a train journey with two bristly persons.

H.H.G. was seething at Toller Bottom.

Ida and Griselda headed to the Kennels.

Griselda never failed to glance at Ida for signs of melancholy. In Ida's face there was a pale and powdered ruddiness. Ida threw her heart over. She refused to be sad. Ida had her hounds, her horses, the dogs at the Grange; her huntsman; her head groom in late middle age; her fourteen-year-old under-strappers; the remnants. Ida had a household. Ida's year remained one of mating and whelping, of distemper, of puppies at walk, of keeping the hunt horses and her own hunters on their legs. Of showing good sport.

'That girl,' Ida remarked to her sister, 'is a daughter of Wastrel '15.'

Had Grizel, Ida wondered, become 'serious'? Griselda, who had once died, simply died, to disguise herself as a man and ride in a point-to-point race.

15   Coast Defence

'Stand up, Mudge, there is nothing so very amiss with her,' said Lieutenant Flower.

When Mudge had got off her head, Dalliance struggled to her feet and gave a great shake. Mudge straightened the saddle and girthed her up again.

She appeared to have emerged sound from her mishap.

Dalliance was to remain on the Heath. Mudge had orders to go off blissfully on his own; and he found, without recourse to map science, 'D' Troop at Three-Hole Farm.

Thanks to Mr Plomer, 'Feather' by nickname, thanks to his imaginative spirit, 'D' Troop's patrols took advantage of the land. Warrender Common was endowed with defiles (hollow roads) and rickety bridges. Philomena refused at a log because she could scent the young of a field mouse in the nest beneath it. She collided with the chestnut.

'D' Troop had been detailed to patrol the high chalk ridge of Canmell Down, where the breeze kept the flies away; and the sheen of the harbour kept company far below.

They built a beacon.

On past the barrows, and on, to gaze down at the outer sea; to dip languorous by the cliff to the shore; and up afresh, on the limestone.

The men released one of the two carrier pigeons that had ridden with them in a basket.

To wilder cliffs.

Half a mile inland, on the Head, they established a look-out post. By semaphore they signalled to an outlying section of 'C' Troop; and freed the second hen. Their look-out posts covered the sea reaches. The pigeons could out-fly a motorbikist.

'D' Troop was recalled to Eldon Heath, along with most of the Regiment.

The Colonel had arrived back from Brigade HQ. Without embarking on the 'perennial contentions' (sword *v.* rifle), he was determined. 'Let us,' he said, 'be fit to fight on foot, and to go into action as mounted infantry, whilst we preserve, with pride, our skill in shock and awe, and the efficacy of the *arme blanche*.'

To his 'comrades of Dorset', whose training had been abbreviated by Coast Defence, these ideas were so much jaw-jaw. They listened loyally.

The Lord-Lieutenant addressed the Regiment. Dammit if he didn't wish to ask for volunteers to serve overseas. Some married men paled. Mudge's blood ran and he thought, not half!

Two-thirds of them stepped forward. Those officers and men who didn't feel able, they would remain to form and train a second line. Since Philomena's first, reassuring glimpse of the Heath, little more than a month had elapsed.

Minus the two troops of 'A' Squadron down at Portland, the Regiment, on 7th October, proceeded with their painted farm wagons and carts, by route march to Creech Camp. In every village, folk turned out to see them go by. Upon the completion of these quaint ardours, Philomena was in good fettle.

The horses, unsettled, having no stall or stable that was familiar, became duller in their sensibilities. They counted on the company of each other. They dozed in fetlock-deep, disgusting mud.

The Regiment (indeed, the Brigade) was re-equipped. Mudge had a new sword. His rifle acquired a bayonet. His saddle gained a new bucket, and Philomena a blanket. Mudge got superior uniform. General service wagons replaced the bucolic vehicles. The wagons acquired mules. The mules acquired decent harness.

The squelch was so ruddy, the squadrons were dispersed upon surrounding villages.

Private Mudge did well in his musketry course. Sixty-nine points out of eighty-four at two hundred yards, and fifty-eight points at a range of five hundred. Philomena was introduced to cavalry drill; 'as did ought to be' said Mudge.

Lieutenant Plomer, O.C. 'D' Troop, proved a handicap.

Mounted, they were to drill first in troop, until they could form line, dress the front, advance in line; decrease the front, form column of sections, increase the front, incline, if pretty raggedly; shoulder, form troop in close order; wheel, and at the trot extend, at the trot close in . . . break up, and rally, be told off in fours.

When they were proficient, and had grasped the meaning of the commands, and could in the absence of commands 'follow the leader', drilling in squadron might follow.

What had baffled the recruits at Eldon Heath, and befogged some other fellows, was gone through slow. Even the paragon Mudge was glad to refresh himself.

It was conceivable that some day the Troop might have to dismount and prepare to fire. They were issued *at last* with ammunition, blank *and* live.

They were instructed in concealing their approach at the trot or the gallop; in throwing themselves off their horses, 'for action dismount', in handing their reins to the one man in four—the No. 3 in each section that galloped the led horses to the rear—and, not omitting to post look-outs, in flattening themselves behind a shred of cover, judging the distance, adjusting their sights, ready, at least *ready*, to fire upon a target.

Philomena was dismayed.

The horseholder was getting them all

infected. Better if they didn't pull up wild-eyed and snorting!

The officer soon blew two long blasts, and the horses set off back. Then it would be, 'Stand to your Horses'; and, 'Mount'; to retire by half troop from a position upon another.

Once, during 'Stables', Lieutenant Flower took hold of Philomena's tongue, he peered at her back teeth, and his fingers explored her gums. Horses that were stiff in the neck were trying, often, to protect a sore tooth or cheek from the action of the bit.

Lieutenant Flower told Mudge he detected no untoward thing.

Mudge had her out in long reins.

He asked her to back by feeling one rein, and alternately the other, persuading first the foot she'd had foremost and then the other to step back; and so on. Unsuspecting, she complied.

By the next asking, it had sunk in: she'd done what she most liked to resist doing. So she'd be mulish. Mudge worked patiently until she forgot her 'silly habit'.

Mr Flower bestowed on her one of his smiles.

There was a big exercise over the Plain. The Dorsets were engaged in it. A detachment of Bucks Yeomanry, with a machine-gun, acted enemy. The umpires were armed with very shrill whistles. 'A' Squadron did well at reconnoitring, and in reporting and in signalling back. O.C. 'B' Squadron 'failed to have recourse to initiative' and 'C' Squadron forded the wrong river.

The 'enemy' retired without loss.

There was practice in taking up a wounded man. Philomena had to stand, first while Mudge, in the saddle, hauled the casualty up across his pommel. Secondly, on his feet, he hoisted the wounded man up and over; mounting behind him.

Philomena was steady at this: her intelligence ensured that she shone at the peculiar.

On the Plain, a chestnut had bolted.

The autumn began to bite. They were entrained, in *pukka* horse-boxes, for the low horizons and bleak winds of Norfolk.

In the lines, Philomena tucked her tail in and was cold.

'A' Squadron went to Houghton Hall. Philomena was gratified to find herself in the stable-yard. A blizzard blew. Frost-nails were issued to the transport horses.

Before Christmas, German ships bombarded Great Yarmouth; and the entire Brigade turned out.

Conker's officer didn't play at soldiers every day of the week. Conker had already . . . from Eldon Heath . . . snatched a morning's cubbing, out with Miss Lupus's. The Master, Miss Lupus, had been thrilled to see the old boy so well-looking. When his duties permitted, Conker's officer followed hounds.

In February, Private Mudge had measles. He was fit for foreign service by the end of the first week of April. They'd been ordered to Egypt; and were issued with Wolseley helmets. By the 8th, shaken all night in tedious railway wagons, the Regiment was at Avonmouth Docks.

16   Jibbing at the gangway

In the train, Nanny said, 'Thank you, madam, no raised pie for me. It sits on the tummy or makes for heartburn. And I can't feel meat pie would be suitable for Amabel.'

'Tomato sandwiches,' said Miss Lupus, 'I knew you'd like those.'

'Oh, but the skins, Miss Lupus, the skins should have been scalded off!'

'They have been, Nanny, there are no skins. Galantine of calf's head?'

'What a messy thing for Amabel to eat, though.'

'Why not look in the hamper? Mrs Cockerell has crammed it with treats!'

'Oh, my, you've put so much thought into it.'

'Is the tangerine,' whispered Amabel, 'for me? Ought I to save it for Peter?' Nanny cast her employer and Miss Lupus a rictus that passed for her usual amiability. 'Better not toss it through the window, dear! Might be

73

understood *ill.*'

On the main line, no part of the journey had to be endured minus corridor. An absence of corridor never failed to induce the child to be 'bursting'.

Neither Mrs Romney nor Miss Lupus ever dreamt of setting foot in a public convenience. They would draw up the motor by a hotel, and march in. Unless there were clumps of gorse.

In a railway-carriage, Mrs Romney and Miss Lupus 'waited'. So too did Nanny. It behoved Nanny to school Amabel's bladder. It would stand Amabel in such stead.

Nanny was conscious that she'd been trained up, as a nursemaid, by the children's nurse to a private household; and not *properly*. Mrs Romney hadn't minded. Mrs Romney had never questioned Nanny's superior knowledge of infants and the small.

Only once had Mrs Romney 'said' something.

At her grandest, Mrs Romney had said, 'The world is divided, Nanny, into those of *it* who lick a fingertip to turn a page and those of *us* who do not.'

This had seared Nanny.

She'd wondered whether Norland nurses licked their fingers; or whether they'd been taught.

Mrs Romney was staunch C. of E. Nanny would have considered it scandalous had she foisted the Methodist in herself upon Mrs

Romney's children.

And Nanny liked it when Mrs Romney was (or chose to be) grand. Being Nanny Romney was agreeable; the tiresomenesses and all. Instinct, as it were, had invited her to study Mrs Romney's speech. She wouldn't have aped Mrs Romney or put on airs. Nanny knew she would look back on her years as Nanny Romney with pride; and with a whatsit tantamount to love.

They were obliged to pass the night at the Rawley Hotel. Nanny failed to get a wink.

The *Koh-i-Noor* was black-hulled. The black funnel didn't help. This *Koh-i-Noor* looked too exotic.

There was bedlam at the dockside. Miss Lupus and Mrs Romney lacked a gentleman to take care of them! Other parties consisted of ladies, in full-length minks and the *infra dig* musquash; and of gentlemen that leant on canes. *Other* luggage was made up of hat-boxes and scientific equipment.

Mrs Romney had left her furs behind.

'What is it, Nanny?' asked Mrs Romney. '*What* have we left behind? We can't stand about in this mill.'

Liberty bodices, flannel, shall we be warm enough? flustered Nanny to herself.

'Easy there!' murmured Amabel. The roan, in a canvas sling, hung her head and her legs shook, poor thing. Nanny was the recipient of a whispered commentary. Nanny whispered

75

back, 'Why ever couldn't she have been led on board, dear?' The roan was lowered ... Amabel was in a fever.

'*Lucky*,' said Nanny, out loud, 'that Miss Lupus is with us ...'

'We are *depending* upon you, Nanny!'

'Miss Lupus will take Amabel and me home to the Grange, and permit us ... I'm sure I'm right in saying ... to stay there, madam!'

'Please, Nanny,' said Mrs Romney. And, 'Let's see where we're situated. My sister has oodles of time. They put out an announcement, you know, asking those who are not sailing to go ashore.'

Nanny had a vision of the dogs, stuck mournfully to Mrs Romney's heels—*Nanny* would have *liked* to have been parked.

'I don't like to disoblige you, madam ... I am positive I cannot go with you.'

Amabel had sharp ears.

Amabel hissed, 'Peter and the blue roan mare mustn't sail away without me. I'll die. Quite distinctly, Nanny, die!'

'Shush, dear!' said Nanny.

'Don't make me die.'

'You retrieve them, duck.'

'The blue roan mare is in the hold!'

Mrs Romney was staring about her with a pleased, intrigued expression. The garrison band had struck up.

'I can't leave her. She has been embarked, I *won't* ...'

'Gracious me, Amabel! We don't, do we, say *"won't"*!'

Nanny struggled not to bite her lips. The red sashes of the lascars caught Amabel's attention. A fascinated Amabel tugged.

Nanny trembled.

'*Do* come along, Nanny!' exclaimed Mrs Romney, at her most winning.

Sheepishly, Nanny stepped onto the gangway. It shivered under her foot.

17 H.M.T. *Cormorant*

Philomena lost Mudge, not merely to measles but now to another vessel. Three hundred and eighteen other ranks were embarked in the liner, *Falls of Kyle*. Only twenty-one officers and one hundred and eighty-nine O.R.s were to board *Cormorant*.

At the dock, the brigade vet checked temperatures and breathing-rate of each animal.

A crowd was gathering; restless and noisy.

The mules, since they were to be put in the worst, the deepest, the most stuffy quarters, close to the engine-room, were embarked first. They were nervy. Water-carts, field ambulance, all regimental transport wagons and two of the Maxim guns were lowered into the hold; followed by the bulk of the forty-eight tons of

77

hay, forty tons in hundredweight sacks of crushed oats; farriers' stores of fifteen hundredweight of bran, six of linseed.

Horses had to tread up a ramp to the main deck.

The mules had descended by yet steeper ramps; to high-step through watertight doors. Some one hundred and sixty troop-horses did likewise. Others were obliged to thread *via* narrow passages to gain their stalls. So narrow were the passageways that those that swung slightly got the bulwark against their flanks. That frightened them.

The ship smelt horrible.

The men exerted themselves to soothe and coax. A little patience would be repaid during the voyage.

Philomena's luck held in her stowage.

The open decks offered free circulation of air. The stabling on the main deck consisted of stalls in eights, side by side together, three foot six inches per horse. Here there was a risk from the weather, too much sea; or a surfeit of spray.

Officers' chargers were comfortable on the Boat Deck. The remaining troop-horses went up into timber stalls partitioned for pairs. Philomena's troop shared the Boat Deck with Conker and other smart fellows, but she was closer to the rail.

All artillery horses were in *Falls of Kyle*.

Cormorant had been a trader on the West

Indies run and provided as awkward a berth as could be imagined. Matting should have been laid across the outside decks and on inside decks. There wasn't the room.

Rolling was better sustained when the forelegs could brace together; though that scarcely helped for pitch and toss. It was desirable to face the boxes and stalls away from the prevailing wind. In the North Atlantic the wind blew steadily, more or less, from one direction. The stalls, in particular, having a heavy, cocked overhang could receive more of a blow from the gales.

The Dorsets were taking to Egypt four hundred and ninety-eight horses. All the chargers and the forty-eight troop-horses, Philomena among them, faced the preferred, port beam. Philomena had the davits of a lifeboat for view.

The stalls had been constructed so dung could be raked out to the rear. The animals weren't to stand in until the hindquarters became raised above the wither: that would be awful. The yeomen were horsemasters, deep in their hearts; and mucking out was a fatigue done willingly, excruciating contortions though it might require; in all but the heaviest sea. In bad seas, no horse might be extracted; not even for grooming. 'Weather' was probable. In the twelve to fourteen days out, feet would not be immersed for long enough to suffer, though the stench be severe.

Four hours and a quarter later, the convoy, with destroyer escort, sailed on the tide.

The crowd raised a great cheer.

18 Philomena at sea

The snag of possessing an impassive face became apparent with the absence of Mudge.

She was bewildered by the heaving; and the cramped conditions. Salt in the air made her blink. Draughts whistled through the cracks. The water had a tang. She curled her lip at it and struck, with her nose, Private Dyke's canvas bucket. There was spillage. Private Dyke cursed her.

He reeked in the regions of his boots.

She ate her rations. A nosebag safeguarded the corn. Hay cocked in front of each stall was a mistake. It was caught by gusts.

Hay-nets were issued.

Hay was also chaffed. Constant small issues of rations were a distraction, and helped the constitution.

Early 'Stables' meant that either Dyke or Saddler-Corporal Bourne would arrive to muck out. Philomena had learnt the measurements of the stall; and how to *lean* on it. The bay mare, three down, panicked every time her rump touched timber.

Horses ceased to munch; or stood, brooding;

mournful; as though humiliated by the nosebag.

And as for exercise ... A little coir, soaked by spray, had been wedded to the clanging deck. To no avail. Too hazardous.

The men rubbed down, assiduous in maintaining the circulation. Tails and manes were sticky; eyelashes gummed. Grey sky filled the heavens, sown with dark patches. There was a swell on the starboard beam. The wind strengthened. *Cormorant* rolled. Saddler-Corporal Borne was green. Borne and Dyke, with eight to do, got another four.

On that breeze, Conker's wild neigh once blew to Philomena: it brought her head up.

The storm clouds tore in.

Hour after hour, the horses braced, propping themselves against the stall; or, in some cases, against their neighbours. They nodded off and jerked awake.

No animal could lie down.

Philomena had been intrigued; then bored.

To her off side, there was a grey, a bay and a black gelding. The black gelding would keep biting the timber bar across the front of his stall. The squawk of the wood and the gnawing of teeth soothed Philomena. Neither Borne nor Dyke cared much; so long as the fellow never sucked wind in. The black gelding wasn't the only one.

Stout timber could bear a lot of that before it weakened.

Inordinate pains were taken, night and day, over welfare. An officer passed the suddenly pricked ears on thrice-daily inspections.

Then the black went off his forage ration.

The ship creaked and shuddered. The tremor accompanied the ship like a horsefly in July.

Philomena stared at waves that reared and broke, and ran away from her for as far as she could see. Rain thrummed on her roof, the rain lashed the starboard side.

When *Cormorant* was off Cape St Vincent, the black gelding took fright, flattened his ears, and started to kick out. His companions gathered every muscle, and racked back and forth. Timber screeched.

The black's pal, the bay, was making a kind of groaning noise. The black gelding burst the front rail from its block. The bar, still whole, spun and skidded into *Cormorant*'s rail, pursued willy-nilly by the black, who tipped up with a hind leg through; dragging the bay after him. The bay bore the welt of a kick; and he required a deal of comforting.

The thuds and the splintering had spread alarm.

Philomena saw the reprobate shot. Philomena's head went up. Her expression didn't change.

That black was the first of thirty to founder.

In the hold, Farrier-Corporal Barnes had stopped up two nights and a day to nurse the chestnut gelding Corky, consoling him, tempting him with mashes of bran and boiled linseed; balling it in the palm.

The horse's digestion was always delicate; and his constitution sometimes. It was dire to see the privation. *Cormorant* had been so crowded. Hard pressed, all troopers ended up hand-feeding their charges.

The farriers weren't so unoccupied as to be sick themselves.

The vet performed a small operation to ease a contracted sheath.

Of the subsequent twenty-nine casualties, one was caused by savaging; three were due to colic, many cases of which had been aggravated by the stalls, for the patient could neither get down nor relieve the pain physically; three by problems of circulation; and *twenty-two* to a distressing form of pneumonia that afflicted those animals with the worst ventilation.

In the narrowest quarters, the casualties were obliged to die standing up.

Until the hawser of the derrick could be carried to it, the carcass had to be dragged and manoeuvred. Back-breaking work. It went overboard; with a drowned splash.

Sight of the convoy had been lost from the first day out.

19 Mrs Arthur Romney

Koh-i-Noor was bulging with top brass. Going out to India. First Class positively glittered. The Chief Engineer had a red face that would have put Griselda off: the 3rd Officer's table was acceptable.

In principle, the amiable Mr Nightingale sat down at eight. Since he himself stood the Forenoon and the First Watch, eight until twelve, he arrived before the hour; wolfed his victuals and ran.

Tiffin was different. He was with them for tiffin. On one day in seven he honoured the lower Saloon.

They made a quaint collection. What these passengers had in common was that they would disembark in or before the Red Sea.

Larshaw's name for Mrs Larshaw was 'Pussy'. Mrs Larshaw should have married somebody else. Her reading was probably restricted to novels and the toshiest verse. She danced. She would be inventive at charades. She dressed well. She would be 'Willing-to-play-sardines'. She was over-gracious and had undying small talk.

Larshaw was clever, a scholar, with a quick wit. Rather pink about the gills. He might be of use. As though he had no teeth at the back, he nibbled, like a rabbit.

'I suppose you'll tell me your purpose in travelling to Egypt?' he murmured conspiratorially.

Griselda tried saying she had a horse in Egypt. This provoked some comic assumptions. Having embarked together at Gravesend, the others were all acquainted. On Griselda's other side was A.P.P. Mulchard, the archaeologist, who must have disliked her on the spot. Griselda expanded.

'Does one think of horses at this juncture of History!' Lady Spence was *en route* to rejoin Spence in Malta; and, because of old Sir John Spence's past appointments, she claimed seniority. Lady Spence was well-preserved.

'In Heaven's name, why one should not, ma'am?' said the General bravely.

'Don't you remember, there were promises made ... ?' mused Griselda in a humorous tone.

'Promises?'

'D'you know, I do, I *do* remember, it comes back to me,' cried Mrs Larshaw. 'The Government had made promises! It was a scandal!'

'Would *any* Government promise to return *horses*?' said Mulchard.

'And it was the Government, or the War Office, that opted not to honour any such undertaking.'

'Mrs Romney sounds very sure of her ground,' remarked Lady Spence.

'It *would* be Lloyd George.'

'What would?'

'The decision to sell thousands of our cavalry and artillery horses to dealers in Cairo. It may be laid at his door.'

'Don't you believe it,' Larshaw said.

'Were you attached to the animal, Mrs Romney?'

'Strangely enough, I can't forget her.'

Mrs Larshaw said, 'My dear, Orientals don't understand our sentiment for our animals, do they!'

'Oh, this isn't *sentiment*!' Griselda was fierce.

Mulchard, although engaged with his neighbour, gave a 'haw-haw'.

'For all I know, I may have to destroy her.'

They nodded.

Mulchard, who didn't like horses, said, 'Quite the angel, swooping!'

He attracted some straight looks.

'Is it not conceivable, Mrs Romsey, that she may be fit and well?' he said.

'Then I shall bring her home.'

'Romney,' said the General. 'Mrs *Romney*.'

Mulchard picked up his napkin. He wiped his moustache.

Mrs Larshaw sighed. 'I warrant you'll search for five years. And you'll be the *sadder* for it.'

One of the two Harrovians smiled at Griselda.

The romantic Mohammad ibn Taha al-Husseini could speak, Griselda had recognized, in a soft, cultured voice: at sixteen he was reluctant to open his mouth.

'Would you have been educated in Istanbul, had the War not brought such things to a stop? Has England been *interesting*?'

'If you'd lived for as long as I have ...' Mrs Larshaw continued, gleefully drowning the polite noises ... 'you'd recollect how carriage horses suffered from our *cruel* bearing-reins in the 'seventies and 'eighties. It was *Black Beauty* ...'

Insisting on her release from horses, Griselda cast Mrs Larshaw a courteous glimmer.

'And now? Have you had a sudden summons home to Arabia?' It was the middle of October.

She hadn't been at sea, and in a liner such as the *Koh-i-Noor* (1,500 tons), for years. Once, going abroad had been a terrific thrill. Despite the gruesome sharing of all First Class staterooms. The Griselda shut away at Bark Hart wasn't the same ecstatic traveller. She focused on Mohammad's face.

He lowered his eyes. These had wonderful lashes.

Lady Spence glanced down the length of the table and gathered the ladies.

The *punkah* above their heads was stirring.

The trouble with Plymouth was that all too soon the weather worsened. The deck rose and fell.

Griselda dropped in on her entourage.

'We shall have Amabel bilious.'

'Oh, Nanny, you may ask for whatever you fancy, whether you see it in the menu or not!'

'Amabel is not used to these great meals.'

'That is why I thought you'd find the earlier sitting convenient.'

'We shall have something more like, I hope, for our midday dinner.'

'Well, yes, the Company must be accustomed to providing for children.'

'Oh, you'd *think* so!'

'Nanny, you'll *enjoy* the voyage!' uttered Griselda, in winning tones. 'I shall be having breakfast with you.' Nanny had been gratified to find herself and the child in the side-cabin ('all mahogany, dear!') to Griselda's own.

Nanny smiled tightly.

'A trifle queasy?'

Every so often, there was a bump.

Nanny shook her head.

'There were two Arab princelings. They held hands between courses. They were at Harrow.'

'Didn't the school stamp on that!'

'They were murmuring to each other in Maltese.'

'Are they Maltese?'

'Bound for Jeddeh!'

Before Griselda swam a round of musical soirées, charades, games; potted palms and dance-partners. She disengaged herself from Nanny; and went back.

20 Sea legs

Nanny was aware that she was sliding, crown-first ... downwards ... and then her crown would rise and she was slipping, toes first ... downwards; and tipping almost out.

Their accommodation amidships and in First Class was supposed to preclude this behaviour. They had been deceived. The Commander had ordered the deadlights to be closed and a seaman, a *Khalasi*, had been round to do it; salaaming. In the night, in near-darkness.

Out on deck, there were crashes. The thickest lines were flailing the bulkheads.

Nanny's skin was raw from skidding to and fro. The sheet that had been soft was starched and coarse. The night-light revealed a peaceful child. Amabel didn't weigh enough to shift with the pitch. Perhaps she rolled a little. Amabel had a smile on her lips.

Nanny groaned.

When she tried to stand she had to lie flat. *Koh-i-Noor* didn't strike Nanny as a stable vessel at all. Nanny's tummy was *disturbed*. She lurched up, climbed into her dressing-gown, and staggered, banging her ribcage, to be sick.

Nanny, valiant, was sick *quietly*.

She watched her supper away, in chunks. White beans. Undigested and awful. There was the diced mangold-wurzel. Her dribble

89

tasted horrid. She wiped her face. Her eyes were hollow. She was still on her knees. With great animosity Nanny watched the sea water's gushing and frothing.

This happened several times until there was no supper left and she was being sick on sips. The ship pitched and tossed, *and* rolled, for the rest of the night. In the morning there was no relief.

Amabel got herself up. Amabel was convinced that she had been born with sea legs.

Mrs Romney entered and said, 'Oh, dear, dear! Riding helps there, Nanny, those of us that ride make good sailors.' And, 'Pity you don't like horses!'

Mrs Romney summoned a drink of water and glucose powder. She said, 'Nanny, you must have something to be sick on.' Nanny concurred.

Mrs Romney held the basin under Nanny's chin. Mrs Romney, with her own hands, wiped Nanny's chin. 'Thank you, madam!' gasped Nanny.

'There are silk ropes with tassels, Nanny,' said Amabel, 'silk ropes lead you *everywhere*!'

'Are there, dear?' murmured Nanny. 'Oh . . . do they?'

'So enormous my fingers don't reach round them. And the table-cloths are *wet*.'

Koh-i-Noor sank into a trough, sailed upwards, hovered on a crest; shuddered, spun, creaking as though wooden-hulled, and plunged. 'I shall be,' said Nanny, 'up in a jiffy.'

'I think you should stay where you are,' said Mrs Romney.

Mrs Romney and Amabel were robust.

Some dry toast was ordered.

Koh-i-Noor steamed, with the swell on to her starboard bow, and waves, driving across the swell, to the beam, all day; for the wind had gone round.

Mrs Romney and Amabel attended Divine Service.

Nanny was shattered. 'My nerves won't stand this!' she uttered. But the sea was not so huge.

By and by Mrs Romney exclaimed. 'If Amabel is to sleep in here, we must get some air in. *So stuffy!* Now, Nanny, a few minutes out on deck will do wonders!' Nanny took Mrs Romney's meaning, and was mortified. Mrs Romney was so kind.

An eternity passed, two nights and a day, before the deadlights were open.

21 'Make much of your horses'

Even as *Cormorant* sailed through the Strait, the condition had begun to fall away. In a surprising number, the bones of the hip, without being worthy of the description of 'ragged', were no longer properly covered.

Muscle in every direction had dwindled and sunk. Spirits had been pulled down.

Apart from a submarine alarm, a day into the Mediterranean, there was no incident. When transports got torpedoed, every blessed horse drowned.

A day's coaling in the Grand Harbour, Valetta, raised expectations; and caused the horses to sneeze. Calm seas, sunshine and sweet breezes were deceptive in April: they sailed straight into a storm. *Cormorant* docked in Alexandria on the 21st. Cloud and a drenching rain greeted them. The men were astonished.

Disembarkation was slow. Seven went straight to Veterinary Hospital. Philomena hung mutely over Mudge.

Mudge led her for miles.

In the dusk of a North African night, in a lingering half-light of this solid rain, the Regiment arrived at Ez Zahriya, for a spell of recovery. Nobody cared for the ground. Everything from cigarette ends to night soil had been stamped in. The fellows were hard put to it to make the horses easy, let alone themselves.

Two horses died. One was destroyed. Three more contracted pneumonia. Five went to Veterinary Hospital.

In roofed carriages they trundled off into a scenery of mud and canal water, lit up by the thousands and thousands of wild duck. Mud-brick houses shaded by tattered palm-trees wafted strange scents into the air. The sky was a pallid blue. Wading-fowl, disturbed by the engine, rose clumsily; white herons, and leggy flamingos. Pelicans. The reflections on the face of a green-glazed delta were black, shadows incised like giant ferns.

Cairo was hotter.

The Brigade went straight into infested barracks; the lumbering, red edifice of Kasr en-Nil. Mudge would mutter to his horse a very great many 'words' on the subject of bedbugs.

The flies hung on the eyes in clusters, and crept from the corners, where the lids met in a lake, familiarly up the brow and down to the lips, where they ate a sore of their own accord.

Philomena was issued with a fly-fringe.

Kasr en-Nil accommodated a territorial battery of the R.H.A. plus three yeomanry regiments and transports.

The Nile rolled by, in dense and unsmiling eddies, the colour of smashed rushes. It was fringed by those rushes, overhung by a rich variety of trees and dotted by the lateen sails of boats; elongated, pointed boats.

The heat was not yet so boiling as to bring out a sweat on a stationary animal. Summer coats were hurried on but without grief.

English hay was scarce. Philomena adored the *berseem*, the last of the lucerne cut in a succession of winter crops before it was fed

93

dried as *dreis*. For bulk, she'd eat the chaffed barley-straw that Mudge had learnt to call *tibbin*. There were, still, for the moment, English oats.

Water had a sweet taste. The orderly trumpeter woke Philomena up; and settled her for the night; summoned her rations; and brought Mudge to her.

There were astounding smells and sights.

Few among the troop-horses were frightened by donkeys; or tinkling bells; and none by mules. It was as well. Donkeys with bells were plentiful.

Soon familiar were creatures with humps, the tops of which, when exposed, wobbled slightly, humps and long, swan necks, small ears, nostrils like eyes, and the eyes of a goat crossed with a spaniel that observed everything and said nothing, feet split between two nails, creatures with coarse hair and scent, harnessed with string-ends to pull carts. In early morning, they paced and padded within trusses of straw or under voluminous burdens.

Lanterns, like so many carriage-lamps, proclaimed their presence after dark. By day, they too rang little bells.

The column had disgraced itself once. A bay mare had reared and brought down herself and Corporal Anson in the dust. There was still a deal of snorting, stopping, sidling and colliding. The horses couldn't know that they might owe their lives to camels; and to the most reeking of all, the bull-camels.

Impervious to the bands, plumes, colours and swirl of the British Army, and to the white plumes of the Regiment's senior officers, horses that didn't bat an eyelid at the flapping, the spectacular or at tram-cars, *objected* to ladies that were a glitter of eyes in a well of black.

In narrow streets, the horses were uneasy below the rustling cracks in lattice that reminded Mudge of Mrs Mudge's pastry.

It was rare that they did pass down narrow streets. Kasr en-Nil lay in the Khedivial quarter. All was spacious there. Motors nudged and honked, with top brass in them. Gharries bowled in a myriad of directions. Mudge had a fancy to spot a 'smart' carriage with 'running syces' in blue or maroon tunics and white nether-garments. But the custom was 'near dead, like'.

A southerly tore at the palm-trees, at the acacia branches; and recollections of the sea made Philomena twitch.

Two horses rejoined from the Veterinary Hospital in Alexandria. Another was destroyed.

For Mudge, Philomena tried hard. 'Make much of your horses,' Lieutenant Flower would say, for 'A' Squadron was busy with drill. Mudge patted her neck and might fondle an ear.

His affection had been earned.

They marched out into the desert, and bivouacked under the stars for brigade manoeuvres. The crisp sand by day was a flame that, reflecting the sun, frizzled up all the dampness from her eyes. Steam rose in clouds from the jingling, sweating troops. At every halt, a blanket would shield backs.

From Kasr en-Nil the Dorsets shifted with the dying sun . . . over the great bridge with its stone lions to the middle of the river itself, to the island, El Gezireh; to the greenery and shade of the Sporting Club and the Agriculture College. The watered gardens, the flowering trees, the birds, the bulbuls that huddled up to each other on a twig, the hoopoes that darted down with crests up and beaks like lances, the doves, the elfin sunbirds and the warblers, the scents and sounds, these lulled the horses; and the patrols sent out were pacific in nature. Garrison duties.

On their third day there, one of 'A' Squadron's died of a twisted gut. Two of 'B' Squadron's succumbed to pneumonia.

Mudge was broiling.

In early July, six were destroyed. Two were cast and sold. Ten were received from Remounts.

Up then to the Abbas Hilmy Barracks; the sprucest, newest and most comfortable barracks anybody had ever laid eyes on (no bugs), at the edge of the fertile land. The lines were sheltered by matting. But the heat was taking a lot out of every English creature. And the camel-shy were tortured. The Command had assembled dromedaries by the multitude at Abbasiya.

In August, lobster red (what with his freckly skin), Mudge was keen to see action.

On the 13th, the Q.O.D.Y. paraded dismounted, in two squadrons and M.G. Section, with packs and transport. A rear party, of squadron strength, was to bide. Farriers, shoeing smiths, saddlers, officers' grooms and the unfit. Mudge sailed for Gallipoli; and Philomena had lost him for ever.

22 The Quartermaster

Nanny and Amabel disposed themselves for elevenses in the Forward Saloon. Once they were sailing through the Mediterranean, it would be *nice* to crochet out on deck. Amabel watched the blue roan mare. The salty wind flipped into her long tail. Muzz, ambitious to 'hear' Amabel's reading, might have heard instead some civil converse.

'A good morning to you, Nanny!'

'Oh, thank you, I wish the same to you, and I dare say you have made the trip many times, Ayah?'

'Did you find the Bay of Biscay rough,

Nanny!'

'Only a trifle, Ayah.'

Nanny was making strides.

'D'you have any idea why Nanny is so reluctant to eat? She *must* take you in for meals.'

Amabel replied, 'She can't abide cockroaches.'

'Is *that* all?'

'What is an *Agwallah*, Muzz?'

'Oh, well, a fireman, I suppose . . .'

The Deck Steward charged with the organization of games and sports was beastly. If Nanny hated colourless cockroaches, Amabel was revolted by musical chairs. Amabel spoke to other children: she did so when neither Muzz nor Nanny was around.

Captain Blunt (the Company called him the 'Commander') got thoroughly 'around' the First Class, buttering ladies and men indiscriminately.

Amabel was suspicious of Captain Blunt. He'd never buttered Nanny. Muzz and Amabel had been invited (or buttered) by Mr Nightingale.

During the Forenoon Watch, as mere passengers, they started from Lifeboat Station 'A' and, riding the roll of the vessel, let themselves be propelled upwards, on the leeward, port side.

'Don't be tactless, will you,' said Muzz. 'A liner can seem tame *to a naval child.*'

98

Mr Nightingale spouted in riddles. 'Oh, I fear, I fear, there is much cloud, how low would you guess, how high, how many miles off us does the horizon *sit*, how many knots is the *Koh-i-Noor* making. Eighteen! Oh, what is our weather prospect, where is the wind. If North is that way, which is South, and East, where is South-west. Oh, I say. Prime! Oh, do go in before you are blown away.'

The wind hadn't seemed that stiff.

Inside the Wheel-house a number of eyes turned, bar two. 'The Quartermaster keeping this watch is Brabin.'

To starboard, in dark blue *lalchi* (his tunic) and crimson *rhumal* (his sash), was stationed a lascar. At a dark, inner throat, an Officer's Steward, in pure white. *He* salaamed. The Quartermaster's glance sank to the compass needle and rose to seaward. Sturdy in navy-blue wool. 'Brabin will show the little girl how he keeps the vessel on course.' Mr Nightingale strode up to the vast window, peered down and gesticulated.

The Atlantic was cold and grey; and heaved without expression.

'The lascar in the crow's-nest sounds the *gong*, for steam or sail, one blow 'to port', two 'to starboard', three for a sail or a light *ahead*, crumbs you *are* bright, when I ring down to the Engine-room I pull this handle, or the lascar does it for me, you can read, read what it says, Full Ahead, Half Ahead . . .'

Muzz made faces at Amabel. The faces said, Go and look! Go and *look*!

Koh-i-Noor juddered and smashed against the swell. Brabin swayed with nonchalant ease.

Brabin grinned.

'Is that a *fisherman*, that black speck, fearfully tiny, d'you know, I think that *is* a fisherman.'

Amabel stared at Mr Nightingale.

'When we are entering port, the heading is called out and the Quartermaster repeats it, or should we change course at sea, he has to keep that needle-point *pointing*.'

'Oops!' said Amabel. Her stride had expanded in mid-air.

'Hallo!' said Brabin, unexpectedly. 'How old are you, missie?'

Mr Nightingale never ceased.

'Shall we enter the Chart-room, I can show my slide-rule to you, and projector and dividers and log tables, the sun reaches his zenith at noon. Pity! But we might calculate and mark our position from our last known position, we work out our speed in knots, oh, this is my sextant-case *and in it is my sextant*, can you see the chart, I shall place a cross about . . . there!'

Amabel couldn't see the chart, and the table wasn't log. Brabin was fair and youthful. She trotted back. Amabel thought him handsome.

'And how old are you?' she asked in a conversational tone.

Brabin laughed. 'Twenty-four,' he said.

Amabel made her gaze rigid. Cautiously she placed her palm on the wheel.

'How far are you going in her, then?' he said.

'We're making for Zeebrugge,' said Amabel. 'It's in Egypt.'

'Oh, duck!' said Brabin. 'Zeebrugge is behind us.'

Amabel looked behind herself.

'Zeebrugge, I've bin there.'

'My father went to Zeebrugge,' said Amabel. 'And he hasn't come home yet.'

Brabin looked terribly sad.

'Ah,' he said. 'Might he have been an orfficer?'

'Uh huh,' said Amabel.

'I were in the Navy,' said Brabin.

'Were you brave too?'

'I hopes as how!'

Amabel digested it.

'Do you know his ship?'

'Of course I do!' said Amabel.

'Pa were in a blockship?'

'I don't think so,' said Amabel. 'He went alongside the Mole. Are you acquainted with the Mole?'

'I'll say!' Brabin said. 'Funny you and me should have so much in common, miss. I was in *Vindictive* myself.'

'He was seen astride the Mole,' said Amabel.

'Led one of the seamen storming-parties?'

'We haven't laid our eyes on him since,' said

101

Amabel, placidly.

Brabin's very blue ones were fixed on the sea.

'I don't s'pose you has,' he said.

'That's why we're sailing in *Koh-i-Noor* to Egypt, to retrieve him!'

'To wot 'im? How old did you say you was?' said Brabin. 'I fought you was clever.' He blinked. His blue eyes were soaked.

'My great-uncle, Uncle Archie, shoots the mole, through the window of his den at Quarr. For spoiling the lawn. There are zebras in Egypt,' tried Amabel.

Amabel wasn't sure whether she believed half she said.

'Oh, so there you are! It's been splendid,' said Muzz. 'Say thank you to Mr Nightingale, and . . .' (including Brabin and the *Khalasi* in a radiant smile) '. . . to the Quartermaster!'

Amabel was heard by those on the Bridge to murmur, 'And *that wasn't* tame.'

23 Lamed

The slowly grilling summer, months in which to acclimatize, and to swallow queer rations, were of help to the horses in Egypt.

When a squadron was formed under the command of Major Sandley to go to the Western Desert, Philomena went with it. They entrained for Dabaa, to quell the Senussi tribesmen. Sandley was Irish. His wife's connections were Dorset gentry. At home, he hunted with the Quarr Hounds.

The force—three composite regiments of yeomen, together with Notts Battery R.H.A., six R.N. armoured cars and a wireless car—patrolled the terrain in the region of the Dabaa railhead.

The oil wells were not threatened. Hugging the coast, they marched towards the little port of Mersa Matruh. Once, Antony and Cleopatra had lolled in a villa at Matruh.

To Philomena, the restlessness was a puzzle.

On the Khedivial motor-road, the column straggled for two miles, incessantly held up, inefficient. Tiring for horses obliged to carry their heads.

In her barley was earth; and blown sand.

Claps of thunder made every *wadi* run yellow.

Nights were starry; days, damp. Reveille was sounded in the dark at a quarter to four. Philomena, blanket-clipped to ward off mange, woke cold and stiff.

Often, Private Cogg (fresh out from England) threw the surcingle over; and banged her elbow. 'Wheely' Cogg's saddle on her chilly back caused her to hump and fidget. The oaf didn't sit firm; he twisted. He *was* heavy; and he rode heavy. Her *numnah* slipped out of the arch, and pressed down on her wither.

Nobody noticed. He'd failed to strap it. At *last*, as punishment, Cogg was ordered to march on foot.

The sun lay lurid and swollen on the horizon. Then Philomena was led in the rear with a sore back.

On 11th December, black tents were spotted. The horses were on half rations. The advanced guard, the Bucks squadron, its scouts not far enough out, was *surprised* by three hundred (or so) of the enemy. The Berks, in support, charged; and sustained losses. Philomena's lot had been held in reserve: they were detached to frustrate the escape. The endeavour failed.

These yeomen were 'reptilian and dopey'.

Philomena herded prisoners: Bedouin were roped to her saddle, to be tugged on in; questioned, set free; and, for their kid-goats, paid.

The column went back to Matruh.

A supply vessel docked in the harbour.

One day, a silent Cogg packed Philomena's saddle with her equipment; and vanished. All the men she knew ... gone. Major Sandley's Squadron had been dismounted. They'd sailed for Alexandria. The officers' chargers set off on land to the railhead at Dabaa.

In Alexandria, Sandley's Squadron, reinforced by a M.G. troop, was recalled to Matruh.

Philomena, trundling from hand to hand in camp at Matruh, sulky, indifferent, had been re-shod cold. The Bucks shoeing-smith, driving a nail in too high, pricked her. She went septic.

Philomena's foot throbbed.

Disembarking at the port, the squadron looked for their beloved horses.

The razor-backed, the scouring, the mangy, the downright lame! That was all they got in their fresh draft. The worst animals. A draft that had been *scraped* from the Brigade!

Of their original horses, there were six.

One was an old pal with a white face. One was Philomena; morose. The third was Corky. The fourth had (though it was harmless) stringhalt. The fifth was a slug. The sixth was nervous.

Six!

Major Sandley waxed rather Irish and went himself to fetch away well-known Dorset hunters.

Philomena was unsound, and to press an unsound horse on the march was unenviable. It was too early in the campaign for the men to be insensitive: riding in the serrefile rank made not a jot of difference. But they *had* no led horses.

Issued to a short, wiry man, who was told to 'save' her, a fellow more the stamp of the faithful Mudge, Philomena was not to see Dalliance again.

Of course Philomena's shoe had been removed . . . she'd been given her former D.Y.

number but the cancellation on the wall of her hoof would have to grow ... and a poultice applied.

Her shoe had to go back on. Orders to march. She would be nodding for days.

His name was Burdock.

24 Algiers

'D'you know, I believe I must be in love again,' remarked Mrs Romney, after two hours ashore in Algiers.

'Oh, madam! I don't suppose you *are*!'

Mrs Romney's laugh alarmed Nanny. 'Dancing, aboard ship, when the deck is heaving, is a hoot ... !'

Nanny's days were filled, what with the sea's being less immense, by children's parties, the conjuror, the playing of the games that Amabel so dreaded.

Nanny said mildly to Amabel, 'Have you seen Mummie with a gentleman?'

'Piles of them!'

'Piles?'

'They cluster and drape their arms!'

'Over Mummie?'

'Over and over each other, like toads, in the urge to be closest to her.'

'Amabel, you're exaggerating! She hasn't gone and fallen for one, has she?'

'Oh, no,' said Amabel. 'Muzz won't.'

Nanny hesitated. This was not the moment to suggest that Mrs Romney, since she was so susceptible, might not wish to soap the weeds for ever and ever.

Nanny wondered to herself how devoted Mrs Romney *had* been. Nanny could imagine that Mrs Romney might have led Daddy a dance! There was the Grazebrook cousin. Nanny wasn't deceived.

Mrs Romney was Nanny's sole prop.

Mrs Romney, in *Koh-i-Noor*, was showing all the signs. She gave trembling snorts to items of conversation that weren't funny. She would sit down beside Nanny and her eyes would wander. Nanny reviewed the personages hitherto described to her.

The General. The digging gentleman. The grizzled, portly Captain Blunt himself. Mr Nightingale. *He* had not gone ashore in Algiers. Neither had Mr Barrow, the Chief Officer. Nanny had heard his voice raised to the lascars: *'Jildi karo, jildi karo!'*

Mrs Romney looked down on Merchant Navy (ex-R.N. but not quite). Nanny glared at the horseshoe of solid buildings, solid and French that lined the quays. Above it rose the amphitheatre of the square white houses of Algiers.

'One has to penetrate the Casbah to discover that it isn't France after all! Would it amuse you, Amabel . . . your first footfall in North

Africa ... Moors and Berbers ... pirates, buccaneers, Arab merchants, and men out of the Sahara! What fun it will be to show you! Goodness!' That was what Nanny believed Mrs Romney to have uttered.

And then, despite the anticipation, Nanny and Amabel had been marooned—on board ship.

A misunderstanding, indeed! 'Nanny, *you* were going ashore with Mrs Aylsebury, the little girls and Ayah!' Such naughtiness, thought Nanny.

Nanny and Amabel had never discovered how unfrenchified the Casbah was, for Mrs Aylsebury (travelling out to India), accompanied by what Amabel *would* call 'the three little ducklings' and Ayah, had assumed that Amabel and Nanny were with Mummie. All Mrs Romney had exerted herself to do had been to take Amabel to look at the *Môle al-Djefna*. As if they weren't tied up to it.

The light changed again. Orange rays lit the eastern Corniche.

That evening, to Nanny's perturbation, Mrs Romney invited a gentleman to her Bedroom.

Nanny, squirming, heard the clink of ice against crystal; the murmur of voices; one of them Mrs Romney's, the other deep. Amabel was asleep.

It didn't last long. The sound of chatter, followed by the lashing rain. Nanny had time to turn the hem of a lawn handkerchief.

25   Taking it too far

Griselda let the mystery of the shore trip in Algiers hang in Nanny's brain; like a sea fog. Of course through playing charades she became ruffled and flushed. Nanny was imagining any *unnatural* glow! Nanny was in a huff about Algiers. Griselda would make up for it in Valletta. The ship would be coaling.

In the year before the War had broken out, she and Arthur had rented a house in Malta.

'Valletta is a diminutive city crammed with magnificent palaces, *auberges* where the Templars, worn to a thread from nursing, laid their heads down and supped, and secret passages ... some secret, some rather less secret ... and hanging gardens, the English curtain, and a pillar on which St Paul ... um, died, darling ...'

'Fancy!' interposed Nanny.

'And then, all over the place, temples that were built by giants, with stone that no ordinary mortal could hew or *move*! And Malta is the home of the cross winds ...'

'Oh, dear!' said Amabel.

'... And ruts like our squelchy cart ruts of the winter in the woods at Quarr, but of pure stone! Dwarf elephant, and dwarf hippopotami, gigantic dormice, gigantic swans ...! And hammering, all night.'

'Giants?'

'Darling, no, hammering from the dockyards. *Our* dockyards. Hammering echoes at night because of the stillness. In the Naval Dockyard, men labour every hour of every day.'

'Shame!' said Nanny. 'No holidays whatsoever?'

To the surprise of General and Mrs Larshaw, Mulchard remarked over cocktails, with a glimmer that he *must* have meant to be less than polite, 'I should restrain yourself, Mrs Romney, in informing your little girl, for I fear what you choose to tell her belongs in the realm of farradiddle. I couldn't help but overhear you on the Promenade Deck . . .!'

Griselda considered 'overhearing' common.

'Mr Mulchard, I feel you must acquainted be with Malta. Tell us your opinion of our archaeological 'finds',' put in Lady Spence. Professor Mulchard was a solemn man. Lady Spence in her prime had been five foot nine in her stockings. General Larshaw radiated consternation. Perhaps he knew Lady Spence.

'Curiosity,' announced Mulchard, 'is a curse.'

They were all startled.

Visibly, they strove to follow his meaning. Mrs Larshaw's lips moved.

The mannish Miss Colley laughed.

Mulchard nodded.

Lady Spence tried, 'D'you know, our richness in the matter of ancient ruins is superior. A little strolling here and there will not hurt. Sir John . . . my husband, y'know . . . suggests the origin of our 'cart ruts' lies millions of years before the Neolithic man to whom they are credited.'

'I ascribe,' said Griselda, 'to the notion of wheeled creatures from outer space!'

Professor Mulchard, sidling like a crab into dinner, failed to recognize a tease. 'I am not familiar with Malta.'

'Malta,' said Lady Spence, 'is celebrated in the arc-ae-oh-logicle world.' A reproof.

'The man's study is ancient Egypt,' Larshaw said, *sotto voce*.

Mulchard pretended not to have heard. He continued, 'In Egypt, I am obliged to listen to many a concocted fable.'

Lady Spence, to Griselda's gratification, rode in with, *'We in Malta* may reckon the pyramids *young.'*

Mulchard was stiffer than his boiled shirt. He eyed his mulligatawny.

Mrs Larshaw leapt in warmly. 'We are all ears, Professor. Where do you . . . er . . . make *your* finds?'

Lady Spence kept her serenity. 'Quite right, my dear, the old Malta hands should not hog the conversation.'

A boom from Miss Colley.

The soup vanished and salvers of sardines hovered over their elbows.

Mulchard whispered, 'Mrs Larshaw, I don't

111

believe Lady Spence can have visited Egypt.'

Somebody snorted.

'On the contrary,' retorted Lady Spence, 'Sir John has corresponded with Lord Carnarvon.'

Mohammad and his brother continued quietly to discuss chemistry.

'Fellow's ears ought never to have been a-flap-flapping in the first place!' The consonants resonated. General Larshaw would have died rather than overheard a private conversation.

'I fancy we should have been aware *already*,' said Griselda, 'of your particular field and period. Do forgive us.'

Streaks of colour high in his pasty features, Mulchard said, *'Pace*, Mrs Romsey, Lady Spence . . .'

'Romney . . .' said the General.

Mulchard put up his napkin to wipe his lip.

'Where is your Chair?' pursued Miss Colley, with the best of intentions.

'You're not tempted to break your journey?' Mulchard was saying acidly to his neighbour, Mrs Romney.

'Professor Mulchard . . .' Miss Colley, loudly.

'Consider me as bound to the mast,' replied Griselda.

'Oh, your horse . . .' said Lady Spence. 'Mrs Romney and her horse!' Lady Spence glanced around; humorously.

Miss Colley sped to safety. 'He must have been *so* well cared for, your horse, in the

Army! We British . . . !'

Griselda inclined her head.

Those whose manners were very good felt a little 'conscious'.

Far too late, Mohammed ventured, 'The 'cart ruts' . . . do they . . . might they not . . . chart the course of the heavens?'

Virtually everybody pooh-poohed this. There was a discomfiting hiatus.

'Gnomic!' said the General.

26   The Senussi

Burdock knew this funny brown mare was making a fuss and he didn't blame her. He was a kind soul.

Unlike Cogg, Burdock was popular with the fellows. He was a trained scout (Scout 2nd Class). Cogg had kept Philomena's *equipment* in order. 'Wheely' Cogg couldn't stop cleaning, shaking, and turning the nosebags inmost out. Inspection didn't affright Cogg. But you had to compassion a sack of potatoes, thought Burdock, that never ought to a-been in the Yeomanry at all.

And 'A' Troop was an altogether decent affair, with Lieutenant Atkinson in command.

Mr Atkinson told them about the Senussi. The Senussi was a tribe and a Sufi Order ('dervishes') at a blow; a big tribe what inhabited the expanses of the desert in the country next door. The Grand Senussi was a religious gentleman. The Grand Senussi himself, Sayyid Ahmed, had been well disposed toward the British. So what a shame it was when he was bribed by the Turk into declaring a *jihad* and mobilizing his swarm against us.

This Jaafar Pasha, a Baghdadi general in the Ottoman Army, had gone and blooming landed at Tripoli with chests of gold, rifles and machine guns, and, after the Italians had fallen back on the coast, had persuaded the Senussi to debouch out of Tripolitania into Egypt.

The Grand Senussi was a *devout*. The Grand Senussi reckoned the British in Egypt were infidels. He was revered muchly by his dervishes. These dervishes was desirous of martyrdom. Armed with antiquated and modern rifles, catapults, knives, fowling-pieces and elephant guns, they were wanting to die. In a fight with infidels.

The dervishes had eyesight in the exceptional.

In the water of Siwa Oasis, where the Senussi were clustered, was the billy harris. But that, alas, never could be counted on to sicken Bedouin.

The Senussi possessed artillery-pieces, and had Johnny Turk to help to fire them. The gun-horses would be greys. Grey was the colour favoured by the Turk. The fanaticals

114

numbered some five thousand, to which you added irregulars.

Tribesmen's sense of honour weren't such as what we recognized. They couldn't be expected to make war-war by the rules of the civilized armies. Not knowing any better. As for Johnny, Mr Atkinson said, as for Johnny Turk, he wasn't fed proper.

The men roared.

They that had been evacuated out of Gallipoli, they waxed less vocal.

The siege of Khartoum by the *mahdi* and General Gordon's heroic death had lodged in the brain of every man, woman and child in the British Isles. Lieutenant Atkinson didn't have to remind his troopers that fanaticals would exhibit *tenacity*.

He allowed the dervish his tenacity.

It was an enemy what derided hardships. Wild. Impetuous.

No matter how damnable the desert was without proper supplies of water, British yeomen ... not to mention Australian M.I. and those grand South Africans ... would be *smacking* the Senussi back to Tripolitania.

Burdock sharpened his sword-point.

In Philomena's belly the sting of an ulcer, from the sand in her rations, started up. One day in January, echeloned on the right of the advanced guard of Australian Light Horse (Gallipoli convalescents to a man), they marched inland, away from the sea and the azure shallows, into driving rain, up to an immense pancake.

The coarse-grained sand, balling, rasped her heels.

The Australians were in touch with Senussi outposts at ten o'clock. As Sandley's Squadron was ordered up, the Australian horseholders tore back through them. Philomena was infected.

There was the delicate crack and boom of 13-pounder guns. The Notts Battery R.H.A. was exchanging fire with the enemy.

Philomena's ears flickered.

She was never close enough up to catch any glimpse of the three hundred Senussi tents.

Burdock and Philomena enjoyed a day of galloping hither and thither, in support of machine-guns that jammed. While Burdock and his rifle were belly down, Philomena was being escorted to the rear; for there wasn't, in the horseholders' eyes, a ridge or a gully to be had. She would be straightaway ordered up again. A day of retiring, pressed by dervishes, who crept round in a skating-pond of mud. A messy fight, that had cost the infantry thirty-one dead, two hundred and fifty-five wounded. The business was decided when the South Africans got into the enemy camp and set fire to it.

Sandley's Squadron was ordered to cut off the retreat. Philomena was weary. It was asking much of the horses.

Much *was* asked. The Senussi vanished into the desert.

Then the transports were adrift. It was a question of bivouacking comfortless.

Burdock was off to be harnessed, in the morning, to an armoured car! He'd been a small farmer, 'twasn't *his* first go in the drag ropes ever. Together with the bay and chestnut geldings, Philomena went with 'Jackdaw' Dawkes.

General Beecham gave up the command of Western Force and went home altogether.

Towards the end of the previous November, shattered, hollow-cheeked, with Lieutenant Flower in command, the Regiment had returned to Cairo from Gallipoli. Of the fellows that had sailed, so many had been slaughtered, or else severely wounded, in the action on the peninsula . . .

At that time, their M.G. Section had been there *still*; under the icy winds. Egypt was balmier. At Mena Camp, by the Great Pyramid, Flower, with a lop-sided grin, had searched for Philomena and Dalliance in vain.

Sandley's Squadron was now joined by the recuperated Regiment. Acting-Colonel Dittis, ex-Indian Army, was known: he'd come out in *Falls of Clyde* as Second-in-Command. The Acting-Adjutant, Lieutenant Murray, was on temporary secondment from the Scots Greys.

Major Sandley's formed 'B' Squadron. Flower was O.C. 'A' Squadron.

On February 1st, total strength in horses was two hundred and ninety-seven. Conker's officer had died in Gallipoli, of shrapnel wounds suffered on Chocolate Hill; but Conker was among these reinforcements.

27 The dragon's tail

Muzz and Amabel liked to stroll around the decks; 'noticing'. Muzz even kept Amabel up, past bedtime, to teach her the stars.

Amabel had ferreted out each and every companionway that was perpendicular. In a passenger liner, these were not many. Amabel wanted to practise; front-first; navy-fashion.

One dropped from the Hurricane Deck to the Upper Deck; although it was barred by a chain.

They were surprised there by Amabel's Quartermaster.

'It's you,' exclaimed Amabel joyfully.

He grinned at Amabel.

'Muzz, he knew Daddy!'

' 'Morning, ma'am!' was all that Brabin said.

So Griselda said, 'Could you have been in the Navy?' She looked at him properly. Sailors adored children.

'He went to Zeebrugge!' cried Amabel.

Brabin swallowed. Trying to get by.

Griselda   regarded   him   with   utmost

amiability.

'My husband? Did you know Commander Romney? What a coincidence!'

Brabin nodded, and nodded again.

'Might we . . . might we have a chat? When you're not busy, perhaps?'

'Crew,' Brabin stammered out, blushing.

'Oh, well . . . Is fratting with passengers *out*?' They couldn't be spotted from the Bridge.

Emboldened, Brabin said, 'There's the Lower After-deck, ma'am, if you'd condescend, that is. If you can find it.'

'I am a very good finder!' And, since Griselda was quick-witted, she said, 'What time would suit you?'

Brabin plumped for the kindness of the dusk.

Griselda said, 'I don't wish to be encouraging you in the clandestine, Brabin!'

Amabel eyed them.

He scuttled away forward.

Brabin turned and Amabel caught the magic phrase, 'Porpoise at the bow, m'm!'

Griselda was hard put to it to know what to expect. She embarked in a spirit of *adventure* on this snatched congregation with 'crew'. It seemed harmless!

With ingenuity, she descended from the Main Deck, set off along the side, negotiated a chain; and emerged aft. A bearer was emptying swill into the wash astern.

The raucous gulls of the Atlantic were

119

absent. There were big yellow-legged birds; rather mute. The throb of *Koh-i-Noor*'s twin screws was heady. The vessel's shudder was magnified. Churned in the wake, the sea shone white. The air itself was rather deafening. Green scum bobbed on the surface. Brabin, smoking a cigarette, stepped shyly out of the gloom. In deference, he bared his head. He stubbed his cigarette and tossed it so that it was carried on the wind.

This was awkward.

'My daughter tells me you were in the *Vindictive*?'

Brabin had been picked for one of the seamen storming-parties. Picked 'special', not expected back, all were volunteers in the raid on Zeebrugge. On'y senior officers was married. He'd gone ... *incommunicado* 'as good as' ... to the remote, secretive anchorage of Swin Deep; waited for the tide and moon; sailed from Swin Deep on two futile tries; been patient.

When finally the cruiser *Vindictive*, under the six guns of the German shore battery, in saturating rain and through a failing smoke screen, was pushed up by *Daffodil* against the outer wall of the Mole ... ripped into by every sort of fire and lit up by searchlight beams and her own flame-throwers, at a minute past midnight on St George's Day, 23rd April, Brabin ... Brabin, crouchin' under cover below, was ready. His pal was killed by flyin'

120

metal before ever they'd received the order.

In Brabin's arms, like.

He blinked.

The Lieutenant-Commander was in command of another seamen storming-party, the first. There was also plucky Marines. *Vindictive* were being shot to pieces. She weren't fatally holed because the German gunners was startled by her apparition out of the fog and she so close up they never got the range. Most of the officers ... while they waited on board they were the most exposed, commanding the stormers ... a majority of they officers had been killed or incapacitated straight off. The funny little ferry-boat, *Daffodil*, had to hold *Vindictive* against the Mole, not a soul would have got ashore else; and how terr'ble a job they was havin' to secure her with grappling anchors. The landing brows, the gangways, what was to take the storming-parties onto the Mole, were smashing against the wall and being shot up. Scarce more than a narrow plank they was, slippery from rain ... and the sea a drop of thirty foot. Only two gangways survived. Demented, it were. The explosions was a horror. What with our Stokes gun batteries, and fire directed onto the Mole from *Vindictive*'s fighting-top.

At the sight of her so close, the Jerries had lost their heads entirely. The damage 'ud have done for her else.

Had the attack failed, not a single one of they blockships would have sailed into the harbour.

Vindictive's gun turrets were shot ragged. Large pieces of the funnels and ventilators was ripping through the air. The casualties was severe. This were, like, afore a soul was ashore. The grapnels failed. They was all lit up, plunged from darkness to white light and back.

Lieutenant-Commander Romney ran onto *his* gangway, what was swaying and resting on the wall only to be pulled away from it, and leapt. Then he were seen, though shot in the face, astride the wall. Commander Romney was *still alive* and on the Mole when the seamen, burdened with their flame-throwers, bombs, machine guns and demolition gear, first started to pour keenly up.

Thetis didn't get all the way to be sunk in her correct position at the lock gates, *Thetis* dragged up the nets and was holed. But she'd cleared a path for *Intrepid* to pass her. *Intrepid* was sunk near to the lock gates, so to bung the entrance to the ship canal, and *Iphegenia* in her correct position, to bring about silting.

From the blockships they got away in cutters ... 'amazin'' ... though they was gassed.

Daffodil had *Vindictive* against the Mole for an hour and five minutes.

With pain, Griselda listened to this (the gist of which she knew intimately), fixed on

122

Brabin's blue eyes; and then unable to meet him in the eyes at all. She ceased to look at his greasy hair. She didn't look at his ruddy skin, or hear the eager tone in his voice. She thought, the wretched fellow is going to savour his tale for the rest of his life . . . the War has been more vivid for him than life itself.

Griselda heard distinctly the bleating of a kid-goat.

She thought, he will claim that Arthur, with a half face, saved him from a burning explosives dump, that he'd rallied to Arthur, the wounded Arthur . . . 'with arf a face he couldn' speak' . . .

Arthur led a charge on a machine-gun position. A number were killed. Brabin followed him through the tangle of huts, bollards, chains, gun emplacements and tunnels.

Brabin was droning eagerly on. '. . . We dragged out Sawyer and Brake before they was charred to death.'

Griselda knew that many of their wounded had had to be left behind. Few came back from the Mole at Zeebrugge.

'One sec' he were there . . . one sec' . . .'

She thought, he is going to spit out some bit . . . some *bit* . . . that I don't know. And he will *enjoy* being in a position to tell me this.

Griselda heard the relish that she was sure he should be forgiven; and she was revolted. *Revolted*.

'Gorn,' said Brabin, 'an' we never saw him no more!'

Griselda, turned to stone, had stopped her ears.

28 Scouting

It wasn't that Burdock saw to her before he attended to himself: every yeoman was dedicated similarly. It was that his solicitude was as genuine as the English yew-tree.

Her ruffled feelings subsided; and she tried hard for him.

The chestnut gelding, Corky, was a cocktailed, iron-mouthed blunderbuss, said Dawkes. Corky wasn't the friend Philomena might have chosen; but after he'd spent (humbly) days and nights at her side, he'd whicker; whenever chance had separated them.

With Dawkes on his back, Corky would stiffen his neck and get his bit just so in his mouth that he might have run away with anybody. A more awkward troop-horse you couldn't imagine. Perhaps it was his good nature that made him a sensible ride. That and his moderate paces. Under-fed he might be, over-worked he might be, but Corky *understood* his work; was an excellent doer, and was up to weight. Dawkes gave him a pull every now and then. That did.

The spotter, assiduous in the skies, reported the main body of the enemy, in its old camp, about ten miles from the sea, a shallow dip up on an escarpment, at the foot of which there was water, in pools, and shade from palm-trees and wild acacia. Despite the January rain, Wadi Maktil was dry. The spotter didn't see every feature from his aeroplane. The spotter was remarkably blind.

Two upstanding battalions of South Africans, four armoured cars, the Dorsets with a squadron of Bucks attached, the Notts Battery, as well as field-ambulances, marched along the coast by the Khedivial road towards Sidi Barrani. The duties of scouting and reconnaissance belonged to the mounted troops.

The Dorsets, *bumbling*, had been late to assemble (what with the canteens and nosebags that cast theirselves off) and had got cursed. They would have been sent back and the Berks Yeomanry ordered up instead, had time permitted.

They halted to bivouac by a *wadi* fringed in tamarisk. A wait for daylight was favoured.

The officer patrols sent out by 'A' Squadron encountered sniper fire. But they failed (somewhat) in the intelligence they brought in.

Out of nowhere, two big guns opened up.

The shells were bursting short. Philomena felt astonishment and alarm. Burdock patted her neck, and soothed her. Corky rolled his eyes. The enemy had sallied out in force.

The Turkish gunners never found the range. The crump of the R.H.A. guns, which she'd heard in January at Bir Sholeh, was no less peculiar. Soon there was silence.

The enemy retreated.

'Off-saddles' wasn't called, and all night Burdock stood to. At this juncture, grave or exciting according to a man's temperament, Lieutenant Atkinson inspected 'First Field Dressings'.

When the dawn broke, and the sun began to show emerald behind the threads of cloud, Burdock received the order to mount.

Corky whickered softly after her.

The scout sergeant, Totterdown, rode up the bed of the *wadi*, and out towards their first outpost. Besides Burdock, they had Critchard and rear point Marnhill. The horses could hear similar stirrings far away; upwind.

They went at a trot.

They attracted no fire. The sun pinked the face of the sandstone of a low, broken escarpment. They circled it and penetrated beyond it. Nobody was there. The ground had been disturbed. Fresh knobs of camel dung were strewn over it. Philomena snorted at those. That was all. Sergeant Totterdown pursued the camel-tracks until the wind covered them.

He had the direction.

126

He was not required to demonstrate this. Signals reported that the enemy, spotted from the sky, was back in camp. A Bedouin village in the bottom by the Wadi Maktil was called Agagiya.

Philomena's girths were slackened: she had her nosebag. Burdock munched on his loaf and bully. Surplus kit was to be deposited at the bivouac, a small detachment of infantry would guard it.

Two squadrons of Dorsets formed the advance guard. They marched in column of half-squadrons. Philomena and Corky, in the rear rank of 'A' Troop, were on the right, therefore, of 'B' Troop; with 'A' Squadron ahead, and 'A' Squadron's scouts thrown forward. Two of the armoured cars were on the right of the infantry; the squadron of Bucks on the left, with the other cars.

Away from the coast, the bleached and skeletal thyme gave out. Tufts of esparto grass gave out too. The sun was more cordial. In possession of a line of sand-hills, and with the wind, rather full of dust, on their cheeks, the cavalry halted at 10.15 a.m., three-quarters of an hour after starting out.

The enemy had entrenched its position and occupied it in strength. The spotter had reported a force of fifteen hundred. The trench system took up a mile. Officers' patrols did recces, to establish the depth.

The South African column was in view.

Their battalions deployed to face the enemy.

The Dorsets' C.O. rode back to HQ for orders.

Philomena and Corky enjoyed an 'easy'. The infantry advanced, with caution. The Senussi ventured a flanking movement. The South Africans dissuaded them.

The cavalry was now ordered to mount. The job was to pen the enemy in. 'B' Squadron to lead.

Advancing south-west, gingerly, in column of squadrons, they drew machine-gun fire. Several horses (and yeomen) were frightened by the metallic yap.

Small parties of Senussi were seeping away.

Burdock and Philomena had to rush forward from lip to lip; Burdock to dismount and take up firing position.

Sun and wind were rough.

A bullet smashed Major Bathurst's hand, glanced off his field-glasses and buried itself in his chocolate tin.

An hour after mid-day, the guns of the Notts Battery opened up. The horses still hung their heads but they stirred, puzzled.

The enemy shifted machine-guns to meet the South African attack; yet the bluff to the rear likewise bristled. A camel convoy was making off south-east. The Bucks squadron galloped to stop it.

Philomena's tiring afternoon had truly begun.

The country was one of blobby dunes; ever softer. Floundering southwards through loose yellow sand, for two hours they harassed the main retreat. They darted repeatedly to the tops of dunes for dismounted action. The range, a thousand yards. Dawkes held Corky and the bay close up.

Burdock was detailed to form one of a scouting party.

They rode each at a distance from one another; either that or spread in a screen. Sharp of eye, as to enemy *and* contour. Each to be mindful of every inch of cover. Burdock was sent back to report. The Colonel did some reconnaissance of his own.

Four times Philomena was hustled to and fro before Burdock was relieved.

The horses, so tested in the troughy sand, had scented two pools of unseen water. They passed between them, and were facing almost east.

The range was increasing. Then, by three o'clock, the enemy was out of range.

The Regiment was halted at the rim of a small, flat plain. Burdock dismounted. 'C' Squadron took up firing positions. A firm, crystalline desert floor appeared to stretch to the foot of a low ridge. Particles of quartz glittered and flashed; and the minute fragments of dead, silver leaf. Hoof-prints were slight where the shoe had bitten into the crust. An officer had long gone at a canter to retrieve the Bucks Hussars.

Nothing moved near at hand except the wind. The horses eased their necks.

Tucked under the horizon, a vast caravan, with an escort of Berber irregulars (in brown burnooses), was strung out. The regulars, the *muhafiziya,* with some Turkish officers and N.C.O.s protected the flank and rear. They were reckoned to have six Maxim guns.

Burdock had established with his own blessed eyes that machine-guns were carried by dromedaries.

Colonel Dittis rode forward, alone, to examine the ground through his telescope. The wind was on his cheek.

In the men's ears, still, burned that pie-jaw ... Four nights earlier the C.O. had told them how awful they were. How shaming.

The wind had dropped considerably. It blew, what wind there was, at the dervish flank.

29 The Commander

Koh-i-Noor's 'Commander', Captain Blunt, thought he had coped with every calamity. He had dispatched many people overboard sewn into white canvas, performed the marriages of fourteen, dealt with stowaways; he had concealed the woes (to do with the Manifest) of his Chief Officer.

Captain Blunt faced Mrs Romney.

Mrs Romney's chin was up.

'D'you see, ma'am,' blurted out the Commander, and his mouth was dry.

Mrs Romney frowned slightly.

The Chief Purser stared glassily into nowhere. Blunt glanced at him for moral support. It was *infra dig* for the lady. However, a witness *of that sort* (Purser's Office) had been essential.

The Surgeon was sitting on his hands.

Blunt was drifting in a stippled sea.

'Mrs Romney,' he said to Mrs Romney, 'was "observed" on the Lower After-deck consorting with a seaman.'

'D'you mean the Quartermaster? The one with the weepy eyes?'

'Good God, I don't look at their eyes!' He pitied himself.

The Surgeon longed to say to her, Shut up! Doing yourself no end of damage! Digging own grave!

'Consorting?'

'Cavorting, if you prefer . . .'

Mrs Romney was silent.

Blunt's lips flickered and said, with an effort, 'Can't have that!'

He said, 'And on *deck*! No better than the ship's whore!'

The Purser squinted at Mrs Romney. She appeared to be staggered.

'Oh,' she said, with a dangerous glint, 'do

131

you have a ship's whore?'

The Commander uttered a blustery noise that might have been 'yes' and might have been 'no'.

He considered that he hadn't responded.

'Only one?' asked the lady.

The Purser wanted to laugh. He drove his chin hard into his collar.

'Not officially!' he interjected.

The Commander glared at him.

'I fear,' pronounced Captain Blunt, in a polar tone, 'I fear that it was noted . . .'

'By whom?' she enquired, with an air of bewilderment that was, the Commander thought, bizarrely convincing. He hadn't had the honour of having eaten his roast beef with her. He'd enquired of Nightingale. Nightingale had choked.

' "Noted" by whom!'

'. . . That you were . . . er . . . kicking up your legs.' He went red.

Mrs Romney gasped, and recovered. 'Is that what your whore does? Kick up her legs?'

'Not *my* whore, ma'am!'

'D'you know . . .'

'You should now confirm or deny your conduct.'

'Oh,' said Mrs Romney.

She raised her eyebrows, and glittered.

The Commander shot the bolt right home. 'I'm afraid I must put you ashore here in Malta.'

Mrs Romney grinned, she actually grinned.

The Purser thought the woman pretty game.

'I regret also that ... I speak for the Company ... you will be *persona non grata* aboard any of the ...'

Mrs Romney interrupted by rising to her feet and turning her back on him.

'Goodbye!' she said.

The Purser was appalled. She was a war widow; the wife of a naval officer; of an officer, so he'd understood, twice decorated! The Purser was as powerless in the matter as his humble stenographer.

When Mrs Romney reached Nanny, the storm in her face broke.

Her lips were, Nanny noted, throbbing and hot. 'What is it, madam?' said Nanny.

Mrs Romney's hand shook, but her voice was steady.

'You and I and Amabel will be going ashore. The *Koh-i-Noor* will sail without us!'

'Oh!' said Nanny. 'Whatever's brought that on?'

'So we should pack! I'll have to talk to the Baggage Steward ... Please manage somehow, Nanny,' said Mrs Romney, with an exhausted sigh.

'What of our luggage in the hold, madam?'

Mrs Romney gave a start. 'I imagine that will continue the voyage to Port Said ... and wait for us there ...'

Her words trailed off.

'I hope the labels stay stuck down. What made us change our mind?' pursued Nanny.

'Oh, once we're no longer on board,' said Mrs Romney, 'I'll tell you.'

'A lot of faith to place in a label ...' muttered Nanny.

Amabel happened to be peeved. Amabel had suffered all the chagrin of a traveller who has missed the fascinating part of the voyage and woken to find her ship in port.

Mrs Romney, in Nanny's hearing, said her goodbyes to few of her fellow passengers.

'The English, Mrs Romney,' said the Harrow boy, 'admire the English. So do the Arabs admire the Arabs. We don't eat horses. We also laugh, and the mischievous tickles us. The Arabs and the English love jokes. The English have their honour, and the Arabs have theirs. We are alike in our sensitive manners. The English count the Arabs among the 'uncivilized', despite their *admiration* for us, and that is perverse.'

'He is saying that Egypt is not Arabia. The *fellah* in Egypt,' said the other, with the luminous eyes, 'is poor indeed. And in the towns the Egyptians are scarcely Arab either.'

'I see,' said Mrs Romney.

'Do not forget it ... when you are seeking your horse. *Insha'allah* you succeed!'

'I realize,' Mrs Romney said, on impulse, 'what it is, why you feel such an affinity to your own horses, why you ... I'll bet you do! ... sit

134

so well and look so natural on horseback: you are like horses *yourselves*!'

The triumph of this was dashed, for horror crossed their faces. 'But, Mrs Romney,' said the one called Mohammed, *'that is an insult.'*

They held out rather limp hands.

Nanny saw Mrs Romney's stare. Bewildered! *'Ma'a salaama!'* they said, and glided away.

30   Amabel creates

Mrs Romney said, in the morning, 'Please, Nanny, could you and Amabel go out for some fresh air? While I grapple with our affairs. You won't become lost, will you? And I feel so rotten I must lie on my bed.'

Although Nanny felt lost already (if thankful to have two feet on dry land), she was obliged to concur. So she wasn't attending.

'Draughty streets, these, I must say!' Amabel listened to a dirge. Nanny's cap was plucked and tweaked. 'Windy here … Too many sailors … I do hope your mother chose us a *suitable* hotel, dear!' And, reiterated, 'I don't know that this is a district for a child of your age!'

'It looks proper,' tried Amabel.

Nanny's nose led her away from Kingsway. She bore leftwards. Towards the open. The two of them found themselves on the ramparts, in the type of spot beloved of nurses and children, in the Upper Barracca Gardens. The walls were grey against the blue and glinting sky. There were grey statues. The air was mild.

'What do you know about 'proper', miss?'

'I'm to visit the Engine-room after we've sailed from Valletta.'

'Mm, that'll be nice.'

'There's a respectable man, Nanny.'

'Don't point, Amabel!'

'In a frock coat!'

'I'd rather not gawp, *if* you don't mind.'

Amabel gazed down at the quay; where, close to the Custom House, a vessel was berthed. The vessel's livery was white, pale blue and streaks of rust.

Tiny figures dodged around the breeches of antiquated canon that had been embedded to make bollards. Amabel caught her breath, for in the buffeting of wind there was uncanny stillness, and said, '*Where* is *Koh-i-Noor*?'

Nanny said, 'This isn't the right water, duck. We were at anchor in the Quarantine Harbour. Don't you remember? They called it a creek.'

'Where!'

'On the other side.'

'*That* other side?'

Amabel pointed.

'Rum place! Quaint, though . . .'

'Shall we go to see the Quarantine Harbour,

136

Nanny?'

'Too far for short legs.'

'Oh, *Nanny*!'

'Don't you like all these Navy ships? What's that in the dry-dock! The Grand Harbour has the arms of half an octopus! Lovely shelter, isn't it!'

'Why only half,' said Amabel doubtfully.

'Besides,' said Nanny, 'it's not as though the *Koh-i-Noor* will be at anchor. Must have sailed last night.'

Amabel goggled.

'I didn't think to tell you, my pet.'

'*Without* us?'

Amabel had sounded aghast.

'What with all the to-do, I never thought!'

Amabel broke out a laugh like a flag. Disbelief.

'Why else would Mummie have said goodbye to her acquaintances? Weren't you paying attention?'

Amabel was too old to boo-hoo. She was bawling; and *in public*. She was carrying on as though her heart would break. Screaming and stamping!

'Amabel, my nerves ...' pleaded Nanny. 'Children don't do this! Sakes, what is the matter? People are about!'

Amabel sobbed. She sobbed and sobbed. Her nose was streaming and she had to gulp for air.

'What anguish! Dry your eyes up before we

go back to the Osborne,' said Nanny, 'do!'

It seemed Amabel could contain herself only to dissolve in front of her mummie.

Mrs Romney pressed a hand to her forehead and said, full of incredulity and indignation, 'Oh, must you, darling? A frightful *clamour*?'

A mere hour later and Nanny's dam must have burst; for she felt it necessary to betray Amabel. 'Madam, it was the 'blue roan mare'. She's left behind her . . . her blue roan mare. Her horse has sailed with *Koh-i-Noor*.'

'Nanny, that would have been *your* packing.'

'The blue roan mare was in a stall amidships, and her groom, a groom-person . . . had a hammock in some nook . . .' mused Nanny aloud.

'Nanny . . . !' exclaimed Mrs Romney, more like her old self.

Nanny's smile appeared.

'D'you mean to tell me,' said Mrs Romney, 'that we've been travelling with a pretend animal?'

Nanny nodded.

'And this Peter. He rides beside or behind us, when we go out on the bicycle. Amabel will *crane*! Don't *you* wobble, madam?'

'Gracious!'

'And he gallops, I think, beside all the railway-engines and motors . . .'

'Do we have Peter with us, or is he still on board?'

'I wouldn't like to venture an opinion,' said

138

Nanny. 'It's to be hoped he is with the blue roan mare or she will starve and thirst to death!'

'Oh, Nanny, oh Nanny!' said Mrs Romney, half crying, half laughing. 'I have left someone on board too. *Quite* precious to me. Bound for Egypt, just as we were.'

'In that case,' said Nanny, appalling herself, 'should we not proceed to Egypt by other means? I trust you'll not mention to Amabel that I've let you into her secret. If you don't mind, madam.'

Mrs Romney didn't take on.

It was the first time Mrs Romney had acknowledged the reality of a 'beau'.

'Have you got your thermometer, Nanny?'

'For you?'

'I think I may be running a slight one,' she said.

III DEFEAT

O patient eyes, courageous hearts!

JULIAN GRENFELL

Some of the wounds the horses had are too terrible to think about.

SUBALTERN, *'A' Squadron, Q.O.D.Y, Agagiya*

31 Nanny imposes

'Why this Lia?' demanded Nanny, in the brusque tones that betrayed to Amabel that Nanny felt herself to be in a hole.

'Because that is where Lady Spence resides!' said the hotel manager. 'The station in Valletta is near the Opera House, where Ordnance Street, parallel to our street, meets Kingsway ... the *Strada Reale*. Handy to this *hôtel*. You may travel in the 10.08 as far as Attard.'

'Will it have a corridor?' said a voice at Nanny's elbow.

'Take first class tickets. I advise Attard.'

'How many minutes?' piped up Amabel.

'Twenty,' he said, without lowering his regard. 'If, Nurse, you feel you should seek out Lady Spence, it is necessary to go to find her. Unless you'd care to try the telephone?'

Nanny thought not.

'There should be *carrozzini* outside Attard station. I am furnishing you with the *correct* address.'

And suppose the driver takes us off into the blue, thought Nanny. 'Does he speak English, this cab driver?'

'He speaks English even to his horse,' stated Mr Azzopardi.

Amabel was subdued. Gripping her, Nanny set off, with her jaw into the wind.

A ticket office was an ordeal. And, 'What tiddly carriages! Reminds me of the railway-engine the Talbots' papa used to run around the garden. A toy, I'd say!'

And, 'Such a mountain of fortification! Quite puts the wind up a body.'

'Does it, Nanny?' Amabel said, mechanically. 'Was it a fib?'

'Was what a fib, dear?'

'The twenty minutes.'

'Never trust a fellow of his stamp! Why?'

'Oh, *Nanny*!' squeaked Amabel.

An obedient Nanny sat on past Birchircara. There were no *carrozzini* at Attard station.

It was a place of country lanes, sprinkled with mansions; palm trees; vineyards; green shoots of wheat in red soil. 'Oh, *what* a pretty part of the world. It can't be so far, you have legs, Amabel!'

Nanny kept enquiring for a location that nobody understood. ' "Liar", is this right for "Liar"?' That made it farther.

She held the jotted address.

A liveried servant stopped in mid-errand and uttered the blessed phrase, 'Nurse, may I direct you?' They took fresh hope. They were soon at sea.

A Maltese greengrocer by his barrow said shyly, 'Help?'

Nanny said, 'I dare say you're acquainted with a Lady Spence?'

'Everybody is,' he said.

144

This was gratifying.

'I'll draw it for you,' the man said. He sketched it on newspaper, over the print.

Then, to add to Nanny's bewilderment, there were monks and things (*monks!*) in the street, too many; in what was a rustical, opulent setting; not at all what she had pictured.

'*Romans*,' hissed Nanny.

Lady Spence inhabited a grand, stone villa. It was one of perhaps six or eight similar. In common with others, it showed an austere face to the world, ornamented by a single armorial escutcheon; and rose, sheer, from the flags of the village pavement; onto which the door gave. 'Rum, I'd say,' said Nanny. Along the top of this front was, incongruously, a Palladian balustrade.

'There aren't any birds in cages,' said Amabel; as though congratulating this Lady Spence, thought Nanny, on her good taste. But it wasn't as though they 'knew' her. Nanny had a duty, and she would do it. She attacked the door.

Once you stepped over the threshold, you saw a jolly garden, ornamental trees; mimosa, creamy jasmine and a lemon-tree with lemons on it; a fountain. The flow emerged from an O in a boy's face and, since his face was turned upward, the jet went straight up into the air. The sunlight burnished the water. The boy might have been swallowing a sword.

Nanny, dwarfed by a row of fat columns, was

145

reassured.

'You never know, these days,' she remarked, 'what is inside.'

Conducted to the terrace, Nanny was stumped by a stare of the most utter, utter incomprehension.

'Well, I'm most awfully sorry, Nurse.'

'Nanny,' said Amabel.

Lady Spence in her distraction glanced at Amabel.

'Nanny, then! It must be difficult for you. Mrs Romney *carried off*, you say? To the Blue Sisters? By the sound of it, she was lucky. The *lazaro* would have been frightful. What has this to do with *me*? We were barely acquainted! Did she not leave the *Koh-i-Noor* in bad odour?'

Nanny was stout. 'My duty is to Amabel!'

'D'you mean you and the child are incapable of *staying in an hotel* in Valletta?'

Nanny refused to wilt.

'It doesn't seem suitable, not to us,' she said.

'It doesn't?' asked Lady Spence, wildly. Beneath the wide-brimmed hat, the hair was streaky and fine, Nanny noted.

'Delirious,' insisted Nanny (the flapping ears!) under her breath. 'Mrs Romney is raving! Not a word of sense to be got from that quarter, madam. Amabel and I are *stranded*.'

Lady Spence was baffled.

'I don't believe you realize, we live here rather "out of the way".'

Nanny kept her lips closed.

'My grandchildren are grown-ups. I don't *have* a nursery any more. No nursery!'

Nanny's pale eyes stared through their spectacles.

Right out loud, Lady Spence remarked to herself, 'I can't imagine what claim they have on me!'

Nanny rummaged her lips around a stubborn mouth.

At last Lady Spence said, 'Won't you sit down?'

Primly, if rather speedily, Nanny plumped down; and tugged Amabel's frock. Amabel, taken unawares, tipped into Nanny's lap. Nanny grasped Amabel's waist and deposited her on a stool.

Amabel straightened her garments, trying to sustain her part without having garnered an inkling as to what her part was.

Lady Spence tried, 'Don't y'see, Nanny, this isn't the house you believe it to be!'

With that cryptic reference to Nanny knew not what, they'd found refuge. 'What am I to say to Sir John ... Oh, well, oh well ... Mrs Romney may not be long in hospital ... it won't be to her liking ...' muttered Lady Spence. 'And do let us pray she is not!'

32 Agagiya

If Philomena was anxious for a drink, Burdock was too. His water was close to drained. He hankered for a brew. He put the thought behind him.

The galloper, 2nd Lieutenant Abury, sent to fetch the Bucks squadron (last observed in vigorous pursuit of recalcitrant beasts), returned; having failed to find them. The South African infantry had been hindered by hopeless sand. The axles of the armoured cars were probably spinning themselves ever deeper.

Clear of the sand-hills and wire defences, the baggage camels of the dervishes loped . . . slowly, slowly . . . across the desert behind that slight ridge. The retreating column straggled for over a mile; three to four hundred yards in depth; camouflaged by a more distant, steep escarpment.

The plain appeared to be even. For over three-quarters of a mile it tilted faintly upwards, dotted with cringed thorn and desultory grasses. The going was firm; without serious hindrance; even if sandstone had worn into shelves and small boulders. There was no cover whatsoever, no undulation or feature.

The sun, slipping down the sky, for in February it set early, was starting to cast its pink light.

Burdock began to look cheerful. The alertness of the yeomen brought the horses' heads up. Philomena, who had been watching an emerald beetle, pricked her ears.

The horses weren't fresh; they were tired. Corky was indestructible. Philomena had eaten, ages ago, two thirds of her ration of seven pounds of corn. What remained to her was in the nosebag slung on the saddle. That saddle bore a rolled blanket, rifle-bucket, scabbard and sword, picketing-pegs, water-canteen, ground-sheet, great-coat and spare clothing, flattened canvas bucket, grooming kit, and two spare shoes. One bandoleer went around her neck, the other around Burdock: he'd used up some of the ammunition. On Burdock's person went his haversack, mess-tin, his own rations. Burdock was fairly lean. She was carrying eighteen stone ten; and had been floundering through sand. The encumbrances flumped, rattled and protruded. Her stirrup iron kept catching the rays of the sun and, wobbling, flashed them at the corner of her eye.

The Regiment was together bar 'D' Troop, 'A' Squadron, detailed to guard wounded infantry. Two men from 'A' Squadron had ridden back with dispatches. Stragglers with exhausted or terrified horses numbered three.

The depleted squadrons gave the Colonel, in officers and other ranks, some one hundred and sixty-three sabres. Pluckily with them too was the A.D.C. sent by General Lukin to urge the Colonel to shock-action. There were four Bucks men. The M.G. Section yielded a further seventeen.

The Bucks squadron was to have formed a second line.

Only the M.G. Section was in support.

The officer commanding 'C' Squadron blew his whistle for the led horses to be brought up . . . the order 'Prepare to Mount' . . . Major Sandley, his complexion ablaze, signalled 'Mount': it dawned on Burdock and Dawkes *fully* . . . what was to happen.

At this moment, the wind died.

Burdock had off-saddled twice, for ten minutes, in thirty-six hours. He'd constantly run his fingers inside the girth to dislodge grains of sand that might have attached themselves to sweat.

It didn't look as though the enemy's machine guns were hastening away no more: the camels had vanished. Burdock was glad of Philomena. 'B' Squadron had lost its decent horses at Matruh and got some poor nags in exchange; yet none of the fellows would have spared a minute for ruefulness.

Hadn't they been living for this!

It remained to those not caught up in it to lament the waste of life and horseflesh.

There could be no covering fire of any description. The horse artillery had been

150

confounded by the terrain. The M.G. Section was not in the right position. The Colonel couldn't continue to slither along the flank, or outmanoeuvre the Senussi rear-guard.

Since 'C' Squadron had been the advanced squadron, the Regiment formed line on 'C'. 'A' Squadron came up on the left, 'B' on the right. In double rank; to extend to eight yards and four.

The unluckiest were those with the regimental transport, miles back. Major Bathurst (Second-in-Command) was incapacitated. 'B' Squadron's officers' mess cook had his very own *arme blanche*, his meat cleaver, and it gleamed with a sort of secret smile.

The horses were expectant.

The Colonel bellowed, 'The Regiment will attack.'

Philomena tossed her head.

Burdock sat down in the saddle.

The element of surprise was not a consideration. The trumpet sounded the Advance. The Colonel's arm, at shoulder height, swung back and then forward.

The Colonel, watchful of the ground, as was proper, rode for a while three hundred yards ahead. Some attributed it to anxiety over their capacities.

The sun had slipped again.

The sand began to kick with tiny sputs.

The yeomen trotted with wonderful

151

steadiness . . . straight into rifle and machine-gun fire. The tingling nerves were only for their horses to sense.

Most of the fire passed through them. Philomena was frightened by the hisses and pings that kept buzzing by her ear. Burdock was so overcome he wanted to burst. His breath was drawn in 'huffs': his mouth was open. Sweating, he was face to face with a thrill.

Despite the depredations on the troop-horses brought to Egypt with them, many of the officers had chargers they, or a fellow officer that had fallen in Gallipoli, had hunted. So many of the yeomen, officers and troopers, had followed hounds in the county! Lieutenant Pedlar, O.C. 'A' Troop, 'A' Squadron, was mounted on a black mare familiar with Miss Lupus's; whilst Lieutenant Treeves was thoroughly proud of Conker.

At seven hundred yards, the Colonel gave the command to draw swords—not confident of his regiment's abilities at the gallop. Philomena was oblivious to the uniquely recognizable whisper of sabres bared from the scabbard.

The dervish line was both a blur and clear to see. The hundreds of white burnooses gleamed.

Turks manned the machine-guns, in a litter of ammunition boxes, the bluish-khaki uniforms and scarlet wrists and epaulettes dull in the bleached mass, the *kamalak* (their headgear) like mud in the midst of snow.

The Senussi banners and pennants hung limp.

The dervishes had knelt to receive a cavalry charge. They were shooting the horses first.

At six hundred yards, when swiftness had become *vital*, the Colonel gave the order 'Gallop'. Few attempted to wait the regulation three paces: for an instant the line was wavery. The jingling had changed into a thrum of hoof-beats. In 'A' Squadron, two bay horses were brought down within a single stride of each other. The coverers pressed up.

The Turkish machine-gunners played very freely across the Dorsets' front. Major Sandley wilted in the saddle. The dust raised was shot through with rosy rays of sun. Burgess sailed through the air, and was himself winged like a flapper. Field-glasses saved a young officer. Horses were crumpling. Riderless horses heaved themselves up, and thudded on with the rest. Philomena was so distracted (she had a curious view) she didn't hear the whump when, at four hundred yards, the files closed for impact and Corky was hit in the neck. She didn't pay any attention to his snort. But she saw the white of his eye. He was stubborn.

She was in a lather.

Then the dervish fire was flying over their heads; and the machine-gunners had been rendered erratic.

The Colonel, on a dying horse, gave the order 'Charge!' at sixty yards. His wounded trumpeter responded.

Burdock's sword came from the slope to the sword-in-line. There was a cheer from every yeoman's throat. Burdock had been filling his lungs for this. (The C.O. snatched up the rein of a wild-eyed bay trooper.) Spent horses roused themselves: ears went back, lay flat; and were pricked again; flattened. With one almighty holler, a filthy racket, the Regiment tore at the enemy . . . The Senussi bawled, *'Ya allah, ya allah! Allahu akbar!'* Far away in the desert the Bucks squadron heard; and hair rose on the backs of their necks.

A howl echoed out of the awful collision. Numbers were turning tail, shrieking, throwing aside their arms.

'B' Squadron had lost Major Sandley. The two senior troop leaders had been unhorsed. Lieutenant Atkinson was seriously wounded. Before it ever reached the mêlée, the squadron had been pretty decapitated.

Burdock sent her straight into the fallen . . . a wounded, Roman-nosed bay swerved across 'A' Troop's front and collapsed. Philomena jumped him, a bay with a white race . . . for a split second, as Conker, for it was he, struggled to raise his head, she met his eye . . . and Private Burdock was using his sword industriously, leaning forward to stick backs, remaining so until the blade pulled out . . . not for nought, all that drill. Her strength lent his weapon a butter-cutting power, and she recovered it for him too. Daggers were thrust at Philomena, and at her reins. Rifle butts reared to club her legs. Her near-hind slipped in a gush of blood. Then Philomena was through them. A camel strode off alone into the desert, making a ghastly noise.

Whilst Lieutenant Pitt of 'C' Squadron and Lance-Corporal Hardy rode down a Maxim; and annihilated the Turkish gunners, one of whom Hardy thrust in the throat, 'B' Squadron, having been instructed in the art of 'charging home' galloped on. 'A' Squadron, having gone through the tail of the enemy, rallied.

The Colonel's second horse, the bay trooper, had been killed under him . . . got in the heart. She'd propelled him into the midst.

His hand was being kissed.

Howling, Senussi had bolted in a multitude of directions. With 'C' Troop, 'B' Squadron, 2nd Lieutenant Childe had been twice shot. In such a rage, he rallied and led seven men into a throng, mowing a swathe until he fell. It was now and in the mêlée that those dervishes that had stood and were cool did the most damage; shooting . . . at the closest range . . . or hacking. Horses that would swerve from a scimitar failed to notice a dagger. Dervishes that had lain flat and let the line gallop over them now came to life: the yeomen that had

155

carried on, and gone too far in a pursuit that nobody had ordered, were shot in the back.

Colonel Dittis and a subaltern stepped up to demand the surrender of the Turkish general and his staff. In their gold lace, *on foot*, these gentlemen were unruffled. One bore a wistful expression: he was German. The cherubic, pencil-moustached Jaafar Pasha had suffered a slash in the sword arm.

The Colonel whistled rather frantically for the M.G. Section to gallop up and assist.

The moral impact settled it.

An escort to the rear had to be found. Jaafar had to be mounted.

Caught in enfilade fire, Farrier-Sergeant Burt reeled in the saddle, tipped, pulled himself up. One trooper clung on in their midst, blinded and bleeding, shot in the eye. Sergeant Burt led his remnants of 'A' Troop, 'B' Squadron, at a canter . . . if it was to give quarter and take prisoners, the spirit underwent an abrupt change . . . to gallop over a nest of *muhafizia*, knocking them over and mauling their cover of three couched camels. The dromedaries seemed to die imperturbable. But once agitated they didn't give in; not when slapped with the broad of the sword.

Dawkes dismounted to wrestle with the surviving camel, which groaned terribly, spat and lunged at him with bared teeth yellow as a smoker's. Dawkes had cut the brute free. As

Dawkes took Corky from Burdock, the brute's teeth gashed Philomena.

Both horses were blowing.

'C' Squadron's trumpeter sounded the 'Rally'.

Dawkes was determined to bag the dromedary.

All of a sudden, the bedlam ceased. An eerie glow illuminated the desert. The M.O. was on his knees beside Major Sandley. It was apparent that the yeoman had sabred umpteen Senussi, kindly dispatching any writhers or twitchers. The blood had soaked into patches and patches of sand, until the crystals on the surface had been dimmed. Unhorsed men, whose rifles had been in the bucket, had made sturdy use of steel.

A chestnut sat up miserably on his haunches.

Burdock had been separated from Dawkes and his prize.

Spent bullets arrived like a spatter of rain. The baggage and its escort of irregulars were scuttling into the horizon behind which the sun was about to die. Some of those camels might have been carrying water and rations.

Philomena wanted a drink.

Burdock's hand was stiff, and trembled. His near-side puttee trailed in shreds.

General Lukin's A.D.C. had been killed.

The lap of Philomena's skin with a gout of flesh was her only wound. But there was shock in the horses' eyes; a blank look. Their ears flickered. Their companions lay with broken bones, or stone dead, with bullets in the heart; or hobbled painfully with shattered tendons; or, like Corky, had machine-gun bullets lodged somewhere; or had cocked themselves on fore-legs, hamstrung; or were treading on their own guts and were still eviscerating themselves; or were bleeding to death. Philomena's nostrils filled with the scents of heated metal and of blood.

A winded, riderless Corky, his nostrils red, his reins slashed, and with crimson drying down to the knee of his off fore, crept towards her and stood mutely there. Burdock leant from the saddle, and collected his halter-rope. '*Drat*,' said Burdock.

The Regiment was ordered to retire a little; and was dismounted. Lack of water and rations would forbid the pursuit.

Philomena stretched her neck; she chucked her head.

Some had the strength to shake.

The General, who, upon the extremity of the hills from which he'd driven the Senussi, had witnessed, as though at a military review, the whole thing, sent up a battalion of South Africans, troops that had that day already with such *élan* attacked, to guard the recovery of the wounded (widely scattered) before dusk; and to drive off the snipers of the Senussi rear-guard that were inclined to creep like snakes to dispatch a last bullet home.

The Turkish prisoners, and a dozen *muhafizia*, were passed back to Western Force HQ. It was to be lamented that three of the Maxim guns had escaped.

The Colonel detailed Lieutenant Bray with 2nd Lieutenant Pitt and a party from 'C' Squadron to search the field; and to liaise with the infantry dressing-station.

Pitt trusted fervently that, despite the sniping, any and all of their wounded would be found before nightfall. The Bedouin were reputed to strip naked the unrecovered dead and even to emasculate them. Pitt trusted he'd see every horse put out of its misery. The horses had paid very dearly; and it was a grief to officers and men alike.

They'd captured two flea-bitten greys. Both entire. A trophy was selected from the sanguinary banners.

The Regiment marched back to the pool in the desert scented as long ago as mid-afternoon by the horses. It was standing water from the rains: the horses, with raging thirst, rushed it and plunged in to their knees. Burdock could brew up and Philomena could at last swallow some bad water. The Regiment was to endure a night of cold, discomfort and elation.

Philomena swallowed two pounds of barley too. Men sought the strength to coax horses that wouldn't touch their nosebags; and to bathe their wounds. The farriers were hard pressed. The Brigade Veterinary Officer was nowhere.

In Burdock's stomach there would be dates; for the Bucks squadron had, as well as prisoners, acquired loaded camels; had wasted precious minutes grappling with these transports. The Bucks had burnt, however, other stores.

Burdock rubbed the crushed muscles of Philomena's back and dusted powder in the camel bite. He wasn't to lie, when he did lie down, with his head in the shelter of his cocked saddle. There could be no order to off-saddle for the hours of darkness. The chilled, pained horses dozed and all were stiff. They were linked.

Of eighty-five gallant horses, eighty-four had been killed or so severely wounded as to have to be shot, and one was missing. Permission to destroy a further eleven had to be denied: they could not (not for more than a few days) survive, but were fit for service.

Most of the latter had been machine-gunned in the belly.

Many bore gashes and had lost blood. A charger had a severed tongue.

Five officers and twenty-seven other ranks had fallen. Five officers and thirty O.R.s had been wounded that day.

The other Turkish general, Nuri Bey, was presumed killed (for Corporal Permain had 'ridden him down and stuck him'). During the

160

night his body disappeared. Perceiving that the dervishes surrendered only to pop up, the Dorsets had sabred them. The dervishes were heaped and they were scattered: three hundred was the official figure. A guess. Pitt knew it was overwhelmingly more.

The Q.O.D.Y. could be exceedingly proud. If a trifle costly, it had been a glorious action. In the morning, they'd bury their own.

Some of the horses had been great pets.

Philomena listened to the noises in the darkness, the jackals, the rustlings of tiny creatures.

33 Sodom and Gomorrah

Lady Spence might have appeared forceful. Early impressions were misleading. Lady Spence was a vague old thing, intent on a serene old age in the sunshine, among a few bright flowers, with Sir John, similarly intent, and Monsieur Hippolyte. His surname in full was such a mouthful that to all he was Monsieur Hippolyte.

Without penetrating to that part of the house, without many words in common with the staff, without any gossiping, Nanny soon discovered that the bedchambers of Sir John, Lady Spence and Monsooer Hippolyte 'gave onto' one another.

They lived *à trois*.

Nanny didn't know a lot about those *ménages*. She did wonder whether or not it was now so suitable for Amabel.

Monsieur Hippolyte was, in truth, a godsend. He claimed to abominate children: he adored them. He chucked Amabel under the chin and pinched her cheeks in a manner that would hitherto have been scorned by her. He told stories, and recited poetry. He called her '*mon petit*' and was teaching her '*Jeanne était au pain sec dans le cabinet noir . . .*' amid gales of laughter.

Monsooer H. kept Amabel amused, whenever Nanny had to go off, frantic and alone, with the Spence chauffeur, to the Blue Sisters in St Julian's, to visit Mrs Romney. A more signal duty nobody could have done: a child wasn't a good omen in a hospital and, as Nanny said, Heaven knew what illness Mrs Romney had contracted.

The Blue Sisters never took in infectious or contagious diseases. After Gallipoli and the War, they wouldn't even admit dysentery. However! Mrs Romney had run a high temperature.

Nanny didn't *think* Mrs Romney's illness 'hysteric'. Nanny's face had fresh cares worn into it.

Amabel would remember that naughty *Jeanne* and the awful punishment for the rest of her life, probably. Fancy shutting a child in a black cabinet! Let alone the dry bread. But Nanny was ever so grateful to Monsieur Hippolyte.

She couldn't understand the attraction. He was a messy fellow near his dotage. Sir John seemed to love him. Nanny thought them all very queer. That, reckoned Nanny, accounted for their location.

Sir John had devoted a quarter of his career to the affairs of Malta and was a friend to her.

Sir John and Lady Spence 'went everywhere' and so did Monsieur Hippolyte. Overlooking Napoleon, Maltese society *and* British society had embraced Monsieur Hippolyte.

Sir John and Lady Spence had shown themselves to be poppets. And there was fresh milk; if you didn't wrinkle your nose at the flavour. In the course of the morning, a herd of goats called. The warm milk got to the pantry while the froth was on it.

On Sunday, Nanny and Amabel were whisked in the motor to Queen Adelaide's Church. Lady Spence waved Nanny and Amabel to a side pew, while she and Sir John seated themselves in the nave's middle pews. Nanny felt herself inured to the Church of England.

The other gent bided at home. He, like the monks, was Roman.

Nanny was able to think better of Valletta. 'Nice steps here!' said Nanny. A multitude of them lined every hilly carriageway.

'The steps are shallow because the Knights had a job to bend their knees in heavy armour,' said old Sir John.

'Well!' said Nanny.

'My knees creak,' remarked Lady Spence. 'Yours should not!'

'*God rest his tender brave young spirit,*' sighed Amabel in the motor. '*God rest his tender brave young spirit.*'

'Whose spirit would that be, dear?' murmured Nanny.

34 Monsieur Hippolyte

'Nanny, any number of people would have been glad to have helped you!' said Griselda, torn between exasperation and weak laughter. 'People who *knew* me!'

'There was no learning that, though, the state you were in.'

'We spent our last, happy year in Malta, before the War!'

'Sir John and Lady S. have been staunch, madam.'

Griselda noticed the furrows were growing in.

'And there is Monsooer Hippolyte. Quite a treasure, I *must* say! There's no accounting for children's tastes, I'm sure. Keeps Amabel in stitches! If not that, she is reading to him from her *Straw Peter*. All of a much-ness, really. He teases her over the pages that you cut out.'

'Tell me,' said Griselda, gazing at Nanny, 'about Monsieur Hippolyte. One of the servants there?'

Nanny looked horrified. 'He's a French gentleman, madam, who ...' Griselda raised her eyebrows encouragingly. 'Monsooer is a dear friend, so Sir John was kind enough to tell me, to both Lady Spence, madam, *and* himself.'

Griselda shut her eyes.

'Oh, you're tired, madam!'

'*And* himself?' Griselda had picked up Nanny's intonation.

'You'd do far better to rest,' said Nanny. She ground her teeth. 'No need to fret. I have our business under control, madam; where we, Amabel and I, are concerned. Though we'd thank God if you were to get well again *swiftly*!'

'I'll be up soon.' Griselda examined her wrist: how scrawny it had become!

'Amabel has got ever so attached to "The Panter"!' remarked Nanny.

Was this a diversion from Frenchmen?

'Sir John tells me his proper name is "Lepanto". And that he is from a long line.'

There was a pause. 'A faithful hound?'

'As befitting a small dog whose tongue lolls ...' explained Nanny.

'What breed?'

165

'I knew you'd ask me!'

'A Maltese?'

As though unable to stand her own touch, Griselda stroked her fingers across her eyelids.

She said, in a thread, 'It seems that nobody could have realized we were coming. Why didn't I write ahead?'

'Well, how could you have known!'

Griselda subsided into silence. Nanny looked at the same time stumped and upset.

'Monsooer Hippolyte and Amabel scarce let a moment go by without chattering.'

Griselda was vaguely alarmed.

She said, 'Lady Spence hasn't so much as been in to see me. It would have been civil.'

'Lady Spence is an indolent lady,' said Nanny. 'And older than you might think.'

'Is she?' said Griselda. 'Well, it's all very irregular. I'm grateful to her, of course . . . Oh, Nanny, I'm mortified! You've foisted yourselves on these people.'

'Never mind that now,' said Nanny.

To fill a hiatus, Nanny observed, 'Sir John is writing a book. He's been at it for twelve years. He's told Amabel . . .'

'Amabel talks to him?'

'That it's to do with "wives".'

' "Wives", Nanny?'

'How they've perfectly *ruined* the Empire. No sooner do the wives arrive from England than the country in question goes Downhill. Or the Grasp on it is enfeebled. You may see it

166

in India.'

'May I?'

'The clubs and cantonments, madam, and such, they are evidence of a snobbery that wasn't felt before. Sir John will not beat about the bush. *Snobbery*. The Mutiny might not have occurred had it not been for the advent of the Wives. Jamaica. Malaya. Kenya. The Gold Coast. Gentlemen deal better with natives, all over the globe.'

Griselda giggled.

'Once the wives descended upon Malta in droves, "tactful government" started to slip, madam.'

'Sir John *discusses* this with Amabel! Are you sure she's relayed it to you correctly?'

'Drinks it all in.'

'And her sorrows? I never understood why the blue roan mare shouldn't have sprouted wings, or cantered on water.'

'Not a syllable!' said Nanny.

'Don't let her adopt a "panter" of her own . . . Did you remember my writing-case, Nanny? What day is it?'

Nanny imagined it was Thursday.

Upon Nanny's departure, Griselda roused herself. When the envelopes reappeared on the bedside table, endorsed 'Gone Away', or 'Not Known', Griselda thought the War had altered Malta. It wasn't as though their acquaintance, hers and Arthur's, had been limited to the Services.

167

Under the jacaranda-tree in Lady Spence's garden Monsieur Hippolyte amused Griselda's small daughter. '*Mon petit*, in fourteen twenty-nine, the Moors sacked the islands. The Moors were vicious to St Agathe. St Agathe's bosom had already been sliced off twelve centuries earlier by a Roman Emperor.'

'Why was St Agathe still alive?' Amabel eyed Monsieur Hippolyte, speculatively.

He didn't notice.

'Somebody must have done some slicing before the Roman Emperor got at her,' she said.

'What are you talking about?'

'The Roman Emperor pitied a person with one bosom and wanted to balance her up.'

'St Agathe could boast but the one. One does.'

'She fell asleep in a mountain for ages and ages!' Amabel blinked. 'For twelve centuries,' she said, 'to be precise.'

'Malta has no mountains.'

'She was in an advanced state of preservation like Lady Spence.'

Monsieur Hippolyte said, 'Shh!' And, 'St Agathe was on the wall of a *grotte*. She is today . . .'

'The wall had its bosoms sliced off.'

'Oh, St Agathe did suffer this all right. And twelve centuries later, the Moors, who were not heathens but Mohammedans, they so disapproved, poor things, of images.'

'Why?'

'Images smack of idolatry. The general run of Maltese can't bear Mohammedans.'

'Because of the bosoms?'

'Let us drop bosoms.'

Griselda, restless and in a bed with long white legs, fretted over her own incapacity.

'When the Moors departed, they left behind their language ... The Knights were handed Malta on a plate. They had offered their lives to Jesus, at sea or on land. If a Knight was too wounded to stand up he'd fight *sitting down*. Some very brave Knights had to do so in the breach in sixteen sixty-five. More Mohammedans had sailed to Malta, this time the Ottoman Turks, to lay *tremendous* siege. And Maltese women boiled water and emptied basins of it onto the attackers ...'

Amabel's mouth opened.

'The Maltese men, although their tongue was mostly Arabic, fought as tenaciously. The Maltese and the Knights saved Malta for Christendom.'

'Did the Maltese women have different tongues?' Amabel got in.

Monsieur Hippolyte gazed at her with a quizzical smile.

'... The Knights, during their time in the Holy Land, had learnt a lot of their medicine from the Arabs ...'

'Are the Knights nursing Muzz?'

'Patience, child! I'm telling you ...'

'Muzz likes men,' stated Amabel, in hope.

'. . . They nursed these Sick of every religion, rich and poor, lepers and people whose diseases smelt so disgustingly horrid that nobody else could have borne to go near them; and fed all of them from silver plate, because silver was cleanest; and they operated with silver scalpels.'

'Ugh! Muzz isn't going to have an operation, is she?'

'. . . Whereas the Ottomans, those of the Great Siege, had mutilated the dead Knights, cut their heads off, nailed the heads to crosses and pushed them out to sea. Corpses were washed back . . .'

'Is a leper in the next bed?' This was said in a small voice.

'Napoleon came and the Knights, frail and weak, were driven from Malta . . .'

'Frail and weak from the Siege? They must have been starving!'

'I'm skipping more than two centuries . . . and Napoleon abolished slavery.'

'Oh dear!' said Amabel.

'Oh? "Oh dear"?'

'Nanny slaves for me.'

'The Maltese believed that he had looted the silver, despite his ideals . . . It transpires today that much was hidden by the Maltese nobles . . . They, the little Maltese, rose up, so fiercely Napoleon's garrison was obliged to retreat behind the walls of the five cities of the Grand

Harbour. Malta asked the English admiral, Lord Nelson, to send the fleet.'

Monsieur Hippolyte rather fancied he was *not*, however, keen on the British.

'You like Lady Spence,' Amabel said.

'Oh, I do! And Sir John I like. And you I like. And I almost like Nanny too! The British promised the Knights Hospitaller that their Order might return, but somehow ... somehow ...' He snapped his fingers. 'Perfidious Albion!'

Amabel nodded sagely.

'The Wives,' she said.

Griselda discovered she'd been in hospital for three weeks.

When Philomena came into her head, the patient turned her face into her own dear pillow, which Nanny had brought in scented with drops of essence of lavender.

Griselda wished Philomena had never been hers.

35 On the march

Philomena's skin twitched around the camel bite. The skin had dried to leather. Farrier-Sergeant 'Burtie' Burt was cursory: he had exceeding worse to attend, and a mash in the flesh of his own sword arm.

Burdock dusted the gouge with boric acid.

The flap wouldn't stick down.

Burdock made much of her. He was exhilarated, for she'd carried him safely through; been ('as the saying went, like') his legs, his glory, the thrust to his sword.

Her head drooped.

With dawn, while a mass grave was dug, the horses could lip a few grasses. The spectacle of wounded horses, knee-haltered to pick here and there among the carcasses, worked tears.

The Bedouin women *would* stalk around the periphery; weapon in hand, baby on back. However, it was thought that the charge of the Dorset Yeomanry had done it. Crowned operations in the Western Desert. The Senussi had been dealt a blow; the decider.

A number of men marched away dismounted. Casualty figures were highest for 'B' Squadron.

General Lukin took 'A' Squadron with him, direct to Sollum; to catch what Senussi might be encamped on the coast and to drive them over the border. Philomena, shedding condition, marched *via* Sidi Barrani. In Sidi Barrani, there was briny water with which to bathe the horses' wounds. The horses had been on half rations of grain since leaving Matruh.

Many were scarcely sound.

From Sollum, most now had to trek the two hundred and thirty-five miles to Alexandria. Twenty horses, with fifteen men, would be entrained at Dabaa.

They assembled to march each day at 9 a.m. The forage issued at Matruh on the return was tainted. Better was urgently requested; and neither denied nor supplied.

Burdock led her for hours at a stretch.

Officers and men were troubled for their horses.

The English hunters suffered first. Short rations. Little proper grooming to rub their aching muscles. Any that fell out, with quivering, filled legs and bloodless lids, had to be destroyed on the Khedivial road. The desert spring started to adorn the road with flowers. The wind that had made a bowling alley of the desert with whipped bushes ... that had died too. At sunset, the rocks glowed rosily, to fade in a violet light.

The banks and much of the bed of every *wadi* were angelic with marigolds and red poppies. They were shaded by tamarisk radiant in a feathery purple. Swallows flew low over stagnant pools. The rocky ground sprouted flat yellow dishes, scented; whilst the dunes were fringed by the fat fingers of succulents, also yellow of flower; and when trodden on, these fat fingers stained the hoofs a deeper brown than any oil.

In a salt marsh, bristling with fowl, pairs of white egrets got up in alarm; while ducks swam a hurried zigzag course into the glow of the sun.

To Burdock, cogitating, it seemed that horses appreciated scenery. Burdock felt sorry that they what had fallen had missed the flowering. Mighty sorry. With the flowering had come sand-flies. Despite privation, sand-flies, wounds and the dying, were it nice for an animal to be alive? Nicer than never to live at all?

Burdock didn't know.

To men and fretful horses alike, friends had become vital; and to remain beside one's friend was a comfort. Dawkes lay naked under the grit, and Burdock missed him.

When the Farrier-Sergeant had looked Corky over, he'd grinned. 'A' Troop still had Corky; but Corky carried Corporal Odstock, who, though wounded in the groin, had not been bad enough to be evacuated.

Corky was not at Philomena's side. Her companions were mares; a black with a white star, and an Argentine roan.

The Regiment gained Alexandria in the first week of April; took a whole hour to cross the lake causeway, and went into 'Change of Air Camp', Sidi Bishr; by the beach.

Philomena was coaxed into the sea. The sea water did all the horses an immeasurable good; and once they'd discovered it was for swimming in, a mite chill or not, they couldn't be got out. Burdock too, having ridden through the shallows and swum his horse, returned later to wallow happily. Corky's bullets, refusing to emerge from his commodious neck, ceased to worry him.

Sick horses were paraded 'stripped, with bridle' at 2.30 p.m. and marched off to the Veterinary lines. Eleven were struck off.

With full rations of barley, with *tibbin* for bulk, the horses that could recover did so.

It was the Regiment that was in pitiful shape, 'the laughing stock of Egypt. No R.S.M. A single saddler ...' Stocks-Moyle, the Trojan who had led the Dorset Yeomanry in Gallipoli, had rejoined to resume command. A trumpeter had been killed in the Charge at Agagiya, a shoeing-smith; and Olive, whom he'd bred.

Remounts and reinforcements fed the poor, invalid Q.O.D.Y. up.

Troops were to be 1, 2, 3 and 4.

In 'B' Squadron, Philomena's 'A' Troop became No. 1 Troop.

In May, the Regiment entrained for Cairo and on up the Nile to relieve Australians and Cheshires in the Assiut District. 'B' Squadron's carriages were uncoupled at Deirut.

The cooler air of evening was full of wing-beats. Water buffalo were suspended in the heat; or submerged themselves to the tips of their muzzles, at which spectacle the horses would snort. Cattle egret dotted the little rectilinear crops (the last before the *haraka*) of the variety of *berseem* that could be cut and cut. Philomena was interested in *berseem*, so

175

sweet when fresh; and in shade, whether deep black or dappled; and in corn, whether ripe or green. She had time for certain roots; little for beans, cabbage, flax and cotton; and none for tubers or onions.

The season for great abundance was over.

The level of the river was sinking.

A mangy wreck of an aged cow might totter under the yoke with a gaunt-eyed camel. Or the creak of water-wheels sent a sparkle and a sudden darkening into irrigation ditches: she never tired of watching the apparition.

Philomena would lick the mud. The horses craved salt.

What she relished was the sugar cane.

Sunken-flanked dogs stood torpidly by the blind walls. Hens pressed their breasts into the dust. Where the last dovecots poked up like whitewashed thumbs, the fertile land, wider on the west bank, abruptly stopped; and there was a step, the Nile's true bank, up onto the desert floor.

Mostly, Philomena's view was of wire, acacia trees and companions.

The dromedary had been adopted for desert patrols, and quiet old Burdock parted from her. He and some other fellows chose to transfer to the 2nd Battalion, Imperial Camel Corps; to accustom themselves to the Bikanir, shipped from India.

Philomena's summer was hot. So hot, the horses were not worked between 8.30 a.m. and

176

4.30 p.m.

She was bitten. She stamped, swished and kicked at her belly.

The men were promised that they should go in parties to 'Seaside Camp'; to Sidi Bishr. Scores got sand-fly fever.

The villagers were friendly. The tribes of the wastes were not. They had to be kept from attacking. Usually, Philomena's nights were passed in the lines behind wire entanglements. She had water, she had rations. She had the flies, the terrible flies of Egypt. Where she had an 'easy' she found shade; Corky was beside her again. The whine and drone of insects meant there was the stamping of feet and swishing of tails, the chucking of heads, from sunrise until dusk. At dusk and all through the night, the haze of mosquitoes. The stars dropped out of the sky; and the great sun oozed triumphantly into it. Or violent dust-storms choked the horses and coated their nostrils in black.

Inspections there were many. Drill was desirable to render the squadron fit for further service. Good Argentine remounts arrived; and, in shock, some American 'mustangs'. Those officers and men wounded at Gallipoli, now well recovered, rejoined. Fourteen officers, two hundred and forty-eight other ranks and one hundred and seventy-six horses had brought the Regiment up to strength.

Philomena saw the Nile flood; and only at

the beginning of October, as the water retreated, did 'B' Squadron leave Deirut.

By November, the Regiment was down by the Suez Canal.

The bell-tents lined the water's edge of the Great Bitter Lake, at Geneffeh. Reveille was at 5.45 a.m. The forage ration for horses was 8 lbs barley, 2 lbs bran, 2 lbs *sacrapaille*, 6 lbs *tibbin*, 6 lbs hay, 10 lbs *berseem*.

Philomena and Corky were picketed to sand-bags, so a heel-shackle was deemed necessary. No horses were to be galloped. Scouts and messengers trotted; unless ordered otherwise. Draught vehicles proceeded at a walk. Unblunted spurs were punishable. A blanket, folded in four, covered the loins between 10 a.m. and 4 p.m. The *numnah* and saddle-blanket had to be spread over the saddle which itself had to be on a rack, and secured by the surcingle. The men scavenged for wood to make racks. Hoop iron, off the bales of *tibbin*, had to be folded.

Dung was taken off down a dung road and burnt.

There was 'sea-bathing' for horses and men; a treat. Fresh-water bathing had been cancelled—that billy harris again.

Corky spared Corporal Odstock the attack of a little hooded cobra hidden in loose sand.

Sixty-two horses, with fifty-four men and officers, disappeared; to the newly-forming M.G. Squadron. The D.Y. was issued with the

Hotchkiss gun. Each sabre squadron would have its own gun team.

Philomena found herself once in the sick-lines, with a discharge from the nostrils.

By March 1917, the Regiment, leading the column, had crossed the Canal via the pontoon bridge to El Kantara. Between Kantara and ancient Pelusium, where once a branch of the Nile had run into the sea, the going grew more treacherous. Somebody had thought of pinning out rabbit-wire over the shifting sand, to make a firm road surface for the infantry.

Gangs of *fellaheen*, Egyptian Labour Force, had been laying railway-track. There were sheds and engine-houses; repair shops; stocks of sleepers.

They were piping water, strained of billy harris and chlor7inated, from the *mayya hilwa*, the Sweetwater Canal.

The Sinai gave off a glare foreign to the Nile Valley. It was not yet unbearable. Cavalry was obliged to plod. Dawdling was liable to strain the horses. The going was easier than expected. Water was bad.

Camels carried it in 200-gallon *fanatis* or 'fintassies' for the men.

Philomena marched with twenty-two stone up. Corky did too.

For a few minutes before sunset, that poignant scent of water suffused the desert. It was of the nature of a mirage: not the eyes but the lips were deceived.

After the order 'Slacken Girths, File Away to Water', they waited and waited and were offered brine.

Horses (apparently) drank more if watered twice a day instead of thrice, and did better.

The harsh wind blew from the south. At the halt in each hour, a moistened cloth bathed the mouth, nostrils and eyes.

There were signs of fierce fighting, and abandoned trench systems clasped many an escarpment. Rocky outcrops were almost transparent, at sunset and sunrise; pink that was muted to purple or an eerie mauve; and quivered. White bones of carcasses had been picked clean, crosses stood at the head of clumps of graves. The salt crust between this ancient caravan road and the sea was blotched a lurid yellow by high explosive. At night the jackals shrieked. Pariah dogs tracked the column, expecting animals to perish; and would lurk on the fringe of the shallow saucer of a *hod*. In the latter, unsavoury spots, the M.O. tried to render the well potable.

To El Arish, it was a patient shuffle; on through bleached dunes. Picketing-pegs worked loose. The horses had to be ringed; head tied to head. They were too tired to fuss.

Before dark the wind dropped. Otherwise it would have been drear. At Wad' el-Arish, the going was firmer; anchored by desultory scrub. A trickle meandered in the bed; blue-flowering tamarisk feathered the banks.

A simple row of boundary stones marked the last of Egypt.

Rafa was massed with barracked camels and their Egyptian drivers. Nine horses had to be cast.

Rafa was put to their rear. The yeomen were in Palestine.

It was a sight to lift the spirits; a tranquil stretch of country, with slight undulations and green vegetation on sandy loam; amid the rarer sloughs. In a collar around the village of Khan Yunis, and dominated by a Crusader castle, reclined a quiet valley. There were wild flowers; mallow, and tiny pimpernels, cones of bindweed, irises and poppies. Honey-bees bustled through the air. Dotted about, the Bedouin farmers were ploughing; with a light, palm-wood share drawn by a dromedary. The harness seemed a matter of string attached to a breast collar of woven esparto: this wasn't the yoke of Egypt. Threaded into the acres of green barley was ploughed land; and ribbons of grass. Birds were twittering. There were lightly waving trees, and streams. Farther off, pillowy hills. It didn't have the smell of home, and the hedges were composed of the prickly pear, but it caused many hearts to feel a spasm of recognition.

The horses gazed upon this prettiness; and blew softly through their nostrils.

36 Ida hears from Griselda

Ida Lupus rode in at her mother's place, Orchard House. 'Do you know what!'

'Ida, you're so precipitate!' protested Ma.

'Griselda writes from Malta that she's been ill, so ill she was carted off to some blue nuns . . . they run a *hospital* . . . and Nanny and Amabel went to stay, all on their own, with a Lady Spence, a fellow passenger, to whom Griselda hadn't much warmed.'

'She was ill on board? Was it grave?'

'Her inside.'

'Eaten something?'

'An inflammation in a part of her anatomy for which she has to be treated by a Navy chap.'

Ma digested this.

'Oh,' she said. 'People like us don't go to hospitals, or to nuns. What was Nanny dreaming of? She should have obtained a sick-nurse.'

'To a hotel? Grizel had got them all into a hotel.'

'I suppose she didn't . . . no, one doesn't have a high fever with *that*.'

Ida quizzed Ma, and grinned. 'The animals do if 'it' has died in the womb.'

'*Was* she? Would she have set off at all? *Could* she have had "a mis"?'

Ida said, soothingly, 'More awkwardness, though! She puts me in a fix.'

'Money,' said Ma.

'Not only did Nanny not settle the account, the wretched establishment kept their rooms and has landed Griselda with a vast bill! She hasn't got it in her heart to be vexed with Nanny. I believe she hasn't even mentioned it. Griselda was raving when she was ill and Nanny felt a duty to Amabel.'

'Thank God for that!' said Ma. 'Why should she have been raving? I suffered one between Roland and you, and I didn't rave.'

'There are medical bills, and the disputed hotel bill . . . and . . .'

Ma said, 'And where is she now?'

'Deserted by old friends and acquaintances and ostracized.'

'*Ostracized*! Griselda? What do you mean?'

'By the stuffy set.'

'What stuffy set?'

'The British in Malta these days.'

Ma was aghast.

Recovering her composure, she said, 'Griselda is exaggerating. I dare say she went out without gloves.'

'Before the War, and are things remembered . . . ?'

'Oh, well, a *faux pas*, equally insane.'

'She has been taken in, she says, by these strangers. She can't bear being beholden. The pity is, Amabel adores Monsieur Hippolyte.'

'Who might he be?'

'And the dog. Griselda feels, though, vanquished.'

Ma laughed. 'Anybody less vanquished!'

'Nanny wants to come home. Nanny saw the First Galley, and described it as having been "unwashed".'

'How funny!' said Ma, heartlessly.

'This Lady Spence is an old girl who has decided to pass her twilight years in Malta. Throughout the War she exerted herself in visiting soldiers and sailors. The husband is composing a scholarly tome. I don't know a Sir John Spence, do you?'

Ma said, 'Does one know everybody?'

'This Lady Spence managed to drive to the nuns, to be civil. However!' repeated Ida. 'Grizel has emerged from illness an invalid and she cannot endure the unsuitability of Lady Spence's household.'

'What is wrong with it? Might Griselda not surrender to circumstance?' asked Ma, in vague hope.

'She was in despair, and on the point. Then as she was stronger she began to brood. About the horses. She is trying to muster the will to . . . um, persevere.'

'Why don't you show me her letter?'

'It would annoy you,' said Ida, frankly. 'She endeavours *not to think of Georgie*. Otherwise she would totter aboard a westward-bound vessel. Duty lies in Egypt.'

184

'Duty again?' said Ma. 'One has no patience with her.'

'The despair almost overwhelmed her.'

'What a pity it didn't,' said Ma. 'If that would have turned her head towards home.'

'Georgie gets a letter week after week from Nanny, I happen to know, to the bottom of which Amabel will have added a word. Georgie's *mother* writes to everybody *bar*. The trouble is, she has drawn on her funds!'

'Say 'no',' said Ma.

Ida sighed. 'I have! I've had to put it to Grizel that my own pocket can pay for *her* rescue. The estate cannot forward her to *Egypt*, or finance her *in* Egypt.'

'And why did she refrain from sending you a telegram! What was her date? I expect she has *solved* her difficulties!'

Ida said, 'Poor Nanny! Don't you agree?'

Ma produced the noise that Lupuses made, not an 'ugh', not an 'agh' or an 'oh', or a 'tut'; but indicative of a disgust that was tinged with exasperation.

37 Rivel

Burdock had sought to protect her from flies that wanted to suck her blood, flies that wanted to sow eggs in her, scorpions that hid in the *numnah* when the saddle was on the ground, and from stings and bites; he knocked lice on the head (louse powder), mange in the winter (calcium sulphide), septic sores (he'd treated hers before his own); had kept her girth from galling; and he'd picked off her ticks. She still suffered twinges from the ulcer, but not even Burdock could have been aware of that.

Wherever camels had been barracked, the sand was filthy with every creeping thing.

Once the tick had climbed up her leg, travelled over her coat and sunk its head, or, if she browsed, gone via her nose to her eyelids or ears, it would, while bloating itself, cause an itch. Burdock, practised with cows, had understood, and been deft. Burdock, in defiance of orders, had left off his pants, and his sores had been born out of the lack of them.

Rivel, who was Troop Sergeant, wore pants but he was less to her liking.

His was one of the promotions so resented by the men who had fought in Gallipoli and in the Western Desert.

In the Nile Valley (where Rivel hadn't *been*) as well as at Geneffeh (where he had) and at Ismailia, the sergeants had employed Arab syces to do their horses and saddlery.

At Deir el-Belah, Rivel, with his unsympathetic hands, not content with that handsome bay, fancied he'd try out 'mealy muzzle 541'. His breath was repellent, his

186

voice loud; and, in Philomena's view, he talked too much; though not to her. He loathed ticks so much he couldn't bear to touch them.

Rivel looked to Private Worden for the care of his horse. Worden hadn't ventured to report him . . .

Sergeant Rivel drew frond-stems a-glow from the fire and poked at the body: the tick was meant to pull its fore parts out. Rivel had supplied a burn already to two horses. In this climate, a tiny burn could turn to pus. Horses rarely kept still, it was in their instinct to swing away.

Rivel was the conceited sort, the sort that would use a twitch for aught, and if there should not be one to hand he'd knock one up with a loop nailed to a stick. 'Don't reckon as how any of you could get fond of *this* gal!' he said, humorously, of Philomena.

Philomena put her ears back at his approach. 'Twas Field Punishment No. 1, for mistreating a horse. Rarest and most blighting of offences. Drill until you dropped. The funny aspect of it was that Rivel considered himself a horsemaster and rough rider. Not even being born in the county could make a man decent through and through.

Deir el-Belah, however, was pleasant; near the sea and well-found, with a grassy *chukker*, and trees, and stores and quality forage.

Eight horses went down with sand colic.

A reconnaissance in force by the Regiment,

across the big *wadi*, into the neighbourhood of Gaza to attract fire and so probe the defences, flushed out a more familiar apparition. A sturdy dog-fox, his white tag bright in the early sunshine, was viewed away in the open, running strongly. A quiver ran through the yeomen. Ears were pricked. A certain officer, inseparable from his hunting-horn, had been heard to blow 'gone away', when very stirred. Discipline held. Not a single holloa escaped Dorset throats.

Rivel was not a hunting man.

Gaza was a white straggle with a bombarded mosque, said to have been a gem, a former church, around a *medina* on a low hill. The barley and the prickly-pear enclosures lent it tranquillity. Like Reynard, the fortifications were strong; and they ran for miles.

Between Deir el-Belah, its waving trees, litter and grazing, and the *wadi* lay flat, stony land.

Wadi Ghuzzee, as it neared the coast, swept majestically. It was deep cut, fifty foot down; in places more. When the stream wasn't flowing, the bed glistened in pools, trickles and springs; until broadening at the mouth into a *sebkha*, or salt lagoon; where flamingos fed, and fishermen threw their nets. Higher up, cisterns had been insinuated into the *wadi*; to be supplied by camel. The descent was treacherous; and, in getting out, artillery-horses ruptured their hearts. Wadi Ghuzzee held apart the desert and the earthly paradise. Like the bristling hedges, if differently, it represented both cover and trap.

The labyrinth towards Gaza had been eaten into, and torn. The leaves bore sickly brown wounds; as though a madman had set about them with a slasher. Without the gaps the prickly pear would have been impenetrable.

The horses that had seen action in the Western Desert had been obliged to endure very little shelling. Their terror now touched many a stouter heart. Many horses had to learn to steel themselves.

There was attrition and loss.

In France and Belgium, Rivel had told his sergeants' mess pals, the natives would a-crept out and butchered the tastier cuts from casualties in the night; from rump and loins special. Rivel was a right fund! Here in Palestine, the Mohammedans, no matter how ravenous, declined to do any such.

S.S.M. Dowdes had regarded him sardonically. Rivel had 'never bin acrorse' the Channel.

Across the Wadi Ghuzzee, the fallen was as rations to the jackals: a carcass in camp, at Deir el-Belah, would be dragged by a mule-team a two-mile to be burnt; on the instant.

The main attack was for the day after they'd seen Reynard away. The Dorsets were familiar with the sight of jaunty Australians. The Australians and the En Zeds provoked Rivel into grinding his teeth (a puzzled Philomena put her ears back).

These fellows had got by some genius, in the fog, around to the north. The fog cleared.

While the infantry advanced, it was up to the yeomanry to bung the Turks' chance of retreat. When required, it was the duty of the cavalry to sacrifice themselves for the infantry.

In Rivel's reckoning, the mare was in a mood to be disagreeable.

Rivel was a fair shot. 'A' Squadron had already gone up in support of the Berks. 'B' Squadron was ordered up too. The ground was dusty, sent up choking clouds; and was spattered by machine-gun fire. In action, Rivel had a moral fibre about him that bolstered them as was under his command.

The horses had an uncomfortable time of it, held in a *nullah*, distracted by the whoomph and rumble of the guns. They were sheltered a little from each searing blast, but shells whined over their heads, or exploded, in puffs of smoke, too loudly in front. Philomena knew the little bay well: he trembled and shook and was so nervous he couldn't break out a sweat. Coated in grit like a miller's in flour, his nose dripped. She lowered her head.

The horses would reach out with their whiskers, under fire, and touch each other with their breath.

Hours and hours of skirmishing left the yeomen shrouded; and the enemy could have enveloped them in the dusk. Three large Turkish columns had been observed to be approaching Gaza. The Brigade was to retire a short distance.

That accomplished, each man started to dig himself in.

The Brigade was to fall back on Wadi Ghuzzee. Philomena was whistled up. Rivel mounted. The sting in her belly was fretting her. She was thirsty and tired.

The Dorset squadrons were in disarray. They'd lost contact with each other. It was a black night. 'A' Squadron hadn't been able find its horses. The dust had settled a trifle. As far as 'C' Squadron was concerned, a Hotchkiss gun, gun horse and ten men had plain evaporated. Extracting the Bucks Hussars and the Berks, their brigadier appointed a rendezvous.

The notion of the fiendish *wadi* beyond it put the wind up. The sheer drop, sixty feet to its bed, was invisible at two hundred yards in the ruddy daylight!

Their South African lieutenant assisted the Colonel. The Dorsets fumbled through the pitch, to find themselves alone at the rendezvous—a well-head with a trough to accommodate ten, beneath three palm-trees and some pitiful tamarisk.

With two nervous pickets posted, they waited, standing to their horses, and waited . . . Watering was started. Philomena was wistful for her turn. She still had nine stone six on her back. Girths had not been slackened. Her eyes were liquid from the grit and dust. For days past, just half the squadron had been unsaddled at any one time.

Not until a glimmer streaked the east did a staff officer ride up.

The Brigade was ordered to cross the *wadi*. The Bucks and the Berks (on account of their blundering) couldn't linger to water.

It was to the Dorsets to cover the rear. The flank guard, a Bucks squadron, managed in error to pass through them.

The Turks were pressing up hotly.

By six o'clock in the morning, the Regiment was being shelled. This crazed some of the jaded horses. The shells burst in fours. The air itself, in the tail of an almighty shriek, was breaking into flashes in the sky at the height of a chimney. A chestnut went down in a sizzle of shrapnel bullets. The chestnut was kicking.

Two other troops of 'B' Squadron retreated at the trot. Held close to the firing-line and the Hotchkiss gun, Philomena had to listen.

When No. 1 Troop did disengage, Sergeant Rivel's coolness in thrusting two casualties (bullet in the ribs and a shattered shoulder) into the saddle was exemplary.

The light was not yet good.

Bringing up the rear, Rivel was, though, in something of a skitter. Philomena knew where the edge of the precipice was. Rivel hadn't seen it; yet he was hanging on to her mouth. He took a pull at the last moment, unbalancing her.

One of her forefeet slipped on stones loosened by the gun horse. She heard a cascade. She made a frightened effort to get her weight on her quarters . . . and failed. The ground gave. Her off-hind went from under her, she skidded onto her flank. The brown mare 541 had propelled Sergeant Rivel out of the saddle (impossible though it was to fall off) and head first down a goat path.

It was greatly to his credit that he kept his temper.

38 Uncle Archie

'Might you have had a letter from Griselda!' asked Ida, suspiciously.

Uncle Archie's cheeks looked a little pink.

He wasn't *so* ancient; but he had the simple, guileless smile. And nobody took care of him, so the breeches that he was industriously wearing out, and out of which he never really changed, had been cobbled together at the crotch with some sort of white cotton lining still protruding. When he sat down, your eyes were drawn to this tongue of white; fearing that you might have to say that his clothes were coming apart.

People stared in every direction but *at* him. He was used to the treatment.

His handkerchiefs began life like snow: they acquired their grubby patina; and couldn't be boiled clean. He plastered one of these handkerchiefs across half of his face, so Ida shouldn't go poking.

'Fresh news?'

He blushed. 'Nanny is in a demi-paradise, waited on hand and foot. Griselda isn't content. *Griselda* is obliged to have breakfast, luncheon, tea and then *dine* with the people. Nanny and Amabel have seen *Ali Baba and the Forty Thieves*. Amabel has been to a party, at the invitation of the sawbones that ministered to her mother. The Navy went to enormous expense and the ingenious use of a dungeon . . . suspended one of His Majesty's ships, out of cardboard and plywood, overhead, and the children all thought they were under water. Voices from deep-sea diving suits, diving suits that were so heavy the sailors in them were unable to move; lots of sploshing and lapping sounds. Seaweed made of silk, and jellies that had been set in fish moulds.'

He added, 'Amabel managed to enjoy it.'

Ida said, undeceived, 'You always have had a soft spot for Griselda.'

'Ah?' he mumbled. 'Well . . . And Nanny . . .'. He hurried on. 'Nanny has got above herself and is being outrageous.'

His eyes seeped and at the corner of his lips

194

there was boiled egg.

'Uncle Archie?'

'I'll do what I like!' he said, with defiance.

'She is naughty.'

He said, 'My dear Ida!' He stopped. He pulled himself together. He said, 'Your sister *is a war widow*!'

'Um . . .'

'You may not recollect, I myself sent Silver and my bay, Lilian . . . and Lilian had been wounded, was never to be sound again . . . home from the South African War, in the care of Trussell.'

'I do remember!' Ida smiled. She shook out her wet things. 'And what a lovely foal you had from her!'

The back passage at Quarr smelt in the winter of damp dogs and isinglass. 'I'm glad . . . it's better . . . more suitable . . . that Griselda should have applied to you than beg from Palsy who has, by the way, hopes of being called upon to sally out to her aid!'

'I am afraid Griselda will fail,' said Uncle Archie. 'Bound to. Let her find that out for herself.'

39 Gaza II

She hadn't liked Sergeant Rivel; yet she felt spurned. Cherritt dearly loved Blissful.

No. 601 Blissy had been wounded by shrapnel, and was ordered to Romani by ambulance and railway train. Philomena, even the Philomena made meek by the War, was not the animal for a man in mourning.

The spotter had been replaced in the sky by a dove. The enemy's *Taube* circled the camp at Deir el-Belah, and dropped bombs that cracked deafeningly into a whirr of metal; swooped to hose the horse-lines with its machine-gun, pursued by rifle-fire.

The men pelted at the horses ... much bunching and humping in alarm ... released the fetlock, seized the rope, vaulted on bareback, and galloped them, nosebag and all, anywhere, out into the desert, away from the lines and the camp, to scatter widely; to freeze. It was like a gymkhana event, with a trumpeter to sound the off.

These were Aussie tactics.

The crate droned nearer, nearer, circled. The *Taube* couldn't see them in such tiny scattered dots. The horses had a chance to go on munching. Then, slowly, as though to collect a rosette in the ring, Cherritt and Philomena would amble into camp.

Whenever Corky was near, she whickered.

A bomb once fell far too close to her. She trembled. Cherritt didn't comfort her. Explosions hurt her ears. Cherritt stared, from the saddle, between those ears; and hankered after a fine chestnut mane. Philomena

196

reminded him of an Exmoor pony, for all she had a free action and hoity-toity manner.

Though their South African lieutenant was a credit and brought off exploits too, the Dorsets, indeed yeomen of every regiment, were keenly aware that they were compared to the Australian and En Zed M.I. The comparison was unfavourable.

In Sinai the Aussies had been sent to fetch in whole *squadrons* of lorst British territorials. So it was said.

The Australians didn't look smart, and they were cocksure.

Once they'd 'learnt they had only one horse' they'd cared meticulously for their Walers. They could see in the dark; and were intrepid and cool. They could manage compass bearings, and stars. They could manage without too. Mysterious.

They had scant notion of deference. They didn't salute their own officers much, let alone all officers. They rode and fought, as the weather got warmer, naked on the top half. They hacked at their nether garments to fashion their weeny cut-shorts; and their legs didn't chafe, nor did the shoulder across which went the bandolier. They were irreverent and blasphemed and didn't go much on church of a Sunday. They slouched in the saddle or loped at their horses' heads indefatigably. No stirrup iron was rubbed up; they kept bits about clean yet not so as to glint. *They* never had, when out on patrol, to seek shade what didn't exist, lest a blooming tunic button gie 'em away.

They were scornful. Cheery to a fault. It irked.

Three weeks after the first big attack, there was the second. The Brigade was in action by mid-morning, in support of mounted infantry, which had been hurled against the Turkish defences of El Atawineh. The D.Y. was held in reserve.

At two-thirty, the Dorsets were ordered up to a position on the right shoulder of some Australian Light Horse. Philomena stretched her legs in the two-mile gallop under shell-fire; not altogether noticing a stream of casualties in mule-drawn field ambulances.

The Australians had suffered, and there was a pervasive whiff of blood.

Cherritt tugged his rifle from the bucket, jumped from the saddle; and she was hustled back for more than a mile. Here she waited until the evening; ears flickering, studying the lizards (emerald green about the head) and the tiny insects.

Closer to Gaza the Turks used gas. Philomena was spared that.

After darkness had surrounded them, the led horses returned to the line and a general retirement began.

The Dorsets were relieved by the Warwick Yeomanry. Officers and men were exhausted and filthy. Six days of fighting, marching and outpost duty.

Camel Corps units had been in that mortifying struggle. Philomena's ears pricked at the sound of a voice she knew well. Burdock was visiting his mates. She heard his familiar burble in the horse-lines. Nearer and nearer.

The Generals, according to Burdock, had 'lorst nerve'; and fallen back, all through the uncertainty of watering! Whereas they might have held out or pressed on. Want of courage, 'twas! She felt his hand on her neck, she scented his breath. Want of resolve!

He spoke to her. Then he was gone; but, in the main, Philomena was glad of the lull.

The sun began to burn, the sand and dust were hot; and sandstorms were whipped by the *khamseen*. Dust would drive into the eyes and nose; into the rations; alighted in an instant in a skim on the water; and made the horses blunder, half blinded.

It defeated the flies.

There was night-and-thirst training.

There was no tracking at home, unless you were a huntsman, maybe, or a gamekeeper. Their gamekeepers hadn't encountered sand, or stony wastes or sandstorms. Or a landscape of two minds: where there was soil it was pastoral and where it was desert it was trappy. The Bedouin guides (who spied for the Turks) didn't understand '*nullah*': it was, like 'syce', Hindustanee.

There were few bushes that twanged, or

199

leaves to be crushed. The Aussies, a-cock on their horses' loins, could needle a scuffle on sandstone as well as a Bedouin. A limestone pebble the size of a beetle told an Australian scout that a troop-horse had carried it wedged from the bed of Wadi Ghuzzee until it had been dislodged by a hoof-pick. Cherritt knew fossils, he didn't know pebbles. The Aussies (savages really) understood maps too; and map references.

Pitwine's section was sent out to observe the Turk; with three days' half-rations in gram and barley.

On the third afternoon, far across the Wadi Hanafish, they lay behind a scorched ridge with their field-glasses (just issued) proudly trained on the orchards and squat white houses of a hamlet they believed was Bir Ibrahim. At least, Pitwine and the others observed the Arab hamlet: Cherritt was on his back, staring through his heels at the horses—tied head to tail several yards below, flicking each other and stamping. The horses needed to water. The men theirselves was deep onto second canteens, and the goatskin was done.

A lark was singing. The lizards basked and a few butterflies pursued their purposes.

Philomena's head had been up for several minutes. Her ears were pricked. The white blaze of Beacon came up with a jerk. Cherritt gave Pitwine a poke. A snake. Sommat like that.

Pitwine departed on his belly. It wasn't a fox. A fox would have been off. Pitwines's rear end appeared riveted. Pitwine's hand said, 'Hush!'

A whinny, not a score of yards off, made them all jump. Cherritt was down to the horses to untie them. Pitwine kept his wits. Pitwine could have shot the bleeder. Johnny Turk bolted, hobbled by breeches, fingers closed on a splashy tin of water. *Water! Winking.*

The horses hadn't replied.

There was a half-hearted pursuit; a yell. Cherritt fancied Philomena spoilt for speed, and a right one.

This little pop left Pitwine wondering, should they have engaged an enemy patrol, and the like.

A week later Bob Cherritt and Bliss were reunited.

40 An adventure of his own

Where the machine-gun bullets had entered, he would carry the dents for life. Nobody imagined that Corky would fail in endurance, or set off a stampede, acquire an unnecessary injury or even abandon a wounded 'Oddy' Odstock. Corky was sanguine. His brand of independence ensured that he was patient and loyal. He wouldn't do what he didn't want to do; but what he did consent to do was more than enough.

Oddy's Section laughed at him, and swore by him: he was a prime mascot.

The Aussies had suffered a lot of losses. Perhaps it was understandable that two of those cobbers in their cut-shorts should swagger through the D.Y. camp on their way 'home' from a neighbouring mess. The mounted troops were scattered by brigade around Deir el-Belah. Perhaps the guard on the horse-lines had been sleepy, or bamboozled; positively *due* to be up before the orderly officer in the morning.

Corky had felt the dew on his back and was standing in still moonlight. There was never silence. There was a gentle jangle, and the noise of breathing. The tiny screams of small animals broke into any reverie; and marching steps did; and scuttling beetles. Snakes approached on their belly, *troopers* upright.

Corky was bemused by an apparition that squirmed along the ground. Since he could scent it, he knew it was a man. It reeked of strong drink. The body rolled over. Corky saw the eyes; the kind of eyes that measured the size of a ditch. Corky was surrounded by horses; and all were alert. A scrawny arm was straining to loosen his head-rope. Another scrawny arm was freeing his hind fetlock; a fetlock that was ringed in white hairs and sore enough to be better for release. There were two of them, then!

A hand fondled his nose; and cracked lips whispered.

The second form kittened under Corky's legs, hoisted itself upright and persuaded him ('C'mon, neddy', sweet as pie) to back until there was room for it to vault and get a leg over.

The first was hauled up behind the second. The second buried its face in the bristles of Corky's hog-mane. They lay on Corky. Giggling. He found himself being neck-reined, coaxed and prodded past his companions and on. A good-natured animal, Corky complied. On, until he was out of the camp altogether.

They were joined by two more savages, similarly glued on the liver chestnut Ruthless. Corky was reminded of children and he was fond of children. Ruth was sticking.

When Ruth felt the legs against his side he jibbed. He weaved, with the rope tugged and laid on his neck alternately.

They evaded the wire of Brigade Perimeter. Now Ruth had Corky to go with he'd gorn. And go they did, for the riders sat up (stifling laughter) and dug their heels in.

The night was filled by fireflies.

If Corky had a hard mouth when bitted, he had no brakes at all in a halter. He wouldn't leave Ruth. And it was only a question of direction.

The Aussies could see in the moonlight.

The yeomen thought badly of animals that

untied their halters and yanked up their picketing-pegs and cast the shackles in order to stray. There had been the wire, and the guard-house. It was queer.

Philomena eyed the investigating officer.

The camp was a mass of hoof-prints. There were suspicions; and these didn't involve horses that had taken it into their noddles to wander. The two missing, Corky and a liver chestnut gelding known as Ruth, bore regimental identification. Their halters were marked as to squadron and troop, 'B1'. Obliteration of the hoof brand would incriminate any soul that had made the attempt.

If Odstock was aggravated about Corky, Awshew had to brush a tear over Ruth, for Ruth had carried him at Agagiya.

It might have been mucky, and involved embarrassing encounters with friendlies; had not Corky been his obdurate self. Nice though the Aussies might have been. For here was old Corky, trotting smartly into camp, his nose up, his tail up, whickering to his friends, having eluded the pound. He sidled up beside Philomena; and at last he let himself be caught. From tell-tale traces, in the bridle on him, it was simple to run to earth Ruth.

For many months, Philomena had had dreams of Agagiya. The sight wouldn't easily leave her. More rarely, she dreamt of whiffs of the *smell*. It had weakened in her memory: she had, after all, never visited the spot again. Not even when the cairn had been built, and flowers that had lit up the battlefield soon after, anemones and marigolds, were picked and laid in memory. Burdock hadn't been in the detachment that had done that.

Her dreams were of Gaza.

Since her belly figured in her melancholy, Philomena was dissatisfied by *tibbin*, and endless gram. Barley supplied in Egypt was dosed with earth; bran had sawdust in it; and the *tibbin* she choked on.

Chickpeas (gram) made horses scour.

The *dhurra* (a mix of green maize in millet stalks) was acceptable.

In May, in a raid by Anzacs and yeomanry to destroy eleven miles of track, six bridges and all the points at Asling Station, two horses were wounded.

Philomena watched as the first horse-ambulance, drawn by mules, with its passenger on his legs in the cart, his white face gloomily over the front bar, and a retinue of flies, halted for water before going on, to the rail-head, which in April had reached Deir el-Belah. Level ground helped. In the second ambulance, a grey mare not unlike Dalliance was strapped down flat, on her side; with a malevolent buzz in her wake.

Philomena didn't grasp the significance. Instinct suggested a piercing neigh. She was silent.

205

To an animal that was interested (incurably) in all about her, there was much to bewilder her.

41 Birds

Nanny knew that Mrs Romney had never been much of a one for the old. She considered them piggy, and her own dear uncle the piggiest. Mrs Romney was left to droop under the jacaranda, glum, feeble and *hideously* embarrassed. Lepanto, too, was denied the pleasure of covering people with hair.

When Lady Spence had said that Amabel and Nanny should be 'shown Malta' (quite as though they were proper guests) and by their hostess in person, Mrs Romney had been sceptical. Lady Spence's chauffeur saw fit to carry a greenfinch on the dashboard in a cage. Amabel could be counted upon to scowl.

Nanny was cock-a-hoop.

Lady Spence first ordained that Amabel, together with her nurse, should view *'the house'*, the villa with the lovely garden that Amabel's daddy had taken for the last year before the War.

'Bumpy roads,' observed Lady Spence. So bumpy that 'Delphinium Cottage', now squatted, to Lady Spence's surprise, in a pool of rubble.

'Greenery,' Lady Spence said, 'is not *usual*. Indeed, within the walls of Valletta, the Grand Masters forbade gardening. Water was conserved for times of siege.'

'Muzz conserves,' said Amabel, chattily. 'Muzz has bottled plums and strawberry jam in the larder at Bark Hart.'

'Shh!' said Nanny.

'No need to shush, Nanny . . .'

Nanny bristled.

In Valletta, a cannon was firing a gun salute. Puffs of smoke were borne by the cross-wind in the rays of the sun like alien vessels in the sky; until each, as strangely and as suddenly, vanished.

'I ought to advise Nanny . . . on no account to snap a Maltese infant!' Lady Spence was out to *amuse*. 'Capture a child in a photograph and the mother at once fears for its life!'

'Mrs Romney has our Box Brownie in her keeping, madam.'

'Maltese churches have two clocks.'

'Do they indeed.'

'One to keep the correct time, the other to muddle the Devil.'

'Well, I never!'

'And you shouldn't expect the Maltese to say, to an enquiry as to health, 'perfectly stout' or 'exceedingly well, thank you', for that is to tempt fate,' added Monsieur Hippolyte.

'Oh, my word!'

Lady Spence embarked on a rigmarole about

tigers and peacocks in the Governor's Palace in Valletta.

'Don't give this Governor's Palace another thought, madam, if you please. Mummie will show us, when she feels up to it.'

Nanny was pondering as to why it was that the likes of Lady Spence, the Monsooer and Captain Palsy said 'Nanny' this and 'Nanny' that after every other syllable, without ever calling each other by name. To each other they said 'you'.

Veil a-flutter, Lady Spence bowed to an elderly prelate in an Austin Six.

Monsieur Hippolyte said, 'Your compatriots, Nanny, assert ... always so superior ... that those citizens who made the furniture and silver and painted the ceilings and worked the marble ... that they have all departed. The little people of today, *they* are not the true inhabitants ... Bah!'

Neither Lady Spence nor Monsieur Hippolyte drew breath. Out of their mouths came chuckles or smiles. The two old birds were egging each other on. Lady Spence and the Monsooer were relishing an outing *sans* Sir John.

Amabel and Nanny were, well, gooseberries.

What there was to find naughty in a discussion of furniture Nanny didn't know.

'Shortly, we are to give Malta the conduct of her domestic affairs.'

'That's nice!' Nanny saw the Maltese busy

with wax, dusters and polishing cloths.

Gaspar stood on the brakes. Around a bend, hidden by the walls that lined the rustic roads, there hobbled before the motor a procession of donkeys and carts. From one of the carts, carrots were falling: plop, a carrot; plop, another orange-yellow carrot; plop.

'It has been suggested that the Maltese speak a dialect akin to the Babylonian,' said Lady Spence.

'Gracious!'

'My dear Constance, I think it's bad *Moorish*,' said the Monsooer. 'To say so, Nanny, is *not done*.'

'Is it not, monsooer!'

'Monsieur Hippolyte has lived in foreign parts.'

'When do we go to Zeebrugge?'

'Oh, Amabel, don't *start*,' whispered Nanny.

'What!' A basilisk stare.

Monsieur Hippolyte said, 'To where?'

'Zeebrugge,' repeated Amabel.

'Where?' said Lady Spence.

Nanny said, 'I think that would be too out of the way, madam.'

'It was marked on the chart,' said Amabel. 'On the log table in *Koh-i-Noor*.'

'In Malta?'

'How they are quaint, our names!' Monsieur Hippolyte threw up his hands.

'She must have seen a chart of the Channel.'

'Ah, Zeebrugge!' Monsieur Hippolyte. His

209

grasp was quick.

'Zeebrugge is in Belgium,' observed Lady Spence.

'And on the chart, where?' asked Monsieur Hippolyte.

'At the tip of Malta,' said Amabel.

Nanny stifled a sigh.

'Birzebuggia!' cried Lady Spence. *'Beer Zay Bodger.'*

'Ah!'

Amabel was gratified.

'Shall we see the Mole?'

'For our *next* expedition, Ippy,' said Lady Spence, 'I'll ask that charming Flags to escort us round the Dockyards. D'you suppose I can summon the vim?'

'Let her mother ...' said Monsieur Hippolyte.

Amabel's nose was out of joint. She didn't have the monsooer to herself. Their motor had smelly upholstery.

'Monsieur may take you, Amabel, to see the Beheading of St John the Baptist!'

'No nightmares, if you please, madam.'

'Caravaggio is gory. Do you *adore* gore?'

Nanny cleared her throat.

'We are going,' said Lady Spence, 'to a temple dug upside-down in the ground by giants.'

'Ought we to confuse her?' asked Monsieur Hippolyte.

'I do hope it's not dirty, madam.'

'It is not dirty.'

Amabel narrowed her eyes.

'Or slippery.'

'There may be puddles. *We* shall not step in them!'

To divert Amabel, the Monsooer got her rapt in an unsuitable operatic story. He drew her hand to him and quavered out one of his arias. Then the pit *would* have to resemble a pond that had drained, whirling, into a sump of petrified mud.

'I've paid sixpence for you to enter!'

'You wouldn't guess how far it goes down!' said the Monsooer.

'The catacombs frightened her,' Nanny said.

'Amabelle, what about Nanny, and her pleasure!'

'I can safely venture to say, child,' stated Lady Spence, 'that you will regret your spinelessness. Missed chances are never regained; and you will tell your mother that you stuck at the entrance to the Halsuflieni Hypogeum!'

Under Nanny's shocked eyes, Amabel burst into tears.

'Madam, Amabel and I might take a turn, and . . . and . . . wait for you.'

The monument's custodian fanned Lady Spence's tickets.

'Good God, Nanny, I've seen it all *before*! They discovered, don't y'know, the 'Sleeping Lady' down there. Even my smallest great-grandchild doesn't quake!'

Nanny was pained.

Monsieur Hippolyte said, 'We must not oblige *la petite*.' He propelled Lady Spence into the motor.

The next beauty spot was above ground. Entrance was *gratis*. Monsieur Hippolyte tiptoed off in his co-respondent shoes. All of a sudden, an oracle boomed (Amabel and Nanny jumped out of their skins), *'Jeanne était au pain sec dans le cabinet noir . . .'*

Lady Spence chortled.

A faint frown rucked Nanny's forehead.

There ensued the inevitable. Amabel couldn't be an oracle because she wasn't a man. Trebles couldn't be oracles.

Nanny glared at a vast stone female. Very bulbous. Fat legs, fat arms, no head, no feet.

'She is so ancient, Nanny,' said Monsieur Hippolyte, wistfully. 'So, so ancient. It is believed she was carved some thousands of years before Jesu Christ!'

'Oh,' said Nanny.

The chauffeur stopped in a village he called Rendi and which Lady Spence said was Crendi. It was past nursery dinner-time. The greenfinch was left to flutter uneasily. The party clambered into waiting carriages. Domestic fields yielded to wild country; the kind that sprained ankles. Their temple . . . quite big . . . for lunch was at least *upright*, in a bracing February draught. The monoliths were dressed to shut the draught out. Clever.

'An *altar*, Gaspar, would be *excellent* for our food.'

Nanny perched primly.

Amabel refused to eat.

'Not even a *patum* sandwich?'

Monsieur Hippolyte's chin dropped onto his chest.

Amabel picked his tomato from the bread and was off to consort with the horses and mule. At this inspired juncture, Lady Spence chose to murmur, 'It's been borne upon me, Nanny, that there was ... *gossip* in Malta, attached to your Mrs Romney.'

Nanny's eyes snapped.

At last she said, 'I don't see as how that could have been, madam.'

Mrs Romney had left not just the *Koh-i-Noor* under a cloud but Malta too, with a reputation that *hadn't been forgotten*; not all through the War; and despite umpteen changes of people?

Lady Spence's glance was one of amusement.

'There *was* somebody! So! Young women are susceptible when their male relations are at sea. It doesn't surprise you or me.'

Nanny pined for safer company.

Lady Spence and Monsieur Hippolyte, restored to full vim by the Burgundy (and packing in too much), wished to stroll to a lower temple.

The Surgeon-Commander had told Nanny

there'd been not a great deal amiss with Mrs Romney bar a severe go of 'flu 'and her nerves'. Mistaken there. Mrs Romney was *nerveless*.

'Stone circle,' quibbled Lady Spence.

'A womb-shaped *temple*,' declared the Monsooer. '*Two* womb-shapes. Do you know what a womb is, Amabelle?'

'No?' Amabel said. 'What?'

'Grand outlook,' put in the censor. 'Isn't the sea blue!'

It was a crystal blue. Their cheeks were whipped.

Amabel tried to lie in a crevice. Over her stirred petals as yellow as Peter's jersey.

'Is that a game of "coffins"?'

Poor Nanny: her disenchantment had been complete.

Amabel hadn't had a thought in her head about coffins. She'd been playing 'oracles'. She'd piped, fatally, into the scented air, 'Nanny has learned herself *lots* about Malta, Monsieur Hippolyte, she pores over books, before she goes to bed. Nanny knows fossils, and the Stone Age, the Bronze Age and the Iron Age, she knows flowers and butterflies and moths, she knows history and geography and heaps of poems by heart. Nanny hides her light under a bushel, *Muzz* says. Nanny can sing too.'

This had gone down badly.

'I expect ...' Mrs Romney said, in a

melancholy frame, '... I expect you noticed the little stone hides ... Positioned like so many gun emplacements.'

'Was the Major here in Malta, Mr Alan, ever?'

'I don't think so.'

'Passing in a ship?'

'I don't think so, no. Why, what makes you ask? It doesn't fit our ideas of the sporting ...'

Nanny's upper lip corrugated into a myriad of endearing rivulets.

'Didn't come on a visit?'

'I'm afraid not, Nanny.'

'It wouldn't have slipped your mind?'

'... Shot and trapped on the cliff-tops ... trapped, the song-birds we love so much and for whose return in England we wait ... I dare say it wasn't meant to be, our own journey, to Egypt ... I think we should go home!'

'Oh, madam! It's your illness that has pulled you down.'

'Or I'll continue alone, and *you* may ... *go home*!'

'I shan't let you sail for Egypt on your own. It wouldn't be fitting!'

Mrs Romney's face lit up.

IV PERSEVERING

Assuming that the cavalryman is, by nature or training, a lover of horses, the necessity of working his horse when it is suffering the pangs of thirst aggravates painfully the privations and discomforts which he is himself undergoing.

GENERAL SIR GEORGE DE S. BARROW, G.C.B., K.C.M.G., *The Fire of Life*

A pathetic sight was often to be seen during brief halts on a long march, for the faithful, tired animals would lie down, with all their gear on, beside their wearied masters, to snatch what brief repose they could.

A. BRISCOE MOORE, *The Mounted Riflemen in Sinai and Palestine*

Even in the barest provinces you get many a little picture that lives with you for life—a chocolate-coloured bank with red poppies against the green of the prickly-pear hedge above it, and a yellow lizard darting across; a river-bed of pink oleanders flush with the plain; a gorge in Judaea, where you look up between limestone walls picked out with tufts of grass and black-and-tan goats cropping at them, the deep blue of the sky over all, and, on the edge of the only shadow, a well, a trough, and a solitary herdsman.

GEORGE ADAM SMITH, D.D., *The Historical Geography of the Holy Land*

42 To Beersheba

Philomena was, without cease, on the move, never staying for more than a few days in any one camp or bivouac. Her rations were supplied by camel. The horizons shifted with the sun.

She went unshod. In this dry climate, in early summer, her hoofs had grown furiously; having to be cut down. She wasn't as well adapted as a native Syrian, or a Waler, or a pampas horse, to the sheer heat given off by soil and sand.

Over strata of stone, all hoofs could get worn. Shoes were issued again. Adequate supplies weren't coming up from Egypt; and the forge-cart ran short.

The Turks sat in Gaza; and along the thirty miles of their front line to Beersheba. Philomena bustled to and fro ... like a separated friend. Patrols ... advanced point, rear point ... outpost duties, musketry, instruction and inspections more than filled the summer; reconnaissance to pinpoint wells, springs and crossing-places for each and every *nullah*.

The twinges in her belly didn't cease either.

There were stiffer tests of courage.

The Regiment formed the advance-guard during a reconnaissance in brigade force towards Beersheba. The Turkish infantry gave trouble: yellow ants poured out to press the cavalry back. Quite especially for 'B' Squadron to retire through, the Turkish guns drew a veil of explosions across the desert.

Philomena, without a kind hand to calm her, without Corky beside her, trembled.

Two of No. 2 Troop's horses were killed. A gelding in No. 3 Troop had to be abandoned with a shattered leg. It was too hot to stop. She'd seen the gashes and the sudden crimsoning of the coat, seen the slow spilling begin of the guts.

Retirement wasn't the stampede Philomena's instinct recommended. Rather, an affair of bursts and stops and dismounted action; so, for the horses, repeated halts; being held behind low rises that dampened the high explosive only a little.

Somehow Corky was unscathed. He'd borne his bleeding burden to safety: 'Oddy' Odstock owed his life to his horse.

When out of range, Philomena was trembling still.

The yeomen prided themselves on their ability to forestall fits of trembling. Four horses had been crazed. An officer and seventeen other ranks, wounded. One animal, pulling his bridle over his head with twists and tugs, breaking from the horseholder, to bolt towards the enemy.

Philomena and Corky, together, went to No. 3 Troop.

No more Sergeant Rivel!

On 28th June 1917, General Allenby—'the Bull'—took over command of the Egyptian Expeditionary Force. Allenby moved his headquarters up from Egypt. A new spirit was abroad. All the yeomanry regiments, other than those unlucky fellows whose sabres had long been replaced by infantry webbing, were, in August, formed into one division, the Yeomanry Division of the Desert Mounted Corps.

Allenby deemed it a necessity to instigate a process whereby two officers—the officer commanding plus second-in-command or one of the squadron leaders—would be posted from the regular cavalry to each yeomanry regiment.

With Murray, from the Scots Greys, as Adjutant the D.Y. had been one jump ahead.

The C.-in-C. got *everywhere*.

Riding in cut-shorts was prohibited.

Allenby sat up, in the front, beside his driver. Allenby was content for driver with a bare-legged billjim in a vest. Every other Aussie was a Bill or a Jim.

Allenby benefited from the earlier reconnaissance and well-mapping, the rail across Sinai and the pipe. He wouldn't hurl himself at Gaza and be repulsed. He had Beersheba in his sights, and a flanking action around the Turkish line.

Beersheba possessed water.

Over weeks, under cover of darkness, forward dumps of ammunition, stores and forage were established. *Far* forward.

Sergeant Rivel was a strategist. Johnny, according to Sergeant Rivel, in the mess, was expecting us to have a go again at Gaza. Allenby wanted Johnny Turk to think what Johnny Turk was thinking.

The infantry was to provide a feint upon Gaza. The yeomanry and the M.I. would follow on the heels of a sudden bombardment by the heavy guns. Each of those had required a team of twenty-four Shire horses, four abreast.

Philomena's sand muzzle was withdrawn. She was free to suck for salt. To gnaw her head-rope.

She went out unclipped. And Philomena relished night marches and the cool, sweet air.

By 1st November, she was so close up that she was picketed in the centre of a square, and went to water at a trot. Yet other mounted troops came up through and Philomena was in the rear when a famous exploit was brought off by two regiments (4th and 12th) of the 4th Australian Light Horse.

To the admiration, through ground teeth, of 'the cavalry', the blighters charged the Turkish trenches—mounted—in the face of artillery, machine-gun and rifle fire, and whilst bombed from the sky; in a cloud of dust, with ... since they lacked the sabre ... bayonets held in the

222

hand.

Philomena and Private Sage didn't enter Beersheba until the evening of Guy Fawkes' Day. On her near side, Corky carried Corporal Duncliffe. Corky was satisfied with Duncliffe. Sage, who was thirty-eight, felt his bones.

Ignoring Sage, Philomena trod, head up, ears pricked, amid the patter of the unshod hoofs, on the road across the field of battle; over barren, craggy desert, through hollows and twisted metal and spent bullets; up through the southern earthworks, still full of the Turkish fallen in their stained khaki or canary tunics. Most fighting had been well to left and well to right of her. These were not the trenches, eight foot deep and four foot wide, charged by the Aussies.

On Philomena stepped, past awkward piles of Turkish horses, teams of horses that had died together, legs and jaws and matted skin, and smashed limbers, ammunition cases, through more uncollected Turkish dead; past assemblies of Turkish prisoners; dead mules; and dressing-stations that still overflowed with wounded Turks.

Not every Turkish horse was dead. They had fallen five and six days before. Nobody had come to put them out of their misery. Alive, they had lost their eyes to vultures or crows. These blind heads were lifted . . . to sink down into the dirt. A tail would swish, a foot stir. The stink was powerful.

223

Two enterprising Aussie shoeing-smiths, with a mule, were getting shoes off; shoes that looked big enough. Few did.

This avenue of carcasses and corpses and wounded was reflected in the depths of Philomena's liquid pupils. Although her head was straight and she moved steadily forward, in the twilight, she could see, as could every charger and every troop-horse, a great deal more to each side of her than a man could; and that view was pretty unobstructed.

To the north-west, far-off aeroplanes had dropped the last smoke balls of the day. A brief hiatus, and then the boo-om of big guns.

Of Beersheba's seventeen wells and two cisterns, some were hidden in courtyards. The enemy had managed to blow up two of these; and two more in part. During the first night, the R.E. had removed fuses; and revived, or brought in, pumping gear. But calculations of Beersheba's water had been out.

On nearing the trough, horses that had gone for twenty-four or thirty hours whickered urgently. It was hard to ration them.

At one cistern, camels had spoilt the troughs: the horses were less particular.

Other units had found stagnant pools, in the *wadi* of Es Sabah, near the viaduct. This was unedifying land.

Half the Corps was withdrawn to Karm.

After watering in Beersheba beneath the cypress trees ... each troop, as it arrived, coming to the troughs ... the Dorsets moved off by the Mukhtar track, north, to defensive positions on high ground. They suffered casualties from artillery-fire. A grey mare was killed. Philomena wasn't to get another drink for forty-eight hours.

The Turks abandoned Gaza.

43   The tub

'How will our luggage find us, Amabel, you tell me that, dear. Our luggage in Port Said ... ? *Not* where we're off to *now*! *If* they remembered to off-load it and didn't take it to India!'

Imran was astonished. There were European passengers. A little girl and her nurse. Since they weren't looking about in any direction but their own, Imran was able to note that the nurse was worn.

'Oh, well, Mrs C. is kind,' said Nanny. 'Whether your mummie shouldn't have hurried home ...' (a sniff) '... What is to say he won't finish with a short leg! Mummie doesn't seem to know which leg is in plaster, even. We'll discover *some* day, dear. You'd think ...'

A piercing voice said, 'Heavens, Nanny! I'm sure Georgie won't. It isn't as though he's contracted I.P. or ...'

'Oh, madam, how can you! And Mrs Cockerell at Quarr is by no means a nurse. Housekeepers aren't. Mrs Cockerell, madam, is pushing seventy and crude.'

'Georgie and Mrs Cockerell have always been *devoted*.'

'That's as may be ...' The nurse sniffed as though sniffing existed to puncture speech.

'Has your letter to Lady Spence been written, darling?' enquired the voice. 'Nanny, do trust to my sister's good sense! If Miss Lupus can cope with a horse in a sling for six weeks she is equal to a boy on crutches.'

'A *complicated* fracture, madam. Why don't you do a picture for Georgie, dear, to go in my letter? Keep yourself amused until we sail ...'

'I do agree, the entire saga is vexatious,' said the voice.

Its owner had disappeared for the nurse then said, 'Draw him a picture of this *tub*! Your mother never does anything by halves, does she ...'

The last remark was inflected by a certain bitterness.

Imran was both fascinated and appalled.

A number of sailings would have offered passages in liners that carried civilians together with British troops. The British government, in repatriating Imran's brother to Egypt, had paid for a berth in a small, paddle-wheel steamer.

The word 'tub' had no significance to Imran.

He thought 'Nanny' might have been applying it to the *Principessa*.

The *Principessa* was streaked in red rust. Even as she sailed, seamen were struggling to paint bits of her a proper white.

Their cabin was on the port side. The bunks were ranged at either bulkhead, in commodious fashion. In fact, his brother was prostrate on a bunk that minute, asleep. A small basin, circular and chipped, but clean, was located behind a solid metal screen.

Through a metal door, there was a shower, a lavatory, a faucet to which had been attached a length of hose. Imran was inured to cramped vessels—in his house these arrangements were situated at the farthest corner of the roof. The idea of sleeping so close!

There was one other passenger stateroom.

Imran discovered that each had a door into the single water-closet. The water-closet had two doors. One was for the *other* passengers . . . A light switch was inside a box with a hinged lid. Persons were supposed to lock themselves in. Not forgetting, afterwards, to unlock in both directions. The faucet did run all right— frothy sea water—with a groan. Unless restrained, it groaned.

Imran shook himself.

He could hear the murmuring of other passengers. Imran, well travelled as he was, had never encountered such a difficulty. He was incredulous.

There was a tang of the sea.

Across the deck were the Captain's own quarters. In what was a passage at the head of a companionway was a door to a room with a porcelain chair-bath people climbed into, to lie in stagnant water: Imran shivered.

The *Principessa* echoed with clangs and thuds; and creaked with the ague of iron. Her home port was Napoli. It was obvious wine flowed in her.

Imran picked up, 'Gone too far'; and, 'Just when we'd thrown our lot in with her, dear.'

There were no public rooms in a merchantman.

Within two hours, Amabel and Nanny had, Imran understood, been installed in the Wheel-house, and were steaming along in a calm-ish sea ('Nice view, I give you, dear!'); Nanny with her knitting, or her crochet. Captain Salvatore Testa was 'gallantry itself, ever so courteous'. *Principessa Ilaria Maria* was a very old lady; her Master had a spot for children; and was much drawn to others that did too. When Captain Testa spoke, in his small English, to Nanny, his tone was a caress.

Imran was scandalized.

The *Principessa*'s passengers dined below in the Saloon. Nanny and Amabel and the lady at the Captain's table; Imran and his brother at the Chief Engineer's. Nanny was gazing at what would, Imran knew, for her be 'two oriental gentlemen'. Imran was acquainted

228

with the English.

His brother's head was bent. His brother, in a European suit, with waistcoat, watch-chain and tarboosh, was eating like a man that has useless taste-buds.

Nanny whispered, 'He's low, and has suffered knocks. Amabel, don't stare, please!' Imran had keen hearing.

But the face of Imran's beloved elder brother had begun to lose its melancholy, his shoulders had straightened and the shadow in the depths of his eyes paled.

It wasn't in Imran's nature to pursue in his mind the dirtiness of the lady's washing habits. He hadn't consulted his brother. Imran had gone quietly to the Chief Officer and asked for a solution to the problem. Imran shot the bolt across on their door to the lavatory and neither of them would undo it before the *Principessa Ilaria Maria* docked—in Alexandria at last.

44   Fateful meeting

Nanny's discomfiture—'with *Gippos*, madam?' —was to Griselda a source of amusement. Had it not been so, she might have been discomfited herself. She was none too partial: gentlemen were gentlemen and belonged in some arctic, quarry-tiled region. She and

Nanny, she'd perceived, had their Libyan steward, Hassan, to thank for the cleanliness of the 'appointments'.

For the absence of enormity.

Quite, quite soon, it dawned on her that she, Amabel and Nanny had the lavatory, ghastly though it was, to themselves.

It was her benign curiosity that led to a conversation with the clear-complexioned one. But the first thing was that, on leaving the cabin, she fell over him.

The water, still glistening on his hands and wrists arrested her. A tasselled towel had been laid out on the deck. He was sitting on his heels at one end of it. His eyes fleetingly rose to hers.

His lips were moving. As swiftly did he tip forward ... until his forehead touched the 'rug'. With a presence cultivated in the hunting-field, she looked away and trod around him. His feet were bare. On the skin to the ankles and shins too, water winked.

Griselda was so surprised that she couldn't for a few seconds gather what it was she'd witnessed.

She told Amabel and Nanny, 'The Egyptian prays outside our door. Not the haggard fellow; the companion. Be *careful*!'

To a situation that, a week earlier, would have been a dream, Griselda was (provided she could keep Nanny happy) determined to adapt herself.

230

When they met in the Saloon, he smiled. A slight smile.

'May I ask your name?' she said to him, in French.

'My name is Monsieur Imran,' he replied gravely.

'I am Mrs Romney.' She expected an obeisance of some sort. He put his hand over his left breast, above the heart.

Griselda wasn't often at a loss.

'Are you travelling to Egypt? And your acquaintance?'

'He is Marwan el-Mansur.'

'Is he so downcast?'

'He has been enclosed in a villa in Malta. Exiled.'

'I had a villa once in Malta.'

'His health is shattered.'

'I'm so sorry,' she murmured, and continued on her way.

Three yards from her, he took his seat. Nanny gazed at Griselda.

'Is there something the matter, Nanny?'

Nanny's eyes, behind her spectacles, were trying to conceal a message.

Griselda glanced at Nanny interrogatively.

A paddle-wheel steamer was cramped and didn't pander. If not an intimate of the Wheelhouse, you opted for Saloon or Boat Deck. Leaning on the rail, Griselda struck up a chat.

Monsieur Imran was shaven and his chin was smooth. He appeared to possess a kind of

231

urbane calm. Imran was not tall; he was well-covered, neither lean nor fat. He might have been thirty. His voice was soft and modest. When, once, she was to glimpse the inner rim of his tarboosh, she would notice it was greasy.

The man was hung about with the scent of orange blossom.

Imran's lashes were curved and thick; yet he wasn't a hairy man. His eyes were dark brown. His feet had been shapely. Usually, his feet were sandaled.

Had it not been for the circumstances, she might have put him down, had she put him down at all, as an *indigène*. On board ship Imran glided around in a *gallabiyeh*. His tarboosh was exchanged for a white, embroidered cap.

Whilst the other maintained a suited appearance, it was rare for Imran to dress, in the boat, for the street.

When she wanted to be, Griselda was amiable. How else could she have taken up with the odd Captain Palsy; or, for that matter, unbended vis-à-vis the two Harrow boys in *Koh-i-Noor*. They would have disembarked at Jedda ages ago. And had her ruminations not turned to Mohammad, she might not have recalled what Mohammad had said about horses; and their being one's friends. Griselda gasped when she contemplated the enormity of her expedition.

Imran began to tell her, in fluent French, of

232

the struggles of Egypt. Egypt, he said, no longer wanted to recognize the Protectorate. Egypt ached for Independence.

The students had made a demonstration at Tanta. A number had become martyrs.

'Were they killed!'

'Cairo is not so safe for you, *madame*.'

He'd stiffened her resolve.

'There are shootings. British are attacked, Baines Bey was murdered in the street. A month ago. The Australian soldiers have inflamed people. Lord Milner has so far accomplished nil. You have been aware of the Milner Mission?'

'I read my newspaper,' said Griselda. 'Who was Baines Bey?'

'An official in the railways.'

'One would imagine him to have been unimportant?'

'He was British.'

'Oh, dear.'

'Zaghlul Pasha, who should form a government in Egypt, is still in Gibraltar. The peace negotiations with Turkey are not concluded. The price of wheat soars. The *fellaheen* cannot afford to feed their families . . .'

'Or their beasts of burden?'

'The price of cotton is low. The *fellaheen* receive money for their cotton that doesn't suffice to buy wheat.'

Griselda exerted herself to charm him.

She started to tell him about Philomena.

'I doubt if our horses were pampered in the Army. They would, d'you see, have been fed, and watered, they were shod regularly, their saddlery fitted, they had no sores on which the flies could worry. They'd never be worked to death. Never!'

He blinked.

Griselda recollected the appalling cruelties meted out to our remounts, by us, in the South African War. She was familiar with those red-maroon volumes, *Cavalry Training* and *Animal Management*, nowadays *full* of the most humane instruction. Sweat-stained and worn, they ended their days in households such as Quarr's. Since the South African War, there had been a sea change in opinion.

'In the cavalry, we look after our horses before ourselves!'

'*Madame*, you mean what, by "worked to death"? We are given horses by God . . .' (he said '*Dieu*') '. . . that we might be helped in our daily toil by theirs. When God wills . . . only then . . . are they dying.'

'You would say 'Allah'?' she ventured.

'Allah, God, the same.'

'The same?'

'Of course!'

Griselda hadn't caught him at it again.

'I do hope,' she said at last, 'we don't . . . Amabel, Nanny and I, our walking in and out of our cabin . . . trouble you.'

234

Imran shook his head, and smiled.

Sometimes Imran was to call her, before he knew of Georgie, *'Umm Amabel'*, Mother of Amabel.

When she next laid eyes on Imran he was with the other man, sharing a hubble-bubble.

45   El Mughar

Fit though they had been, they began to suffer. Those that had been shod were spared the cut heels and bruised soles. A hundred and forty-nine were nodding at the walk, and more were trotting short. Lameness was tolerated. It had to be.

Philomena had no heat in any foot and was sound. Her hoofs were worn.

Farrier-Sergeant 'Barny' Barnes and Farrier-Corporal Rodder took four pack-mules off to Beersheba. Rodder might have managed pig with his field-forge (at present believed to be split between two dromedaries in the transport) and made up some sets. The mules returned with every prime acquisition bar shoes.

The Regiment was moved out without watering.

At midnight, Philomena waited with twitching lip, imperiously, near one of those two-hundred-foot wells the contents of which were wrung from them by telegraph cable and bucket.

One hour and thirty-five minutes later, her troop approached. In her battle to be allowed time to swallow, Philomena failed to notice Sage's solicitude.

They came up overnight to Khirbet Resik. They spent the morning in support of infantry of the 53rd Division.

Philomena had to gallop wide out on the flank in a great arc, only to be hustled to the brow of a hill and denied the view. The country had undulated first in barren creases; and then downy. She was tiring. Occasionally, she could snatch at grasses burnt to the weight of a feather by the sun in the summer.

Three were killed, two wounded.

The led horses of an entire mounted brigade threaded through them to the rear. Wells had been polluted. Three hours elapsed before these same animals returned.

In late afternoon, Sage watered Philomena at the trough by Sheriah. Philomena thought Sage was useless. It added to her anxieties, her impatience, her weariness. Philomena wasn't to get another drink for fifty-four hours.

Swift though the pursuit was—to intercept the Turkish column—there were, for Philomena, hours of carrying her head, sudden bursts of activity; shuffling, shattering marches and thirsty halts. As the crow flew it was sixty miles from Beersheba to Junction Station: the

Yeomanry Division would cover a hundred and ninety miles; and the Australians many more than that.

In the rear, there was a turmoil of movement and manoeuvre; a positive miracle of supply and of stray transports.

Sage was timid with maps, he never connected topography with squiggles. He could tell they were zigzagging. To Huj, the scene of sterling action. From Huj to Simsim. A hot wind blew up from the east, with a sting. Very dusty.

Two horses foundered.

Great rivulets had striped her coat in sand. Her thirst burnt her gullet. Private Sage patted her. Ignoring him served to distract her. From El Falujeh, they gained both the coast road at El Medjel at 1 a.m. and a three-hour halt.

Perceived in fact to cause sore backs in these circumstances, the cavalry practice of regular dismounting to ease horses on the march had been generally discontinued.

Amid the swirling, and the gusts that made the horses blunder into each other, Philomena began to see, and hear, explosions. Nevertheless, the carcasses that sprawled were of oxen and horses between traces and beneath yokes. They'd died peacefully. No guts, no limbs, no terrible wounds. For fifteen miles, there was to be the reek of blood; yet no blood. And the hoopoes, undeterred, still rose and flew and fell and pierced the soil.

Sage coughed, choking.

Soon the whines and bursts and earache started again. Sweat darkened her shoulder. She stared and stared. Tears seeped from her caked nostrils. She had dirt in her eyes.

Mud-brick walls, blind villages, reared up through this weather. A flock of goats, their lop-ears drooping and their eyes three-quarter shut, stood obediently in the charge of a child, to cross between the squadrons.

Askew on a hilltop, a small plantation of pine bent and streamed.

A retreating army had abandoned a cart without a wheel here, a dead camel there; an endlessly ebbing tide of squalor.

Philomena and Private Sage were famished. Not only shoes, not only water . . . where were the forage wagons . . . Sage was in a lather about ammunition. At noon, he fed her a pound of gram and few handfuls of *tibbin*. He exuded a clumsy kindness.

Philomena rummaged, aggrieved, in her nosebag; tail tucked down hard; beyond fidgeting; too tired to stand *without* fidgeting.

Sage reckoned the top brass had laid aside consideration for the nags. He knew it didn't do to think any such. But Sage never missed a chance to seize on a titbit for her, or at halts to let her snatch at withered grasses.

Philomena's eyes, winking over the nosebag, were stony and remote.

They were off, Philomena's troop, to execute
238

a swift, flanking reconnoitre; to draw rifle fire from the two mud-brick villages or tantalize a machine-gun into giving its position away.

More exertion.

There was no enemy to be shoo-ed out. The enemy was absent. The twinges wouldn't let Philomena's belly alone; and the *sharki* wouldn't abate. All were scorched. Being out in it was like being licked by a cow. The bar of her mouth was dry and the bit was irking the gum.

The stars peered through the haze of the *sharki* and were stronger until they shone with proper zeal.

Philomena was game.

By the next morning the enemy, eluding them no longer, was massed to fight just below a bristling ridge that was scythed in two, at an angle, by the sunken course of Wadi Katrah, a tributary of Wadi Jamus. The northern, greater portion of the heights was commanded, on an outcrop, by the settlement of El Mughar.

The place called Katrah perched opposite. Beyond Katrah there were orange and lemon groves.

El Mughar was encircled by prickly pear. A rocky cascade descended to fertile land.

Across the unbroken, deceptive plain snaked the Wadi Shellal el-Ghor.

Plantations of pomegranate offered scant cover. There were vineyards with leaves the colour of dark red wine; wrinkled trails of passion fruit, and of melon.

Turkish machine-guns and infantry defended every bulge and hollow along the ridge, until, on the extreme left, two more villages were resisting a dismounted attack. The Turkish guns at Katrah were being bitter to our infantry.

Philomena and Corky had an easy in the orange groves of Yebna. Fifteen wells graced Yebna. The scent of crushed fruit assailed nostrils. The men scattered peel, and the horses trampled it.

Duncliffe and Sage were stood to, and mounted. Philomena and Corky found themselves assembled at the fringe of the trees and were startled by the order, 'Direct Gallop Depart'.

They hustled downhill.

Two sections at a go, the unshod, jaded horses (of five squadrons, two Bucks squadrons first and then the Dorsets), under artillery fire, had to cross the gap; to file *via* sheep-tracks tricky with loose stone into the stifling bed of the Wadi Jamus.

The wind had dropped and the air was over-still. The warm sun had begun to lower itself in the sky.

Philomena waited patiently. For an eternity, they remained formed up in a single rank, deep in the ravine. The sweat dried. Private Sage swung into the saddle. At three o'clock, scurrying across their front, a Bucks squadron . . . A frenzy of distant crack-crack.

Duncliffe's section filed up into the precarious open. Philomena's ears went back. The Berks Battery R.H.A. was firing over them from Beshshit. An incoming enemy shell shrieked. The cavalry had begun to issue from the *wadi* so the field artillery of the 52nd Division was popping the ridge.

The rumps (rather hollow) of 'A' Squadron, at a laboured trot, were already pounding the dust. With the farthest to go.

The Colonel led 'B' and 'C' Squadrons. Hotchkiss teams on the left flank. In column of squadrons, extended to five yards, at a distance of two hundred feet.

This wasn't un-reconnoitred terrain. An officer's patrol (a Bucks subaltern and his groom) had raced a swarm of machine-gun bullets in a three-mile arc. He had reported to Brigade HQ a lack of cover for led horses.

So the ridge had to be galloped.

The noise was shocking. The flashes and puffs in so many directions dazed Philomena. Our own machine-gunners had crept along in the Wadi Shellal and were firing upwards.

They were exposed; there was not a dip, not a wall, not a bank.

Their cover was the billowing dust.

The unshod horses tended to peck on sharp flints. They were somehow held up.

Corky snorted. A man had grasped

Duncliffe's stirrup. The hand went. A riderless grey kept pace on Philomena's off-side. A large insect, in an angry buzz, collided with Philomena's shoulder. The going was stonier. An almond plantation trundled by.

Philomena's cleverness kept her from stumbling.

A shell blasted a hole in the cloud that was 'A' Squadron. There was shying and swerving; leaving casualties and shattered ground. Then they vanished altogether.

Philomena crawled from a dry cataract of the Wadi Shellal.

They were to gallop the last thousand yards. Her wind was drawn painfully. Beneath her hoofs, burnt grass was crushed.

Saddles were being emptied.

Corky got his head down. For exhausted horses, weak from thirst and from hunger, these were the longest two miles. The chestnut sobbed. A ghastly, groaning wheeze issued from a bay mare.

To the right, two of the three Bucks squadrons had ridden to the crest. Sun glinted on their naked steel ... two battalions of infantry below the bluff, to assist ... And the Turks had revived.

'A' Squadron was gaining a spur to the north.

Dismounted, the men of 'A' Squadron hurled themselves with fixed bayonets up the rough, twisty paths; to be raked by rifle and machine-gun fire. Their horses rocked on splayed legs, with hanging heads, dreadfully blown.

Some lay down.

Several hundred yards to the right of them, Duncliffe's section, *her* section, in No. 3 Troop, 'B' Squadron, was one of three ordered to dismount. Philomena, still clear-sighted, heaving, with a burst blood vessel in a nostril, noticed that the leading troops of 'B' Squadron were thrusting, swords drawn, in zigzags up the terraces and donkey-paths. But the horses were breaking their knees.

The officer and men of No. 2 Troop's Hotchkiss team scrabbled after them. Philomena saw the cow hocks of the bay gun-horse: his legs were shaky.

Philomena, at the foot of the outcrop, had felt her reins go over her head. Corky was not far off.

Sage was gone.

The suddenness never failed to puzzle her.

They were to be held in dead ground. Philomena distinctly heard the yelp of a dog in pain.

She was distracted.

The guns of the Austrian artillery, embedded in the curve of the Katrah contour, had got the range on the held horses below El Mughar; and one of 'A' Squadron's was screaming.

The ground was not so dead, and (closer) a shell with a long fuse exploded late . . . and low.

Then Philomena didn't know what had

happened to her. She didn't know that she was terrified or that her companions were plunging; were frantic.

She *felt* the linked horses, as if against her flanks; yet all, and the ashen-haired corporal, had disappeared.

Her ears ached. She had her head down and her breath had stopped. Her ribs slowly swelled. She was trembling: her skin and flesh shook in great rivulets of fear. In front of her Corky was lying on his side, his head was nodding; as though he'd been dozing in a meadow. The chestnut was between them, and was dead. Philomena's rein vanished beneath the chestnut. She jerked her head up, but nothing gave. Eight other horses were down. A ninth was down but, dazed, with forelegs that were stumps. Philomena blinked.

Painfully, her wind returned. Her coat was spattered. Her legs supported her. In her gullet, the hump of her tongue was close to choking her. She coughed.

Corky whickered.

She answered him.

One of the horseholders was twisted and silent. Philomena realized that another man was sitting up and staring at her. With his hands he was pawing and pawing at his tunic, in which his First Field Dressing was hiding. A splintered bone poked through his breeches.

Shrapnel had torn through all these creatures. Philomena couldn't release her head. Her feet were sore, the off-hind throbbed rhythmically. She was unscathed.

She was oblivious to remote sounds: the push of the Lowlanders on El Mughar; the jingling of the Berks when they came up to clear Katrah.

Twice the trumpeter sounded 'Rally!'

She stirred; restless. She understood him.

Even through the fighting, she could identify the dromedary that was getting the wounded out (it groaned loudly when asked to stand) and carting them from the M.O.'s First Aid Post to the dressing-station.

She waited for Sage.

Instead, the Regiment's led horses approached from the rear. They veered off. The faint jingle melted.

The sun had not played for some while on her back. It must have been sliding closer to the horizon. She glimpsed the flashes of a heliotrope—signalling high above her. Stretcher-bearers came with a horse-drawn sledge and took away the men.

She couldn't see the sledge horse or its ridden companion. She could scent them.

A medical orderly put his hand on his hip and gave Philomena a kind, sad smile.

Insofar as she was able, rolling her eyes, she looked steadily at him. But he didn't understand.

Then the sun had gone. It was still light. Corky laid his head down and sighed.

She distinguished the steady tump-tump tump-tump of a dispatch-rider. The trotting receded in the direction of Wadi Jamus.

More bearers came and went. She pricked one ear forward, listening to their muttered conversation.

Somebody, whom she couldn't see, patted her. She thought she heard, with her one ear, the Squadron Trumpeter, thin and high above her. The other ear was deaf.

As darkness fell, Corky died.

Philomena stood, with hanging head; ears back. Several times she tried to tug the rein. She assumed she'd been tied up. She waited for Sage.

She was alone. It made her uneasy. She was longing for company. But she couldn't whinny, not the sort of shrill whinny that would have carried. Not with her head down. She whickered again. The remote hum of a motor. The jackals began to prowl. She waited for one of the horses to lurch to his feet, shake himself and come nearer.

None did.

A rumble of mess carts, field kitchens and ammunition wagons. Far, far off.

The moon shone bright; leering in the sky.

No bombardment, no whistle of machine-gun fire or the thud when it met the chest or rump of a horse, no snap of rifle-fire, had beaten her into accepting the loneliness of that night.

Philomena nursed a sullen desperation for water. The beam of a searchlight swept towards her; and over her. Illuminated for an instant, the chestnut looked black. She could see him well enough.

The hush enfolded them.

After the dawn would come birds. With her head pinned, she was vulnerable.

The moon had set when she heard Captain Flower. Revolver in hand, and accompanied by his Farrier Sergeant, he'd been to 'A' Squadron's horses, those that had suffered in the open and those shelled below the spur. The brigade vet was busy in El Mughar with cocaine; dressings; and captive bolt.

'It's Philomena!' said Captain Flower. He seemed sad.

She twitched her ears. She tried to roll an eye at him. Her neck ached with cramps.

'I've known her ever since we were at Eldon Heath,' he remarked.

He had his revolver in his hand but he hadn't cocked it. He was worn out himself . . . yet out among these horses. Ages before the detail to retrieve equipment.

Her ears flickered. 'What is amiss?' Captain Flower asked Philomena. 'Truly!'

Philomena, on four legs, was the picture of an animal with a severe abdominal wound. He squeezed his boot between the chestnut and the bay and reached her side. He cupped her ear. Her ear was warm. A hand ran over her

247

near-fore and near-hind. He strove to balance himself against her, and his pith helmet touched her belly.

They tried to drag at her reins. Or to manhandle the carcass. Then they unbuckled her reins from bit and bridoon. While they were backing her, she got a hind foot on something; and she groped in panic: she was determined to struggle out. Flower slackened her girth. The Farrier Sergeant stooped to take Corky's reins to give to her. With the rope of her headstall, they led her away.

Only the fading of memory itself would allow Philomena to forgive Flower a croak of laughter.

46 The marble

A child with a blue roan mare in Egypt had a lot of worries too.

Nanny had pleaded, from the deepest bottom of her being, to be delivered from the mortification of this w.c. There'd been not a whiff. '*Men!*' she'd say to Amabel. The last thing a body wanted was to get a whiff.

Muzz and Nanny had been scrupulous in unlocking the other door. The anxiety had done little to help their insides.

Nanny had tried to steel herself to watch the lock.

Nanny couldn't detect that anybody *ever* turned it. In a mysterious way (said Nanny) her prayer had been answered. For the door was not a party door, after all!

Or, if it could be, it wasn't, not for now.

Muzz slept with her head in her arm ('I don't think, Nanny, we have to stand on ceremony, you and I').

Nanny had often seen Muzz in bed at Bark Hart. In bed but awake. Nanny said Muzz muttered and stirred in her sleep. Nanny was surprised.

The 2nd Officer, Mr Oliviero, administered to ailments aboard ship. To divert Nanny, he produced from a handkerchief a stone like a calcified peach-stone and declared it disgorged, upwards, by a seaman. When Nanny had recovered from the horror, she was able to sustain a conversation. 'Rum!' declared Nanny. 'Rum?' repeated the 2nd Officer. 'Peculiar,' said Nanny.

The 2nd Officer was *boring*. Amabel courted the Chief.

To visit the Engine-room you had to descend, and descend; and (Nanny thought) *descend*. The Chief, a quarter Scottish, half Italian, a quarter Greek, conducted them himself. It was a Meccano set of iron stairs, stairs with treads you saw through. The din was hollow, as though it could be louder and was muted out of consideration. Voices clanged against the metal. These regions were stuffed with giant pistons that thrust and pumped themselves to and fro. It was just like being shut in with a railway-train.

Nanny stayed at the top.

With aplomb, Amabel clambered below, on the punctured steps. The engine room wasn't so very deep at all. The piston rods were level with the paddle-wheels on port and starboard beam, and driven by steam from two boilers. The paddles splat smoothly. The Chief had an open deadlight through which the uppermost section of the wheel could be watched.

At the two stokeholes, wiry firemen, fully clothed, with glistening hair and corrugated faces shovelled coal into two glowing mouths. The coal fell forward in shuffling landslips.

'Work never cease-ah,' bawled the Chief Engineer.

His uniform clung to him.

There was the other end of the Engine Telegraph. Amabel had seen the ceramic handles of it and its white tin face in the Wheel-house. A face much friendlier than *Koh-i-Noor*'s one.

The shudder of the paddles filled both eardrums quite pleasantly.

Amabel thought, Nanny is calling but we can't hear her.

Which quarter of him was Scottish? The Chief awed her. He grasped her arm and pushed. The furnace changed water into steam and the steam drove the pistons that turned the paddles that persuaded the *Principessa* to scuttle along at nine knots. Alexandria was four days out from Valletta. The Chief beamed.

They climbed back. Nanny was hopping from one foot to another.

As they squeezed through the watertight door onto deck, the after funnel snorted a plume of black smoke.

Amabel, in gazing up, dropped her green marble. This marble, unless stabled, lived in her right hand. It was busy rolling ... as swift as a bat flew ... over the deck and into the scuppers.

'Nanny!' she squawked.

47 The Judaean hills

It had taken heroism to ride beloved horses to death. For, of the eighty-three lost, some thirty, 'lacking water and rations' (weak, parched and starved), had been foundered.

The night had been busy on the narrow ridge of El Mughar. The Brigade had captured two field guns, fourteen machine guns, taken prisoner eighteen officers and one thousand, three hundred and seventy-eight other ranks.

'A' Squadron, despite their having been overtaken in the assault on the crest, had suffered the heaviest casualties in horses and

251

in men.

The Regiment had acquitted itself with distinction.

The Adjutant, Murray, badly wounded in scrotum and right buttock, had turned one of the eight Turkish machine guns downhill upon the mass of the retreating, for which he would be awarded the M.C.

Another popular officer, though not to die at once, had sustained mortal wounds.

Nine O.R.s killed, forty-three wounded.

Now and only now were the Aussies and En Zeds to accept the yeomen as worthwhile.

It had been perhaps significant that the G.O.C. the Brigade had in August relieved the previous one; whilst since June the new divisional commander was a short, cheerful man, Indian Army, with a bald head that bothered itself about horses as much as it did about men.

For Philomena, there was chagrin. She'd quite thought Captain Flower had been going to take her to water and give her a nosebag. Instead, she'd had to hang about. Then it was blameless Sage, with his boils, who moistened her lips.

For many of 'B' Squadron's horses there'd been an hour's browsing on the north flank of the ridge. El Mughar had the one well. Not every horse got a drink. At 10 a.m. there was an advance, under heavy shelling (no wounded), across the plain to the Jewish

252

settlement of New Akir. They slipped into the orange groves, and, in consequence of the horse losses, rested all day. There was one well at Akir too, sixty metres deep, but with an engine.

Private Sage trudged to an outlying dwelling, at the risk of his life, and requisitioned some charcoal-baked *'khobz'* (Sage didn't know the Yiddish). Bread! Coaxing her to feed ... feed from his own mouth; and the mouths of the section.

In the evening, they passed through the Arab village.

There could be no respite. Neither for the Turk, being chased north, nor for the Brigade, pushing on towards Junction Station.

There was no let-up for Philomena or the lightly wounded. The losses had been great. There *were* no led horses.

Gamely, if grudgingly, Philomena did her best for Sage.

All the next afternoon, they bore the shell-fire from Abu Shusheh. This ridge, with Abu Shusheh on its northern redoubt and ancient Gezer on the southern, glowered equally, as it had throughout the centuries, upon the port of Jaffa and the gate to the Vale of Ajalon.

On the 15th, the Brigade assaulted the cheese-like ridge; scrambling up it dismounted, with their horses. Sage, who would have given much to save her, ran beside Philomena, panting. The Dorsets had to ride down the big guns at Sidun from the rear; pelting at their horses' heads. Sage tripped and sprawled headlong, jerking Philomena to a halt and making her gasp. Almost as a relief to her came the general order to mount and the cantering through the awful boulders and scrub.

Some of these Turks cowered.

The Regiment was vastly proud of its valiant horses.

Sage ached to garner more forage from the country; or . . . from another regiment. They were thirty-five miles from the rail-head. Philomena was lame, on and off; and shocked. Her hunger had gone beyond the keen. She had a throbbing in the near shoulder.

The poison of prickly-pear thorn itched and festered in the skin.

The daily ration was supposed to be nine and a half pounds of crushed gram. The issue had been 12 lbs for two days. There was no *tibbin*. Digestion, in the absence of bulk, was affected.

Gram was thirst-making.

Philomena still went unshod.

A gelding had been abandoned in the advance; left standing. He'd called after his friends until they were out of sight. An officer's belated recollection that there could be no confusion over stolen animals in the hands of the Bedouin saw permission to destroy him sought from the C.O. and Barnes sent back.

254

They rested at Ramla for three days. At the water, Philomena was given long enough to swallow.

There was no rest for a certain Farrier Quartermaster Sergeant and two Farrier Sergeants, or for their horses—away to draw supplies in Deir el-Belah. Distressingly, they would catch up, three days later, empty-handed.

South African mules were issued. Already shod. Nobody in his right mind would have begrudged them their shoes.

Sage was short of rations himself. He made much of Philomena. She was supercilious. Philomena was thin. Every rib was hollow. Sage made her saddle to fit by folding blankets. Like many, she was scouring. 'Darn thik gram.' He groomed the stickiness and smelliness out of her coat. The horses had got in lathers, although their coats were retarded. Her skin had lost its suppleness; it clove to itself.

Sage begged the saddler to mend a thinning strap and to repair stitching. He bothered himself no end. It was a strange circumstance in both Palestine and Egypt that the grease from the coat kept saddlery supple, in prime nick.

At Ramla, eight were destroyed.

The lack of drink had taken its toll. Some of the Australian regiments had waited eighty hours.

Since her sand muzzle had been withdrawn, for the march on Beersheba, she'd been watered on average once in every thirty-six hours. Her rations had been meagre. She had been carrying up to twenty-two stone. The yeomen wondered at the horses; and took courage from their endurance.

Nosebags had to be employed as muzzles. The horses were eating their head ropes.

General Barrow wanted them lighter for Judaea.

The front-line transport, the mule-drawn ambulances, hospital camels that evacuated the casualties on either side of their emaciated humps in cacolets, dromedaries covered in putrefying sores, mange and on shredded feet, now to be frightened by the wet rock, for they slipped and broke their legs, or to sink in mud ... even the indestructible little donkeys, 'Allenby's white mice' ... beasts and men, the unshod horses of the Dorset Yeomanry, all had worse before them.

The mange spread to the Egyptian camel-drivers.

Philomena marched towards Jerusalem. It was deceptively pleasant. The sky was cool. Not until they'd passed beneath Abu Shusheh and struck off to the east, through the spurs of the hills, and could look back and see neither plain nor sea, was it in the least grim. The winding altitude seemed to grow out of nowhere.

The rain closed in.

There were almond groves. And orchards of plum. Pomegranate. Tiny squares and ribbons of fields; sheepfolds. And olives; only ancient olive-trees on the terraces; with swelling fruit. If the disused track consented to keep to the floor of the valley, it was strewn with fallen limestone. Beside it would be ancient houses, circular, with a room for the flock and an outer stair to an upper floor. All ruins.

These were sites that suggested a well, a cistern.

The road ascended through long-derelict terraces. It clung to a knobbly plateau, exposed and windswept; and lacking a smooth inch. Cyclamen sprouted from the crevices. It descended, between caves, or tombs. The villages were so lonely, so barren, it was surprising a soul lived in them.

The horses got a canvas bucketful each at a makeshift dam.

Mud sluiced down the hills. The transport wagons tilted in holes up to their axles; and turned about.

An artillery battery squeezed back down, pursued by other wheeled transport. This was impossible. Pack-mules and pack-camels, hastening up, would attempt to pass the column in the dark. The Army had bought thirty thousand baggage camels in Egypt and saw no reason not to make use of them.

Staggering how camels strode across flints;

257

retained their *sang-froid* on precipices.

The ravines that debouched from the mountains sent tons of water onto the valley walls. The streams began to rush. They would turn too dangerous to ford.

The road dipped, and the torrents with it, to a *wadi*. Philomena and Sage, fording nevertheless, filed between and around the unstable boulders in the bed.

The rain did rinse the paths of the blood of the camels' feet.

Even the sheep and goats were absent. It was uncanny.

The donkeys tripped on: no officer's batman was obliged to forgo his ride. But the pack-animals, being urged, lost their footing. Dromedaries expired.

The dismounted flank guard of each regiment was obliged to clamber over decaying terraces; slither on shiny, petrified mud in which were imprisoned the prints of dinosaurs; grapple with rock-fall and stone-fall, caves and crevices.

In the night, since picketing gear had been dispensed with, the horses were ringed, in the mud. They couldn't lie down.

The softer their feet, the worse it was for them.

The village wells were inadequate.

Sage shivered under his groundsheet. 'Billy' (General Barrow) had wanted to spare the horses the weight. Sage had no great-coat or

258

blanket packed on the saddle; no spare clothing; Philomena carried no blanket under the *numnah*. Sage would have sacrificed his own under-garments to pad Philomena's saddle on the wasted muscles of her back had he not recollected the seams.

Soaked, Sage did so compassion his horse.

Within thirty hours, it was reported that the leading regiments were in contact; ten to twelve miles ahead. Or ten hours: it was the same.

The fellows could swear it was clear as an egg on a plate that the Turks held in strength the Beitunia ridge that commanded the Jerusalem-to-Nablus road; with cavalry, artillery and infantry. It put the wind up them that they could have toiled past Turkish machine-gun teams concealed in caves and infantry units that went and ambushed our rear-guard.

The main attack fell instead on the Yeomanry Division's most advanced outpost, at Zeitun, on the western extremity.

However, something was happening on the left flank, for at eight o'clock in the morning 'C' Squadron was ordered rapidly uphill; to counter-attack. 'B' Squadron to fall back and support, followed by two troops of 'A' Squadron.

'C' Squadron's held horses were able to retire safely. Philomena and the horses of 'B' Squadron were, weirdly, ahead.

259

It was a heavy-legged No. 3 Troop that pursued Johnny; and found itself engaged on the slopes of the Zeitun spur. The fighting was still fierce when the Colonel was wounded at one o'clock.

Throughout the afternoon, in a narrow defile, Philomena hung her head.

The rain had stopped and a rainbow stood in the sky.

Led horses were being shelled elsewhere, and going down in a dreadful tangle and panic. Their vital spark was vanquished in the ubiquitous puffs of smoke. Here all was peaceful.

Before he was killed Sage had seen her easy and had waited—humble—for that droopy lip and the closeness of nostril and breath that would have told him that his rubbing her down with his fingers gratified her.

Philomena never did reward him.

His teeth had been chattering.

48 Monsieur Imran

Amabel's green marble raced across the deck; taking small tosses and bounces. It had reached the rail and was rolling, it would shortly go for ever. The slap of Imran's sandals might have startled Amabel and Nanny. He was swooping ... his *gallabiyeh* flew ... He

260

stood up with the marble in his hand.

Nanny smiled.

The child was more inscrutable. She said 'thank you!' prettily; and he withdrew.

Imran hadn't revealed to Mrs Romney that Marwan was his brother. Imran didn't seek to pour out what was private.

Mrs Romney asked whether 'Imran' was the name of his family or his 'very own'. His own.

He judged that her interest in him lay in his uses. Imran was content. He wished to accord her all the kindness and courtesy he possessed. That didn't lead him to enlighten her in all that which she didn't know.

Imran continued to pray outside the cabin. The lady didn't, however, stumble over him again.

Ten months ago he'd woken in the night, sat bolt upright and said aloud, *'Allah!'*

He now prayed; prayed five times a day; and he observed two days of *sawm* in each month. Fasting was healthy; it made you feel light-headed and clean.

Imran hadn't informed the lady that there was little unusual, or untoward, in him. He regarded the fire of the angry devout with indulgence. Imran himself burned for Egypt's independence, but without the skill to enflame his fellows that had dispatched his brother Marwan to the Seychelles, and to Malta. He didn't confide to her that he revered education.

261

Imran had kept Ramadan in every year since—his own desire—the age of nine. It was customary; his father and mother and his brothers and sisters did so. He'd been like every boy he knew, like many men; always full of love for Allah.

Then Allah had intervened, waking him from an unremembered dream.

The passage of his life had run on; with a new sense of calm, and purpose.

Why should he have told Mrs Romney that he was married! The lady hadn't asked. Or that he had two sons? Tahar, four; and Khalfallah, two. She hadn't asked. Or that his beloved father lived; and his beloved mother. Or that his sister Hadeh suffered from a wasting illness; and his small sister Firdaus had lost an eye to disease.

The lady hadn't asked; and, had she asked, Imran would not have told her very much at all; nor, if pressed, would he have perceived the slightest need to tell the truth.

The truth was private; precious, not to be squandered; rather, to be honoured. From Allah nothing was hidden.

Honour was inviolable.

As a Muslim, as a Muslim man, he could look upon the lady benignly. Nothing could ruffle his sense that to be a Muslim was to be lifted above the Nazarene—the Christian lady. In his calm serenity, Imran was agitated beyond words by one consideration only; for the British were in the *ascendant* ... more crushing, more educated, sophisticated and favoured.

Imran was aware that the British were in Egypt to tantalize her struggling inhabitants.

49 Wounded

The road that had been in existence since antiquity was an abomination. No assault on Jerusalem by this route had succeeded *in* antiquity. Or ever. Or by any other road from the coast. The native guides were unreliable.

Had the Turkish line of communication between Nablus and Jerusalem been cut, horses would have become essential. Barrow had weighed their distress against that necessity. But the yeomen, fighting like the fellows of the 74th away to their right, as infantry, were hampered most severely.

By evening the Turks had obliged Billy to contemplate a retirement upon Beit Ur el-Foka.

The Turkish forces had already—before 'B' Squadron's farriers, saddlers and lightly wounded could file out with the horses—taken back a lot of ground; thrusting forward their nine-pounder mountain guns by mule.

The horses of the entire division were to be evacuated; to Ramla and Ludd. Officers' chargers, mules, donkeys to remain; and some of the emaciated camels. Ammunition-trains of donkeys had been ordered up. Pack-camels were required to carry light machine guns; and cacolets. When they collapsed and died, their shivering Egyptian drivers had an inclination to die beside them. The Egyptian fallen, flapping blue cotton and wet, were not uncommon.

Philomena trod after her companions solemnly, delicately, round one of these casualties. The *fellah* had been hit. His blood had painted a tiny plant. His hand clutched a crooked cigarette. The contracting of her nostrils ... the staring at the leaves ... The *avoidance of leaves* had distracted her.

Johnny had spotted the movement out of that sheltered crack, Wad' Ilmesh, of 'B' Squadron's horses. Our artillery, too, would shell led horses with alacrity.

The screech of the shell went unheard. The nine-pounder's was a higher whistle. It was attended to by one of Philomena's fractured senses. Splinters of furnace-hot metal whirred into her belly and stifle. Cannoning into warm horseflesh, she went down at once. With a ghastly plunge, she was up again. She grunted, and swayed. She would have bolted. 'Whoa, whoa!' Pain scalded her leg; instinctively she kept trying to put weight on the foot.

Five of her companions had been killed; and a sixth was at once put out of his misery.

She was on three legs; dead lame.

Her wounds attracted a cursory inspection. The flesh of her off-hind quarter was torn and dirty. The damage to her belly was less important.

Progress was slow. That saved her. The pace of the column was a death march.

The fuzzy brown camel, barracked at the Field Ambulance collecting-station, had luminous eyes; dark and weepy; eyes in such extremity. Blood had seeped up between the two big nails of his feet; and had dried.

Camels showed no fear under fire. That indifference, or bravery, didn't serve them when they slipped, or did the splits like giraffes, they were frightened. Their humps were cavernous.

With her coated gaskins, her stinky coat, her belly moist with blood, Philomena ought to have been helpless enough. But if she was to be evacuated, she would have to be walked.

There were the wounded.

None of these people, not the brigade's vet, Captain Joyce, not even 'B' Squadron's own farriers, could attend to her. Something ... chivalry, for she put her ears back at the stretcher-bearers ... made her stand: a man was being poked and heaved into Sage's saddle. Tied to it. A boot was shoved into the iron, and looped to the surcingle. A left arm was strapped to the pommel. The bandaged right had been shattered. It hung limp. It had to hang to balance him. Round his neck was the empty sling. In shattering, the right leg beat the arm. Perhaps he ought never to have ridden. His face was a mush. Two puttees were rigged (an empty rifle-bucket helped) to support his wounded side. It was that or be a sack of oats across the saddle. The stirrup-leather was pulled over her wither.

She still carried Sage's sword. Sage's precious morsel of kindling that smelt of the fresh oranges at Yebna.

Philomena, in increasing pain, fumbled and juddered, together with the forty sick, starving, thirsty and unshod horses that had been asked to carry casualties, down the terrible track.

Fresh boulders had been washed onto it; and any vestige of paving had been eaten from it.

Her chap was swooning. Every sway, every jerk back upright, seemed to taunt her strength. Many of the men keeled over the pommel onto their mounts' necks, where they clung. Some dug their hands into the breast-plate, like children embracing their ponies; or fastened their teeth in the hog-mane, causing themselves septic bristle-sores ('they Aussies mun a-keep full manes for the *purpose*'). They drew warmth from their mounts.

In front were forty more.

It was too much. After two miles, Philomena's hind legs slipped, landing to her horror against a carcass. Her burden issued an unearthly groan. She was down on her injured

266

side, and his.

He was cut off her. They had to impel her to struggle, so as to release him.

He was youthful, this casualty they called Pardoner, his tanned cheeks were a peculiar white; and he spat out, 'Thank 'ee!'

She didn't see him again.

Philomena couldn't get up. She was permitted to fall out . . . to follow like a dog. She rested, dazed, and her head nodded.

The rest had stiffened her. She scrambled to her feet and stood there. A passing Farrier-Corporal Pitchford came with a smile, and took her rein. Then she mustered her strength. She was coaxed on among the horses of 'C' Squadron.

The Yeomanry Division had been covering a front of four miles with barely a thousand men. It was reinforced by the Australian Mounted Brigade, 7th Mounted Brigade and, brought up in forced marches, a brigade of infantry.

On 28th November, the yeomen were relieved.

In the Judaean hills, repulses were reversed. The line was held. In December, a push from Kuryet el-Enab on the road up from Jaffa, plus an encircling movement from Hebron and Bethlehem, was to squeeze the Turkish Seventh Army out towards Nablus. General Shea would be offered the keys of Jerusalem. On 12th December Allenby would walk

267

through the Jaffa Gate.

50 Evacuation

Only at Ramla (without the two Mobile Veterinary Sections that had been there) did Philomena receive an anti-tetanic injection. Her temperature was taken.

She was struck off the strength of the D.Y. She no longer belonged.

At dawn, she began her journey. At her side plodded a black gelding. He held his head askew, for he had shrapnel lodged in his brain and his near eye-socket was oozing. He'd been peppered in eighteen places; some stitched. The healed bullet-dimples in his neck would have been from previous action.

Two men conducted thirty horses.

These, in pairs, were tied to a rope that went from the head of the column, which was led by one man, to the tail, where the second man had his hand on the last, near-side horse. The slowest and most severely wounded were placed to the fore: their pace determined the pace of all.

Philomena and the black were the fourth from the head. They were asked to stagger forty miles, on their worn hoofs, carrying their wounds.

The rail-head was approaching Wadi

Ghuzzee. Those unable to walk went by ambulance. If unfit to stand in the ambulance-cart, they were destroyed. Nos. 306, 59, No. 477 Chips and No. 821 had been left to recover at Ramla. If they could. There *was* an ambulance (unavailable) with a tilting floor that conveyed, for short distances, a horse strapped on its side.

Horses on their feet stayed in a better frame of mind.

The plain was awash. Philomena could spare little interest for the transformation. The water, where it was held up, had spawned. Fish swam in it, and reptiles. Cranes and storks stood in the olive-trees. The sky alternated heaviness with blinding blue; and the rocks turned all the colours of opal. The horses' feet were soothed by the coolness. When these had been submerged for several hours, the water induced more pain.

Every halt was a search for higher ground.

When the sun glinted on flood water almost as far as the eye could see and no motor transport had passed for six hours, the conducting party debated. The column might be swirled away. Difficult to go back, hard to proceed. Imperative to distinguish flat water from the fast-moving.

The casualties browsed feebly.

Philomena marched in a daze ... her lameness more crippling than ever. Spanning Wadi Ghuzzee was a new, wooden bridge.

She had luck. She could have been entrained as far as Romani. Sent to Veterinary Hospital at Deir el-Belah, Philomena found herself by the lake, sheltered from the desert and sea winds by palm-trees; fig-groves and acacia. Venerable fig-trees grew right to the beach, and ancient vines clambered over them.

A warm, bran mash, redolent of boiled linseed, would not be forthcoming; but there was tempting *berseem*.

She was off her feed. She'd stopped eating. She was drinking her water. Perhaps the weather had saved her. She'd been chilled in the mountains. Across the Philistine plain, the wet, although miserable, had washed her wounds.

Her fever rose.

The veterinary patients were separated into 'infectious eye diseases' (isolated), 'mange and intestinal parasite' (isolated to a degree), 'sand colic, festering sores, injury to the feet' and 'shrapnel- or bullet-wounds'.

The battle-wounded were divided according to whether they were to be stitched up (in most cases this would have been done in the field) or operated upon. Or were to recover under a policy of non-interference. To delve after the bullet or metal splinter was antiquated. Either the foreign bodies would be expelled in pus or they'd be encysted within the body.

A horse unlikely to be returned to service

was a lost cause. The black, with his eye gone, was a determined old thing, and might pull through; even if his days as a troop-horse lay in the past.

It wasn't the metal that had entered Philomena's belly, low in the flank, that had to have attention. It was believed not to have careered into or through the large intestine. Her fever and refusal to eat boded ill in this respect. There was no exit wound.

On an empty stomach she'd been scouring: to stop it, she was given a drench. She had always objected to taking medicine in this horrid way. She was obliged to gulp, and did so with a very disagreeable face. A good sign.

Her fever abated.

A splinter of bone was pricking through the broken skin below the stifle joint. The trek to Deir el-Belah had made the injury worse. The flesh around the shrapnel entry was turning a morbid blue. Cocaine was the principal relief for stitching, and minor surgery; whilst, for worse, chloroform put to sleep. They drew the splinter; and inserted a tube to drain pus.

Rest was a help.

In the end, it would be Philomena's fitness that would have the greatest bearing on her ability to withstand the infection, and to repair her own body.

Many of these horses were so exhausted as to be vanquished in spirit entirely.

Indian cavalry, in the finest tradition (under

fire, with cover nil, it saved life), might have horses trained to stretch out their necks on the ground. But so far the Indian cavalry hadn't arrived. Yeomanry horses were simpler creatures.

They drew the bone splinter. And, within the twelve-hour, confident she'd get up, Philomena was glad of a long lie-down.

Philomena was strong. She mouthed the *berseem*. It was too rich to be ideal for invalids; yet palatable in comparison to gram. At Deir el-Belah in December there was grass. There were paddocks: she could be loose. There was no threat from the sky. Our aeroplanes flew energetically overhead. The army vets and the Egyptian syces were kind to her.

By January, nineteen cavalry regiments were encamped around Deir el-Belah.

Although Philomena might never have seen the Dorsets again, and she had no such right, she was issued back, convalescent, to the Regiment. Somebody must have valued her.

She was shod. The supply situation had been rectified. Rations were excellent. Both horses and men had gained a respite; and began to put on lost condition. In February, there was the scent—so poignant—of almond blossom.

51 The pilot

'Thomas Cook will be meeting us and conducting us to Cairo,' remarked Muzz to Monsieur Imran. Nanny called him 'Mummie's hanger-on'.

'May I give you my card? We shall be putting up at this *hôtel*. Do you know it? Do come! I could so do with your help!'

This was said with one of the smiles she employed to slaughter men. Muzz didn't smile at Amabel like that. There was a *most* special smile for Amabel, and for Georgie. Georgie had been slaughtered anyway, at a young age. As an infant, probably. Amabel was keen to copy the slaughtering smile in order to slaughter Peter. But Peter was her slave. So Amabel was saving it up. Some day, Nanny had said, Amabel too would slaughter men. Then, 'Do I have to?' asked Amabel.

'Particularly,' said Muzz, addressing Imran, 'if there is a risk of our being shot.'

Nanny was minatory. 'Bound to be a step up, isn't it, the next place we stay at, after the *Principessa*! Not but what, madam, Captain Testa hasn't been kind.'

Griselda considered the little voyage had been a godsend. Nanny had been rendered less rampant. Amabel had been amused. She herself had made a great saving in expenditure. Griselda smiled.

For several hours, as the *Principessa Ilaria Maria* thrashed the Libyan Sea, the coast, if it was indeed present, had been too low and too hazy. Dusk had taken all hope away. The fourth night, falling, had revealed all manner of shipping. Lights, green and red, white, were passed; winking. On deck, the seamen were busy at the hatch covers. The *Principessa* raised her derricks. The air had changed. Griselda said, 'D'you smell Africa?'

Griselda tingled with excitement.

Amabel was allowed up late. Griselda wanted Amabel to be able to remember Egypt. Amabel's face was a closed book. She was such a curious child.

Amabel and Nanny departed for their privileged refuge. Captain Testa had said Amabel could, once they were standing a mile off the lighthouse on the Pharos peninsula, see the pilot taken on board. Griselda thought that Amabel could just as well have watched from the rail amidships; beside her mother.

The stars made Griselda think of Ma. She craned her neck. The *Principessa* was sailing through waters known to any that had studied the Battle of the Nile; whilst the moon floated in the deep sky. And Napoleon's windmills, did they still line the shore?

Standing at that rail, with warm February air on her cheek, waiting and waiting for the port to approach, Griselda had known that delicious sense of being pulled in two directions: she was unable to wrench herself away, wanting it to last forever; and yet she longed for the arrival to end (they weren't to disembark at once but to sleep on board) or to lie down until it did, to awaken at the dock in the Inner Harbour.

There was a newer light. There were two, some hundreds of yards apart. So faint that they kept vanishing.

Alexandria seemed insubstantial; and from it emanated no night noises. Griselda had to imagine that a city occupied the darkness. She rubbed her eyes.

There was a wind from Greece.

She heard the moan of a buoy to port. The vessel was losing way. The leading-light of a tiny craft bobbed towards her. Could this be the pilot? The *Principessa* was still far out. The thrashing of the paddles had slowed; and the thump-thump of the pistons. The shudder was a quiver.

Griselda, pressing on the rail, saw that the steps had been lowered over the sea.

The pilot jumped and gripped, and scrambled nimbly. An invisible somebody would greet him and conduct him to the Bridge.

Shrinking against the bulkhead, the two Egyptians huddled; the prisoner in his European suit and tarboosh (he bowed); her chum in several flowing layers, tarboosh and white turban, and graceful of gesture. Griselda wondered, for a moment, whether the prisoner would feel restored; and what relation they might be, the one to the other.

The *Principessa* already had way on her.

52 'It's Philomena!'

Philomena had no recollection of Sage, and didn't pine. Awshew was less of a *sensitive* fellow. She knew him of old. Philomena and Awshew went, together, to No. 2 Troop, 'B' Squadron.

The Regiment had suffered in the mountains. The rations had been so short; the cold so bitter; and as for the fighting, it had proved both bitter and deleterious to morale. 'Officers and men are one in their admiration and affection for the horses', noted Captain Flower, in a letter. It wasn't the officers on whom fell the toil of looking after them.

The winter had been wretched.

Camp was to the west of Belah; out on the Dar Sineid road. There was leave to Cairo; by a passenger service on the line. Two brigades had got together bobbery packs of hounds, divided the country between them. They ran the jackal six to seven miles. There were 'Brigade Sports' days. For the men, wrestling on horseback, a tug-of-war on horseback (which few horses appeared to relish); and such.

In March, 7th Brigade would be holding a steeplechase meeting at Deir el-Belah. Dorset officers could still field three well-known pointer-to-pointers. Otherwise there was to be no galloping or wastage of horseflesh. Manes were to grow (flies). Legs were not (strictly not) to be clipped. 'Billy' Barrow's orders.

Remounts were trained industriously.

The Regiment moved to Gaza, to Esdud and twelve miles on north. A regular Hussar officer arrived to take over command. At the Nahr Sukereir, Philomena managed not to die. Two horses did. A failure by the yeomen to grasp that wild oleander (*'laurier rose'*) was as poisonous as laurel. The *wadi* was duly denuded of it; and the plant burnt; and the carcasses were dragged to the animal burial area.

Being at Sukereir didn't prevent several officers from declaring for the 'Palestine Grand National'.

Philomena attended the races, travelling by rail; and much enjoyed herself: a keen spectator, head up, ears pricked, tail flicked by the wind off the sea. Her Captain Flower and his chestnut thoroughbred, Echo, came home an honourable fourth.

At the time, Flower had appropriated her, 'borrowed' her, for Turnham. Her quarters with Captain Flower's chargers were comfortable. Philomena listened for the trumpet sounds she loved.

Turnham had laughed at her.

She couldn't bear being laughed at. Yet he treated her so thoughtfully that her feelings were soothed. Whereas no troop-horse was permitted to go above a trot, she could canter a length behind Echo or the grey Arabian, Festoon. She, Philomena, who had once sought to get her nose in front.

Turnham might be sent off alone with a message. Philomena was *appreciated*. Her stifle joint was stiff, and gave her twinges. She wasn't the horse she had been.

Then Captain Flower's personal establishment was up to strength with the return to fitness of Turnham's cherished Aidos. The acquaintances of 'A' Squadron were left behind and Philomena was in the lines again; back among the horses of 'B' Squadron; many of them unfamiliar to her.

She bore the *utmost* disappointment and chagrin.

She would bump into Turnham. Still Turnham spoke to her. She was without expression. He did notice the umbrage, but he was a busy fellow.

In April, they were at Deir el-Belah. The Bucks and the Berks went off to be converted into machine-gun companies and go to the Western Front. Replacing them in the Brigade were two exotic Indian Army regiments, the

2nd Lancers and 38th Central India Horse.

The 2nd Lancers, in particular, were frightfully smart. They'd come from France. In no time, they'd taught baffled remounts splendid tricks; and at tent-pegging the cry of '*Yi-hai*!' sent a shiver down the spine. The Indians rode at something under ten stone seven; so sopped up the best of the Syrians too light for yeomen.

There was no shortage of remounts.

Nine yeomanry regiments had been withdrawn from Palestine. 'The Bull' had lost, also, two entire infantry divisions; five and half siege batteries; nine more British battalions and five machine-gun companies. He had been deprived of 60,000 battle-hardened troops. Infantry divisions arrived from Mesopotamia and India; and their transport drivers had to be trained. General Allenby damn near saw his crack Australian Mounted Division off to France too. The Australian and En Zed units of the Imperial Camel Corps Brigade were converted to cavalry.

The Dorsets were issued with their customary drill tunics for the summer, but with tin hats as well. The horses drawn from the influx were satisfactory. The tin hats were far too hot.

The Second-in-Command had been invalided home. A Major Grazebrook was posted to them from the 8th Hussars (Irish connections). A Grazebrook had hunted with the Pitt brother killed in action in Gallipoli: Alan Grazebrook . . .

It was the very same.

This officer had regarded the mare measuringly, in the course of parades. Many a *dark* brown had a mealy muzzle. A washier brown was a less common colour. Saddle marks, galls and injury had left white in her coat. His fingers wandered over the dents in her quarter and belly. A quality brown mare, with a mealy muzzle, an intelligent head and a neck the set-on of which was, a trifle, perhaps, quaint caused him to search his memory. Until, one day, he sauntered over to gaze at her in the lines; felt positive, and said, 'Isn't it Philomena? What is this horse's name, Trooper?'

Many a Prince or a Samson was Bobby or Blackie. Philomena had remained Philomena.

Grazebrook's face (long lashes and raddled cheeks) lit up!

The migrating storks flew overhead and there were blooms of every kind. The almond blossom had been displaced by fleshy green nut-cases. It was a time, in Palestine, of scented evenings, and of burgeoning insects.

V ENDURING

With these advantages in numbers, in efficiency, and in spirit, a victory was to be looked for. The manner of that victory—the boldness of the design, the sureness of its execution, the completeness of the enemy's ruin—make the operation a strategical masterpiece.

The plan was daring, but simple.

COLONEL A. P. WAVELL, C.M.G., M.C. *The Palestine Campaigns*

On the way we passed the column of Turkish transport carts with the animals—mules, donkeys, oxen, standing patiently in the shafts. It is more than probable that they were enduring hunger, thirst and fatigue, but there was no time or possibility to attend to their wants. I do not know what eventually became of them. God forgive us the suffering which, in pursuit of our own selfish aims, we bring to the animals over which we have been given dominion!

GENERAL SIR GEORGE DE S. BARROW, G.C.B., K.C.M.G. *The Fire of Life*

I hated to remember but could not forget.

MRS GEOFFREY BROOKE

53 Nanny in Cairo

Philomena had been for so long in her mind that Griselda still looked about herself with amazement, riveted by exotic scenes, the scents of dust, charcoal smoke, dung ... She was so frightfully *interested*. She'd catch her breath and think, Philomena was here! Then, Philomena *is* here! And, Nanny too is here!

Griselda would never, ever, have questioned the necessity of keeping Nanny (reunited with her sewing-machine) happy.

Griselda *always* devoted much time to it.

Nanny had taken against the harmless dragoman sent by Cook to conduct them from the ship at Alexandria to the hotel in Cairo. They owed to Cook the retrieval of the baggage.

The Gezireh Palace ('In the old days a Khedivial *palace*, Nanny!') had, however, gone down well.

The Gezireh Palace wasn't as dear as Shepheard's or the Semiramis. It was as natural to Griselda to lash out on what was cheap *in relation* as it was to dwell at dear Bark Hart in utter eccentricity and minus one's indoor servants.

Nanny glowered with favour upon the garden, its bougainvillaea, its gingko and jacaranda trees, its leaning palms, its light, its shadows. A band played in the garden twice weekly. Sumptuous public rooms mollified Nanny, and ... beyond the gilded pavilion ... so did the position beside the Nile.

Soon Nanny would be speaking of profligacy.

The sun, rising over the Mokattam Hills, caused the stone of the distant minarets to glow rosily, and bathed the nearer, more cosmopolitan buildings without penetrating the Nile's serpentine green.

Nanny was within two steps of the gardens of the Aquarium, a perfect spot for children and their nurses. Amabel and Nanny could stroll to the lush perimeter of the Sporting Club.

Griselda herself was still unwell.

She believed she was grappling with the various obstacles. One engaged, with ease, servants. Through the good offices of the chief *sofragi*, the Gezireh Palace's magnificent personage, Griselda had hired a country girl to minister to the nursery.

Soon after the dawn ... when the *fellaheen* began to pour, radiant with produce, across the Kasr en-Nil Bridge, trailed by dromedaries, discernible by legs and heads yet in every other respect ambulatory bundles (Griselda couldn't hear the tinkle of their bells, they were too far away), and donkeys that bore baskets of gasping vegetables ... there might be an ox-cart in this procession and there were horses ... shortly after this, the girl was delivered.

Day after day, alone with Nanny, Munia unwrapped her head (a cotton shawl). On her forehead was a tattoo, and brass earrings stretched her ears. Too shy to speak.

Griselda had said, 'Nanny, please don't hide your light under a bushel, I know you have your own way of communicating, common language or no!'

Nanny had tightened her lips.

So Nanny, who hadn't cared for male servants (and in the most intimate performance of duties) on board, was, Griselda assumed, cock-a-hoop!

'Munia's chaperon is a husband, madam,' observed Nanny.

Griselda owed her introduction at the Sporting Club to a letter from the *Koh-i-Noor* flame ... 'Nanny, such acquaintances can be *noble*!' Griselda buttered up the Secretary and, as a non-resident visitor ('Sounds like a bird'), was offered the loan of a polo pony, Moti. Delightful! That left Amabel.

Griselda hated to think that her children might grow up without riding, hunting, shooting for boys, fishing, without the knack to train a dog or blow an egg ... Nanny was proficient in the last of these.

It wouldn't have mattered had Georgie (dear Georgie) not been able to boil an egg. He was a better timer than the clock. The very contrast with Bark Hart made Griselda laugh. A man to wash their clothes had been employed, and a syce for Moti, a retinue floated in and out of the hotel on Mrs Romney's business, or crouched in attendance on her wishes.

This, it seemed, was customary.

Less of the thing was the lack of 'a sign' from Mrs Larshaw.

Amabel was having bad dreams ... never mind that. Amabel and Nanny's bedchamber had a window onto the inner garden. The fall of the water in the fountains would cool the child's brain.

While Amabel, in a straw hat, dabbled her legs, or stalked birds in the shade, or read to Nanny, stumbling, *Pilot*, from *Pilot and Other Stories*, that highly-strung, kind, precious being might knit, or do her crochet, in a cushioned, palm-wicker chair, sipping lemonade, *grenadine* or strong Indian tea.

Nanny gazed anxiously at Mrs Romney on occasions that grew more and more numerous. The inspection tried Griselda.

True, Griselda had been in hope (Monsieur Imran might have had his uses too). More particular uses than the flame—she'd had three scrawls from Colonel Black, written from Wady Halfa! Too far. Wady Halfa was in the Sudan! At the Second Cataract. Even if she did rather long to lay eyes again on him ... her dancing partner ... her flirt in Algiers.

More uses, perhaps, than Farrier-Sergeant-Major 'Dusty' O'Connel at the Abbas Hilmy

Barracks.

Griselda had bumped into Larshaw in the Club. At General Larshaw's instigation, the farrier sergeant-major had presented himself and professed himself able and willing, when duties permitted, to accompany Mrs Romney in her 'pursuit'.

O'Connel knew Cairo and possessed rudimentary Arabic. She felt dubious about O'Connel.

She took him to inspect Moti. It was O'Connel who saw that Moti had been taught to lift a foreleg to beg for sugar.

Griselda could have sat down with Imran in the Gezireh Palace, and ordered coffee. Ironic that she could take O'Connel into the Sporting Club (certain areas), and her syce, Shams, entered, 'in his capacity'; for Imran would have been barred.

In 1914, the High Commissioner at the time, Lord Kitchener, had engineered the resignation of the pasha Members. He'd suspected them of anti-British chatter. These days, five or six cultured Egyptians, superb at tennis or polo, were welcomed.

Nanny thought breakfast in bed spoke of sloth. The cold, cross gaze of Professor A.P.P. Mulchard had suddenly lent breakfast in bed an appeal. The last creature Griselda wished to lay eyes on was using the Gezireh Palace (in preference to the Mena House) as his base.

Mulchard was a different man.

A period of triumph, of commanding an army of Egyptian labourers, donkeys and English adorers, in full ardour, with sieves and cataloguing, photographs, identifying and dating, had soothed his digestion. Possibly A.P.P. Mulchard did know of her disgrace. He couldn't have realized how unjust. He was such a funny fellow: he rose to his feet, smiled thinly; approached her to say shake hands.

Mulchard scorned the Sporting Club.

In the *Principessa*, she hadn't 'placed' Imran. With her new knowledge, she thought he might belong in that stratum known as the *effendi* class. Egypt was in ferment. The Protectorate was on the point of being abolished. Which was what she, Egypt, had demanded. Allenby, present High Commissioner in Egypt, would be back any day. And the Gezireh Palace was a haven.

Nanny had said, 'No need to wrap yourself up in the nursery.' Griselda dined alone.

The obsequiousness was in such contrast to Imran's dignified composure. The hotel's people practically kissed the floor. As for the shopkeepers (under their fancy English fascia boards), Griselda thought they *did* kiss the ground.

Dinner invitations came.

She looked for Imran in vain.

Gharries congregated from dawn to dusk by the Gezireh Palace and the Sporting Club. There were horses with army brands, the NZ

288

of the New Zealand regiments, the broad arrow and over-large initials of the requisitioning officer that marked Walers. The broad arrow of the British. All these brands were cancelled by the welt of the letter C.

One bay gelding, lovingly turned out, had so hollow a back he had to have been thirty-five. Other horses were not so lovingly harnessed, were galled; smart though they were with swinging throat plumes. There were the smaller Syrians, bred in Egypt, with Arab blood; and other brands (a five-pointed star was frequent).

Griselda noticed that the breeching (broader than breeching in England) was *not* too tight.

And, as the distant, dawn cavalcade over the Kasr en-Nil Bridge surged, daily, beyond the great lions on their columns, Griselda never even turned her head.

54 'The man to see'

Griselda crossed the Nile in a gharry and, at half past eight, stepped into Rawlinson's office. The sun was large and golden. Light was reflected across Rawlinson's clutter; although his windows faced to the west.

Rawlinson, being as large as the sun in his own importance, was in crumpled suit and tarboosh. When harassed, he pushed the tarboosh askew. On his desk lay a fly-swish with a fine, kid-covered handle and loop; and grey horsehair. Rawlinson grated his chair. Shaking hands seemed to cost him an effort. Griselda was determined to be civil.

Rawlinson snorted.

('Passionately caught up in his job, my dear, and you shouldn't confuse his manner with his years of instilling humane ideas. He creeps about *at night*, risking his life.') At dead of night, all the crocks emerged like bats; and Rawlinson courted murder. Day or night, Rawlinson didn't dare approach the stone quarries. In the stone quarries toiled pack-animals, in dreadful dust and heat, to convey stone up to the road; where it crashed into carts, to which were harnessed horses only marginally less unfortunate.

('If you know this . . . knowing this . . . ?' and 'Oh, no, Mrs Romney, one tries to *forget* . . .')

Old troopers and artillery-horses had strength and courage. ('Their uses are first exhausted in the streets. When *extinguished*, they go to the stone quarries.') Just as the broken-down English thoroughbreds descended from glory on the racecourse to servitude.

('After the unspeakable struggle, my dear, of the War, you fritter your energies on *horses*? Of course, it *was* a scandal at the time. Caused an outcry!')

Griselda was disappointed in Rawlinson. It

was not to occur to her for weeks that he and she shared sympathies.

Rawlinson had been responsible for the inspection of civilian animals in Cairo, and for the enforcement of regulations and law in respect to their protection. The new government had taken up the reins of Egyptian civil administration at the highest level, and Rawlinson's function was merely to be Secretary to the S.P.C.A. and to the Agricultural Society.

'The back streets,' he said, 'are not for you! Do you not read the newspapers? It is a time of unrest. One horse among thousands? Dead, I suppose. Or in Alexandria, Tanta, or Siwa; or in Upper Egypt!'

He squinted at her.

'My advice to you, ma'am, is not to meddle. Don't want to provoke an incident! *On board ship with the Larshaws*, were you not? A wee bird, yes ... Mrs will advise you ... if you let her. Pushy Larshaw. She'll do the trick. Put you off the notion and turn your head for home!'

Still Griselda smiled.

He gobbled in silence. The veins of his hands pulsed.

Spurred by a presentiment, she had written to Georgie, *I may run into danger. I pray that Amabel and Nanny will be safe and that you will look after them.*

It all at once seemed unduly pessimistic.

291

Griselda did rather long for him, her companion of the washing-up. Three weeks ago, the R.A.M.C. chap had been shot in cold blood in the Ezbekiyeh! The other day, a harmless Australian railwayman called Crick.

'Mrs Romney, for how long have you been in Egypt? How *could* you understand?' And in a kinder, gruffer voice, 'But you don't know what you're asking.'

Griselda said she thought she'd be back.

'Drive out to Gizeh, why not? Climb the Great Pyramid . . .'

It was a favourite ride. The acquaintances were forever trotting out along the acacia-lined causeway.

Griselda, being Griselda, chose instead to visit a dealer's yard. O'Connel was summoned.

Griselda and O'Connel, together, picked their gharry.

Mr Seiyid Salaheddin el-Bari, or Abu Abdelkarim, was a genuine character, who had addled a sum in supplying the British Army (reliably) and buying remounts cast at Abbasiyeh, said O'Connel.

His premises may have been handy to the Barracks, but Abu Abdelkarim knew English ladies.

He had three pure-bred Arabians for Mrs Romney and Sergeant-Major O'Connel to admire. Quality animals. Griselda, staring about her, letting her eyes wander past Abu Abdelkarim's considerable presence and bare, brown feet, would inspect *every* horse, every mule, every jack; every jenny.

The jack donkeys were dearer than jennies, and uglier. These donkeys had big sores on their knees, and down behind their legs; great, white, oozing absences of skin. O'Connel remarked, 'They fight with each other, hobbled or no.' The wounds were bites.

Griselda grew dejected.

A dozen had sores on their rumps. 'Children! They whack them, and whack them, in the same spot,' said O'Connel. One donkey was a collapsing blancmange. And a bay gelding with a star had a suppurating wound under the saddle that made Griselda sick at heart. 'From the Pyramids!' said Abu Abdelkarim. He let this sink in—the implication. Trippers. 'I deplore this, *madaam.*'

Philomena wasn't there, at all events.

Griselda bought, for Amabel, a grey jenny donkey. 'Muzz' chose the name. 'Be on your guard, darling, you mustn't get *fond* of Humbug!'

Amabel squinted. Full of doubts.

Shams, their *syce*, made Amabel laugh. He had a droopy moustache; yet his black hair was in tight curls. On his head was a cloth (skimpy), and he tied a rakish belt around his *gallabiyeh*. He wasn't a Cairene. He was *bedawi*, from the Western Desert. Ex-prisoner-of-war. Shams had been syce to some 'ruddy sweet cobbers'.

Too late to have said that he was unsuitable!

Donkey saddles in Egypt were odd affairs, with a bulbous leather pommel, a hump. The rider was thrust onto the animal's loins. Griselda begged an army saddler to make a felt saddle, with crupper and stirrup leathers; and a bridle with a small snaffle.

The minute Amabel was let off the leading rein, Humbug executed an about-turn; and those narrow, annoying hindquarters would tootle. Getting the better of Hum would do wonders for Amabel; and for Amabel's grit.

Nanny's sewing-machine was enjoying Cairo. They'd been to a shop in Suleiman Pasha where Nanny was destined to find herself an honoured customer. On wonderful new materials, the sewing-machine twiddled away, and its smocking and ruffling attachments issued happy little twangs as they emerged from the box.

'Egypt' was all going swimmingly. Griselda felt at a loss.

55   In the Jordan Valley

Finding Philomena had warmed his heart. His heart was with the 9th Cavalry Brigade in France; although he'd met with nothing but kindness. And then he'd spotted Conker. Alan

Grazebrook had written about them—Griselda's horses—to his aunt.

Patterson, the South African, hadn't remembered Conker; but Flower had. Conker had been killed in the famous Charge at Agagiya. Flower was positive. The bay with the Roman nose was soon proved to be another.

Philomena was much changed.

She couldn't be called hollow-backed. There was a finer, angular look about most of the horses. Her eye was less brilliant. Alan Grazebrook laughed, rather, over the whole notion that she should be going strong here in Palestine. She had seen action and been wounded. Years as a troop-horse had told on her. Her mouth couldn't be what it had been. He didn't doubt that she'd been 'ruined'. He trusted she'd get through the War.

If Philomena recognized him at all, she didn't perceive in him her saviour. There were umpteen of him; slight, neat officers with bushy moustaches, open faces and drawn features, who smoked their baccy in pipes. They chewed the mouthpiece, and every so often examined the teeth-marks absently.

The stolid Awshew, had she but known it, might have contrived to have had himself issued, instead, with a sensible bay mare whose hoof had borne the brand of the Royal Bucks Hussars. Major Grazebrook was aware of this.

So Philomena had some reputation, then!

Awshew was a funny chap. He hailed from

the back streets of Fawernbridge, so he wasn't one of 'they knowing strappers' or whippers-in. His seat had owed more to the fairground until it had been worked upon in the *manège*; and would never be a joy. He'd never learn light hands. But he didn't ride heavy. Early in his service he'd done a punishable thing. He'd failed to strap a pack up proper, off of the loins. He'd had to drill for four hours; in rotten heat. He was now a creditable shot; and a resourceful soldier.

When, late in May, the Regiment marched to Gaza and on across the Philistine plain, to wind up the Jerusalem road, looking back at the minarets of Ludd and Ramla, bivouacking on the pass at Kuryet el-Enab, where seven horses were struck off; through Jerusalem by 6 a.m. and on up *via* the Mount of Olives, passing black tents of glowering Bedouin, to look from the red rocks and dull, crystal sand onto an inland sea, far below, it was Awshew who marched at her head or, a wiry ten stone two, in the saddle.

The descent into the Jordan Valley was peculiar. The air pressed, and rose; arriving like waves. It disconcerted Philomena. She met a new midge, at that altitude; a tiny jumper: it settled in the ears, and bit and bit.

Gritty, red-grey crests seemed to pull themselves up short, to teeter over the abyss. The bumps and elongated ridges of the wastes were corrugated by the bottomless ravines.

Mountains shimmied faintly in the haze to the east. The column, with its halo of steam, descended; around curling bends.

When they'd sunk, yet were not nearly at the bottom, the road split. The cavalry had chosen the shorter route. The R.H.A. and the transport would go round.

The afternoon was horrid.

Other brigades had marched at night the twenty-seven miles from Enab to Jericho. Philomena noticed the shadows of the wings of birds of prey. They bivouacked. There was no water for the horses; who could, however, scent it.

Three more were evacuated.

They marched at two, by moonlight.

Philomena could see the road, the abyss, the tumbles of rock, the rearing of cliffs and in the strata the mouths of caves; saw them for what they were and not for what they weren't. Awshew, unseeing, paid no attention to topography.

Grazebrook was in a curious state, over-sensitive; and the unexpected presence of Philomena had made him whimsical.

They watered at Wadi Kelt. Awshew filled Philomena's canvas bucket. She pushed away the dust with her lip. They crossed the skirt of the white, salt delta; and they were held up, in readiness to move at four hours' notice. Four nights outside the cluster of awful houses that was Jericho. Veterinary inspection in the

297

lines ... and six horses were struck off the strength.

The Regiment encamped two miles north of Jericho. The horse-lines were within range of the enemy's big guns.

The Lower Jordan Valley defied description; with or without, thought Grazebrook, a nod to censorship. Vultures watched it.

Three miles away, in the dense, sweating jungle of the gorge and its tangles of bleached flotsam and thorn, there were partridge, hares and wild boar. In the right season. There was also a plague of mosquitoes, in the gorge and here on the dust; centipedes that could pinch so severely that a man might die with blood poisoning; the worst scorpions, black spiders the size of two mice; and, whereas the least scrape, Major Grazebrook had been told, would have produced anywhere in Palestine 'a nasty', these sores were such that the M.O. never stopped; and men went down with ailments, or off to hospital fearfully ill. Sand-fly fever was too jolly prevalent. These beggars could get through all but the most stifling of mosquito-netting.

Their ground was composed of flour. The horses raised a cloud of it whenever they stirred from the lines. They were watered in darkness, twice in every twenty-four hours, some four miles away at canvas troughs filled from the Wadi Kelt; since the billows that followed them caught the attention of enemy artillery-spotters. Nine horses were killed whilst watering. Philomena didn't see this. Other mounted brigades watered to the north, with serious losses.

The tin hats, issued to officers and men, were fatuous.

The 6th Mounted Brigade became 10th Cavalry Brigade. And the G.O.C. was moved sideways; to the grief of all.

Forage for the horses was mediocre: 6lbs of crushed barley, 4 lbs of gram and 12 lbs *tibbin*. Unless *boiled*, barley was daft. So said the knowing to Awshew. Chickpeas? Diabolical!

Grazebrook's chargers enjoyed shelters of bamboo and bulrushes. Philomena didn't have the luxury. Indiscriminate cutting of branches was forbidden. Awshew had protected her spine from the sun. She was piled with folded blankets. Yet all wheeled transport had to be shielded from the blaze.

The spokes shrivelled and got loose, else.

Whenever Awshew off-saddled, he stretched Philomena's bridle pommel-to-cantle (with bit at the pommel), and secured, by the surcingle, a blanket over it.

Awshew was everlastingly digging and wiring. There was no Egyptian labour. Then, so many were sick, or bitten, or stung, that Awshew was looking after six. One hundred and thirty degrees in the shade. It did him in . . . Once in a while, he summoned the go for housey-housey, or for to sing along.

Funnelled from the north, a wind blew grit in a swirl from sunrise until about half past ten; when it dropped. A furnace-like heat stifled every mortal creature for half an hour or so. Until the sun dropped, the south wind blew all the grit back up the valley, laced with salt.

Other days dawned so still it was horrible.

The horses were better unshod. Their shoes heated to burning. A rifle that touched the coat *singed* it.

Philomena bore the flies; stamped and swished her tail and shook her head. The sand-fly hurt the worst. The ordinary flies *looked* ordinary but the fly-fringe was feeble. Like a rounded black wart, a cluster would sit on the eye. The sweating meant that the flies perched, from poll to croup, on the twitching skin of saddled-up horses. Flies sat on top of flies. When Awshew went over Philomena with the sweat-scraper he scraped flies. The horses were tired, and morose.

Their dung was burned. Camp rubbish was buried.

Patrols were tediously hot. Or they might be hot though not tedious ... Outpost work and guarding bridges and fords took them southwards, from the tropical gorge to the glare of the white salt pancake onto which the tons of water of the River Jordan, green and sinewy, spilt; never, in summer, to reach the Dead Sea.

The shingle and rocks around the Dead

Sea's shore were encrusted in salt. The valley floor was desolation.

When Grazebrook laid his head down, he couldn't breathe. The sulphurous stink seeped even through the groundsheet. He wrote to his aunt at Toller Bottom about the more uplifting scenery; the mountains, the monastery like an eerie . . .

It was a victory: no Europeans had ever, *ever*, maintained a presence in the Jordan Valley in the summer. Nor had English horses. Our forces were holding the bridgehead at Ghoraniyeh.

56 A toe in the water

The spring in Cairo was ravishing. Griselda was determined. These two thoughts remained uppermost.

Amabel had been the first to spot Imran. As though at home, in what was an *imposing* hotel, he'd penetrated, conducted there by a *sofragi*, to the garden terrace, to look for them. Such informality had surprised Griselda. Not annoyed her.

He proved to be an excellent escort. Griselda found herself spending much time in his company. Their acquaintance seemed unsullied and sunny.

Imran had little interest in horses. He

assumed that she should go where she wanted to go, more or less. That would suit. Imran had his own priorities for her. Imran guided her into mosques, and showed her how to allow felt over-slippers to be placed on her feet, shoe and all. He himself removed his shoes, facing the soles one to another.

She visited a number of Islamic sights. His gaze would grow liquid and eloquent.

He was also a merry companion. He was keen to talk, to ask questions, and, while never losing his refinement and politeness, he made no bones over such domestic practicalities as the workings of people's insides. At times ('Is Nanny intact?'), Griselda's eyebrows shot up. But she chose to smile.

Imran showed her Fatamid minarets; Ayyubid features and Mameluke. He taught her how to tell the different Sufi orders apart, by the colour of the turbans.

Imran took Amabel and Nanny to the Citadel. At the entrance, there were two-horse gharries. In the streets, Griselda had to whip her head round to allow her eye time to take in every detail. After a while of it, this whipping round was a sort of tic. *Ranks* of gharries were simpler.

At a glance it had been no worse than Naples; *not* that she would wish upon any animal of hers a retirement to Naples.

Gharry horses appeared to be, after a long, rapid trot, pretty done. They were, on the

302

whole, sound. Their harness, on the whole, fitted, and was supple. Some were poled up too tight. It was plain that they were groomed. Coats had a bloom on them. And in moments of rest the sweat-scraper was used. Elderly gents abounded. Griselda thought, the gharry-drivers must take a pride in them. Why else copy the Hussars?

'Hussars!' asked Imran.

'The throat-plume. These cab-drivers must have admired the gay throat-plumes of our chargers. So sweet!'

'If you go into the Museum of Egyptian Antiquities you will notice these plumes.'

Griselda felt foolish.

He'd rarely counter an assertion.

To match the exotic throat-plume was the black silk and the bejewelled *barku* of the ladies of the upper orders. The Copts, Jews and Syrians went out unveiled.

Griselda began *truly* to picture Philomena's life in Cairo.

Philomena had never been broken to harness. Poor darling! Her mouth had been rather good.

How Philomena would have hated the jerk on the reins that, in all countries, distinguished the peasant 'whip'! Philomena would have jibbed and been stubborn. The lash of the kurbash would have landed on her rump.

Cairo wasn't hilly. There were *slopes*. Small boys hit with their hard sticks donkeys that

303

were trying to hold back carts.

The donkeys were driven bitless. There was a chain over the nose. There was a wide noseband. The noseband *could* be covered by the chain. Generally, it concealed what the chain did to the nose. The chains ate into the nose-bones to a depth of quite half an inch.

Donkeys went about, if spared the dinner plate on the rump, with a grievous nose. Suppurating pus.

Three grievous noses, harnessed abreast.

'Why does nobody turn to stare?' said Griselda, in the square outside the Gami' Sultan Hasan. A return to the Citadel without Nanny.

'Stare at what, *madame*?'

Scavengers flew overhead. The kites.

Griselda frowned over her first foal (winter foal) in the august surroundings of the Abdin Palace. The exhaustion in the face, the wobbly legs, the mysteriously deformed spine. Griselda was to puzzle over these roach backs.

It wasn't to dawn on her, not for weeks and weeks, that burdens might be put on them.

If Griselda did have Nanny with her, she would, of course, draw to Nanny's attention the costumes, the mill, the fortune-tellers; artisans that tap-tapped on brass or stitched red shoes. She and Imran exposed Amabel to killims, carpets, jewellery. Amabel, wielding her very own fly-swish, struggled not to gawp at dwarfs.

304

Griselda's eyes were drawn to creased and cracked collars, and their tufts of escaping straw. To the sheer weight of the harness saddle. The saddles were high, of painted wood; *for show*.

Gharries had brakes. Worn brakes. Egypt lacked drag shoes, or skids. The flat-bed carts and trolleys, without brakes, weren't held back by breeching either. Shortened shafts shot forward on their little chains (pole chains) and a horse or donkey could be thrust bodily on or up; hoisted by the belly-band.

Imran had volunteered to take her into every gharry stable. To visit every dealer. He barred Amabel and Nanny.

Gharry stables were beastly. Dark and stinking. Bedding was unheard-of. Griselda pitied creatures that never had a proper chance to lie down.

In England there was still firing. With numbing and the greatest care afterwards. Griselda didn't like it; but it could and did answer for splints. When she saw the suppurating handiwork of quacks, in this climate, Griselda herself burned.

There was an old bay, with gaunt intelligence: he'd caught her once near the Abdin Palace (the first foal) and once at the door of the Semiramis (where she'd gone, as one did, to drink green, mint tea). *Whickered* to her, remembering her sugar lumps.

Awful.

Beyond the Bab en-Nasr, a bright chestnut was lying dead, speared by a splintered shaft.

'It is necessary,' Imran would say. 'It is necessity.'

Perhaps the horses knew that the call to prayer, that exquisite, curling sound, brought a rest. (At noon, *Madame* could be entrusted to a delighted Syrian Christian shopkeeper.) For some minutes, they hung their heads, lost in their own world of endurance and misery.

Or, with the bridle and rusty bit removed, they ate their nosebags. Nosebags, which, in the effort to search their every cranny, they buried on the ground.

'But *never* to hear a kind word spoken, Nanny!' Griselda said.

Griselda had four crumpled photographs. Artisans, after what was to her a tedious exchange of courtesies, were glad to gaze and give serious thought to Philomena. Once, Griselda discovered she'd bought a handsome Turkoman carpet, from Mosul, with colours of deepest red, sea-blue and cypress-green.

She was even to buy a shroud.

A rather lovely shroud.

Imran took Griselda to Heliopolis and Ma'adi; to Gizeh, to the University, to the Zoo. To Masr el-Kadimeh.

Train, electric tram, gharry, boat.

Griselda was 'pulled' by the streets within a stone's throw of the Citadel. To the *suk*, noisome; to the scents of spices. There were secretive cafés she couldn't enter. Music seeped thinly like steam. To the crunch of iron-bound wheels, the rumble of hide-bound; and the dim weaving of the purblind, the stumble of the lame, the clink of worn shoes.

Imran puzzled her.

She thought, he worships me.

And when he returned her (wrung out) to Amabel and Nanny, she only had to wander out in the evening to the Nile ... to see a flying chariot (novel pneumatic tyres) on the Kasr en-Nil Bridge and whooping youths that would gallop an empty vehicle.

57   In the rear

Jericho had been entered by Ausdiv on February 21st, 1918. The Q.O.D.Y. had not been in the Jordan Valley at the time of the raids on the east bank, in March and April, towards Amman and the Hedjaz railway.

In the second, mounted infantry, infantry and cameleers, troops from three divisions, had crossed the Jordan, climbed the ghastly tracks and occupied the town of Es Salt, filling its hospital with wounded, all of whom had had to be evacuated, trickily, that same evening.

These were reverses.

Australian Mounted Infantry regiments

(some) were absorbing sword drill in six short weeks, with typical *brio*. Given the *arme blanche* they'd hankered after.

There were no horse casualties when 'C' Squadron, in pushing an outpost forward, was engaged by the enemy. Captain Pitt retired his squadron two hundred yards; drew his sword, rallied his yeomen and forced a withdrawal.

Two horses were killed when Lieutenant Fitzpaine, a sergeant, a trumpeter corporal and Private Dilks charged two Turkish gun-teams. Three of the four laid down their lives.

In a skirmish in June, another officer was lost. Poor Phelps.

Fifteen horses, with shrapnel wounds, were evacuated. Twenty-four had, cruelly, been scythed in the lines.

Then the horses of 'A' Squadron, with a single shackle on the foreleg, *bombed* by the enemy, pulled up their pegs, stampeded and blundered into wire. Three were destroyed. Ten were lamed; having strained their pasterns.

Turkish cavalry to the north was reputed to have its own horse-lines in trenches, and underground in caves.

None of this could Alan Grazebrook relay, in his pleasing hand, to his aunt. Irene Romney. One couldn't tell one's aunt that the troopers called the Ghoraniyeh bridgehead 'Gonorrhoea'. So he said that Griselda's mare was well.

Philomena had been lucky. She hadn't witnessed these scenes of mayhem. Horses that went bravely into action responded badly to being shelled while eating their nosebags. They heard an incoming shell before a man did. Experience might have taught them the different sounds of nine-pounder, thirteen-pounder, fifteen-pounder and bomb: the *effect* confused them.

Philomena dreamt of shell-bursts and screaming. Of galloping at guns that raged and blazed. Of yelling. Of singed whiskers. Of hurting ears; and abrupt silence. Of a trooper, sword in hand, leaning, standing in his stirrups, his weight's shifting, twisting in the saddle. Her saddle. She was thirsty.

The horses licked the salt.

Infernal vigilance in hygiene kept down the incidence of malaria and tummy bugs. Sores and septic bites had to be bandaged. More than the yeomen in the climate, the Indians sickened. Their devotion to their horses was touching; and they employed sand-carts, drawn by a pair, to drag in concussed and wounded horses. Or they carried them on litters, at shoulder height! Theirs was a tradition of veterinary care in the regiment, which Grazebrook admired.

Patrols from both Indian regiments distinguished themselves.

At the end of June, the bigger flies were dying of heat.

Grazebrook reeled from a succession of woes. A scorpion sting, a septic thumb, a go of dysentery. He remained on duty.

Ten horses were evacuated to the Mobile Veterinary Section.

In July, the Dorsets were relieved by Hyderabad Lancers.

Indians weren't to be called 'natives'. Officers had to instruct their men that natives were 'native to a country', Indians were no more native than anybody else.

Thirteen horses were unfit to march. One squadron (mercifully not Philomena's) saddled up one hour and twenty minutes before parade, tiring its horses.

Most other units went to Desert Rest Camp near Bethlehem. Ras Deiran was more distant: it lay on the nose of a hill near Ramla. On the march, Philomena sulked. The air was better for the lungs but her sand muzzle made her cross. Philomena was moody; although she had long ceased to come into season.

She was grazed for an hour every day of her five weeks at Ras Deiran. They were all inspected by a senior Remounts officer. The Regiment took part in a night-time, tactical exercise 'in the field', in 'pursuit of a defeated enemy'.

And the D.Y. went deeply to the rear; to the south of Esdud.

On 10th September 1918, and in the dark, the 4th Division, minus yeomen, marched from the Jordan Valley; away from the pocked, sorrel cliffs.

Tents had not been struck.

Philomena was not there to watch, in the dying heat of September, the picketing out of phantom cavalry, fifteen thousand dummy horses in great, meandering lines. She might have been too listless to snort and stare at dummies made of straw-stuffed canvas and bamboo, and furnished with rugs and nosebags.

The trails from the 'horse-lines' to the Wadi Auja and the Wadi Kelt were to be swept at every dusk and at every midnight to raise the customary billows. The forage to feed the dummies had been requisitioned, and its transport laid on. New bridges had been thrown across the Jordan; and raids by Lawrence and the Sherifian Arabs on the Turkish lines of communication to the east would succeed in enticing reinforcements from Nablus and the Turkish Seventh Army.

To the West Indians would fall the most tedious duty devised. Marching down repeatedly from Jerusalem to Jericho. To be returned by lorry, in moonlight.

Motor transports trundled similarly. Turkish agents in Jerusalem 'knew' that Fast's Hotel, in the Jaffa Road, was to be the forward HQ. Wireless traffic was maintained.

Turkish observers were able to swear that three cavalry divisions, a complete infantry division, gun batteries and other units were in their camps as per usual. Turkish Command anticipated an attack in the Upper Jordan Valley and on the heights of Moab.

The 4th Division, its days made hideous through heat and flies, and fractured sleep, in five wearying stages spirited itself under cover of darkness to orange groves, inland from the sea. Philomena, marching from Yebna by night on the 16th, and having bivouacked at Ramla, found it there.

In the air hung . . . excitement.

58 In a pickle

Amabel had a life of worry.

She hadn't wanted Captain Palsy for a stepfather. Amabel didn't want a stepfather at all. Nobody could take the place of her father. Muzz's keenness for men was the greatest disaster.

All the grown-ups, Nanny, Aunt Ida, her two grandmothers, they'd all whisper over the latest man in tones of dread and exasperation. It irked Amabel. They laughed, they shrugged. They had no idea how thunderous it would be, were Muzz to take it into her head to inflict a *sham papa* on Bark Hart. Bark Hart was perfect without. If her own couldn't be there.

Bark Hart knew.

Amabel thought Bark Hart was waiting for him.

The sun in Egypt was hotter. Nanny's temperament was so far equal to it. Amabel liked to watch the *fellah* who sold starlings by the Nile, under the trees on the site of the outdoor Gezireh market. Starlings were sold live. Otherwise, the blade of the knife sliced across the front of their necks and they were dropped back in the basket with clouded eyes. Some took longer to die than the rest.

It sent Nanny all of a quiver. 'Because, dear! Because!'

Muzz's 'men' always made up to Amabel, tried to sit her on their knees. Captain Palsy was drear. When Amabel had asked, 'Does he kiss you too?' Muzz had answered, 'No, darling.' Amabel *supposed* that had been true. Muzz put great stress on what was required of you. Only white lies. A smaller Amabel had gone through 'a phase', and Muzz had been caustic.

Caustic soda ate the big in the Bark Hart drains.

Amabel spared Peter much of her anxiety. Cairo was a game for the blue roan mare. Cairo had no verges. Amabel took Cairo as she saw it. Every Tuesday, the snake-charmer enticed the snakes from beneath the *shagara* bushes of the Gezireh Palace. This was entertainment that even Nanny could enjoy. Quite as reliably, when no one was paying

313

attention (Amabel, in common with every European child in Egypt, was positive), the snake-charmer, before his departure, restocked the garden.

Amabel wasn't alarmed by Imran. She'd been very alarmed by the dashing Colonel. A smitten Muzz had done a lot of dancing with *him* on board *Koh-i-Noor*, gone ashore in his company, *alone* with him, in Algiers. A freshly smitten Muzz was always dotty. It wore off a bit, then she wasn't so bad. Nanny hadn't got a whiff. Nanny, who had packed a spare pillow for Amabel, would have gone on and on. It was unheard of for Amabel to wet her bed. Thinking about Daddy (and despite the night-light), she soaked her pillow.

In her sleep Amabel dreamt that Nanny went to a place. To a place.

That was all.

Amabel liked being consulted. Muzz asked, 'Has Nanny found her feet, darling? What do you think?'

'I think she's cock-a-hoop.'

'Really!' Muzz was pleased.

To Muzz, Nanny would drop remarks, 'Major Grazebrook, Mr Alan, he must have been here in Suleiman Pasha ...' or 'knelt down in All Saints' ...' or 'played many a *chukker* at your Club ... !'

And Muzz would reply, 'I suppose so!' Muzz's mind was on Philomena.

Nanny couldn't guard Muzz.

314

Amabel didn't admire the dashing ones. She considered that all colonels ought to have had their cheeks corrugated in action. Colonel Black could dance beautifully, he was Irish and light on his feet. The War might have weighed on him. But, no, he'd been gay. He and Muzz were gay together. Instead of riding with Amabel, Muzz rode with *him*. Wouldn't *Georgie* have guarded Muzz?

Muzz had promised to ask Amabel's permission, and Georgie's, before foisting a body on Bark Hart.

Nanny's social engagements took Amabel's eye off Muzz.

There was Fraülein Knoblerhof, nurse to the children of Gamal Pasha, three country girls under her. Nanny said Austrians were strict. There were diplomatic families, and army families. Nanny Gough was pert. Nanny Maitland was pert too. That was enough for Nanny. There weren't many families. They hadn't come out.

Nanny struck up with Miss Welch.

Nanny didn't suggest for a moment that Muzz and Miss Welch would have rubbed along. Miss Welch was governess to the children of an Alexandrian skin doctor, a Greek; who was in Cairo to be consulted.

'Greek . . .' said Nanny guiltily.

That very next Sunday when she was leaning forward and half-closing her eyes, in the pew at All Saints', Muzz even thanked God for

315

Miss Welch.

Miss Welch wasn't present. Miss Welch was chapel. She had a wart. Miss Welch's employer worshipped a Greek god. The acquaintance 'blossomed'. Amabel and eight-year-old Spiros, or Spiro ... Nanny muddled his name and so did Miss Welch ... went with Nanny and Miss Welch to spread tracts to the law students. Nanny considered this interesting.

The tracts were Miss Welch's. She hadn't written the tracts herself. She said she'd drawn the pictures. Amabel considered this unlikely, for the pictures were bad and how could Miss Welch have obtained her position?

The Egyptian troops had turned out to help the police. None was mounted.

The garrison regiment of Imperial cavalry, before Egypt herself posted guards on embassies, was the 8th Hussars. There were four cavalry regiments in Egypt. Muzz had explained that regiments went out to India *via* a tour of duty in the Near East. Our old horses, cast and working in the streets of Cairo, still pricked their ears at the sound of trumpet or bugle. That made Muzz awfully sad. Miss Welch was not bothered. Muzz had said some other war-horses had been deafened. *That* was sad.

The law students, bemused, dropped the tracts. The flimsy tracts got trampled. Nanny reckoned it a waste. Amabel couldn't hear what they said. Amabel was bored.

316

Nanny hadn't a notion as to what all the to-do was about. She muttered, 'Starch does wilt so in the sun, dear.'

The crowd heaved and shouted.

Spiros sucked his thumb.

Nanny hadn't witnessed a demonstration before. Let alone a riot. Miss Welch pointed to the fervour of the Egyptian 'educationalists'! When, in the distance, there was shooting, and shouting, Miss Welch set her chin. Miss Welch was deaf to protest. Nanny said, 'Amabel, hold my hand tightly, we don't want to get lost, not in this bedlam.'

And, tremulously, 'Mummie might be vexed.'

Nanny was out of her depth.

Miss Welch had temerity, so pushed a tract at a bearded student. Amabel watched the semi-translucent globs land in the dust at Miss Welch's toes.

'I do think, Miss Welch, we should be going on!'

'Our duty as Christians, Nanny. Keep your nerve!'

The mob surged towards them. Nanny bit her lip, and swooped on Amabel. Tucked Amabel under her arm. An appalled voice was speaking in Amabel's ear.

'Nanny,' it said, 'follow me!'

'Oh, it's *you*!' gasped Nanny.

Amabel changed hands like a parcel.

Wildly, Nanny sought Miss Welch and Miss Welch's charge.

317

Amabel was hitched on Imran's hip now, and she clung to him around his neck. A human wheelbarrow sped by them. The legs and arms divided between friends. The faces were ablaze, with grief. Weren't they pulling him apart? His clothing around his middle had been crimson. 'Oh, they aren't very expert at first aid!' cried Nanny.

'The *soul of kindness*, that Imran!' breathed Nanny presently to Muzz. Nanny had recovered her colour.

'*No more Miss Welch*,' said Muzz.

Amabel waited patiently for Philomena to be found.

59 Going through the gap

The horses of two divisions, relishing the shade, had been concealed for almost two days within range of the enemy's big guns, in the Arab-owned orange groves that clasped Jaffa in a rich belt. The irrigation channels delivered water. The sea breezes fanned the dark leaves. Otherwise, in daylight, not a thing stirred. No fires were permitted; not at any hour. For miles around Sarona and Selmeh the groves teemed with cavalry; and its mules, donkeys, ambulances, horse-drawn and motor transport. Bulbuls rubbed shoulders on the branches.

Infantry camps, maintained on half-battalion

strength, had, with no outward alteration, filled up.

Our forces had supremacy in the air.

To face eight thousand unsuspecting Turkish infantry and one hundred and thirty guns on the Plain of Sharon, Allenby had massed thirty-five thousand rifles, three thousand sabres and three hundred and eighty-three guns. Regarding his Mohammedans—Ramadan was at an end. Four infantry divisions were to punch through on the coast; and the 4th and 5th Divisions of the Desert Mounted Corps to pass through them—the 5th Division along the beach. The Australian Mounted Division, in bivouac back at Ludd, would follow.

A kind of pincer movement towards Nablus by XX Corps in the hills alerted the enemy: it didn't alarm him.

Closer at hand, Awshew saddled up before dawn, and stood to; ready to march at 0455 hours from their leafy orange grove. It was September 19th. *Their* easy, Philomena's and Awshew's, had been for five and three-quarter hours, merely.

The horse-artillery batteries had gone up. They would rejoin their brigades in the advance. The infantry, deployed to positions from which they were to attack the first trench system, started quietly to move. At 4.30 a.m. the big guns opened up.

Turkish Seventh Army HQ at Nablus and

Eighth Army HQ at Tul Keram were bombed from the air. The Air Force also disabled the telephonic and telegraphic exchange at El Afuleh, cutting communications to Turkish Army Group HQ in Nazareth.

The big guns shook the earth. Philomena, in the dark, was very surprised to see the velvet sky explode. Out to sea, there were flashes, orange and green. Two destroyers, *Druid* and *Forester*, were bombarding the coast road.

After fifteen minutes, thin bands of sky, like slits in gummed eyelids, paled over the eastern heights.

Intricate and daring planning would bring the head of the 4th Division to a little over two miles from the Turkish trenches ... and without masking the artillery. The 5th Cavalry Division had been on the pale yellow sands since the evening.

A moving barrage was laid down at 100 yards per minute. A swift, general advance was ordered. Across the Front, the forward units of the infantry marched behind the curtain of fire—the Turks in turn shelled abandoned positions and the incoming shells exploded harmlessly.

Around Philomena, birds still fluttered from their night-time roosts.

Barrow had issued the order, '*Spare neither horse nor rider*'! But 'Billy' Barrow never ceased to consider the horses keenly. Upon them rested so much.

None was carrying more than seventeen stone. Twenty-one pounds of it was crushed barley in a nosebag and in a sandbag. Under the saddle were two blankets. For Awshew, one iron ration, two days' emergency rations, two water-bottles. His great-coat and tin hat did not come; nor did his spare clothing; nor did picketing gear. A further day's rations: relegated to a limber-wagon. Thereafter the Division was to live off the country; requisition *and pay for* forage and rations. Philomena had been freshly shod. All surpluses had been handed back to Ordnance at Ludd. Grazebrook was restricted to one pack-horse; his batman to a white donkey.

Soon after six-thirty, they got to a purposeful river, thirty yards wide; and they crossed by the Khadra bridge. Ten bridges had been thrown across the Nahr el-Auja. In earlier 'training' exercises, pontoons had been constructed and again dismantled. An informer would have noted little untoward.

Philomena was watered here. Awshew off-saddled. She was given a small feed. They marched from the Auja, into dunes, at 0730 hours.

By the time they assembled in brigade mass to the rear of the 7th (Indian) Infantry Division's attack, the 60th, 7th, 3rd (Lahore) and 54th Divisions had rushed the Turks.

The trench system occupied a soft, shallow ridge, to a depth of about three thousand yards.

The front troops of the 60th had overwhelmed its western end at speed, in order to establish a bridgehead on the Nahr el-Falik, at the seaward end of the second.

Pioneer parties had gone in on their heels. The wire was being cut, and the first trenches filled or ramped.

The 5th Cavalry Division, hidden by cliffs, began on the instant to go through.

Barrow's Fourdiv, two miles inland, and exposed, was obliged to wait until the enemy had been cleared out of the entire length of the second defences, two miles on.

At eight thirty, Philomena and Awshew moved forward; to halt one hundred yards from the marked track. To Philomena the tang of high explosive was stifling. The infantry had planted red and blue flags. At two minutes to nine, the advanced guard (Jacob's Horse) of the 4th Cavalry Division flowed into the gap.

It was an extraordinary moment.

Philomena and Awshew filed over the 'bridges' of earth and through the Turkish works. Their Brigade was third through. Most of the wounded had already been got out. Those waiting had been stripped of their weapons.

Unexploded ordnance was a hazard. The horses had to pick their way, even on this marked track, across splinters of timber, nails, twisted metal. Major Grazebrook remarked that Richard the Lionheart had defeated Saladin between the two Turkish trench systems.

After negotiating the second of these, plus the Nahr el-Falik, the regiments re-formed in open country.

No gap could have been more satisfactorily punched; and no cavalry could have passed into enemy territory with more glee!

Awshew hadn't been bred either a horseman or a soldier and had learnt these skills painstakingly: his cheerfulness *leapt*. To Major Grazebrook, who had manoeuvred his toys and marbles through the hummocks of a mump- and measle-contagious eiderdown, it was a thrill of undisguised immensity. Philomena sensed the mood. Philomena went with a will.

Grassy ground rolled over downy hills, cut into by harmless marshes. There were trees, groves and crops for cover. If stretches of tight sand would make harder going for the limbered wagons, it was perfect cavalry country.

The Division was able to push forward with speed. The Turkish infantry were in a state of hectic retreat. In mid-morning, the advanced guard sent back two hundred and fifty prisoners. Captured vehicles were constantly rumbling towards Philomena. A rabid fox, swaying and red-eyed, had to be shot.

They were hoorah-ed as they passed through

the most forward units of the infantry, 60th
Division. More the roar of a race-crowd than
the war-cry of a charge.

Whooping made the horses step out, and
many an ear flickered.

Another exhilarating stretch. There was a
halt at Umm Sur, due west of Tul Keram; by a
watercourse.

Over the Plain of Sharon, the sun was at the
zenith.

Philomena failed (unaccountably) to get a
drink. The horses were hot; sweating. She was
given her nosebag.

To the rear, those fellows of the 60th, with
the former cameleers of the 5th A.L.H.
Brigade, were swinging east by now, towards
Tul Keram and Messoudieh Junction in
Samaria—in the second stage of the operation.
The 7th Division was heading for Et Taiyibeh;
the 75th for Et Tireh. Already the 3rd had
faced right and would assault the Tabsor
defences, and carry the villages of Jiljulieh and
Kalkilieh. The 54th, with the French Palestine
Contingent, north of Kefr Kasim in the hills,
were encountering some of the stiffest fighting.

Throughout the afternoon, the scouts
reported bodies of Turkish reinforcements.
The cavalry had orders not to engage them.

The Nahr Iskanderun (known to be salty)
was forded. The wide marshes would be a trial
to the transport.

At six in the evening, a halt for three hours—

tactically, three precious hours—was supposed to allow every horse water, a rest and a feed. Swiftness of movement was so crucial.

At El Medjel, ten miles to the rear of the rest of the Brigade, the yeomen found the *wadi* was a trickle. The *wadi* ran, according to Major Grazebrook, into the Crusaders' 'Dead River'. At 8 a.m. Philomena hadn't swallowed to the full. Waiting now, she broke out a sweat; afresh. At 7 p.m. she was satisfied.

The Brigade, meanwhile, around the railway-station of Kerkur, had but two deep wells. Some squadrons were dispersed to the villages.

Other brigades fared similarly.

At the end of that warm day, with a long night ahead, there would be doubt in the mind of General Barrow as to whether all horses had got a drink.

Barrow's orders had required 10 Cav to march at ten o'clock, to lead the Division over the Musmus Pass. Through some shocking muddle, brigade orders were rather different. The Brigade had expected to march at eleven thirty. The advanced guard, the 2nd Lancers, moved out only at a quarter to nine, to wait five miles on. An apoplectic General Barrow, visiting Brigade HQ, discovered the mistake for himself.

It wasn't to be the sole blunder.

There were four routes through the Samarian Hills. Napoleon (explained Major

Grazebrook) had taken the westernmost, to Tel Keimun. Between Napoleon and Barrow's 4th Division, the 5th Cavalry Division got what was a commodious passage.

The summit of the Musmus Pass was 1,200 feet above sea level. In fourteen miles, the road rose from three hundred feet, to descend to five hundred and fifty. The six-mile defile, after the last village, was narrow and V-shaped. The Turks had repaired the surface, but it was stony. A couple of machine guns, on the heights: that was all that would be needed to hold them up.

Philomena bustled from El Medjel: she was tired but game. The Indian regiments had destroyed three distressed, of theirs.

The moon was bright; so bright that the shadows loomed and leered bizarrely. Out of Kerkur, marching late, the Dorset Yeomanry led. Awshew knew that ahead of their squadrons, in column of half-sections ... ahead though obscured, rode the G.O.C. and officers of his brigade staff. Just ahead again were the Brigade-Major and, in flapping sandals at his horse's shoulder, a native guide, a Christian.

Ahead of *them* were the 2nd Lancers. The 2nd Lancers, having sent back a message, were awaiting orders.

To the rear, in touch, the Central India Horse. Then the leading regiment of the 12th Cavalry Brigade.

Philomena found herself on an agreeable, sloping track. It wound from the railway-crossing, northwards, through olive groves. The gnarled trunks were black. It was Awshew who thought one of these looked human.

The horses pricked their ears at whispers of the night.

The olive-trees were behind them, a hamlet and its nervous inhabitants; and pine-trees draped deep cloaks over the horses in front of her. There was a spell of fair country; redolent and rustling. The horses, well within themselves, walked and sneezed and blew through their nostrils; and the column jingled on.

60 Mulchard hospitable

Cairo, from the crack of dawn, and the crowing of cockerels, Cairo . . . never dropping off . . . whirred, what with the call of the muezzin, with hoof-beats, bugles, motor-horns, and braying donkeys. Then there was the smell of drains and flowers, and the hot stillness, and the wind. The wind was splendid for the lateen sail of the felucca.

If Nanny had been anticipating ructions there would be none. Griselda was stricken by conscience.

'I'd rather you cultivated nicer people,' she

murmured; and left it at that.

Griselda, herself revelling in a ride out to the Mena House and a gallop in the desert, followed by breakfast in that illustrious hotel, saw a Nanny in need of distraction. When Professor Mulchard issued an invitation for Mrs Romney and party to visit him at Dahshur, Griselda leapt at it. Unsuspicious (she would afterwards think), Griselda and Nanny got up before six in the morning.

Mr Johns-Kelsall fitted Nanny's ideal. He was far too youthful to prove 'awkward'. He spoke Arabic. He was brown but shaven. Johns-Kelsall had been spared from the dig to usher them into their railway carriage. In Griselda's estimation he was an ass.

The trip as far as El Bedrasheen was spiffing.

On the banks of the canal, *fellaheen* were fishing with line. Griselda was able to show Amabel the elephant-grey water buffalo; and the silver, long-horned cattle; and water-wheels. The lebbek trees, with their sweet yellow flower, shaded small irrigation channels. In the neat squares and rectangles of *berseem*, pure white dots were spaced in scrupulous fairness. The cattle egret. Flocks of doves swept the sky. The soil was a wonderful, friable, red-brown.

Nanny, who hoped to add the rufous warbler to the list, and so was wishing for a quiet stop, seemed content.

Up in the glare, there were glimpses of the

328

Sakkara pyramids. Griselda had taken Nanny by electric tram to Gizeh. These days, the Sphinx was not half smothered.

Mulchard had sent his motor to meet the train. In no time (a while) they were coughing through the village of Dahshur.

Poultry and mangy dogs scattered. The mud-brick hovels were uncanny in their stillness. Soon there was no dirt road. Had she thought about it, Griselda would have expected dromedaries or donkeys. The Rolls Royce, without hesitation, advanced onto the desert floor, and climbed a *vaguely* beaten track onto the plateau.

Sand was heaped in small, crested billows, and in shallow dunes. These broke into thousands of ripples, into which were softening trails of animal prints. Some very decayed pyramids, like so many couched camels, reached to north and west as far as the eye could see.

The breeze was whipping Griselda's cheeks.

The desert carriages of Gizeh were absent. Horridly visible were trippers with camel-drivers from Sakkara.

Mulchard's camp was primitive. He had tents. In the tents were rugs. He had chairs worked from palm frond, and crates for tables. Planks on trestles supported either 'finds' or refreshment. The squalor was unmistakeable. There were too many persons in bare desert, and no bushes.

329

The scorch kept Nanny's motoring veil over her face. Amabel squirmed.

The Pyramid of Two Angles, or the Blunted Pyramid was, Mulchard said, thought to have been the earliest of the pyramid tombs. His excavation wasn't *within*. Whereas other, more showy Egyptologists hungered for the fabulous, Mulchard's nose had led him to a site to the side. He'd been convinced he would uncover ... a mortuary temple and, yes, a modest tomb!

Lumps and bumps on the bedrock.

Here he'd invested his whole winter season! Griselda maintained her expression of absorption. She took out her pocket compass: the Blunted Pyramid was fifteen degrees out of alignment with the Stone Pyramid. The falcons, now familiar to her, mewed overheard.

Nanny, unusually, stared into the sky.

Griselda could hear that Nanny was telling Amabel about Snofru, mistaken in his geometry, and out in his angles. Often, Nanny surprised Griselda. Instead of leaving his *ka* in the *Stone* Pyramid ('higher than Cephren's at Gizeh'), his choice had fallen on his old, dear *Blunted* Pyramid, with its two entrances and singular appearance.

Amabel wanted to go inside it.

Well, yes, he had picked up some extraordinary objects, artefacts and jewellery, Mulchard was murmuring.

The Stone Pyramid lay three-quarters of a mile behind them to the north. First, everyone had an appetite. Over lunch, Mulchard uttered remarks about the new Egyptian government. These gentlemen were determined to put *restraints* on the distinguished Englishmen, Germans, Italians and Frenchmen, who devoted their energies and their instincts to Egypt's 'past'. That was how Professor Mulchard saw it. The new Egyptian government had acted to stop antiquities from leaving Egypt. Such *hubris*!

The government didn't bar entry to Snofru's Stone Pyramid. It asked half a *piastre* each.

Nanny thought she would rest, if Mrs Romney didn't mind.

There was a scramble up to gain the mouth of the thing. And an unending chute, a wooden ramp to the bottom (below ground); and steep. Amabel's legs gave way. Johns-Kelsall had to clutch the child to his chest.

The stepped roof of the chambers might have been built yesterday. The lamps of the guide and of Mr Johns-Kelsall cast the eeriest shadows.

The third chamber smelt of corpses.

Corpses and drains.

To Griselda, who'd nourished a vision of the blue roan's being stuck in the pyramid, the brilliant light of the desert came as a relief.

To HQ for an early tea.

Professor Mulchard took Amabel's hand,

and pulled forth a little marbled-cardboard drawer. On its bed lay a collection of scarabs, mostly of a very dull colour, the colour of bone. Only two were blue, and two were a whitish pale.

'Dung-beetles,' he said.

He picked them up, one by one, to show Amabel the folding of the legs. Some scarabs had differently folded legs.

The blue were of *lapis lazuli*.

'The early scarabs were not incised with hieroglyphs. They were just as sacred, though. Perhaps even more so. The beetle coats her eggs with her own dung and the male rolls the dung-ball about with him. The ancient Egyptians of the Old Kingdom were astonished by the beetle's habits and saw in the dung-beetle's ball something of the awe they felt about the sun that, having set, never failed to rise again. Isn't that interesting, child?'

Amabel was amused by beetles.

'I shall choose one for you,' he said. 'D'you see, you may, if you wish, thread a cord through it and have it around your neck! It is far older than you. Roughly, four thousand nine hundred and ninety-seven years older!'

'Fancy!' Nanny was heard to murmur.

He chose a plain colour.

Griselda approved, absently, Amabel's stuttered thanks. Looking for Philomena had made Griselda sad. *Looking* made her sad. It was time to turn for Cairo.

Mulchard was to send them in style, in the Rolls Royce.

The sun had passed over the Nile and across the top of their heads and was lighting the crests and the collapsed pyra-mids. As they approached Sakkara they could watch the Step Pyramid blush. The desert was full of colour; rose and blue and violet. Griselda forgot Philomena.

The wind had died.

To the east, just there, the crops of *dhurra* and *berseem* were laced like lattice pastry with inviting black shadows. The conjunction of water channels, green crops, flowers and burnished sand was unearthly.

Griselda felt grateful to her *bête noire*.

Then, when they at last teetered on the horizon, with the Great Pyramid in sight below them, the Rolls foundered again.

It was dark.

The first stars had been out for a while. There'd be a half moon. Amabel was dropping. Griselda—she and Nanny were too—put up for the night at the Mena House. Willowy Mr Johns-Kelsall could take himself off, knowing he stood high in their estimation. Mrs Romney was capable of taking the electric tram.

A light supper was served in their rooms.

Three days later, at the Gezireh Palace, Mulchard padded softly towards her, to ask whether he might add a couple of cases ...

'crates, Mrs Romsey, 1'8" deep, 2'6" long, 1'6" broad' . . . to her luggage. He was 'aware' she was accompanied by 'boxes of horse medicines'.

Griselda recollected the conversation at Dahshur. 'And yours contain horse medicines?'

After a pause, she pleaded female incompetence.

61 'Spare neither horse nor rider'

General Barrow came up with the 2nd Lancers at half past eleven. The reconnoitring, armoured cars returned at ten to midnight. Barrow ordered the 2nd Lancers to press on, into the Pass, unsupported; to secure the debouch onto the Plain of Megiddo. A road the Turks would be seeking to stop up. It was bold work. For the narrowest nine miles, although the Lancers had scouts forward, flank guards were not to be thought of. The little, genial, bald-haired General waited for the column to appear. It did not.

He was beside himself.

By the time his Australian staff officer (Australian of course) riding a weary charger, had tracked and located them, the Dorsets were more than four miles in the wrong direction. And the Central India Horse had filed off after them. And the leading regiment of 12 Cav had too.

Barrow ordered the remaining regiments up to and into the defile. The 10th Brigade, once back on the right road, would fall in at the rear of the 11th. Philomena couldn't know it, but they'd again allowed themselves to get lost. Perhaps the fault *had* lain with the Brigade-Major's dependence on a native guide ... They wheeled by the head, to stumble across stony country on a compass bearing. That night she toiled eight miles farther than she need have done. Bungling had deprived Barrow of three hours.

Eight empty miles.

Musmus, in the onomatopoeic Arabic, mimicked the suck of a swallowing gullet, a slurp. Its road was stonier still. For twenty minutes, Awshew panted at her head; pitying himself.

Mortification was felt in no small measure by the Dorset's South African officer, Captain Patterson; who had always guided the Regiment in the dark. This ruined any recollection of history. The great Pharaoh Thothmes III, Vespasian, Saul, the biblical armies, Greek, Saracen, Crusader, they *certainly* hadn't all wandered off to the north; and worn their horses to no purpose.

Another chagrined party was to scurry *back* through the Musmus: the dislodged Brigadier-General.

The 2nd Lancers, meanwhile, attached to

335

the 12th Brigade, had found no ambush, no trap. No machine-gun fired from salients to slaughter them. The Turkish guard at El Lejjun—ancient Megiddo, by the biblical Har Megeddon—was sitting down, with arms piled.

Philomena saw the first rays, slanting across the mist in the Plain of Esdraelon, of the sun.

To the north-east, a far, snow-topped mountain was the grandest thing in sight. Mount Hermon. Grazebrook, who had studied (as had his Commander-in-Chief) George Adam Smith, muttered to himself, 'hanging like the only cloud in the sky'; which truly it was.

A shower, in a hiss and a hush, cleared the mist, and rinsed away their sweat and dust. As the mist dispersed, Mount Tabor rose serene, encircled in a halo. The horses gazed down with interest upon fresh scenery.

Far below, pouring spectacularly over the Plain, were the 2nd Lancers, the 12th Brigade minus one regiment and the leading regiment of the 11th. Another column had encroached from the north-west in similar dramatic fashion: the 5th Division.

The course of the railway was being picked out by a snail of a train.

As, four or five miles away, the Indian lancers were met by a force of six companies of valiant if breathless Turkish infantrymen, with twelve machine-guns, not an echo of the distant action floated up to Philomena. The

336

lancers charged superbly.

It was over in a few minutes. The joy of spearing some forty-six Germans and Turks! They did take prisoners.

Philomena descended. Her knees juddered.

The brooks and streams that had looked tiny began to glint between crushed stubble and green shoots of wheat. Orchards and pastures could be made out on the Nazarene slopes; and the oaks on Mount Tabor.

The yeoman brewed up for breakfast at Lejjun.

Once she had gained El Afuleh, Philomena had an easy amid the din (demolition explosions catapulted grit through the air) until a few minutes to one. Awshew saddled up and stood to his horse. The Brigade was reassembled. The D.Y. for advanced guard.

Philomena had to trot.

Awshew was asking her to go, and go, and go.

They halted at Esh Shutteh; having covered eight miles, walking and trotting, in an hour and a quarter. This pace was kept up for a further nine. The need to beat the light was paramount. Most scouts and the flank-guards had been drawn in. A cloud of blackish soil enveloped Philomena and Awshew. The view across the Vale of Jezreel was deceptive. The land suddenly slipped and sank in terraces. Here, said Major Grazebrook, Gideon had made the first night attack recorded in history.

The horses were stiff and aching. Awshew flexed his feet in the irons; and his bottom in the saddle.

They were outside marshy Beisan at half past four. Philomena had to gallop the railway depôt and its howitzers. Awshew held her together.

Many horses had exerted themselves in the herding of the two thousand prisoners. Twenty-six horses (straight from the Jordan Valley) in the entire Division had been foundered. Our mounted forces had suffered not a single casualty in men. By midnight, *via* Jenin and the Pass of Dothan, the first units of infantry would be gaining Afula.

Philomena was deep in the rear of the Turkish Seventh Army. A very long way indeed from the British lines of supply. From the orange groves of Sarona, in thirty-six hours, she'd done seventy-eight miles.

Philomena was watered. She finished her rations; the last until the wagon came up. Awshew, tired as he was, exultant as he was, rubbed her down with all the solemnity of an old trooper.

It was warm. Awshew slapped at mosquitoes on his neck.

Philomena had no notion that two Turkish armies might be rushing back upon her.

62 A warrior

The graveyard at Up-Nyland held little appeal (Amabel was trying to decide where she wanted to leave her *ka*). To Griselda's dismay, Amabel went on to wonder where Daddy 'would' leave his *ka*. 'With us,' stated Griselda. 'To have a care for us?' 'Oh, decidedly so!' And Amabel subsided.

Amabel would grow out of her dreams. Nanny considered that, big though the child was, Amabel wasn't perfectly convinced that Daddy had died. Amabel, in dreams, 'heard his voice downstairs in the drawing-room'.

Griselda tried not to fall into fits of dejection. At times, it seemed that all she was doing was wrong. 'It's not Philomena': these words she uttered often. She would walk away. It was dreadful when the horses gazed at her, or pricked their ears at the sound of her voice; horses in distress. She was astounding herself.

She always carried sugar-lumps for them; and they were pathetically grateful.

Unless, rigidly staring, far gone in pain. Then she'd send a message to Rawlinson. Never knowing whether or not he'd responded.

She saw Walers and horses that could have been Irish, and short-legged, square horses from she-knew-not-where, and the horses from New Zealand. She saw the English hunter types. Griselda also saw herself abandoning them.

The cancelled broad arrows.

She saw the native *baladi* (the 'Syrians' of Army parlance); and once-fine Arabians; or English thoroughbreds that had been imported, in 1910, 1912, say, to give pleasure; and she saw herself refusing them, and abandoning, them too.

She saw horses that were looked after with a modicum of 'sense and expense'; and others that were not.

Griselda was having bad dreams; premonitions. Mulchard had, on board ship, spoken of her as the 'angel swooping'.

The horse-medicines went with her. The English lady could doctor sores and galls, administer worm powders and drenches; clean wounds; poultice heels; hand out fly-fringes obtainable in Egypt. Where Griselda felt dismally weak was in cases of severe abscess, and in the proper treatment of eye diseases. Deformity of the feet was man's work.

She *could* doctor. Monsieur Imran quite failed to persuade people of the fact.

Griselda wasn't enjoying herself.

Rawlinson was supposed to ensure the beasts of burden were provided with water. Summer had begun to blaze. The matter of a drink was beyond her.

Her own inaction made her weep. A figure of speech: tears were foreign to Mrs Arthur

Romney.

Allenby was High Commissioner. His motor swirled, every day, past and through the horses that had served under him in Palestine: did that not strike the great man?

Griselda had been introduced—she moved in Residency circles—but hadn't brought herself to tackle him.

One day Imran led her into the Gamaliyeh, into a street of tradesmen, carpenters, wheelwrights, of vats of tar that bubbled and frightful fires beneath, gasping poultry in baskets, heaps of iron scrap, baskets of coal and a camel butcher. Since the houses were premises and not lived in, the street was more open than usual to the sky, and no balconies shaded the shattered paving.

These were gharry stables they'd visited before.

The outer wall was whitewashed, and a low horseshoe arch, wide enough to swallow a carriage, led down into a dingy courtyard. Three sides were composed of stone sheds that might have housed forty. This was the usual airless, closed-in, reeking hell. There was nobody. No animals stirred.

The rake was too steep for weary legs. No bedding. The dung had been stamped into a midden-like cake. Emerging from the dinginess into the glare of the sun would put a strain on the eye. The lack of ventilation and the ammonia harmed wind, and interfered with digestion.

'Oh dear!' moaned Griselda. Horses feared to enter dark places.

'In the corner,' said Imran. 'Look!'

Griselda had once seen a blindfold camel that turned the wheel to draw water from a deep well. When told to halt, the camel had halted so totally that the poor creature had seemed stuffed . . .

The mare was brown. She did have a mealy muzzle. She was about 15.2 hh. Her dock was long, and on her near shoulder was branded the letter 'C'. In her neck on the off side, in the muscle above the artery, was a healed wound.

She was skeletal. One eye stared from a hollow socket. The other was filmed. Dried pus had collected on the lashes. Her lips were marked, as though by cuts and welts; and suppurating. Her neck was hollow. Her back was hollow. The ribs were threadbare. Her hips poked upwards in a dry hide. When pinched, the skin cleaved. Her legs were scarred and gaunt. The cannon bones and tendons were a mass of lumps. She was resting her near foreleg, pointing it. Each hock was swollen. The hoofs, still shod, had grown out; overlapped, and split. They were grotesque. The flies buzzed on the dung and perched all over her. On her flank, they formed a ball. Griselda had to push them to get them to move. Under the flies was a ring of raw flesh.

The creature turned her head.

It wasn't Philomena.

Griselda said to Imran, 'We can't leave her. I can't leave this one.'

Imran said, 'Why *this* one? What else can you do!'

Griselda registered that Imran was grave.

'I'll have to buy her. How much would your acquaintance want for this wreck?'

Imran drew breath.

'Where is the fellow?'

Imran was tepid about horses. Griselda knew that. His courtesy, however, was immense. The skeleton mumbled a sugar lump, and dropped it.

There was no life in her.

'Sheer starvation,' said Griselda.

Imran recoiled (a faint waft of orange-blossom). 'I had hoped she would end your search, *madame*,' he said.

Griselda persevered. The sugar lump passed the lips, and the teeth. The jaw worked. The smallest crunch. No more. The sugar was melting onto the tongue, perhaps.

A faint bubble of slaver appeared.

The solitude of the mare and the lack of persons about lent a curious atmosphere to the scene.

Griselda felt the foreleg.

Imran stroked his chin.

'There is a calcified lump on the cannon bone, it has had time to mend a little, but I

343

doubt . . .' A gnawed end of halter rope hung from the mare's head. She had eaten all of it she could reach. She was loose, by her ring. Griselda broke out into a sweat.

Griselda tried to get the animal to take a step. The poor thing did respond. Ponderously . . . a step. Two steps. 'This won't do,' said Griselda.

She patted the sticky neck.

Imran sighed.

'I'm afraid you must fetch Farrier-Sergeant-Major O'Connel.'

'For what?' asked Imran.

63 Understanding

Imran knew that Mungy Lassa'ad was sitting over a *kanun* and a pot of tea, observing them. Imran had seen the *kanun*, the rose-decorated teapot on the burning charcoal, had pictured all. Nothing had been visible.

Mungy Lassa'ad emerged with deference; eyes alight, if warily.

Mrs Romney obliged Imran to negotiate. 'But what will you do with her?' asked Imran.

'Please negotiate a price.'

Imran glimmered a warning. 'She is not worth it.'

Mungy Lassa'ad, proprietor, named a preposterous sum.

Imran felt torn. He had not been acquainted with Mungy Lassa'ad.

Imran spoke softly to Mungy Lassa'ad.

'Will the horse live until tomorrow?' Imran asked the lady.

'Yes,' said Mrs Romney.

'Is this mare fit to walk?'

'Not really,' said Mrs Romney.

'The *effendi* says she hasn't worked for three months.' Imran was flattering Mungy Lassa'ad.

'I'm not surprised.' Mrs Romney clenched her jaw.

The price was lowered.

'Ah, *please* don't go, *madame*!' Imran said.

'May you be offered tea, honoured lady?' said the proprietor, in English. The mare was on the road to recovery, she was a good, strong animal, one that he had not much desire to sell.

Imran stared at nothing.

'May the animal have a drink?' interrupted Mrs Romney.

'*Madame*, you must *accept* the tea,' said Imran, in French.

'We shall pay what it will cost you to get another horse,' she said. Imran hid his own delight. 'Then we shall go away to bring an ambulance!'

The deal was concluded with rapidity. Mungy Lassa'ad looked suitably disgruntled. 'I shall arrange water for the horse,' he conceded.

'Where is your water?'

'The well. Cistern.' A wave of the hand.

'May she have water *now*?'

Englishwomen were so forceful.

'Yes.'

'Monsieur Lassa'ad is a good person,' remarked Imran.

Mrs Romney said, stubbornly, 'Starvation causes pain.'

'Is it not better?'

'Better than what? Why not even enough water?' she murmured. 'Thirst causes pain.'

Imran said, 'The English take into their hands what should be in God's hands. You slaughter. With us, no slaughter.'

'Indulge me,' said Mrs Romney to Mungy Lassa'ad. 'I hanker to watch the mare drink.'

Imran shivered.

The horse was blubbering into the water's surface when Mrs Romney remarked to Imran, 'I'm so sorry, I must ask you to go on your own to Abbasiyeh.'

Imran, usually, was in charge. Mrs Romney might not have been aware of this. But it was so. Events never quite slipped beyond his control. He didn't enjoy himself when they were starting to slip. It was one of those occasions. He was aghast.

'What will you do?'

'I stay! Please do this . . .' There was little of the commanding in her voice. More, a throbbing calmness he couldn't resist.

346

'*Madame*, I cannot, you will be ... *unescorted.*'

'Well, for a little while.'

'Will you not be afraid?'

'At the English barracks you will find Sergeant-Major O'Connel. I shall scribble a note for him. He will accompany you. With a horse-ambulance, mules and two of his Egyptian orderlies, I've no doubt.'

Imran considered. While she bent over her pencil and paper, he took in the enclosed yard and its one narrow entrance. O'Connel might not be at all grateful to be summoned.

Imran pitied Mrs Romney. If she was afraid, she didn't show it.

He thought the English soldiers would be scared.

'*Madame*, I cannot leave you alone in this place.'

Would she oblige him to yield?

Spectators were sidling in, one by one, to stand in profound, expressionless silence. There was some peculiarity in the lack of greeting.

Imran didn't have to examine the faces to know. These were *Egyptians*. There was not a man there that didn't respect Imran's status with the English lady. It would not have surprised anyone. Nor would it have occurred to a single spectator to bandy Imran's business about: Imran was conducting the lady in Cairo, and on terms that would remain imprecise to the lady herself. Recognized to be the son of his father, Imran attracted esteem.

Imran looked helplessly at Mungy Lassa'ad. Mungy Lassa'ad drove the spectators out ... They were alone again.

Mrs Romney, in the dark stable, was serenely cleaning the nostrils with a damp cloth; also the corners of the eyes.

Imran was expressionless.

'I have asked the Farrier Sergeant-Major to bring his humane-killer. To be on the safe side. He will take the mare in his horse-ambulance to Gezireh.' She turned. 'He'll do it *for me.*'

Mrs Romney laughed.

'I shall *stay*!'

Imran's lips parted. Gracefully, he smoothed the sleeve of his European suit. Imran would slaughter a lamb at *el 'Id*. Cattle hoisted by a leg with throats cut were a common sight. Horses often died in the street. Imran had never seen this humane-killer. An English word, said in English ... or was it, like 'syce' and 'gharry', Indian ...

'Oh dear, *do* get on!'

Imran passed like a shadow into the brilliant sunshine. Mungy Lassa'ad had retreated to the teapot. If the lady would not go to the tea, the tea would come to the lady.

Imran made no attempt to hire a gharry. He walked purposefully to the Khan el-Khalili. He seated himself in the recesses of a favoured café. He ordered coffee. There wasn't time to settle. He imagined instead some delicate essence ... fruit, peel, or zest ... thrown on the charcoal of a *shisheh*. He listened, as he drew imaginary smoke through the water, to the bubbling.

He strode back to Mrs Romney.

'It was in the hands of *Allah*,' Imran explained to the lady.

Mrs Romney opened her mouth to speak.

'I was able to spot the reluctance of your English sergeant. The soldiers are frightened. Of being trapped by the crowd.'

'Piffle.'

'*Madame*, you can't get them to understand us. You ... you, *madame*, understand us.'

'Augh!' said Mrs Romney, exasperated. And, 'We shall have to lead her. While you were away, I persuaded your acquaintance to procure her some wetted bread. 'I *think*,' said Mrs Romney, 'this horse can reach Gezireh.'

Mrs Romney seemed haunted and rash.

Bread? 'Bread! He wanted *flous* for it?'

'I gave him money, yes.'

Imran was appalled that she could have revealed even to so distinguished a person as Mungy Lassa'ad that she carried money. 'People very poor,' said Imran.

He took a breath; and smiled unhappily.

Their journey was hard. The horse went slowly. So slowly. The horse laboured. Mrs Romney's patience was greater than Imran's own. She held the halter, and coaxed. Imran, sometimes stroking his sleeve, idled before or beside her. He marvelled at her courage . . . of which she had too much (it was unbecoming). On every side, there were stunned faces, there were swift, startled looks, and glassy. That was all.

The horse collapsed and died quite close to el-Hosein. Even this occupied ten minutes.

Imran, forced to promise to attend to disposal of the carcass, handed Mrs Romney into a gharry. She had refused the first one.

He watched until she was borne out of sight. He spun on his heel and *went*, swiftly. Mrs Romney would go back to Amabel and Nanny.

The ragged children would still ask for her at the Gezireh Palace, with 'news' of brown horses with mealy muzzles. Imran, from then on, would shun her.

The fascination was gone.

64   Griselda disturbed

The Griselda with Amabel and Nanny at Dahshur had been accompanied by another Griselda. One of these persons simply hadn't seen the thin horses and the battered donkeys that toiled in Mulchard's service.

It was the Griselda that had driven with the *Koh-i-Noor* flame—Rory Black, on a flying visit from the Sudan—into the Mokattam Hills for the sake of the sunset. It was the most *romantic* view of Cairo, with the sails of the feluccas tiny and the minarets. The Griselda that had been invited together with Amabel and Nanny to Mrs Vandeleur's picnic in a marvellous *wadi*, reached from Helwan. Amabel and Nanny had picked up fossils. The Griselda that loved gymkhanas, dances and fun.

One Griselda *enjoyed* herself.

Twice, riding Moti, she'd been arrested by carcasses in odd situations, carcasses with the twists of rope hobbles still scarring the hide. Nevertheless, it wasn't natural to 'see'. This whipping round at every sound of hoofs, casting one's eyes hungrily, for it was impossible to take everything in at a glance, and she felt more like Amabel, who took ages to drink in every snake or monkey ... and being attentive always ... It wasn't normal behaviour.

Griselda was *charmed* by Cairo: where on *earth* would an hotel have put up so smilingly with her odd visitors, Imran's informants! It wasn't unknown for an animal to be presented at the portals of the Gezireh Palace (the fountain fed a water trough), a weak, starving, courageous horse with a cancelled brand. Griselda would send a *sofragi* for the medicine-chest.

This Griselda was stricken.

Feet would be heated, there would be heat in

fetlocks. Swollen knees, scarred knees. Staring ribs. Scars, galls, more abscesses. Griselda could have shown people how to poultice. It was possible to buy Army hoof-picks, Army sweat-scrapers, in the *suk*; but not mackintosh. Her supply of mackintosh was by no means exhausted. Poulticing was foreign.

Permitted to give away her hoof pick, she did so more times than she could count.

Griselda had arrived at the conclusion, confirmed by the Egyptian vet at the Sporting Club, that not a few horses suffered from laminitis. The fault didn't lie with the richness of their fodder. The laminitis was due to the concussion of the feet on the hard road.

It was said that the running syces had run in the eighteen-eighties and nineties with eyes a-pop. Hitherto, the life of a running syce had been one of graceful dancing before the horses of pashas. The British had shipped fast-trotters to Egypt and driven at such a pace as to place their syces in danger of being trampled. In those days, running syces damaged their hearts. In consequence, now, there wasn't a gharry-driver, an *arbagi*, in Cairo that didn't push his horse to trot as rapidly as could be.

One district she couldn't . . . 'you mustn't' . . . visit was the fish market, El Was'a, a stone's throw from the Ezbekiyeh. Several miles the other way, to the south-west, beyond the Mosque of Seiyideh Zeinab, was the

Slaughterhouse; and streets full of forges. Griselda couldn't venture there either. Shoeing was execrable.

There were butchers elsewhere. Camel legs, splintered on the cannon bone, the amputated feet propped casually against door or arch, never failed to make Nanny gasp.

Bovine heads, at eye level, didn't unsettle Nanny so much.

The Gezireh Club's vet, Dr Mohammed Usama, had served during the War with the Imperial Camel Corps Brigade and was engaged in the creation of a veterinary faculty at the University. He had a gentle manner. Her impression was that he wanted Mrs Romney (in all admiration) to go home.

Being naive, she'd asked him, 'Are you a Christian?' His surprise was patent.

'Moslem, *madame*,' he replied.

A week before the start of the holy month, a police inspector, Bimbashi Cave, was murdered.

Her syce, Shams, was inspired to observe that Imran, during Ramadan, would be in a position to seek out a *vast* number of paupers to whom to give alms. She knew that Shams had been jealous of Imran. It was customary to seek out paupers in Ramadan.

Griselda ignored Shams.

Having opened his mouth, and having too little occupation, with a single polo pony to look after and a donkey, even if he was impelled to run (ignobly, since Humbug and Amabel required him to bring up the rear), a reckless Shams pressed home.

'*Madaam* make Imran bleeding rich cobber.'

Griselda had long learnt to shut her ears.

'When you walkabout to hunt neddy, Imran paid.'

'I don't pay him, he is far too superior,' said Griselda. '*You* I employ.'

'Imran don't say, sod *baksheesh*. Imran say he blessed. Allah pleased with Imran.'

'I expect Allah *is* pleased with Imran.'

'More *baksheesh*, more alms for poor people, more Allah pleased.'

'Most unlikely!'

'Heck!' said Shams. 'Heck! Imran bleed all these children.'

'What children?'

'*Madaam* pay children.'

Griselda had been appalled by how many sullen horses, and foals, were in the charge of boys that appeared to be no older than eight.

'I reward information. I reward my children. I must! How could it be fair to do otherwise?'

'Imran tell his slave to go *shuftee* for children. Children reward Imran.'

'Really? Imran looks for the children I reward? Imran has a slave? A *slave*? Is this a tall story, *ya* Shams? For how does this, um, *slave* find my children?'

Shams goggled.

'Children in Cairo.'

'Yes, but . . .'

'*Everywhere, madaam* dole out *baksheesh*.'

Imran was *sordid* . . . ? Griselda was mystified.

'*Madaam* buy *killim*. Imran *baksheesh*. *Madaam* news of horses. Imran tell slave. Imran never lay finger on *baksheesh*. But Imran *baksheesh*.' Shams glanced at her. He made sure she was listening.

'What do you mean, "*slave*"?'

'Mr Shams slave *madaam*. Moti.'

'Oh, I see! Imran has a *sofragi*.'

'Pukka *sofragi, la*. Not *pukka*.'

'This *is* a tall story . . .'

'*Madaam* find sodding gelding when she seek mare.'

'Well, it's true I find a grey when I've told everybody my horse is a brown.'

'*Baksheesh*!'

Griselda was taken aback.

She thought, should I have offered Imran a wage? Risked a *faux pas*? She'd never have dreamt . . . his aid would not go unappreciated, but . . .

Shams shrugged.

Did Imran line his pocket? Griselda would be large-minded. 'Imran has to live,' she said flatly to Shams.

'Imran has wife and two sons. Imran, he Abu Tahar.'

'Nonsense!'

'Wife the daughter of Hafez Ahmad.

355

Mumkin beautiful and good.'

'Why "possibly"?'

Shams stared. 'I never ficky seed the lady.'

'I don't think I should attend to you!'

'Four girlies!'

'And your language is *disgusting*.'

'*Madaam* go to Rawlinson Bey. Rawlinson Bey . . .' and Shams pulled down with his finger the cheek below his eyelid.

'I'm willing to believe you swear out of ignorance!'

'Rawlinson Bey travel everywhere, he know every well-head what water neddies, he know all dealer, *arbagiya*, all. Rawlinson Bey loose, scour mighty . . . shitty breeches . . . for fear enter stone-quarries. And if with squaddies he bring riot. So, he don't!'

'*I* shall have to visit the stone-quarries.'

'*Madaam*, if you not loose you *murdered*.'

'Oh, dear!'

'No *shuftee*. Stone-quarry evil.'

'That cannot deter me!'

'Amabel bloody weep!'

'I dare say!' said Griselda, humorously. 'I shouldn't be saying this to you, *ya* Shams . . . Mr Rawlinson was less than civil. He told me not to poke my nose into what shouldn't concern me.'

Griselda had put Rawlinson down as a misogynist.

He'd half risen from behind his desk, with grotesque manners, and hung there in the air, half risen, half seated, as though unable to persuade himself to get up and escort her to the door.

65 The palaver

'We mustn't mope!'

'I'm not moping,' said Georgie.

'The heat of summer will drive your old Muzz home. She can't keep Nanny and Amabel in Cairo.' Uncle Archie was abrupt with children (better with girls). 'Besides . . .' Uncle Archie shook his head. He wouldn't say what he'd been about to say.

Georgie was out of plaster; had been for a while. He was still lame. He knew there was 'worry' over him. Uncle Archie had been dragooned into coaching him. Uncle Archie (though a *scholar*-soldier) was so monumentally unsuitable as to cause Georgie many twinges of sympathy. This was what had induced Georgie, with his God-given cleverness, to idle away hours on horseback or in the water of the pond. No matter how much he missed 'them', Quarr was much to Georgie's liking.

Letters took a fortnight. Sometimes as little as eleven days. By mid-May, Muzz must have telegraphed to Uncle Archie for a loan. Georgie was aware of the hum.

'They sleep under mosquito nets, do they . . .' had remarked Grandma, in one of those fatuous, if innocent, remarks for which she was famed.

With Palsy due to arrive at any minute, the family congregated, much to Uncle Archie's fright, for a conflab. Aunt Ida had been decent enough not to have excluded Georgie.

'Griselda is saying that Nanny and Amabel ought to come home. With the blue roan mare!' said Ida. ' "Blue roan mare" scratched out.'

'What blue roan mare?'

'Why scratched out?'

'She must have rescued one of our horses.'

'Scratched out?'

'Has she mentioned a blue roan mare to you, Archie?' asked Grandma.

'No. But I've been expecting her to transport dozens home. Hundreds.'

'Why scratched out?' repeated Georgie.

'*Have* you! Good God!' exclaimed Grandma.

Aunt Ida said, 'That or remain in Egypt to minister.'

'Not in front of the child.'

'I'm hardly a child.'

'Aren't you . . . ?' Aunt Ida cast a kind smile at him.

'Nanny gives Griselda concern. She writes that Nanny's head is heating up. Grizel is afraid Nanny is going to do something unwise. If she could imagine what, she could act to forestall it.'

They howled with laughter.

'And Amabel has seen a eunuch. Not a snake-charmer, or a performing monkey: a eunuch!'

'In what circumstances?'

'In the street, perhaps?'

'Could she have gone to a diplomatic reception?'

'A eunuch at a diplomatic reception?'

'Oh, well, an Ottoman affair. The Sultan became King in March.'

'Griselda steers clear of that set.'

'How dreary!'

'Nanny hadn't known how to explain, so Griselda told Amabel the man had been gelded.'

Grandma Lupus made an 'Augh!' noise.

'Amabel needs a governess. Since the War, you people,' observed Grandma, 'have grown *slack*!'

'Nanny is a vital stay, Ma,' said Aunt Ida.

Uncle Archie believed that all the heart had been driven out of parents to ensure their children grew up *educated*. All this day-dreaming in the woods in drab brown shifts. It was Uncle Archie's belonging to an earlier age that had made him incapable of resisting Muzz when she asked for money. Of course he was also rather touched, and peculiar. Uncle Archie said that something had happened between the South African War and the Great

War.

Englishmen had come home chastened by the suffering inflicted upon the remounts. American remounts, soft, in the wrong coat, without training, after a sea journey out of New Orleans ... entrained for cold uplands, within two days of disembarkation obliged to march with the column ... Such animals could last but three days before foundering, falling out. Some hussar regiments had gone through in horses four and a half times their strength in men.

Since 1904, successive Inspectors-General of Cavalry (junior officers in South Africa) had rewritten the official principles of cavalry training and animal management.

Uncle Archie said that the Royal Agricultural Society had not allowed docked foals to be exhibited in the show-ring in 1900, or yearlings in 1901, or two-year-olds in 1902. Bearing-reins were, by then, out of fashion for carriage horses and frowned upon. Thoughtlessness, whether in the hunting-field, on farm or highway, was condemned.

It had been a beginning.

'How your Muzz exercised herself over animals, when she was a child!' would say Uncle Archie.

Remembering Muzz, a *radiant* little girl, lighting up all their lives, before Georgie's grandfather had gone and died, he, Uncle Archie, couldn't deny her the help she needed now. He, Archie, had never joined those who had been critical. 'Hampering your father's career, indeed!'

Hampering? 'Why hampering?' had asked Georgie.

'Held against her. It's been a bone. Don't know I ought to be babbling to you like this. They were rather too *young*, that was all!'

Aunt Ida broke in on Georgie's reverie. 'One of us has to fetch Griselda.'

There was silence.

'Retrieve Amabel, retrieve Nanny, remind Griselda of her duty here ... you know she does dote on you, darling, though she might appear careless ...'

Georgie nodded.

'... and drag her away.' Aunt Ida swallowed. 'It always has been ... well, *whimsical*.'

'If Captain Palsy will go ...' muttered Grandma.

'Rather much to ask!' said Uncle Archie. 'Is the fellow fit?'

'Will Griselda thank us?' said Grandma.

'I can't go. Uncle Archie cannot. Uncle Archie dispatches funds! I don't see that you can, Ma. If we were to send Arthur's mother, Griselda would be furious. I know you're fond of Grannie Romney, darling, but Muzz can't stand her! *Fatal*!'

Georgie said, 'I could go with Grannie.'

They pondered upon this.

They shook their heads.

'She's too groggy. Besides . . . on that pin of yours . . .'

Uncle Archie all of a sudden scrambled to his feet: he was making a bolt. He had excellent ears.

'. . . And what if I do help her out . . . *quite* my own affair . . . !'

Ida looked up.

'I want Grizel to do the trick,' was his Parthian shot; in a strangulated voice.

Grandma was embarrassed.

'Jack Palsy,' said Aunt Ida. She sounded weary. 'The deluded man is about to tell you, Ma, that he has telegraphed Griselda two hundred and fifty pounds. And he is, yes, offering to sail for Egypt. It isn't as though he's a friend of *ours.*'

'What a complication,' said Grandma.

'Why?' remarked Georgie. 'No fear she'd marry him.'

'That is what bothers us, Georgie,' they wailed.

66   The Household Cavalry

It was a stiff Philomena that ungummed her eyes, with a start, minutes before Reveille. She was sore in the leg. She was tied by her head-rope to a metal rail in the marshalling yard, between Wideawake and Loppy. Philomena pricked her ears.

The horses were too overworked and underfed to offer injury to each other; but the march had melted all enmity between Philomena and Wideawake.

A big, black mare, with a star, raw-boned, not carrying much flesh at all, No. 933 Wideawake was 'a character'. Until the Household Cavalry had been dismounted, she'd served with them in France. Unless they were *humbler* Philomena didn't take to mares.

The two had vied with each other in the Jordan Valley; ignored each other on the march through Jerusalem to Ras Deiran, and during the weeks of rest at the rear. They had made faces, lunged, poked, humped (beyond squealing) and taken no pleasure in the company of the other. It was one of those mysteries: it was as friends that they'd reached Beisan.

Wideawake had a colic pain in the large intestine. They lacked *tibbin*; and green fodder. Wideawake stamped; and she looked round at her belly; several times.

The Farrier Sergeant gave her a cold enema. Before eight o'clock, 'B' Squadron was trotting out on the Nablus road as far as Wad' el-Jar. That managed to ease the black.

Awshew was achy. For an unsalubrious district it was a lovely morning. The sun shone warmly on them. The bay gelding in the rank behind them had been cold-shod in the night.

363

Heading *south* made the horses think they were off home.

When the outpost their troop was to relieve was come upon, and Awshew dismounted, he (unusual for him) patted Philomena. Heartily.

Philomena and Wideawake, flank to flank, were led by their horseholder, Crowcombe, three hundred yards to the rear of the Regiment, where they dozed and rested a leg, and were allowed to mumble the heads of dry weed.

Beisan had supplies of barley and gram. Philomena carried twenty-one pounds of grain. Spotters had been posted on the hill at Beisan and could see to the thorn thickets of the River Jordan.

In the early hours of the 20th, Nazareth (the enemy's Army Group HQ) had been surprised.

Awshew had to be on the go. They all stood in the way of an orderly Turkish retreat. It was No. 4 Troop, though, that was detailed for escort duty. The Turkish rank and file smelt, to Awshew, dirty but unafraid.

At dusk, mounted patrols were formed. A substantial Turkish column led by top-brass motors was nearing. 'B' Squadron, with its two Hotchkiss gun-teams, prepared to fight. 'C' Squadron, in the direction of the Jordan, held a line on the left.

A squadron of Central India Horse came up in support.

The lie of the land provided the led horses with cover.

Grazebrook, not able to guess the depth of the Turkish column, correctly took over the command of 'B' Squadron from Captain Patterson.

Turkish riflemen tried to break through around the flank. A diversion, for the sake of their motors on the metal. Patterson relieved his feelings by dashing off to a troop of C.I.H. to urge a charge. But the *braggadocio* of the enemy's generals was popped.

Crowcombe confided to Loppy, Wideawake, to his old chestnut and Philomena that if they thought *Arabs* didn't behave gentlemanly to Turks, they had to clap sight on the *Boche* N.C.O.s what kicked and swore terrible; even at little Johnny Officer.

By three in the afternoon of the next day the Brigade had sent back to Beisan two thousand, eight hundred prisoners, and untold vehicles and wagons. The Dorsets had lost no horses. Two men killed, and a third shot by a sniper.

Philomena was glad of a few lulls. Patrols and mounted escort to bodies of dejected cavalry gave her bursts; and there'd been no 'off-saddles'. Once, she was sent back to Beisan only for the order to be countermanded.

They were ringed at night. It wearied them. Wideawake was scouring.

Awshew now seemed given to smiling.

And to slapping his neck. The D.Y. went to Ain el-Beida and returned.

The Division was to march to Deraa. General Barrow to rendezvous with the Sherifian Arabs and intercept the Turks' Fourth Army. The Brigade bivouacked at Jisr el-Mejamieh (hot and sticky), where the Yarmuk flowed into the Jordan.

Twenty-four hours in advance of the main column, the 10th Brigade crossed the bridge to march the sixteen miles, and 2,700 ft, up to Irbid. The road was bad. It first traversed ill-drained ground that steamed. Rising into the mountains of Gilead it was littered with sharp stone. Tired horses had to be dragged at a walk. Clouds had been collecting and turning blue. A clap of thunder signalled a downpour. This ceased abruptly. It had left the slopes slippery for the horses; and the gullies treacherous for wheels. A rainbow. The road curved round an outside contour, on the windward side. Grotesque rocks stood sentry.

There wasn't a tree to be seen. As though in pain, broom and thorn lay prone.

For four miles, Philomena plodded after Awshew along a ledge that dangled over a chasm. Basalt outcrops, jutting from the limestone, had to be inched around. Loppy fell out, having cast a shoe, others, ahead, had to be passed on the precipice; and the shoeing-smith, doubled up with nails between his teeth.

Wind buffeted them from the north. They'd

366

been sweating; and they were cold. Wheeled transport had got stuck at a collapsed bridge. On the tops, wherever stone had been cleared, red plough. There were ruins of a life far grander; a shattered aqueduct, a carved lintel.

Awshew thought it the rottenest place in Palestine.

Philomena carried rations for one day for herself, for two days for him. Both he and she were *famished*.

67 A goose chase

Often, in Ramadan, she found Shams asleep in the straw. Worn out with eating and smoking in the night.

Griselda was astonished to receive a civil message from Rawlinson. He'd spotted a brown mare with a mealy muzzle; at a place close to Lake Timseh. 'I don't much care, Nanny,' said Griselda, 'to drag you miles.' Privately, she meant to keep Amabel and Nanny under her eye. The motor, plus driver, was ordered for six o'clock. Griselda asked for a hamper.

They would take Shams: he could sit in front. She utterly refused to see why any other escort was called for.

Shams was keeping Ramadan. Their driver, Fathy, was keeping Ramadan. Griselda wondered why she hadn't insisted on a Greek driver. She couldn't fathom how anybody dared be operated upon, or have a tooth out. Also, in all courtesy, she would have to contrive to feed their party out of sight. Griselda began to think it a headache.

Amabel was happy: Fathy was pronounced 'Fat He'.

Amabel hoped for crocodiles.

They had the sun on their shoulder. The city was subdued; after the animation of the night. They slipped through Abbasiyeh, on the road to Zagazig.

Broadly speaking, the route parted the delta from the desert. Since this was the very edge of what was lush, the huge flocks of birds were diminished. Nanny was gratified to spot pelicans, and, she *believed*, a black heron; and masses of duck and small fowl.

Their party tripped into the Hôtel Bubastis in Zagazig.

Shams and Fathy got out of the motor, wrapped up their heads, lay down in the shade . . . and were fast asleep.

They'd covered half the distance.

Fathy now took the road due east along Wadi Tumilat. Efforts were being made to irrigate the land to the north, to reclaim it for the delta. On the right a verdant ribbon kept pace.

Shams and their driver had to stop to pray at noon.

Amabel had to stop for the fourth time to be

sick. Shams and Fathy averted their eyes. Nanny had devised a vast length of cloth to enclose the child in the open. She didn't employ it for sick.

The Mayya Hilwa was a vision of tranquillity. Banana, loquat and mango groves enticed travellers into the gardens and town of Ismailia. Griselda's heart thumped.

It was half-past one.

It was hot. Seven and a half hours! And no breakdowns. Not even a puncture. A hundred miles on the road. Shams unjammed his eyes. Nanny seemed stout. Fathy steered the motor aimlessly.

Griselda strained to inspect what horses were about. Ismailia was shabby; if quaint.

The steamer station on Lake Timseh had to be forgotten, unfortunately. Fathy, by asking and asking, and enjoying inordinate conversation, his elbow laid negligently on the wound-down window, obtained a view of the Suez Canal.

The picnic-basket was duly borne into an establishment. The proprietor was Italian. This was better ... ! Amabel mesmerized Italians.

They were all three pleased with the view. The big ships slipped through the desert like a scalding knife through butter. The Canal was ripping! Amabel forgot crocodiles. 'Why were you sick in that motor? Professor Mulchard's didn't bother you!'

'The leather was too new,' said Amabel.

'A shame the bank on the Sinai side,' remarked Nanny, 'is so heaped. I suppose they had to put the diggings somewhere.'

Griselda couldn't go to sleep in public (although she had the terrace to herself). She opened her book. Nanny's chin sank. Eight times, gharry horses passed: eight times, Griselda leapt up, to stare.

Then nobody stirred until four o'clock; when Griselda woke with a start.

They withdrew to wash, and tea was summoned.

'I suppose the *sofragiya* are inured to watching us eat in Ramadan.'

Griselda was seized by a thought: she hadn't planned this competently. She'd rushed to be intrepid. It was going to fall to Shams to get Philomena to Cairo *by train*. Another thing: she trusted Shams, she didn't trust Fathy.

The hour was nearer.

She pictured their voyage, after the nursing of the old girl, Quarr in high summer, the clumps of Michaelmas daisies where Amabel hid. Christmas tea; her darling Georgie. Griselda believed the memories of the horses in Egypt would grow less . . . less of a wrench. She'd tried so, to be dispassionate. In her head they still lived, they'd had faces, lips, that chestnut, so eloquent, the purblind bay, the sightless camel, the bewildered foals; children that earned in piastres *per annum* no more

370

than she spent on sugar-lumps for a week.

All . . . somewhere.

Rawlinson had advised her to go to the gharry stables shortly before *El Maghreb*, the sunset prayer. In Ramadan, every gharry returned to stables early (they'd emerge again). Every *arbagi* wished to be with his family to break the fast. She had the address. They had to set out to allow Fathy *time* to find it. And what if some of the drivers chose to go straight to their houses?

Fathy had ideas of his own. He claimed the address didn't exist; could not have existed. He set off for Cairo.

Griselda grew furious.

She was also anxious. 'Make him turn round, *ya* Shams!' Griselda gripped the *kefiyeh* where a tassel fell on the collar of Fathy's uniform. And he was *so upset*!

She brushed her hands with distaste. Shams had been at fault. The entire expedition was farcical.

Gharry stables in Ismailia were unlike the gharry stables of the Gamaliyeh. Instead of Stygian darkness, there was light; too much light, for there seemed scarcely any shelter. Enclosed behind high mud-brick walls that did cast some late shadow, the yard was square. Horses would be tied up to eat their rations, said Shams, and hobbled to wander until break of day. Except in Ramadan.

'Why hobbled?'

'Custom,' said Shams.

Not a soul was there.

Griselda sat ... silent ... in the motor. 'Camp stool, *madaam!*' said Shams.

'In the street?'

Griselda sat on, although Amabel clambered out. Round the corner trotted two horses, and one of them was brown, a light brown, with a mealy muzzle, a poor, broken-winded, ribby mare, with flaring nostrils; making a noise.

The *arbagi* stared curiously.

The lady didn't stir.

'Are you going to get out, Muzz?'

Griselda bowed her head.

Nanny said timidly, 'It was Philomena, then, was it?'

Griselda said, 'That was a Marwari, I think, with scimitar ears. Indian cavalry! Fourteen hands, perhaps. Philomena wouldn't have looked remotely ...' The voice trailed away.

Fathy breathed heavily. He was tired.

Half a mile out of Ismailia, Fathy, of his own volition, drew up beneath a very lovely tree. It had large, orange and pink flowers.

The muezzin's call was threading the air. Stools were unfolded. The hamper was opened in the boot; the wick was lit, and flamed blue; and the men withdrew with their mats to wash and to pray. When that was done, they moistened their lips, and swallowed two or three mouthfuls from their water bottle. They had acquired native bread; no doubt filled with *ta'miyyeh*. They didn't wolf, they ate slowly. They smoked several cigarettes.

Griselda, deposited without ceremony on the bank of the Mayya Hilwa, the Sweetwater Canal, took out her sketch-book and set about recording the scene (bloated dead dog and all) for Georgie. Thought of him made her eyes water.

Fathy jumped up and waggled his finger.

She pretended absorption. Quite soon, though, she looked the other way. Griselda felt worn and disappointed. Precious hours in Ismailia squandered . . .

Amabel was done in.

They suffered two punctures and Nanny was furrowed. Zagazig it had to be. For the night!

68   The last hurrah

As day broke in a magpie sky on the 27th, the yeomen came up and formed the advance-guard. Still some miles, what remained of the thirty-eight from Jisr el-Mejamieh, separated them from Er Remteh, ancient Ramoth-Gilead, on the *hajj* road to Mecca. Philomena was puzzled: there was haste in the air.

The previous evening, to secure the water supply at Irbid, the 2nd Lancers (commanded by an officer senior to the dashing hero of El Afuleh) had charged without reconnaissance or support. Costly and inglorious. However, in the dark, the Turkish flank guard, five thousand strong, of the Fourth Army, bolted. 10 Cav was grateful for their nine tons of barley and herd of live cattle (duly attached).

For six miles Philomena marched on a broad, unmetalled surface. Rock falls caused delays. The horses hadn't been watered. They shambled along with hanging heads.

Awshew, again at her head, was sorry for himself. His boots were cut.

The sun was malicious.

The enemy was standing to fight on a ridge that defended the railway at Er Remteh. Two troops of 'A' Squadron were digging out fresh road-slips, poor fellows, so as to escort prisoners back to Beisan. No. 1 Troop, 'B' Squadron, was absent on brigade reconnaissance. Two troops of 'C' Squadron had got fired upon from outlying houses and withdrawn smart-ish. Having gained higher ground, they were dismounted for action.

Out of the town, three hundred blooming Turks advanced, brazen, with four machine guns on carriages. Awshew grimaced. Captain Pitt hurried up the rest of his 'C' Squadron.

Philomena, with her keen ears, might, above sounds of rapid firing, have been aware of the whereabouts of those dismounted men disposed behind knolls.

The broken country favoured them.

In the rear, Captain Patterson commanded

one troop of 'A' and two of 'B'. His orders were to charge if the chance arose. Those of the Central India Horse were to turn the enemy's flank below the escarpment.

A party of Turks, fifty of them, galumphed forward to occupy the dead ground below 'C' Squadron's position. Patterson, through his field-glasses, noticed how cocky Johnny was. Their shoulders were braced confidently, and their discipline was tight. Quite unlike the demeanour of the half-starved mob so far encountered.

Awshew stood to his weary horse. Awshew mounted.

Patterson was swift to form his little force in a column of wings—two troops in line, in two ranks, with a troop in support. Philomena had her head in front.

The order to draw swords was immediate. A 'Direct Gallop Depart' was ineligible but Awshew dug in his spurs. The horses, like startled drudges, rallied their last ounces of strength.

The rise concealed them and would have muffled even the sound of them. And then Patterson, at the gallop, shouldered to the left. To the Turks it must have seemed that the yeomen had materialized very suddenly on the flank.

The horses had to scramble down scree and jump boulders, thorn and holes. Far from blenching at the flashes of sunlit steel, the

Turkish force turned to meet them; and was just able to redirect its fire.

Patterson's sword-arm said 'Charge'.

Philomena was galvanized by the roar that issued from the throat of Awshew. Old war-horse that she was, she *bucketed* over the rocks. Awshew hurt her mouth. Loppy pecked heavily . . . and found a foot. Philomena saw the soldier that reared up in front of her; his rifle seemed to fling itself up into the air, the bayonet glinted; he reared up only, rather to her dismay, to be knocked flat beneath her feet. She snorted.

The air was full of smell and noise; and then it was done. Not a single saddle had been emptied. A lather broke out on her shoulder. All fifty Turks there were killed or surrendered.

This action knocked the stomach out of 'em by noon.

All the more upsetting, therefore, that in taking the surrender of Turkish troops that had shown a white flag from a house, one officer should be mortally wounded, two other ranks killed, yet another officer and two troopers wounded.

Accounted for, at Er Remteh, had been the last officer and trooper in the Regiment to have been childhood pals.

In consequence, every household was turned out onto the street and the village searched.

On this day, three horses had been killed.

Two were chargers; one of which, a dark brown mare familiar to hunting folk, had gone all through the campaign unscathed. Five had received light wounds. Those losses were in addition to one officer wounded; and, of O.R.s, nine wounded. With one, it was mortal.

Philomena was anxious about her feed.

She was off-saddled and the horses of No. 2 Troop were able to enjoy an hour's grazing. Then the Regiment's limber-wagons rendered up the captured barley.

The Divisional Commander arrived.

The unforeseen upshot was that the march was halted for the night. General Barrow always had a care for the horses. Many had looked to him to be utterly done.

Awshew's section got little rest. On second-outpost duty, they could peer down on their goal. Awshew saw fires, threads of smoke through the moonlight.

At seven in the morning, a general advance on Deraa was ordered.

Philomena and Wideawake snorted and stared at the squalor. The jaws of a jack donkey yawned wide in an agony of some kind, a squeak fluted from his mouth. Deraa was bedlam. In particular the Turkish wounded of an ambulance train had been stripped naked by Colonel Lawrence's Arabs, in retaliation for beastliness to women and children; and many throats had been slit.

It wasn't what the yeoman liked.

The 10th Brigade remained in Deraa. Philomena got some handfuls of *tibbin* while Awshew was on first aid to the Turks. They marched to bivouac by the Roman aqueduct at Dilli; and rejoined the Division on the 30th.

The uplands of the Hauran were drear, devoid of trees, and windswept, yet must, Grazebrook thought, have yielded bushels and bushels of grain. Each village was rich in circular threshing-floors. Constant artillery-fire harried the Turkish Fourth Army in its appalled retreat. Over the next three days, Major Grazebrook himself put three hundred and twenty-one injured or wounded animals out of their misery.

Other officers wasted ammunition similarly.

This was as nothing compared to the slaughter on the 31st in the Barada Gorge. With orders not to enter Damascus but to feel round it to block the roads to Beirut and to Homs, the advanced machine-gun units of two brigades of the Australian Mounted Division (the 5th A.L.H, those former cameleers, and the 3rd) were traversing ground that sloped away to their left. A reconnoitring sergeant galloped down this slope ... to see the earth about to open in front of him. He observed railway, road and torrent. It was a gorge along which scuttled a great column of Turkish troops.

The machine guns of the En Zed squadron and the *mitrailleuses* of the Régiment Mixte poured in fire. Upon the German gun-teams piled the escaping, higgledy-piggledy thousands, an approaching train suffered the ripping up of its every carriage roof, while the fire directed on the tail of the column (as the machine-gunners could see it) ultimately persuaded those to the rear to turn about and pelt. Five thousand surrendered. The mounted units of the two brigades had been unable to descend. No other action would have been possible. Grazebrook was in ignorance of all that.

The Turkish Fourth Army had been driven north from Amman and the east bank of the Jordan, the stragglers of the Seventh and Eighth overwhelmed. The Australian Mounted Division had swept straight up from Tiberias. The 5th Cavalry Division had crossed to threaten Damascus from the south, and was now in advance of Barrow's 4th Division.

Damascus was entered on the 1st October by the 3rd Australian Light Horse Brigade and on the same day by Feisal's Arabs.

Philomena knew that Awshew was running a temperature.

Awshew's head ached. His crusty cheeks went pale. He was shivery. He gazed dopily at Mount Hermon (swimming towards him, way off on the left hand) and longed to lie down.

On October 2nd, they bivouacked.

In the morning, the yeomen gained the Ghutah, the gardens of the city.

Philomena and Wideawake were picketed in a blissful vineyard. Water rushed clear and cold nearby. Fig-trees and espalier apricot shaded them. The vines had no vigour; yet on these still hung the deep, pale clusters of grapes.

There was wonderful forage.

69 The *dahabieh*

Her venturing to Ismailia, with an Egyptian syce for escort, was held to have been folly. Griselda had gone beyond the line. *Still* there was no sign from Mrs Larshaw. Griselda had heard that Pussy Larshaw was going home. The knowledge she'd put from her head was bound to have to sink in: on May 15th, the Gezireh Palace, like the Mena House, closed for the summer.

Egypt *seemed* cheap, yet was *not*. Griselda had been obliged to beg Uncle Archie for a loan.

Awfully stupid, though, to practise false economy. The gilded splendour, inlaid marble floors, grand staircase, terraces, the sheer sanctuary of the Gezireh Palace had suited Nanny, and Amabel had been happier in Egypt than Griselda could have dreamt. Amabel's sickness hadn't lasted. Griselda wouldn't order that *noxious* motor.

In Ramadan, you were far more aware of how Arab Cairo was.

There were so many Greek and Levantine merchants, and Griselda patronised a French bookseller in the Shari' Kasr en-Nil, she bought stationery and picture postcards from a Swiss, her photographs were developed by an Egyptian Copt, a Turk made her gloves; her visiting cards were done by an Italian Jew; she and Nanny made use of the Circulating Library in All Saints' Garden; and Nanny favoured an Austrian haberdasher! Austrian!

For Ramadan, the mosques sprouted gay awnings and tented forecourts, light shone through walls of the big lanterns. A whole street existed the year round to make tenting. An excited throng heaved every evening in the little lanes around El Azhar and the mosque of Seiyidna Hosein; and indeed in every Arab quarter. The Arab shops kept limited hours. Gharries plied all night.

Philomena, in each and every Ramadan since the War, would have toiled night and day.

The continental tourists, never in number voluminous, had dwindled. There were soldiers behind sandbags around unexpected corners. Griselda, pursuing a Philomena beyond the Tombs of the Caliphs into a cemetery slum, was met with hostility; glares so vivid that Shams was *petrified*.

She'd gone too far.

Pack-mules and camels trekked through the city, markets seethed, horses plodded between the shafts of charcoal-carts and oil-carts, gharry horses trotted their hearts out. The donkeys, with their dinner-plate sores, pattered, bells tinkled, drivers shouted '*shii*'; bent and burdened the children hissed. In Ramadan, boys would light squibs and throw them at the feet of horses.

There was always a burst of laughter.

The old war-horses didn't flinch. Griselda was inexpressibly sad. The animals in Cairo were used to being a target for humour.

Processions abounded.

She saw dervishes in the white turban of the Kadiriyeh order.

It was Nanny who engineered the offer of the *dahabieh* for three months; and it was one to be jumped at. Nanny had been talking to Mrs Burnaby. Mrs Burnaby had heard all about Georgie, Quarr and Bark Hart. Mrs Burnaby was plump and good-natured.

Amabel and Nanny would be contented in the *dahabieh*. Mrs Burnaby's *sofragi* would do as much as lay in his power to attend to their every want. The situation was peaceful. Moti and the Sporting Club were within easy reach. Munia could still wait upon the nursery. Griselda wouldn't have such an outlay. *Dalila* was the most *darling* little houseboat. Major Burnaby was in Alexandria, and would deal with hiccups.

At 'Low Nile', *Dalila* lay at the bottom of a sloping bank, brushed by cypress, tamarisk, stiff palmette; oleander, bamboo, mimosa. Rushes feathered her bow. In the magical twilight, the swifts that were stationed above the old *medina* seemed to fly out; out over the Ismailiyeh, the Nile and the island; on purpose to salute her. She was painted china blue. She had a shallow, cream-coloured roof, and lattice rails. Each room had a window, a screen, and a glazed door, through which muslin curtains billowed, on to a deck veranda. Inside she was hung with gilded chandeliers. Her outer simplicity misled. Like a horse in the Army, she had a number. *Dalila* was No. 173. Mrs Burnaby's Nubian *sofragi*, who burned incense in miniature versions of the brass burners at the Gezireh Palace, forbade Nanny her Flit-gun. He was interestingly hung with amulets.

'Daddy will take to *Dalila*,' Amabel was heard to remark into thin air.

'Oughtn't we to deal with . . . um, "Daddy"?' Griselda asked Nanny.

Nanny took up Amabel's lessons instead.

70   The political officer

Dalila had a snag. The blue roan mare couldn't manage (as she had 'managed' in the garden at the Gezireh Palace) and had to be stabled at the Sporting Club. Otherwise *Dalila* was perfect. The *bawwab*, whether awake, or asleep on his palm-twigs across the gangplank, guarded them day and night. In Ramadan, too. Nanny made Amabel promise never to touch the water of the Nile.

At her mooring on the west bank of Gezireh, in Zamalek, *Dalila* was secluded from Nile traffic. To have been by the Semiramis might have been the most *chic* but it wouldn't have suited Griselda. *Dalila*'s riverine neighbours were pretty villas; whilst a *chanteuse* had the boat downstream and the Russian Trade Delegate the upstream one. Nanny objected to neither.

Because of the breeze along the river, they all felt cool in *Dalila*. Breakfast, lunch, tea and dinner or supper came piping from the Oasis Restaurant. Aly doled out the *baksheesh*. The supply from the waterworks was laid on by hose.

From Griselda's point of view, there was another advantage. Visitors were received elegantly on the upper deck. Her bedroom *cum* private drawing-room was below. They all went downstairs to bed. *Most* romantic.

'Have some sense!' said Rory Black. 'It's plain you haven't been to Greece. Or to Ireland! Nowhere on earth could the breeding of horses be attended with more skill, and yet the poor can be ignorant, entrenched in archaic practices, and *seem* stupid. The

English have the fervour of the converted. Not such ages ago they were driving urchins up chimneys by burning coals in the fireplace.'

He was in Cairo, blissfully, on a week's leave.

'Would it have been better to have burnt wood?'

'Your daughter . . . to the life!'

Griselda said, 'In the War, our horses would have been, well, not pampered but *cherished*! I *know* it!'

'Do you?'

'Umpteen chaps have told me. Chaps who fought.'

Did Griselda suppose, asked Rory Black, that in this War nobody ever had to beat an artillery-horse to get it out of a ditch? Foundered a beloved charger? Or that on the Western Front distressed horses hadn't been swallowed excruciatingly into the mud? That the screams of horses hadn't been ignored?

She shook her head, not wishing to hear.

In the early morning, they rode. The two of them. To the parade grounds at Abbasiyeh. Or out along the raised road to the Gizeh pyramids. Rory supported her in her painful scrutiny of the desert carriages; with their hide-bound wheels.

'What nonsense to say these people are poor! The families in the villages close to the Pyramids have been stuffing their pockets for decades! The dragomans sit down in their finery in the Mena House to have tea . . . well, perhaps not in Ramadan . . . with the richest potentates, and the most well-heeled British.'

'Potentates?'

'Even in the War, with the Mena House an officers' mess, you know they did excellently. Don't tell me they are poor. I expect the camels have frightful sore backs and holes in their humps, beneath that gaudy saddle-cloth. They have the most expensive leather-seated saddles . . .'

Rory Black was kind to Amabel. He was the nicest man. He liked to put Amabel up on Moti.

Rory Black was a fine horseman.

'What can the child learn from that Humbug?' he observed.

Heat and flies were gathering. The huge fan swung round and round. It was more difficult to get rid of Nanny and Amabel. Sometimes Griselda had the *dahabieh* to herself.

After all . . . he couldn't accuse her of having led him up the garden path.

Tirelessly (selflessly) he took her out to Old Cairo; took them all, in magical late afternoon light, to the island of Roda to show Amabel and Nanny the Nilometer; though there were no gharries at the rank there. Respectable places. He twisted Rawlinson's arm. He questioned her informants, so she didn't rush off to a bay or a gelding or a salmon-marked Waler. The stream had dwindled to a trickle. He went to have a chat with O'Connel.

Like Amabel, Rory knew what you said to beggars. *Allah ya'tik*, apparently. Since God *hadn't* given much to them, it seemed to be to rub salt. In Up-Nyland, there was an old crone whose nose was finished off by two-inch stalactites.

'Dear one, your girl could be in some remote village in Upper Egypt, or at the very least in Alexandria.'

'Rawlinson was of the same opinion.'

'Don't you admit it?'

'I've *been* to Alexandria! I went by train, from the Gezireh Palace. Nanny was a brick. I left them by themselves . . . for several nights!'

Griselda clung to instinct. She felt she *knew* Philomena was close by, and waiting to be found.

Rory Black said, 'Dearest, you don't *want* to find her, do you! That's the truth of it.'

She was silent. Offended.

Often on the faces of horses she saw expressions that she never *wanted* to see again.

Almost with bitterness, he said, 'Of the poverty of the *fellah*, you have no comprehension whatsoever. There is no pity in you.'

Riding past the Abbas Hilmy Barracks, once, as the four lovely, descending notes of an orderly trumpeter floated through the air, they noticed that a pair of gharry horses threw up their whitening heads.

'What is being sounded?'

' "Feed" ', said Rory.

Pity? What was one to *think*! Horses that would have pawed and whickered.

Rory's intimation that Imran was dangerous made her insubordinate. (And *if* Imran had been so fearfully *money*-minded, why the absence?)

'The association with el-Mansur is deemed unwise.'

'With *whom*? Our prisoner?'

'What "prisoner"?'

'We had an exile with us on board the *Principessa*.'

'I see!' Rory raised his raven eyebrows. 'No, the other.'

'I'm not acquainted with any other, I'm afraid.'

'The brother. I recommend you divest yourself of him.'

Griselda digested, speechless. Imran?

'Besides, no *"effendi"* should take you to such localities!' Rory had trowelled onto the 'effendi' a certain irony. What shot into her memory was Imran's ambiguity in speaking of Mungy Lassa'ad.

'Localities!'

'Where you go.'

'Don't be absurd!' said Griselda. 'And how can you have any notion of where I "go"?'

Rory stroked his moustache with the ball of his thumb.

The sliver of moon was saluted with an

exuberance that must have made the horses believe themselves back in action. The whines and pops of fireworks were mingled with a *feu de joie* (although the weapons, or so Colonel Black was heard to tell Nanny, would have been illegal) and the entire population relished the holiday. Bank holidays were, Rory Black remarked to Nanny, the tradition in Egypt. For Rosh Hashana too, and for the Coptic Easter.

'Fancy!'

A *feu de joie* had last been executed in Britain at Aldershot, during a Royal Review, he thought, in the latter part of the nineteenth century. A wave of fire into the air sped along the line of infantry. Must have looked grand!

'I never knew that!'

Nanny, of course, had greeted the dashing Colonel with rhapsodies of approval. An English gentleman, or in this case an Irish cavalry officer, was *manna* to Nanny, despite the aroma.

When the fireworks crackled to mark the sighting of the new moon, his leave was at an end, and he had gone. Griselda breathed again; although she did miss the fellow, rather.

Amabel said, 'Were you *friendly* with him?'

71 Bab Zuweileh

An expedition with Muzz and Shams was always delayed while Muzz looked the gharry's horses over. Muzz when dissatisfied was capable of jibbing. And the *arbagi* was capable of taking offence. Where Nanny had doubts about upholstery and 'scents', these were 'of no consequence'.

Brushed aside.

Amabel should see Egypt, Muzz said. This meant leaving Nanny's stamping-ground of the Nile, the quarter of Ismailiyeh, from Suleiman Pasha to All Saints in the Shari' Bulak, and the Ezbekiyeh. From the Ezbekiyeh and El Ataba el-Khadra, the Muski led into Sikket el-Jedideh, together the longest, narrowest thoroughfare imaginable; and that led straight on to the Shari' esh-Sharawani.

The day was neither Monday nor Thursday, yet the Muski thronged. Nanny got taut in a throng.

The throng *moved* on its feet, moved, moved, moved, in every hue and black; and when blessed carriage-horses split the throng, like a tongue, the throng's 'apparel' got fanned by the spokes, the throng's feet were in peril. To add to Nanny's ordeal, the shops that crammed the Muski weren't, despite their fascia-boards, Nanny's cup of tea.

Shams was no longer ill-clothed or a scamp. He'd grown as important as Mrs Burnaby's *sofragi*, Aly.

Shams glided ahead of Muzz, and Egyptian merchants stepped into the gutter for her.

Nanny and Amabel, in Muzz's wake, might not be so lucky.

Nanny, in her starched uniform, cap and antiquated motoring veil, her hem eight inches above the soles of her stout shoes, attracted vague glances: at Amabel people positively smiled.

Nanny was in dread of 'losing' Muzz.

And then Nanny would be scared by a *'dahrik, ya sitt'* and a loud hiss behind them. In Egypt, people that wanted to clear a way for a handcart or load called 'mind your back, lady'.

Shams said camels at night had lights.

The Egyptian ladies were addressed as *'hanum'*; and, occasionally, timid and respectful voices called Muzz that. Instead of *madaam*. Nobody would *ever* address Nanny as *'hanum'*. In the Ezbekiyeh, nobody said *'hanum'* to Muzz. In the Muski, they might.

More to Nanny's liking was the Citadel. Especially as the sun was sinking towards the pyramids.

Amabel liked to be relieved of the tiring-ness of the walk up the Muski. It was too much for her legs. She preferred to be 'conveyed'.

Muzz had promised not to inflict the Gamaliyeh upon Nanny. In the Gamaliyeh,

391

Muzz had found the darkest, stinkiest stables. Today Muzz wouldn't be diverted to the street of the booksellers (Amabel 'collected' old English picture-books). Muzz (single-minded) was fond of 'penetrating'. They'd dive through the incense *suk* to show Amabel the Bab Zuweileh.

Outside the great mosque of El Azhar, British soldiers watched from sandbags. Muzz was not so interested in British soldiers either. Muzz was looking *everywhere* for Philomena. In fact, Muzz had developed gimlet eyes.

She would peer into alleys. Muzz was embarrassing.

Bab Zuweileh had a gory history.

It was buried in the heart of ancient Cairo but it had been a gate of the Fatamid city. This meant little to Amabel. It was the Marble Arch of Cairo, a place of execution, of hanging. This meant more. When you strolled beneath the stones, the corpses dangled over your head. The corpses were in the past. A child could picture them. Nanny Ironside, in Cairo with English grandchildren, had considered Muzz scandalous. Rarely, the wife of an Egyptian pasha would go into the old *medina* or force a passage through the *suk* of Khan el-Khalili.

Europeans often did, said Muzz.

To the right of the Bab Zuweileh, as Muzz, Nanny, Amabel and Shams emerged through it, was the street of the saddlers. Muzz at once became engrossed in feeling the weight of saddles for horses. Saddles with, she said, *such* heavy trees. One had a tree of iron, one of wood. The saddler's wares were brightly coloured, beaded and beribboned, and Amabel fancied a halter for Hum. Plaited, silky red rope, so soft and thick.

The sun danced through chinks.

Muzz turned to call softly, 'Nanny!'

Amabel didn't know what happened. One minute Nanny, with a wistful face in its round spectacles, was adrift behind them, the next Muzz had half spun, dodged out to see . . . to be sent flying by a blow from a gigantic bundle, under which a small boy, eyes down, was bent double.

Nanny *ran*, she truly galloped.

Muzz had gone flat on her face in the dirt.

Women surged forward, and pulled up, transfixed, in a small semi-circle. Shams went to Muzz more swiftly than anybody; the saddler quick behind.

Muzz got onto her elbow and stretched out a supplicating, ripped glove.

Nanny and Shams hauled at Muzz. Nanny had never touched Shams's hand before. Muzz's face was awful. Amabel knew that Shams had palms that were dry and nice.

'Oh, madam!' exclaimed Nanny.

The semi-circle melted.

That was all. Muzz's knees had been hurt, but she didn't say. Little pieces of filthy straw clung to her. Her frock had suffered.

Then Nanny said, 'There!'

Amabel was shocked.

'Least said, soonest mended.'

Muzz smiled.

Nanny said to Shams, 'Shams will conduct us to a gharry.'

Threading back, wounded, through the *suk* in the direction of the Gami' el-Azhar was hard. Falling down at the Bab Zuweileh, where there were no gharries, was a thing we didn't do. The spices made Amabel sneeze.

For the first time *ever* Muzz climbed into a vehicle without inspecting the horses.

72   Baalbek

Philomena should, with her long service, have marched in triumph through Damascus. A composite squadron went from each regiment. The Dorsets were led by Captain Flower. Awshew had been feverish, and at the last minute the bay gelding had gone instead. Damascus was dusty and the guns raised more of it. Philomena was far better off; with her nosebag of grapes.

Awshew was a-tremble. She sensed the illness, and scented it; and it fretted her.

No sooner had they arrived than they'd shifted for ease of supply. Now, after three days, the Division left Damascus altogether.

Within five miles a stench entered the men's souls.

It outdid Deraa. Headway had been made in clearing; and a burnt tangle of vehicles, ammunition wagons, motors, railway-carriages, limbers, field-kitchens, lorries and gharries had been dragged to the side. Coming from Paradise, Grazebrook saw he was riding through the chilliest regions of Inferno; although it basked under a hot glare. The very name, in Arabic, indicated a place of extraordinary iciness. In mid-river, the current ran swiftly. Where it cut at the rock, carcasses of beasts hid corpses; as though the contents of the road had bulged right across the intervening railway tracks. Vultures hopped and waddled. Otherwise, only the flies moved; and the shadow of jackals. A terrible silence fell on the column. There was no noise, apart from the oily rush, the tread of hoofs, the jingle ... and the faint breathing ... the breathing-in and breathing-out ... of horses and men.

Awshew resented flies that landed on his lips after they'd been gorging on putrid flesh.

Out through the open, rock country, he sat slumped in the saddle. The order to dismount took him by surprise. He almost fell off headfirst. He trudged beside her, surreptitiously hanging back to keep himself up by the flap.

At the next order, Philomena halted of her

own accord.

Awshew stood bemused: his hand was detached by Crowcombe; who off-saddled for him and rubbed her tired back.

The brew-up revived Awshew. The sweat beaded on his forehead; his eyes were glassy. At Zebdhani, on October 9th, in a thunderstorm, Awshew was carted to hospital. Philomena was indifferent. She was past caring even for her own fortune.

Mosquito bites in Beisan, and the fortnight of bad hunger on top, had induced Awshew to incubate the malaria germ; from which he'd escaped after months in the Jordan Valley. It was to rob so many of their health; now fortitude was no longer essential.

Crowcombe himself soon stewed on too tiny a ration of quinine and stumbled around, half delirious, in an effort to minister to his fellows. In the course of three days, the subdued No. 2 Troop was diminished by a half; and still there were the poorly chaps, who struggled among the flourishing to look after the horses.

The A.V.C. Lieutenant was treating Wideawake for scouring again. She was so thin and poor that Crowcombe was mounted on Philomena. Wideawake was thought to be about seventeen.

Philomena had gone out of Alan Grazebrook's mind, rather. He was bound to have been, and to have remained, distracted. His charger had been killed at Er Remteh;

machine-gunned and bleeding to death, the black gelding without a speck of white on him, Fez, had gone quite half a mile, and perhaps saved his master's life.

Once or twice Grazebrook had clapped eyes on her.

He'd had the glimmer of an idea that he might (for he had the prescience to realize he'd be posted back, and presently, before the Dorsets were demobilized, to his own regiment) . . . he might take Griselda's mare with him to England.

It was the least he could do for the old girl. And would it not delight Griselda!

All the surplus horses of the Division were detached for the time being at Shtora: two officers from the Dorsets and thirty-three other ranks remained behind to look after a hundred and sixty-three. Wideawake was one of them.

At Baalbek, proper rations replaced grapes in nosebags.

Barley. Philomena had never understood the waywardness of feed. At last there was *tibbin*. Ground by her back teeth, rolled on her gums, there was *substance*. There had been tasty green leaves at Damascus and at Zebdhani too; but 'make-do'. Oddities. Philomena hadn't been a fussy eater.

Baalbek nights were bitter. Days were scorched by wind. On the horizon was a fringe of squat, white mountains. She was pleased to be given two blankets. It didn't matter by whom. She was watered, she was groomed, she was lightly exercised. She lay down a lot. The cold, soggy mud did her no good. Many of the horses failed to put on any condition.

None was to be clipped.

Alan Grazebrook pencilled a letter to his aunt, in which he sent a message to Arthur's widow. It never occurred to him that his aunt might not pass this on: his undertaking, his promise, to use every exertion to get Philomena cast early; so she might accompany his grey on the voyage home. He'd been attached to Arthur.

Do tell Griselda! he scribbled; never doubting that she would.

Tremendously tall ruins ... he went on. Ozymandian, he fancied. So near. *Kept pretty busy.*

Alan Grazebrook had been twice wounded in France. His chest was not all it might have been. The Spanish 'flu epidemic hit the Regiment. What with malaria and now this, no fewer than eight horses owed their welfare to the devotion of each able-bodied man. Philomena dozed. Allenby, 'The Bull', pressed on to Aleppo. The 4th Division was too weak to move. In camp at Baalbek, the men had only their thin khaki. An icy wind funnelled out of the north-east. Grazebrook had a great-coat. He had two minutes lost in contemplation of the stars on the night of the

30th, the night before the day the Armistice was signed with Turkey.

Grazebrook collapsed; and was taken to the crowded 'English Hospital' in Damascus. The Colonel visited him; and was shaken to perceive that life was precarious. Pneumonia galloped in on the 'flu and, although, delirious, he fought it bravely, five days later Grazebrook died.

73 Mrs Romney clears up confusion

Nanny had long suspected that Mrs Romney wasn't what her late husband the Commander would have called 'in good frame'. There now followed a rum circumstance.

Nanny and Amabel were alone on board, with the *sofragi*, when they were startled by a loud hail from the bank. They heard the steps of a lithe individual on the gangplank, which tended to bounce slightly. Voices. The steps receded. Aly emerged with a salver.

'You can't abide telegrams, can you, Nanny?' The innocent mite.

Nanny and Amabel were helpless. Nanny didn't trust summonses from abroad. Aly laid it down and Nanny advanced towards it. This snake was clothed in the envelope of the Eastern Telegraph Co. Somebody had written on it (beautifully) the name of the *dahabieh*

399

and 'Mrs A. Romney'.

'I shouldn't worry about it, dear. Probably one of the dogs.'

'The dogs, Nanny!'

'Don't waste a thought on it.'

'Dogs don't send telegrams.' A wavering tone.

'Has to wait for Mummie. Let's get out the Picture Lotto!'

Nanny and Amabel had ages to wile.

Mrs Romney returned, wan and exhausted. Mrs Romney wouldn't even open it before she'd washed and had some sustenance inside her. When she did look at it, she said a word. 'Damn!' said Mrs Romney. Mrs Romney wailed to Nanny, 'I never needed him to *arrive* . . . let alone *die*!'

'Who, madam?'

Nanny was fairly startled.

'Captain Palsy, the wretch, sailed out to me in s.s. *Proserpine* . . . how was I to know, I'd have stopped him . . . and he has dropped dead. Can you credit it, Nanny!'

Mrs Romney was *furious*.

Amabel's eyes popped.

'Heart! An hour into Alexandria. Hadn't even disembarked. Military Hospital.'

Mrs Romney gave a groan. Not of sorrow, that was plain.

'I didn't want a death on my conscience.'

'Were you very fond?' temporized Nanny.

'What, Nanny?' said Mrs Romney. She

400

pressed her knuckles into her cheek.

Nanny said, 'I never did think you'd put Major Grazebrook behind you.'

It seemed to be Mrs Romney's turn to stare, and say, 'Who?' Mrs Romney focused her eyes upon Nanny's quivering lips. 'Alan Grazebrook?'

Dazed!

'The very last thing you did, before we locked the door at Bark Hart, was to hold those scraps of letter in your hand. The ones Mrs Romney senior had unearthed for you.'

'Her Human Ghastliness.'

Nanny said, 'Tut-tut.'

'I expect Philomena was in my mind, you know.'

'How you drank in his sighting of Philomena! And then his misapprehension about Conker.'

Nanny spoke of 'Philomena' and 'Conker' as she might have spoken of Artemis and Apollo.

'I was so touched ... He was planning to bring Philomena home. Had the Spanish 'flu not got him first ...'

'Was that all?'

'When he died, I was cut up. The Commander and I had both been fond of him, yes!'

Griselda smiled at Nanny.

'I live to see you settled.' Nanny had almost called Mrs Romney 'dear'! 'I've begun to wonder whether you might ... should we stay on a mite, for it to ripen ... marry Colonel

Black. Though, Amabel and I, we do feel this heat!'

Griselda blinked. 'I couldn't marry a Roman Catholic.'

And then, 'What are we talking about!' She laughed. Rather miserable.

'The poor Captain,' said Nanny, 'poor Captain Palsy.'

Mrs Romney said, with a deep frown, 'All this, for Philomena!'

'*Shall* we be going home?'

'A little longer . . .' whispered Mrs Romney.

74   Griselda Romney is a fool

One of the charms of Zamalek was that everything was mixed up. When Amabel and Nanny went for their constitutional, they admired private gardens, statuary, fountains; could be inquisitive outside shops that sold dried apricots, spices and nuts, or chandlery, or ripe fruit; hover by doors that led into dark pharmacies; and they were perfectly safe. Towards the Imbaba Bridge, and the island's northern point, there was dry marsh, with warblers and frogs, bumblebees, basking lizards, sloughed snakeskins.

When they passed Mr Demetrios, Nanny unbent, responding, 'Good morning'.

Mr Demetrios made papyrus. He occupied

his front entrance. In the back, behind a curtain, five drudges hunched, elbow-to-elbow, in a dismal light, illuminating banana leaves. Mr Demetrios sold his 'papyrus' to Si' Issa. This Si' Issa was rich. Si' Issa was mysterious . . . Griselda hadn't paid much attention.

Imran had once (quaintly) shielded her from an 'excited' stallion.

Now, across the mud street from Mr Demetrios's, beside a bay *baladi* mare (dish face and star) in the shafts of a flat-bed cart, a stripy little creature was planting itself like a stock on four legs. Amabel was entranced!

Some premonition made Griselda hold out an arm to bar the child. The load was unsecured. Rough-hewn palm.

There was a lot of jabber.

Mr Demetrios had gone in.

A spar of palm had been thrust through the spokes of the wheels. Wouldn't chocks have served better!

With no warning, while a third tugged her by the head, two *fellaheen* (they must have been at the Gezireh market), scarcely bothering to shift her mule colt, set about the bay; belabouring her hard with their kurbashes, amid shrieks of '*shii, shii, shii*'.

The wheels had started to roll. As the spar rose rearwards and jammed, the wheels stopped turning.

She threw herself into the collar, straining every wasted muscle to drag the cart forward.

Griselda abandoned Amabel.

Calling out, 'Stop it!', and *'Kif! Kif!'*, Griselda strode across the baked mud. *Imperative* to show the men they'd forgotten their palm-wood spar. How *could* people be so dense!

Two cringed at this intrusion. Another (Egyptians were always so polite) harangued the lady.

Neither party grasped a word that was uttered.

Griselda, with her own hands, struggled with the rough, dirty wood. It was wedged.

The mare was trembling.

Mr Demetrios shot from his door, spectacles in fingers.

Stupidity existed the world over. Griselda knew that. Where animals were concerned, it was one's duty to enlighten it. Griselda asked them, in clear English, to back the mare. She went to the mare's head herself. The head flinched. The harness was so inadequate, and the vehicle so unhandy . . . Griselda pointed to the shaft.

Nobody moved.

'Senseless! Senseless!' Griselda's gestures said.

She was grudgingly obeyed.

Now the spar could be drawn out. Without fuss.

Amabel piped, 'Muzz, they *meant* to brake the wheels!'

'What can you know about it!' snapped Griselda.

Mr Demetrios woke up. *'Madame,'* he pleaded, 'must desist. It is the custom.'

'What custom?'

'They test the horse's strength. A bargain has been proposed. It is necessary for the purchaser to discover how far the cart can be dragged.'

Various misty recollections flooded Griselda's brain.

'On locked wheels?'

Rawlinson spent his life in trying to stop this. Of course.

The injustice welled up in her. Boiling, she had a sense that gloved iron fingers pressed at her temples. More jabber broke out. She had caused genuine bewilderment. The boldest buckled his belt around his waist again. Mr Demetrios spoke to them sternly and said to Griselda, 'It belongs in the horse market. Better you go back to Nanny, *madame!*'

He added, in a conciliatory tone, 'These good men didn't understand you. How else is the strength to be tried? It is vital.'

'How young is the mule?'

Mr Demetrios chivvied them away, saying, 'Take your mama back to Nanny, miss.' There seemed little to do but to leave. Griselda felt quite awful.

Recounting this, Griselda said, 'And I expect the *baladi* had to go through it all over again. I

405

have brought that *about*!'

She despaired.

'The horse market, Nanny. I ought to investigate the horse market. *That* is what our hunters endured. Every time they changed hands.'

'Si' Issa is called Jesus,' said Amabel.

'Is he . . . ? Who is Si' Issa?'

Remarks to do with the spent warriors and how they were, though spent, 'strong' . . . Odd remarks regurgitated themselves.

'*You* know . . . he buys the papyruses from Mr Demetrios. Did Jesus's donkey have sores?'

'What?' said Griselda, unhappy. 'I don't know, darling. I've never thought about it.'

Nanny interrupted, 'This long face won't do, madam. Egypt is getting you down.'

Griselda found it galling. Nanny's familiar spectacles, sparkling concern, swam into view. The obligation to sacrifice Philomena so as to take Nanny home, having nobly to shoulder her own duty to Nanny, *such* an eventuality *had* seemed conceivable. On top of Palsy's keeling over. That her own hopes would collapse had never entered her head.

On June 14th, abruptly, Griselda gave in.

75 'Goodbye to the horses'

Baalbek was a bleak spot. Winter clothing wasn't issued until the third week of November. Some men materialized from hospital. Reinforcements arrived; from the 2nd Cavalry Reserve. Not men of Dorset. The Division marched on the 27th for Beirut, taking two days, *via* Shtora to pick up the horses; and Ain Sufar.

Philomena was glad of her coat. There was snow in the mountains.

10 Cav established camp at El Aluzia; within wind of the sea. It was necessary to post flying sentries. That obstinate fellow, Awshew, had not wanted to be slipped underground. Philomena and Awshew, well forward of the perimeter wire, had to deter the natives. Otherwise troop-horses were not to be taken above a walk, in camp and out. Messengers had to comply unless ordered by an officer to trot. Draught horses were always to walk.

Captain Flower, *pro tem*, was O.C.

Reveille was sounded at 6.30 a.m. Roll Call was at 6.45 a.m. and Stables at 7 a.m. Breakfast wasn't until 8.15 a.m.

Awshew was never present for Second Stables. He'd volunteer for fatigues that took him. He'd rather dig a drainage ditch or form one of a wiring party. Awshew was dying for demobilization. He couldn't wait. Awshew gazed at Philomena as though he saw the engine at a sawmill.

He wasn't a horse man born.

The horses were paraded stripped, in headcollars, and placed in groups: 'under twelve', 'over twelve' and 'captured during operations'. Philomena was fourteen. She was thought to be thirteen.

The officers followed hounds (not as *pukka* as those packs at Aleppo and Tripoli) and got up a steeplechase. There was boxing for the men, a tug-of-war. Concerts and pantomime. Some of Philomena's friends in the Regiment had already been invalided or posted home. The South African, Patterson, still commanded 'B' Squadron.

There was another big inspection, this time by top brass of the Veterinary Service.

After Christmas, demobilization started.

As spring struggled out of winter, Awshew was about even less. He'd go daily in a dismounted detachment that guarded the Turks at the P.O.W. Camp. It wasn't he that looked after her. The strength of the Regiment had been swollen amazingly. Philomena and Wideawake were 'done' with less solicitude.

One of these strange new buggers lammed a chestnut and was severely punished. Another killed himself by drinking creosote.

With the baking sun of earliest summer,

there was a first hint. 'B' Squadron's little Mr Egmont disappeared alone, bareback on his flea-bitten grey; and walked in with his bridle *clenched* in his hand.

Then he sailed.

Officers were given the chance to buy their chargers before May 15th. Soon, like thunder after lightning, there was a general mood of unhappiness; almost of outrage. And not only here at El Aluzia. The Camp hummed with perturbation.

Fellows back from leave had reported sightings of billjims with tears on their cheeks. The Aussies were said to be writing poems. Poems! Australians! Crayoning pictures! Crying angry?

They blamed the War Office. The quarantine regulations of the Dominions that had precipitated the wretched thing. Their neddies couldn't go back with them.

No such difficulties pertained in England. *Shipping* was scarce. To save cost was an object. To show gratitude to the horses was not an object. It was murmured that the Secretary of State had decided the matter himself . . . or it was the Prime Minister himself.

General Barrow, who had a tender heart for horses, was said to have made *furious* protests.

On the day of the fatal inspection, 'B' Squadron's horses were passed, one by one, before the C.O. and Captain Patterson. Two

409

senior Remounts officers also attended; and that A.V.C. Captain with freckled hands. These were accompanied by Farrier-Sergeant-Major 'Burtie' Burt.

Of the twenty-two thousand cavalry, transport and artillery horses in the Near East at the end of the War, there were to be four classifications. That was according to QMG. 4, the Remounts Directorate at the War Office in London.

To be placed in 'A' category implied that an animal was fit for active service; aged twelve or under; or over twelve regardless.

The 'B' category meant 'up to some work'.

Patterson wanted to place every single one of theirs in 'C' or 'D'. Sickening though the outcome would be.

Burt knew Philomena. He and she had been in the Charge at Agagiya. He and she had been wounded. He and she had been in hospital.

Australian troopers, in Syria or back in Palestine, had risked court-martial. They'd ridden, like Mr Egmont, out into the desert, or to a lonesome hollow, and the neddy had 'put a foot in a hole'. Except that they'd had their saddles in their arms.

'Billy' Barrow was said to be turning a blind eye.

A rifle meant shooting a horse in the heart. It took a degree more resolution than with a pistol. Warrant officers and sergeants had it easier. It was that or know your dear old companion, that had saved your life over and over, was to go back to Egypt, to be sold to dealers.

The billjims had known Egypt. The yeomen knew Egypt.

Feelings ran high. Perhaps yeomen were more biddable than billjims. Perhaps Awshew wasn't that bothered.

Wideawake was in no state to be sent anywhere. She was all bones, ragged-hipped, sunken-eyed, hollow-backed; her coat stared and her skin was stiff; there was no lustre in her. She was blind on the off side. She was over at the knees. She'd been struck in the shoulder by a flying tin of bully beef in the action at Er Remteh. Bone spavins were forming. There was something intestinal. Captain Patterson and Farrier-Sergeant-Major Burt agreed she was 'D'.

They smiled at her.

Wideawake's pal couldn't be deemed antique. They havered over Philomena.

She had been wounded.

She stood for quite ten minutes. Once she turned her head and looked thoughtfully at Burt.

The vet approached again and his fingers again felt down each leg. She'd had knocks. She wasn't unsound. She'd been a good do-er. Her age was 'in her favour'. Philomena was a 'B'. Burt was visibly apologetic. That earned him a vexed glance from the senior Remount officer.

A whole week later, Wideawake was led off. Philomena whickered.

The 'C' and 'D' category horses were picketed together, and had their shoes removed. Those with manes were hogged. The hair of the tail was clipped until their docks were bald. They looked a sight. Each was watered. Given two sugar lumps that the S.Q.M.S. had managed to procure, all were 'made much of'. They enjoyed a last nosebag.

They were not unfamiliar with the sound of fire. But they had to be shot in the lines.

For this reason. Their carcasses were to be dragged a mile off, stuffed with straw and set alight as usual. It was the will of QMG. 4 that first they were flayed. A horse's skin was not thick. Couldn't be dragged without damage.

Seven pounds of salt per animal had been issued; to preserve the hide.

This was a rotten job, for horses understood, and, as the shots approached, would tremble.

The bravest didn't tremble.

Philomena called for three days.

What was puzzling was that Wideawake had answered her, wasn't far. And then wasn't answering any longer.

The 'A' and 'B' categories had been returned to duty.

In early June, the Regiment paraded mounted; and, although Remounts would be sending Field Sections to collect small numbers at a time, said goodbye to the horses.

Philomena was led away from El Aluzia, without knowing, really, what was happening to her.

76   Imran

'Shall we see him?' asked Amabel.

'I don't expect so.'

'I do want to say goodbye.'

Griselda said, 'I do, too. Do you know where he lives, or how I send a message?'

'No,' said Amabel, severely. 'That's poor.'

'And how could he know where we are! Help Nanny to pack, will you!'

It seemed that Imran did know. The sightings were fewer, but the trickle of informants had never quite dried up.

A slight, trim figure in his pale suit, waistcoat with watch-chain and watch, neat tie and tarboosh (Griselda hadn't laid eyes on him in Cairo in any other dress) and with his smiling demeanour, smelling of orange-blossom, Imran strode on board *Dalila*.

How many months had gone by since they and Imran had slept with a common bathroom between them?

'How are you?'

'*El hamdu-li-llah!*'

'And your family?' Griselda was learning. She had no idea of what his family consisted.

'*El hamdu-li-llah!* And you, *madame*?'

Griselda acknowledged that they were well. The *sofragi* brought coffee and Imran sat there in *Dalila* and told Griselda that he might have found Philomena.

Griselda was sceptical.

She'd got her hopes up and, often, they had been dashed. How she'd missed Imran's company! He had never stepped over the line. Their concourse had never been anything but proper. His eagerness to hear her opinion on any number of topics had been endearing. So very much had she mourned their falling out.

She laughed. She rose from the edge of her chair and went to get her hat. Griselda was thinner than she had been when he'd last escorted her anywhere.

'May we come with you?'

Griselda looked at Imran. 'Nanny might prefer to stay, darling.'

Imran could have shaken his head.

'This may not be suitable for you and Nanny! For Nanny in particular.'

Amabel's expression was not insolent ... more, resolute.

Nanny said, 'Is it suitable for *you*, madam!'

Griselda would take no notice.

'I won't be in the way,' stated Amabel.

Griselda shrugged. She said, tactfully, 'I think, all the same, Nanny has her hands full in

414

Dalila.'

'I might want to *go!*'

'In that case, better you both stay!'

But Griselda relented.

Amabel leapt on the spot.

Aly was asked by Imran to fetch a gharry. The vehicle procured was ('Regrettable', said Imran) a one-horse *calèche* with a sweating grey between the shafts; and Griselda, Amabel and Nanny, after the inspection, got into it. 'We shall be squashed.'

Griselda had been 'squashed' with Imran in the old days.

A lean, finely-bred, flea-bitten grey, with an intelligent head, and the broad-arrow brand cancelled by the letter C on his near quarter. The horse-medicines and the hamper of refreshments rode with them. Shams would be taken up. The sun was bald.

The gharry-driver, the *arbagi*, took a pride in his charge. He was for whipping his horse to the fastest trot. Wildly the throat-plume swung . . . Griselda found herself wondering at the strange beauty of Cairo and the strange ugliness of its animals' existence.

The *arbagi* threw argumentative remarks back at Imran.

A nudge from Amabel.

'Can you understand them?'

'The *arbagi* doesn't wish to drive us where we are wanting to go.'

Griselda glanced down.

415

'I wouldn't be willing to swear to it,' said Amabel.

Once over El Kubri (lovely breeze off the Nile) they bore right-handed; passing the Ministries. In the district of the Ministries, the city was at its greenest and some said fairest.

Then the railway-line to Helwan was on the right ... Es Seiyideh Zeinab ... 'I oughtn't to have let you persuade me, darling!' ... Three separate squads of Egyptian policemen, still commanded by their British officers.

Imran fished out his watch.

'Please may the horse *walk!*' Presently Griselda said, 'I might have ordered a motor.'

Amabel gripped the squab. The upholstery was split and a mixture of horsehair and straw poked out. The wheels creaked, and made a dull, rolling-upon-cabbage-stalks crunch.

Nanny tucked the corners of her mouth in.

'Bear up, Nanny!' said Griselda. 'Won't you sing to us?'

Nanny pitched her sweet voice for their ears alone, *'Early one morning, just as the day was dawning ...'*

Splendidly incongruous.

Another long trot.

The camel and horse-drawn traffic was more hectic. It was a mystery as to how the tinkling bells made themselves heard above the hubbub. There were no motors. The houses grew humbler, the trudging populace greater. Interleaved with streets were dismal patches of dirt, in which hobbled donkeys drifted, and acacias drooped. Their horse was blowing. He stumbled. 'Do impress upon the man we don't need to be rushed like this!'

They were attracting stares, amazed stares.

Griselda said, 'Tell me, *ya* Imran, do you have a servant?'

'An old woman.'

'Old woman?'

'A woman helps my mother. She has been with us ever since I was small.'

'Oh,' said Griselda. 'Do you live with your mother?'

'It is my father's house,' he said, surprised.

A dread took hold of her; Griselda, the most optimistic of creatures. I've made myself unhappy, she thought. Amabel held her hand.

'There was a murder here last night,' remarked Imran.

'Not in front of Nanny. Where are we now?'

'Don't mind me, madam.'

They were approaching the mosque of El Abdin.

The grey, labouring, dropped into a walk again. Shops, kitchens, and barbers, and vats of tar, butchers and rows of flat-irons, blacksmiths. A *sakka*, a water-carrier, ambled beside them. There were potholes. The flies were atrocious.

Their gharry-horse sighed.

The Citadel seemed peculiarly near.

'Are we going to Fustat?'

417

'Almost!' said Imran.

'If it is Philomena ... I fear this may not be ... she couldn't be anywhere more ancient in Cairo,' said Griselda. And, 'We, you and I, have never entered these parts.'

'Have you visited El Amr ibn el-'As?'

Griselda said absently. 'I shall do so.' She added, 'Without you to guide me into mosques ...'

The pace was resumed.

'I am sorry,' said Imran. 'Without me it is not difficult.'

Amabel gazed from one to the other.

'And if Amabel is urgent, there is a place, Nanny,' he said.

'In a mosque!'

'Close by. Naturally. A clean place.'

'How practical,' murmured Griselda. 'Have you arranged for the animal to be in?' she asked, after a moment.

Imran folded his hand on his watch.

'What is the smell?' said Amabel.

Griselda was familiar with slaughter blood. It wasn't that.

'The tannery,' said Imran. 'The smell is from the tannery.'

Griselda was thinking, oh, the endless procession of misery, possibly I *have* had enough. A four-wheeled trolley of household furniture, drawn by a single horse, was in view, over a little brow. The furniture was preposterous; towering; precarious; as though

418

chucked up to the last brass pot.

Ears back, the gallant soul was straining, in breast harness, to get one leg in front of the other. One painful step followed another. It was as though the leg would never manage to fasten the hoof to the road ... trembling ... let alone entice the load one step forward. The horse's face broke Griselda's heart.

Griselda said to Amabel, 'Wouldn't you think *two* trips ...'

Their gharry had gone on by before Imran had called to their *arbagi*, '*Min fadlak, ya 'arbagi,* turn around ... turn around!'

This proved to be not a straightforward manoeuvre. '*Yallah!*' said the driver. O God. The furniture was at the bottom of the incline. The iron-bound wheels lacked brakes. The load was too heavy for the horse to hold back. Persons were required to hang on for grim death behind. The trolley could have run forward and toppled the horse. Still Griselda hadn't understood.

Her face was puzzled, but she said, mildly, 'Have we gone wrong?'

The furniture, which Griselda loathed with a passion, bore off into an alley.

'Are we *stopping*!'

Shams jumped down. 'That old mare was brown, Muzz,' observed Amabel.

The figure of a small boy appeared from the top of the pile. He began to hand down the possessions; perilously. Before the horse was unhitched. (Griselda's mind continued to register . . .)

The nose jerked. Expecting to be hit, or hurt.

Stiff, lame, without kindness, the poor thing was taken out of the lowered shafts.

77 Philomena

Griselda had always imagined that there would be blinding recognition. That Philomena would prick her ears, perhaps whinny. Horses did remember, and did pick out people. Not after eight years? Griselda had imagined she herself would *know*, on the instant.

As though taken unawares, disbelieving, she remained seated in the gharry; shocked.

The mare stood, unattended, with hanging head, and splayed legs. She didn't rest the off-hind, on which she'd been quite lame. She had no legs to stand on. A filthy rag was knotted around the near pastern. Pus had dried into it.

The men had, without washing, formed a line on a carpet that had been rolled out in front of the building, or warehouse, whatever it was, the doors of which gaped behind them. Imran (Griselda's jaw dropped) had, in his tarboosh and European clothes, joined them; so had Shams and their *arbagi*. Tacked on to the line were three small boys. There, all waited.

Forever afterwards, Griselda would associate the finding of Philomena with the muezzin's poignant cry for the prayer of *Ad Dhohr*. To Griselda, who didn't use words lightly, the *shahada* had its own beauty.

Nobody objected to Amabel.

Amabel had taken some of her mother's sugar lumps, and was talking to the brown horse.

In that moment, the animal came alive, nudging the child about her body; and Amabel was laughing, because the muzzle tickled her. A little girl had offered a forgotten treat. The sugar was crunched loudly, one lump, rolled around the rusty bit; and then another lump, slavering, and a third.

As for the flea-bitten grey, his whickering had gone unheard. He took a step, and then several steps, reins looped on the dashboard; carrying the grown-ups.

Nanny emitted a timid squawk. The *arbagi* glanced in their direction, startled, but saw no harm. Feeding his horse a tit-bit. The English did that.

Only when there was no more sugar did Griselda leave the vehicle.

The eyes were dim and filmy. The sockets were sunken. White hairs flecked the coat; which was swollen with sweat. Dark, sour, latherless sweat. There wasn't an inch that wasn't sopping.

Sweat from the heat. Sweat from pain.

There wasn't the least glimmer that Griselda was recognized.

About the head the white hairs were many. The whiskers were oddly scorched. Saddle marks. The forelegs bore a profusion of white rings; old scabs had broken open. Both knees were puffy. The knees trembled. Behind the elbows were festering galls ... and she hadn't yet been unharnessed.

The back was hollow. The spine was deformed over the loins; as though, when her bones had been green, she'd carried a pack that had been beyond her. The ribs were corrugated. The belly was tucked up. On the off side, between hip and stifle, and behind the stifle, up to half an inch deep, there were dents. Must have been wounded. Bog spavins, both hocks. To Griselda, it appeared that the near fore had been fired, and then not tended. The suppurating burns she'd seen in her travels had healed over.

A confused babble broke out.

The shoes were hideous. Cramped pigs of iron overshot the heel. The hoofs had been boxed by rasping. Although the near-hind one was skewed under her.

'Never had a foal,' said Griselda to Amabel.

'That *is* a mercy,' tried Nanny.

The grey breathed on Amabel; and dislodged Amabel's hat.

His harness was ill-fitting: Griselda was fit to burst. It was imperative not to lose her head.

'Climb out, Nanny,' said Griselda. 'Take my hand.'

Imran now took charge. The lady should see the brown mare free of harness. The alley was squalid. Nanny hummed. It was the hum of anxiety. Nanny didn't know she was doing it. The business of unloading the trolley went on. The *arbagi*, who'd been astonished, backed up his horse; not ungently.

Imran seemed to have a way with his fellow men.

Griselda felt grateful.

Quietly, Imran saw to the small matters. Shams was permitted to unharness the mare. 'Where was she stabled?' asked Griselda. 'Is there no water for her?'

Girth marks, further saddle marks . . .

The *arbagi* even rummaged in his box for a sweat-scraper.

Imran replied, 'Is this your horse, *madame*?'

The supposed owner girded himself. Amabel gazed at her mother. Imran said, 'Her name is *El Gulbeh*.'

'What is that?'

'She is named after the scar from the wound she has from the War.'

And their *arbagi* threw in, '*Inglizi remount*!'

Griselda understood.

She thought she always understood Imran.

The eye was Philomena's eye, however dulled. The mealy muzzle was flecked, and the corners of the mouth caused Griselda to

423

wince. The brow was Philomena's. The ears. The mane ... Griselda couldn't say whether the mane fell as Philomena's mane had, for Philomena and Conker had been kept hogged. The head was hanging on a scrawny neck. An emaciated ghost of Philomena's conformation.

Griselda said, 'It's Philomena.'

And Imran said, '*Hamdullah!*'

'Oh, *my!*' Nanny said.

Through Imran, Griselda paid three *gineih*.

Philomena had been knee-hobbled on a patch of dirt. Was that to be *believed*? Her only companions had been jack donkeys. 'Entire donkeys? With a mare? Are you sure?'

'The donkeys' knees are fastened.'

'Hm,' said Griselda.

Griselda for an abstracted moment pictured a mare in season in the midst of entire donkeys that were hobbled with their heads also shackled to their knees.

'I ought, you know, to see the dirt.'

'He says that it is far.'

Griselda hesitated.

'Do you take her *today, ya madame*?'

'How can I go off without her, I dare not!'

Amabel stared from one to the other.

'Why else did we bring Shams!'

How was the carter to proceed? To earn *fullous*? To feed his family.

Griselda said that the carter now had enough *fullous* to buy another. She choked over what that implied.

'Philomena never *did* have a friend,' she remarked to Amabel.

The grey (Griselda was warming to him so) fixed the child with eyes that were still bright. Pigment had gone from his lips. Griselda was preoccupied with the next hurdle. That of getting Philomena back to the Sporting Club. The *arbagi* was ready to tie her on behind.

('Will *this* one walk to Gezireh, *madame*?' murmured Imran.)

A Shams *ahead* could rest the mare, said Griselda. They would all halt. The lady herself wouldn't be obliged to crane her neck to watch progress; hood down or not. The time was half past one. The distance was judged to be five miles.

Griselda was wrung out; Amabel, flushed.

'*Insha'llah*, no mishap,' said Imran.

Griselda said, 'Where is the nearest drink for the animals?'

There was a cistern by the northern entrance to the Slaughterhouse.

'In order to water the horses we have to . . . ?'

Imran nodded.

'Very well,' said the lady, and, 'We shan't go above a *walk* all afternoon.'

It was Nanny's turn to be appalled. Griselda brushed a hand across her forehead.

The grey's bit was removed from his mouth. Shams shared between the two the barley bran he'd brought wrapped in a cloth. He

425

moistened it with water from his own *fintass*. Shams made balls in his palm. Their eagerness was pathetic.

While the syce fed them, Griselda untied the 'bandage'. She eased it, and snipped it, from the dried pus. She couldn't bathe the mess beneath. She spread ointment on lint and supported it with crêpe, taking that over the fetlock.

A crowd had collected across the end of the alley.

Griselda straightened herself, drew a breath, and said, 'I can see I shall have to offer for our dear grey ...' His was a sound horse, a *good* horse, protested the *arbagi*, full of years of work, and strength, worth forty times more than the crock.

Tears in his eyes. Perhaps he'd been fond of the animal.

'I fear it will take me some weeks, to nurse them fit for the voyage. Then we shall all go home together.'

Amabel said, 'The blue roan wants to stay in Egypt.'

'Without us, pet,' said Nanny, humming.

78 Goodbye old friend

As their ill-shod misshapen hooves felt the deep *tibbin* bed beneath them, there would be another doubting disbelieving halt. Then gradually they would lower their heads and sniff as though they could not believe their own eyes or noses. Memories, long forgotten, would then return when some stepped eagerly forward towards the mangers piled high with *berseem*, while others, with creaking joints, lowered themselves slowly on to the bed and lay, necks and legs outstretched. There they remained, flat out, until hand fed by the syces.

MRS GEOFFREY BROOKE, *Diaries*

In Philomena's whickering there was the throb of anxiety.

She had shuffled and stumped the five miles back, but she hadn't trusted her swollen knees. On deep *tibbin*, at the Sporting Club, she stood, occasionally swaying, shifting uneasily, turning her head whenever anyone came or went. Philomena had the polo ponies for company. With that, it was clear she wasn't satisfied.

Griselda repeated, 'Philomena never did

have friends.'

Philomena was eating fitfully: she greeted her feed with eagerness, lipped at it, then the eagerness died. The painful whickering went on for three days, four . . .

Griselda said she had to go and look for this stable companion. But she didn't go.

'Philomena's head is too big,' observed Amabel.

'That is because her skull has no flesh,' said Griselda.

The *arbagi* had promised to bring the flea-bitten grey at eight-thirty the next morning. He had driven off and vanished. Griselda said she was bound to search for him, too, for had they not grown attached to the horse . . . and she would beg Imran to pester the Cab-drivers Association. But she didn't do that either.

'Where is that Imran when you want him,' said Nanny.

Dr Usama cared tenderly for Philomena. Griselda, triumphant, furnished her sister Ida with the details. *The man is excellent*, Griselda wrote.

Philomena lay down, with a grunt; and didn't get up for an alarming number of hours.

The child crouched in the bedding; until Nanny drew the line.

Shams slept with Philomena.

Griselda tried to offer Dr Usama coffee at the Sporting Club. Knowing it would be 'not done', despite his being vet there (Seifallah

Youssri Pasha might play polo with the Prince of Wales!), he declined, hand on heart.

Nanny had consented to stay on, past the date of Georgie's birthday, so Philomena could be in a condition to sail. Georgie wrote to ask for a red tarboosh with a tassel. Humbug would pass to the Burnabys.

'Is that all?' Griselda sighed. 'A tarboosh? Can't we be imaginative, Nanny!'

Imran visited them in *Dalila*.

Now there was no Philomena to find, there seemed to be awkwardness. As though, Griselda surmised, what they'd had in common had withered. Griselda was tired. She spent all available time at the Club. Once, when he came, Nanny was there on her own. On another occasion, no one. He had brought a volume of engravings. Griselda recollected the passionate reader, the Imran that talked about books. Griselda was ashamed to think she might have caused him chagrin. She did write to thank him, but she had no address. Shams took the letter.

Her knuckles went to her forehead: her concern was for Philomena.

Impatiently, defiantly ... Griselda arranged for Aly to bring a flask of coffee from *Dalila*. Amabel guessed Dr Usama to be aged about thirty-five. Griselda walked Philomena out, gently in the grounds. The lovely green things and the flowering trees were full of dust.

Griselda did hope Amabel hadn't picked up

Shams's awful language.

Dr Usama couldn't make Philomena well.

'The poor darling,' said Griselda.

It wasn't that she was lame on that hind leg with the damaged stifle. The farrier had done what he could for the deformed feet. It wasn't that her eyes were clouded or that, in moving her head, she peered. Dr Usama said her vision was 'restricted'. They had treated her for worm. It wasn't that. If she *had* been pining, she'd ceased to pine. She still wasn't eating properly. It wasn't teeth. It might have been intestinal. Once, she'd been machine-gunned in the belly. They were reluctant to put her through an exploratory operation. The septic galls had healed, and the leg infection more or less.

Griselda couldn't *live* in Egypt. It wasn't to be contemplated. She thought of Georgie.

One day, Griselda asked Dr Usama to put Philomena down. Dr Usama didn't say it was repugnant. Dr Usama would have advised it. He nodded, his round face full of fellow-feeling. He said, 'Since we cannot subject her to a voyage, it would be kinder, *madame.*'

That day, Nanny had Amabel.

'Mummie's spirits, duck,' said Nanny, 'have been dashed. Will you bear up?'

'I'm sad,' said Amabel.

Griselda was with Philomena.

Shams held the headcollar rope. When Griselda, unable to steel herself, turned away,

Philomena, attracted by the sudden movement, pricked her ears. She was dropped—almighty flump—by captive bolt. After a few seconds, the heart stopped.

Philomena never saw England again.

Dorothy Brooke and The Old War Horse Memorial Hospital

In 1930, Brigadier Geoffrey Brooke (later Major-General, C.B., D.S.O., M.C.) was given command of the British cavalry contingent in Egypt. His wife accompanied him to Cairo.

Out of sight, unnoticed, long unfit to go in harness in the smarter districts and in a pitiful state, the war-horses were still gallantly attempting to do the work asked of them. Most were very aged. Virtually none could have been under twenty-five. Many were thirty or more. In that climate, they lived on and on.

Mrs Brooke had never been able to forget their story. They were so out-of-sight that at first she thought they'd perished.

Dorothy Brooke saw in the eyes of these horses that which she could only have interpreted. She expressed it in language that was perhaps more characteristic of her time than of ours: she saw eyes that were pleading for release from extreme misery and pain.

We, in our culture, are accustomed to a recognition that there is a limit to endurance; that, if suffering can't be alleviated, creatures need that suffering to end; and that, so far as animals are concerned, we have a moral

433

obligation to do something about it.

Whether or not we are correct in concluding this, we cannot know.

A contrary opinion is so foreign to us that we are apt to think it mere callousness.

Dorothy Brooke appealed for funds in a letter to the *Morning Post*. Whilst carrying out, as the wife of the senior cavalry officer in Egypt, quite other, social duties, she set up a Committee and established stables. She searched for and bought up the warriors, gave them a few days rest, with a *tibbin* bed, and comforting feed. Then they were put down. It was she who noted the impassioned nature of the friendships the horses formed with their companions in adversity.

Out of the twenty-two thousand sold in Egypt, she was to find five thousand alive.

A few, very few, were sent home.

Every week on a Thursday, during nine months of the year, for four years, Mrs Brooke selected the twelve to be destroyed; and, on the Friday morning, she watched their humane dispatch.

Mrs Brooke never sought to condemn those who had cared for their animals so inadequately. That she had to ignore the plight of the native horses gave her unspeakable grief. Her duty was to the horses 'we' had left behind. But the rule was relaxed, and further crises of conscience ensued.

Dorothy Brooke's Old War Horse Memorial

Hospital became The Brooke Hospital for Animals, and it is still working in Cairo . . . and in Alexandria, Luxor, Aswan and elsewhere in Egypt. This large charity, based in London—and universally known as The Brooke—is now in Jordan, India, Pakistan and Ethiopia. It has projects in collaboration with other agencies in Afghanistan, Kenya and Guatemala.

These days, the aim is provide free veterinary care, education and training, so that people who depend on horses, mules, and donkeys for their livelihood have fitter, happier animals. The Brooke's vets try to eliminate arcane practices, and offer ingenious alternatives to old customs. Mobile teams take clinics to brick kilns and rubbish tips, as in Egypt, and to markets, villages and tonga stands. As in Egypt, national directors, speaking local languages, head operations. Local staff work in the field.

The message may be buoyant: the need is immense.

Mrs Brooke appears to have wanted to see the toiling animals gone from the streets of Cairo—gone altogether. Today, toiling *people* bring their animals to the Brooke because they know they will get them back. Perhaps Dorothy Brooke would have understood how, over the years, this policy has grown to be the only sensible one.

The Brooke (in the spirit of its founder) is deeply prosaic and practical.

As for the yeomen ... Necessity demanded that their horses were worn out in the service of their country; deprived, sometimes severely, of food and water; that they carried too much, and were worked while lame and even after they'd been wounded. The cavalrymen and mounted infantrymen cared about their horses, they owed their lives to them and they had been trained to keep welfare uppermost. Horses respond to kindness; but hardship is hardship.

In Egypt, the descendants of the war-horses live on.

* The Brooke,
30 Farringdon Street,
London
EC4A 4HH.
Tel. +44 [0]203 012 3456
www.thebrooke.org

Sources, spellings, licence and permissions

The Dorset County Record Office and its archivists enabled me to extract much vital information from the fragmented papers of the Dorset Yeomanry and the Regimental Order Books held there. I must thank, too, the staff of the Reading Rooms of the Department of Printed Books at the National Army Museum, the Imperial War Museum, the National Maritime Museum; the Picture Library of the Royal Geographical Society, the eccentric Keep Museum in Dorchester, the Greater Cairo Library and the National Library of Malta. Mike Hoskin, Cultural Development Officer at the Dorset County Council, gave me access to the painting by Lady Butler, *The Charge of the Dorset Yeomanry at Agagia, Egypt.*

In chapters concerned with military action, spelling of place-names is taken from those established by the Battles Nomenclature Committee set up after the War. Otherwise, versions are used that were current in the Army—and there were inconsistencies. For obscure localities, the transliteration in Regimental Order Books tended to reflect the varying ability of individual officers to grasp what had been named to them in Arabic: on the whole these have been disregarded, and the English spelling reconstructed from the likely Arabic meaning. Certain names, being common, crop up again elsewhere.

For 1922, I have used a transliteration that would have been familiar to the British residents in Cairo at the time.

The names and the personalities of officers (unless very senior) and men are fictional.

I have taken some licence. There is no record that any sections from any troop of 'B' Squadron were dismounted at the foot of the Mughar ridge. 'A' Squadron, which *was* dismounted, did suffer the highest casualties in horses and men.

There seems no doubt that the supply of shoes caused serious concern for the Dorset Yeomanry after the Third Battle of Gaza, and that many horses were going lame. From the scanty evidence, it has been difficult not to conclude that the Regiment actually marched into the Judaean hills with some or many of the horses still unshod. The blood from the camels' feet is well documented.

The extract from *My Horse Warrior* by Lord Mottistone (General Jack Seely), published by Hodder & Stoughton, is reprinted by kind permission of Lord Mottistone C.B.E. The extracts from *For Love of Horses, Diaries of Mrs Geoffrey Brooke*, edited by Glenda Spooner and published by The Brooke Hospital for Animals, are reprinted with kind permission of

The Brooke. The extracts from *The Fire of Life* by General Sir George de S. Barrow, published by Hutchinson, are reprinted by permission of The Random House Group Ltd. The extract from *The Palestine Campaigns* by Colonel A. P. Wavell, published by Constable & Co., is reprinted by permission of Constable & Robinson Ltd.

R.B.

Maps

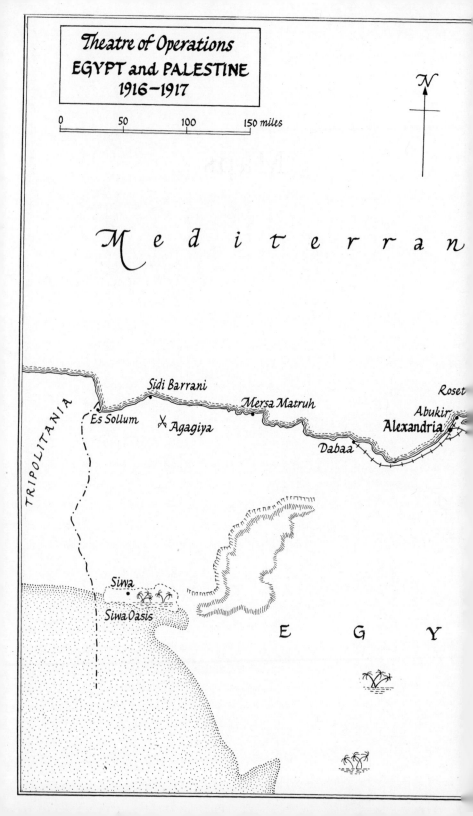

Theatre of Operations
EGYPT and PALESTINE
1916–1917

N

0   50   100   150 miles

M e d i t e r r a n

TRIPOLITANIA

Sidi Barrani

Roset

Es Sollum

Agagiya

Mersa Matruh

Abukir

Alexandria

Dabaa

Siwa

Siwa Oasis

E   G   Y

CYPRUS
Tripoli
Baalbek
Beirut
Damascus
Mt Hermon
a n Sea
L. Tiberias
Acre
Halfa
Deraa
R. Jordan
Nablus
Amman
Es Salt
Jaffa
Jericho
Jerusalem
Gaza
Dead Sea
Rafa
Damietta
Port Said
Beersheba
Romani
SUEZ CANAL
El Arish
Katia
Es Salkieh
El Kantara
Kossaima
Ismailia
L. Timseh
Zagazig
Bitter Lakes
HEJAZ RAILWAY
Giza
Cairo
Geneffeh
Suez
Sakkara
ahshur
SINAI
Akaba
iyum
to Medina
Gulf of Suez
Gulf of Akaba
T
River Nile
Deirut
RED SEA
Assiut

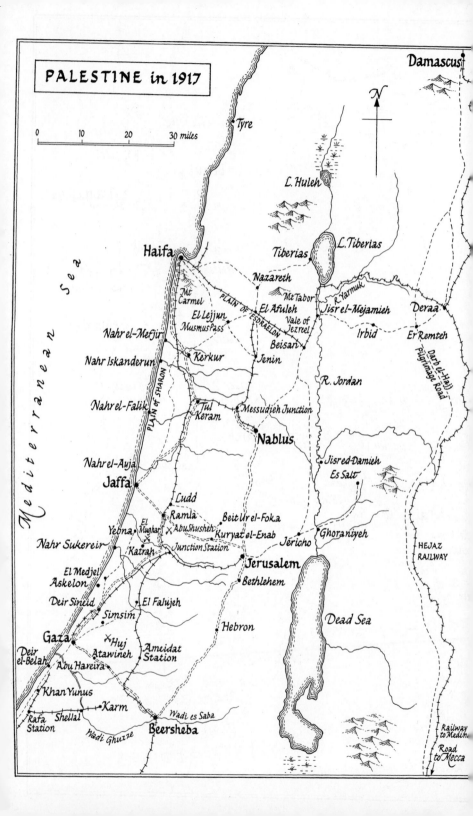